# DIRTY LAUNDRY

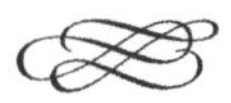

LAUREN LANDISH

Edited by

VALORIE CLIFTON

Edited by

STACI ETHERIDGE

Cover Models: Matthew Hosea & Nin Coleman.
Photography by Reggie Deanching.
Edited by Valorie Clifton & Staci Etheridge.

# INTRODUCTION

**Join my mailing list (www.laurenlandish.com) and receive 2 FREE ebooks! You'll also be the first to know of new releases, sales, and giveaways. If you're on Facebook, come join my Reader Group!**

**I'm a reporter, and I've got the best assignment in the world–get dirt on the hottest country star on the charts, Keith Perkins.**
**The sexy beast who rocks those tight jeans like nobody's business.**
**I'm supposed to learn all of his Dirty Laundry, his deepest and darkest secrets.**
***Without* sleeping with him.**
**Easy enough, right?**
**Wrong.**

I mean, just looking at him makes me wonder what those big, rough hands could do to me. With a voice that's one part velvet and one part growl, it's hard for me to sass him when he melts me into a puddle with a single look.

And when he sings?

All bets are off.
He owns the stage . . . and maybe some naughty parts of my body too.

But he's notoriously single and notoriously private.

Given his status as a walking sex god, neither makes sense. Something is amiss, and I'm going to figure out exactly what it is.

But if I'm not careful, I might just become his **dirty little secret**.

## CHAPTER 1

### ELISE

"Yes, sir. I'm on it, sir. By Monday, of course." I sigh, rolling my eyes as Donnie, my boss, somehow manages to both ream me out for not delivering yet and make me feel like I can totally accomplish my latest assignment.

I'm not sure how he manipulates people so well, but he does. It's a gift, I guess.

Hanging up, I look at myself in the mirror, making sure my disguise for today is in tip-top shape. I'm not famous, but my face is known enough that I want to be sure I'm not recognized. My blonde hair is tied up under a dark brunette wig that falls down in perfect mermaid waves, my usually slightly made-up face is fully done like I'm some YouTube makeup tutorial, and I'm dressed in casual clothes that scream money in quality, not flash. I've got on the one pair of designer jeans I own, a perfectly slouchy tee, and a fluffy soft hand-knit cardigan.

With the addition of my huge sunglasses and heeled booties, I'm off . . . looking just like one of the other millions of twentysomethings, out for coffee and to run errands. Which is exactly what I need, nondescript from the masses.

It's nowhere near my normal look, but that's what makes it a great disguise. Glancing at my watch, I realize I'll need to take a cab if I'm making my first observation point on time. At least I can turn the receipt in for reimbursement because taking cabs all over the city is definitely above my pay bracket.

I hope Donnie isn't going to be a prick on the expense report this time.

After a quick ride, I order a coffee and a blueberry muffin before sitting down at what's become *my* table over the last week, taking out a notebook full of scribbled notes. To an interested observer, I'm working on a movie, or maybe a TV show, or something similarly vapid. I assume an aura of 'don't-fuck-with-me' and pretend to work, which makes a great cover because I am actually working, just not on what it seems.

Keeping my head still behind the shades, my eyes move left and right, not missing a thing. From the obviously morning-after coffee date, to the mom juggling two kids while bribing them with muffins that look just like mine and will put those two into sugar overload in ten minutes, to the old man reading the paper. I've worked long and hard on these skills. They're more vital to my career than the ability to type quickly.

It's not long before my target appears. Keith Perkins, the country music star who's topping charts and winning awards left and right. He walks in to order his morning cup o'joe. He's not really in disguise, just wearing jeans and a t-shirt, but the missing cowboy hat and tennis shoes instead of boots seem to be all the disguise he needs to go about unrecognized in this town. Then again, this isn't a big country town. I bet he couldn't pull this off in Nashville without getting mobbed.

He tells the barista his name is Kevin instead of Keith, but I don't think she even looks up. In fact, I know she doesn't look at him, because if she did, she'd be drooling like I've been for the last five days since I started my assignment.

There's something about the way he moves, like coiled power waiting to spring into action, that makes me hum with anticipation. Combine that with a build that's tall and wide-shouldered, with powerfully built arms and a tightly muscled waist that's so narrow that he can't wear normal jeans without squeezing his thighs and leaving his waist baggy . . . the man's walking sex on a stick. He's infused with energy in such a way that you can't help but wonder what he could to with it.

*Or what he could do to me with it.*

I shake my head, a small smile tilting up one corner of my mouth. As if. That's never gonna happen. I'm not the sort who gets wooed and swept off her feet by handsome stars who then proceed to wine and dine me before making my toes curl. No. With my job, I have a better chance of my name ending up pinned on a voodoo doll than my body being pinned to a bed.

My job is to follow Keith and watch that fine ass and dimpled smile as much as possible to find out his secrets. Once those secrets are in hand, I'll write a damn good story for the online gossip rag I work for. It's not my dream gig. Hell, I've hated it at times, but it's interesting and pays the bills. I wanted to be a real investigative reporter. I wanted to follow in the steps of Woodward and Bernstein, exposing the back-alley machinations and dirty laundry of those who really deserve it. Those in power who are trying to fuck the average Joe.

Too bad most of the reporters on that gig are just as dirty as the assholes they're covering. So I get to watch and report on celebs. But it pays the bills, so here I am lusting after the mark I'm following in preparation to expose all of his dirty laundry to readers who circle like vultures. Sometimes, I feel sorry for people like Keith. He's not into drugs or acting like a jackass, and I've even listened to his music. It's music to make you feel good. And make my panties wet, but that's his voice. He could read his grocery list and I'd be all ears.

Knowing his routine, I start to gather my things, ready to follow out a few seconds behind him. As he walks out the door, questions run through my head, mental preparation for what's coming. *Where are we going today, Keith? The recording studio? Maybe the quiet spot at the gastropub you like to write at that has those bacon cheeseburgers that I have no idea how you eat and still have a six-pack? No jelly there. Or maybe just some errands? I could really use some errands so I have more to complete your picture.*

He doesn't answer, of course, but I carry on the conversation with myself as if he does. *Sounds good, I can learn more that way. Maybe after your errands, you can take me home and fuck me stupid? Make that tight ass of yours good for something . . . pounding into my needy pussy. How's that for a plan, Keith?*

God, I need a man.

It's been months since my last boyfriend, the bastard. While I'm known for being a spontaneous, up for anything kinda girl, I don't sleep around and have pretty discerning taste. Which, of course, is how I find myself fantasizing about Keith's ass as he walks down the street, sort of looking down as he walks, maybe to hide his face from the public or maybe because he's got his own internal dialogue going. It's too much to hope he's thinking about the sexy brunette in designer jeans and sunglasses he saw in the corner of the coffee shop and how he'd like to take her home and make all her dreams come true, but fuck it, I'm allowed to fill in the blanks here.

He pauses in front of a store and looks back, so I step over to a potted plant in front of a store as cover, jostling the sidewalk traffic flow as a younger guy on rollerblades yells at me, "Watch it, bitch!"

I scowl, not wanting the attention, and quickly bury my face in my phone but sneak looks out the side of my sunglasses as I catch my breath.

*Focus, Elise. Get your brain out of the gutter and do your fucking job!*

Suitably chastised by my own more responsible half, I continue on, following Keith into . . . a grocery store?

Wouldn't have expected Mr. Fancy Country Singer to be buying his own food. With online delivery and personal assistants running rampant around this town, I just never imagined him buying his own jars of basil pesto. Still, the fact that he does is cute, sweet, and maybe even a bit humble. I like this down-to-earth potential tilt to my story, so I sneak a few pics of him pushing his cart around the store, an old-fashioned piece of paper in his hand as he goes over his grocery list.

Following at a distance, I grab a few things totally at random as cover while I try to scope out what he's buying to see if there's anything interesting that'll tell me his secrets.

Bread . . . boring, it's not even fancy, just plain old wheat bread. Steaks . . . no surprise, although I wish I could afford a nice rib-eye every now and then. Speaking of USDA prime beef, God, I could take a bite of his biceps. Yummy. Milk . . . so 1990. Wait, not milk. He's buying milks, two different kinds of milk . . . skim *and* whole, a half-gallon each. And the skim milk is that special type for people who are lactose intolerant.

That's unusual, right? I mean, if you drink milk, you're not likely to go for two drastically different fat contents. Unless he cooks? Maybe the skim is to drink and the whole is to cook?

Hmm, could be. But then, why the lactose intolerant one? I've tasted it myself, and no matter what the makers say, it's crap compared to the real thing.

I keep following as he walks . . . into the feminine hygiene aisle. *Jackpot.*

Why would a notoriously single man, one whom women literally throw themselves at and are routinely rebuked, be buying tampons and pads? Because he's not single anymore! The little news ticker in my brain rolls by . . . *Hearts break all across*

*America as Keith Perkins confirms he's off the market, ladies. News at ten o'clock.*

He's stockpiling his house. By the looks of the third box of goodies he tosses in the basket, he's got damn-near a full medicine cabinet in there. I sneak another pic for proof and follow him up toward the front of the store.

Choosing the line behind him, I consider maybe taking a chance to say something. It's risky, but I might be able to tease some nugget of information out of the potential encounter. After setting his items on the conveyor belt, he looks at me.

I smile my biggest, flirtiest smile, expecting him to see stars. This smile has gotten me into more private rooms, parties, and information trades than I could say . . . unless you're paying.

But from Keith, nothing. Not even a returned smile. His eyes slide over me and then back to the conveyor belt as he watches the little display show each item as it's rung up.

How rude!

The whole encounter, Keith ignores me and barely speaks to the cashier. Most of the noise is grunts and mmm-hmms coming from him in response to the cashier's chatter. She doesn't seem to know who he is either. I get that we're not in a country town, but do none of these people listen to country music? Or music period?

You wouldn't think he'd be able to take off his hat and be incognito, but apparently, he can. Clark Kent, eat your fucking heart out. He pays—cash, I notice—and grabs his bags, disappearing out the door in a hurry. Shit, did he make me?

I pay for my mismatched bread, soda, and candy bar and hustle out behind him, wishing I hadn't grabbed that bag of tater tots as part of my cover for going down the frozen food aisle because it wasted precious time telling the cashier I'd changed my mind about them. I'm so busy looking left and right down the sidewalk, trying to find his bald head above the crowd, that I don't notice when he steps out right in front of me.

His chest is like running into a brick wall, bouncing off a slab of iron hard muscle that barely gives. I cry out in surprise, more of a startled squeak really, but before I fall, he captures my arm in a tight grip. For a split second, we're in tight proximity and I can feel the thrum of hot control resonating from him, and it makes me drunk. Suddenly, I'm aware of where my hand is, and it's cupping something big, warm . . . and I bet it would get even bigger if I had a chance. I feel my face heat and am momentarily thankful for the caked-on makeup to hide the flush racing along my cheeks.

The makeup can't hide the shiver that rushes through my body though, straight to my core as I'm reminded once again how fucking sexy Keith is. "Oh my gosh, I'm so sorry," I finally squeak out in a voice that's about an octave higher than I normally have. "I wasn't watching where I was going."

It isn't until I'm finished that realization hits me, and I start praying this was accidental. The last thing I need is his figuring out that I'm part of the press and that I've been following him.

Keith looks down at me, no small task considering I'm five seven in bare feet and usually feel part Amazon by the time I get high heels on. Even in running shoes, I can stand eye to eye with the average man.

As I look up, though, I realize I could wear my highest heels and he'd still be taller than me, still be able to bend me over and fuck me senseless. God, every thought I have of this guy is about sex. Either I'm really that desperate to fuck, he's that sexy, or both. Either way, I need a new vibrator. Hello, Amazon Prime, you are amazing. Two-Day shipping? Yes, please!

Luckily, my traitorous eyes are covered in sunglasses so he

can't know what I'm thinking, but regardless of whether he can catch my vibe or not, he doesn't seem impressed.

"Well, maybe you should watch where you're going then," he half growls, steadying me for a moment. "This isn't the sort of place for daydreaming."

Without another look, he strides off down the street. I stare at him, too shocked to even stammer a reply.

*What an asshole!* I think for a split second before I realize that yeah, I was following him, but he didn't know that for sure!

A tiny thought jumps through my mind, reminding me how hard his body felt, how strong his grip on my arm was as he kept me from falling. And yes, the feeling of what's inside his jeans, even if it was only for a microsecond. For a moment, I'm torn. Should I keep following him? Or now that he's had eye-to-sunglass contact with me, would that be too suspicious? I decide the risk isn't worth it. Besides, I think I have exactly what I need.

There's a woman in Keith's life. It isn't me, but that doesn't mean I'm not going to tell the world about it.

Get ready, Keith. Your dirty laundry is getting hung out to dry.

# CHAPTER 2

## KEITH

"What the fuck, Todd?" I explode into my phone as I do my damndest not to hurl my computer across the room to shatter into a million pieces against the wall. "Have you seen this shit?"

Through the phone, I hear Todd, my manager, trying to placate me. "I know, Keith. And I'm sorry. I'm looking into it as quickly as I can."

Quickly? I'm paying Todd a lot of money to make sure this isn't something that needs to be handled quickly. In this particular matter, I've made it clear that this should *never* be an issue. "Todd, the headline is 'Keith, who's the girl?'" I fume as I keep reading. "Fans want to know who's captured the heart of the rogue country star. Why would they even think there's a girl? I'm not dating anyone. Everyone knows that."

Todd sighs, and in my mind, I can see him now, sitting at his antique oak desk, the little vein in his left temple pulsing to his heartbeat. "That's just it, man. Everyone knows you don't date, and that's . . . odd for a celebrity of your success. I tried to get you to do some image work . . . show up for a few awards shows with another star, but nooooo, you didn't want to hear it. So people get curious."

I've heard all of this before, but I hate being fake. There are too many wannabes and fake ass people in this business for my liking as it is. I refuse to be one too.

"Well, fuck everyone's curiosity. My private life is my own. I sing songs, I make records, ones that have won some pretty sweet awards. I put on concerts, and we've done some damn good shows, I think. But that's it, I'm not available for public comment on my private life. I don't ask what they do with the life-sized posters I sign for them, and they don't get to ask what I do in my home."

Todd clicks into business mode, no longer trying to appease me, beginning the same conversation we've had over and over again for all the years we've worked together. I didn't hire him because he's a friend but because he knows the damn business. "Keith, there's nothing to be ashamed of here. You went grocery shopping and bought supplies for your daughter. Maybe it's time you tell the truth."

I inhale deeply, counting to ten before I let it out, willing it to calm me. It's maybe only slightly successful. "We've talked about this. No. Carsen is only twelve years old, and I want her to have as normal a childhood as she possibly can. If people know about her, she'll get hounded nonstop. She'll need a security detail to go to school, for Christ's sake, and never be able to grow up on her own. Never mind the fact that people are going to do some simple math and figure out that I fathered a child when I was still in high school. That'll start a whole other heap of questions, ones I don't want to fucking go into. The public isn't entitled to know about her, to have an opinion on what she's wearing or how I'm raising her, or fucking bring up her mother. No."

I can hear the resignation in Todd's voice. We've had this argument too many times. "I know. And I understand. It's gonna happen at some point, though. She can't stay hidden forever."

I chuckle darkly. "The hell she can't. If Hannah fucking Montana could pull it off for years, so can I."

Todd groans. "That was a fictional Disney show. And let's face it, I doubt you want your daughter doing what Miley Cyrus is doing in the real world now."

"I know it's fictional, dumbass. But I'll make sure Carsen has her fairytale Disney ending. She deserves that."

"Fine, fine, I can see I'm getting nowhere with you," Todd says, the exasperation with me obvious. His tone changes to one intended to be more placating. "Really, Keith . . . is Carsen okay after all of this?"

"Some bitch reporter made my little girl's first period into an expose about how I've supposedly got some new fucktoy. Ten million people now know what brand of fucking maxi pads I bought for her!" I growl, pissed off. "How do you think Carsen is doing?"

I hear Todd gulp and have a little mercy on him. He's kept my situation secret for nearly five years, a century in celebrity terms. "Sorry, man."

I shake my head, sighing. "No, it's okay. She's doing fine, mostly. She didn't realize that the feminine shit was what brought up the questions. Thinks it's just the usual speculation."

Todd hums, and I can hear the steel in his voice. He's a damn good manager, a good man overall, really. "I'm gonna fix this. I'm not sure how, but I'll see what I can do."

"Do your best. And do it fast, Todd." I grunt as a goodbye before I hang up. As soon as I do, I realize Sarah, my older sister, is standing in the doorway and likely heard everything I just said.

Sarah's leaning against the doorframe with her arms crossed, her long brown hair hanging down nearly to her waist, the same color as mine if I didn't keep my head shaved by choice. "Little rough on Todd there, weren't you?"

I can see the disapproving look in her eye, reminding me so much of Mom. We both got our height and physique from her, although thankfully, I inherited Dad's wide shoulders, or else I'd look like a ripped string bean.

"Not really," I reply evenly. "It's his job to handle things, to make sure nothing like this happens. But it did, so now he can fucking fix it. Fast."

Sarah sighs, giving me an amused eyebrow. "Why didn't you just call me? I could've gone to the store and there wouldn't have been an issue. You know, if I go buy maxi pads, nobody gives a shit."

I sigh, feeling trapped. On one hand, I know she's right. On the other hand, every time I'd have to do it, I'd feel like the world's shittiest father. It's a no-win situation. "I know, Sarah. And you know how much I appreciate everything you do . . . for me and for Carsen. But I'm her dad, you know? She needed something, and it's my job to provide it, so I went to the fucking grocery store. It shouldn't have been a big deal."

I plop to the couch, elbows on my spread knees and my head hung low. It's been hard, raising a little girl without her mother, no help from her grandparents, and only my big sister to turn to. I can't even ask more from Sarah. She's a beautiful young woman with her own life to live. It'd be unfair for me to demand she be even more of a surrogate mother to Carsen. And no matter what . . . "I just didn't want to be a failure of a father."

Sarah sits beside me, putting an arm around my shoulder like she did when we were little and I had to turn to her for comfort in the bad times. "You take good care of her, Keith. No doubt to anyone who knows you two how much you love that little girl. She has everything she needs right here with you, but you don't have to do it alone. I love that girl like she's my own. Damn-near raised her right along with you, remember?"

I place my hand on hers, patting it. "Thanks, Sarah. I know you love her, and I don't know what we'd have done without you all these years, but I hate that something that should be simple, like getting groceries, just isn't anymore." I sigh. "Hell, maybe I need a break. Just step away from the spotlight for a few years until Carsen gets older?"

Sarah shakes her head. "No chance in hell. You have worked your ass off to chase your dream, Keith. 'All those years' you're talking about? I remember them too. I remember you working days at shitty job after shitty job before singing nights. I remember my working a full-time job and bringing Carsen to some seedy places to hear you sing when she was just a toddler. I remember you holding her to your chest with one hand, writing songs with the other while you hummed her to sleep at night."

I smile slightly, remembering those nights too. "She couldn't sleep as a baby unless I was holding her."

"And she still loves you just as much," Sarah reminds me. "So all that hard work? You made it, Keith. You got your dream, and you need to grab onto it with both hands and hang on tight for as long as the ride goes. Because you know what the rap god says."

I nod. Sarah's always been more into hip hop than I am, but I know the lyrics. "When the run's over, just admit it's at an end."

"And in the meantime, get as much as you can out of it," Sarah adds. "So yeah, it's awkward right now, and the fact that something happened that is beyond your control is killing you . . ."

I try to interrupt to disagree, but she talks over me. "Please,

Keith. You're the biggest control freak I've ever met. And this hit you out of left field and you don't like it. But suck it up, buttercup. It'll blow over, and trust Todd to make sure it does. In the meantime, you know you've got a moment, maybe two or three. Hang onto them and give you and your daughter the rest of a life together afterward."

I huff, knowing she's right. "Fine. You're right. As hard as I've worked to make a career singing, I'll give it all up in a split second if it's bad for Carsen though. You know that."

Sarah smiles, reaching up and rubbing my head like she used to when we were kids. "Of course you would. But look around you, Keith. She's fine, goes to a great school, has great friends, lives in a gorgeous house like nothing we could've ever imagined when we were kids, and is happy."

I smile, looking around. You could probably fit our childhood home in just this room. Hell, this house has more bathrooms than we had rooms back then. We've definitely moved up in life since those days.

"Thanks, Sarah," I finally say, leaning back and relaxing some. "You know how to make things sound right."

She nods, and I'm struck by how far we've come, brother and sister against the world. Needing a lighter moment before those childhood memories take over my brain, I tease her a little. "You sound just like Mom."

She grins, sticking her tongue out at me. "Well, thank you. I'm choosing to take that as the compliment I'm sure you intended it to be."

I laugh, giving her a side hug. "Yeah, definitely a compliment, Sis."

# CHAPTER 3

## ELISE

I can't quite be sure, but it feels like I'm floating into work as I walk down the sidewalk. It's only been two days . . . but what a two days. I knew that story was going to be hot. I was ecstatic when Donnie agreed to give me the top header with the biggest page square footage and a big byline on our site's homepage. I've already snapped screen grabs of it for posterity. It's tabloid trash, but one day, those disguises and stalker skills are going to land me my dream job as a real investigative reporter.

I'm not picky, obviously, considering what I'm doing now. But I would like to do more than tabloid celeb hunting. Still, it was some damn fine surveillance if I say so myself. Well, other than when I ran into Keith. That was some newbie shit there, but he didn't seem to figure out I was a reporter, at least. If anything, he probably thought I was just a fan girl trying to get an autograph or maybe cop a feel . . . which I certainly remember, even if that was a tidbit I couldn't publish in order to cover my ass.

Wonder if he's still trying to figure out who at the grocery store scoped him out for the expose?

I pause for coffee, greeting my coworkers Maggie and Francesca as they linger around the pot waiting for refills. They look like a study in opposites. Maggie is tiny, a deceptively curvy blonde who rocks the nerdy-librarian look while maintaining an appearance much younger than her twenty-five years. She's a little shy but a total sweetheart once you get past her armor.

Meanwhile, Francesca is an exotic and willowy brunette who carries the practiced presence of her younger years in pageants. She never fails to mention she was second runner-up Miss Teen New Jersey. No wonder I detest the bitch sometimes.

So they're polar opposites in personality, with Maggie being more shy and reserved to Francesca's extroverted cockiness, but coffee is the eternal common denominator.

Francesca sips her coffee, toasting me slightly. "Congrats on the country singer story, Elise. Got everything you could want with that one."

The words are right, but there's a cattiness to her tone that's always there with her. She's always a bit chilly with anyone she perceives as a threat and sometimes an outright bitch if she doesn't get her way.

I pour myself a mug and make sure to keep my voice neutral. "Thank you. It was hard work so I'm glad it paid off."

She laughs, putting more meaning to words than I'd intended. "Oh, trust me, I do plenty of hard work for my stories too," she says as she almost disgustingly slurps down a mouthful of coffee, hinting at her meaning. "It pays off in some ways more than others."

With a wink, Francesca refills and sashays to her desk. I shake my head as Maggie half chokes on her coffee as she finally gets the meaning. Leaning in closer, she stage-whispers. "Did she just mean . . .?"

I smirk, giving Maggie a glance. "Of course. She's totally been fucking Donnie to get the prime stories. Has been for months. Why do you think her reports are always from fancy parties, galas, and red carpet events? Hello, preferential treatment. You seriously didn't know?"

Maggie blushes a little and shrugs. "Well, I knew she was doing something to get Donnie's attention, and the rumors are always flying. But she's so casual about it, just throwing it out in conversation."

I grin, smacking Maggie's arm. "You're so cute when you go Dorothy Gale on me. Remember, hun, this ain't Kansas. Besides, I can't say I'm jealous. I'd rather work for my stories than get them by giving Donnie blow jobs under the desk. Can you imagine the dust bunnies under there? And eww on sucking his gross dick. I like my facials at the spa, thank you very much."

I half-feign a full-body shudder of disgust, and Maggie laughs. "Ew. Now I'll have that image in my head all day. Thanks a lot, Elise. You suck!"

I grin, blowing Maggie a kiss. "Well, in the right circumstances, yes, I do suck. Even been told I'm pretty good at it. But I think we've established that it's not happening here."

I scan the room with a pointed finger. "Yup, not happening, not happening, not happening, and never, even if he was the last male on Earth and we needed to repopulate the species. So . . . what are you working on now?"

Maggie laughs again, brightening my day. I love making Maggie laugh and blush. She's so easy since she's a bit innocent, and I've got no shame in my game and generally give zero fucks. "Nothing great. I'm currently looking into a senator who's supposedly cheating on his wife. But I've been undercover as a copy-making volunteer in his office for two weeks and haven't seen anything other than a man who works too many hours. Seems like a bust."

"Sorry about that. At least he's not cheating. Hell, that alone would likely make me vote for him, considering the options lately."

Maggie grins, nodding. "Yup. He's even polite. I've been wearing my cutest tight skirt and blouse whenever I go by, and he keeps looking in my eyes."

"Maybe you don't have the equipment that entices him?" I ask, making Maggie laugh. "What? He wouldn't be the first politician to reach across the aisle for entertainment."

"Nah," Maggie says, smiling. Waving fingers at me, she walks off. "See you later, babe."

Refilling my coffee to the top, I head to my desk too but am sidetracked by Donnie's yelling. "Elise! Get your ass in here!"

Damn, you'd think a great prime story would at least get me twenty-four hours of peace, but apparently not. I consider saying as much as I sit in the chair across from Donnie, but when I see how red his face is, I decide to leave it be. Fuck it, I don't need the headache. "What's up?"

Donnie's in a pissed off mood for some reason. "You've got proof on the Perkins story?"

I nod, confused but answering anyway. "Of course. Pics of him in the store, putting things in the shopping cart, including maxi pads in the hygiene aisle, and then again at the register for a close-up. Why?"

Donnie sighs, running his fingers through his thinning, greasy hair, and again I'm reminded why I could never get to the top the way Francesca does. I might be a girl who enjoys sex, but I've got standards. Donnie ticks none of my boxes. "I just hung up with Perkins' people. They want a retraction and correction."

My jaw drops open. It happens in our business from time to time, but it's never happened to me. I'm too damn good at my job. "No way. I followed him legally, pics are in public places, thus legal, it's obviously him, and I didn't say anything that could be libel. It's all true."

Donnie smiles, relieving me a little bit. "I know. That's what I told the guy who called too, but I just wanted to check."

"I appreciate that you had my back," I tell him honestly. Donnie's a sleazeball, but he's a dedicated sleaze. He won't back down from a story he prints unless he has to, and that usually involves lawyers. "So, what now? We're obviously not pulling the story, right?"

Donnie shakes his head, reaching for the bowl of jellybeans he keeps on the corner of his desk and popping three into his mouth. "No, actually, when I told him that wasn't going to happen, he had another idea that's pretty interesting. He proposed a series of interviews, probably three or four at least—but maybe more—with Perkins himself."

Perkins himself? At the words, my pulse quickens. I can't seem to keep my thoughts about him not tied up in how fucking sexy he is. "Really?"

Donnie nods. "They're doing some damage control and wanting to write their own narrative about his life. Control the narrative, you know?"

"That sounds great!" I exclaim gleefully, and not totally professionally. "When do I meet with him?"

Donnie laughs, almost like he's amused I'd ask. "I'm thinking Frannie can take this one, Elise."

My jaw drops. Oh, hell no! Giving the best initial slots to Francesca because she's giving you her slot? I get that . . . but to take a story from me? "Like hell! This is my story . . . a follow-up from my expose. It should go to me and you know it, Donnie."

He narrows his eyes at me, not liking that I questioned him, but I'm right. This is my story. A small piece of me wants to stamp my foot and yell *Mine*! but since that's not likely to get me what I want, I quickly figure out a different tactic.

"Donnie, look. This story should go to me, and I know you . . . appreciate Francesca's work," I choke out, almost gagging to have to say that, "but she's going to be busy with red carpet events for the next two weeks when those new blockbusters come out. You know those comic book movies make big bucks and get big stars at the premieres."

Donnie makes a humming sound in the back of his throat, seemingly in no hurry to hand down his decision while I'm waiting on pins and needles. Do I need to bring up the fact that the whole office knows Francesca's using her . . . assets to get ahead with head? Finally, Donnie speaks. "Okay. You can do it. Interviews with Perkins, and I want all the dirty details, ins and outs of his life, all of it. Can you do that?"

I nod, relieved. "Of course!"

Getting up to leave before Donnie changes his mind, I stop at the door when he calls my name. "Hey, Elise? Just FYI . . . Perkins is pissed as fuck for the story because everyone knows he's majorly private. And he'll know who you are from the byline. You might have six feet three inches of raging cowboy to deal with. Be ready. And get those secrets."

I nod, my mind focusing on the words *inches* and *raging*. "Yes, sir."

# CHAPTER 4

## KEITH

"I can't believe you think this is the best way to deal with this," I growl at Todd through the small screen on my phone. He cringes slightly at the vehemence in my voice, even though he's a thousand miles away and probably thanking the fates for inventing FaceTime. It's not really his fault. It's the upper management at the record label that decided on this hair-brained scheme. He just has to play the messenger, and he's the only person available for me to take out my frustrations on.

So I do, copiously. I need to hit the gym and relieve some of this stress. "Really? How is an interview going to make my life more private? Sing songs, play music, go the fuck home . . . that's all I ask."

Todd sighs at the repeat of the mantra that's been the driving force for my career for the last few years. Yeah, I tour, but always in the summer when Carsen and Sarah can come along. During the school year, I play one-shot TV appearances or so-called "secret shows" where it's marketed as a last-minute gig and usually stuffed with radio personalities and listeners who win tickets. It works for me because I'm usually only gone for a weekend before getting back home to Carsen and my quiet life.

Todd calls it 'keeping my name out there' . . . like I need more promotion. I've got the career I've always dreamed of if the nosy paparazzi would just leave me the hell alone.

"Do we need to do this when I can be there to wrangle you?" Todd asks, deciding to just say fuck it and ignore my protests. "Or can you do this on your own and not be an ass? This is happening, like it or not. The label's already told the paper, and if you back out—"

"Then the shit really hits the fan," I growl. I'm this close to calling his bluff. What stops me is the fact that if I don't talk to this paper, the label will, and not everyone there understands my need for privacy. "Fine, fuck it. I'll be a fucking gentleman."

"Good," Todd replies. "So make sure that you represent yourself in a way that won't make the label folks shit their pants. Okay?"

I sigh, feeling like a deflated balloon. "I'll be fine. You know I can bullshit and be charming when I need to be. I get it . . . follow the party line. No woman in my life, obviously. Stick to promoting the new album and next tour. Nothing too personal."

Todd winces, and I can feel the other shoe about to drop. "Well, not exactly. We sold them on the idea that this is an all-access interview series, and—"

I cut him off, nearly losing my shit again. "All-access? How the hell am I supposed to keep Carsen a secret if it's fucking all-access?"

Todd rolls his eyes. "As I was saying, we call it all-access because then it seems like you're giving them everything, but then you corral them some. There are going to be personal questions. Answer them as honestly as possible without giving anything away that you want kept secret."

"And if they pry into areas that I don't want to talk about?" I ask.

"It's called playing coy, for fuck's sake. Every actress in Hollywood has been doing it since they invented film! You give a smile, a deceptive answer, and let your charm deflect. But by telling them and viewers that it's you completely uncensored and open, they'll hopefully quit asking questions. Especially when they see you're just a nice guy who wants to keep to himself, living out his dream of country music."

I laugh. He's got a few points. "That actually *is* true, so I think I can sell that. Okay, honest . . . to a point. Charming and genuine. Promote. That it?"

Todd claps his hands together, satisfied. "I think that's probably a tall enough order for today. You good? Really?"

I take a big breath, trying to focus. "Yeah, Todd. I'm good. Thanks for talking me off the ledge. You know I hate attention like this already, and with Carsen, it's hard to keep from freaking the fuck out."

Todd, who's kept my secret well, nods. "I know, Keith. Everything you do is for Carsen and for the music. That always shines through, even when you're being an ass. That's why I'm still working with you."

I laugh. "Naw, that's not it. You just like those platinum albums on your resume and my pretty-boy face."

Todd barks out a laugh, getting up from his chair. "Yeah, that's it, of course. Your mug. Speaking of, you'd better get cleaned up. The reporter will be there at four. Dinner service arrives at six for you two to take a break, and then interview number one ends at eight. I'll help you arrange a few things for steering, but if you think you're good, I've got a decent trio that's looking at becoming a bunch of solo acts."

"Why?" I ask as I run through a mental list of what I need to do . . . starting with locking Carsen's room. Thank God she's got her own bathroom.

"Same shit as always. One thinks she's better than the others . . ."

"Damn. Good luck," I reply, thinking about one thing. In four hours, a reporter will be asking me questions, digging into my past, my thoughts, and my heart.

It sounds like hell.

As soon as I hang up with Todd, I work like a madman, calling in for an emergency cleaning from my housekeeper as I scrub every trace of Carsen from the common areas. After that, I plaster a smile on my face and get dressed to kill, hoping that at least my country boy charm can carry me through some of this train wreck.

When the doorbell rings promptly at four o'clock, I force myself to inhale deeply a few times, attempting to calm my nerves. The most important thing is that Carsen is over at Sarah's for the night and I've got a plan in mind for an 'all-access' grand tour that goes nowhere near her room.

You never know just how eagle-eyed and sneaky reporters can be. Carsen's door is locked, so if the reporter checks it, she'll probably think I've got some red room of pain hidden upstairs. But honestly, I'd be better with that than if she exposed Carsen.

I open the door and am immediately struck stupid. The woman standing on my front doorstep is gorgeous. She's tall and lean, but with curves in all the right places, barely contained in the slim-fitting dress she's wearing.

Her blonde hair is pulled back in a ponytail, fully exposing her high cheekbones and the graceful length of her neck. Her blue eyes hold a hint of amusement at my obvious freeze, and something tickles the back of my mind. She seems familiar, but I think I'd remember a woman this beautiful, even if I only glanced at her for a moment.

"Mr. Perkins?" she says after a moment. "I'm Elise Warner from The Daily Spot. I'm here for the interview."

I nod, but I'm still checking her out, if I'm honest, blood rushing to my cock instead of my brain, so it takes a second for what she said to sink in.

"Wait. Did you say Elise Warner? As in the reporter who started this whole clusterfuck in the first place?" I fume, and she nods. "Oh, fuck this."

Before I even think about it, I slam the door and walk off into the house. She should know to leave it alone, walk away and maybe send someone else. Someone I don't want to crucify for fucking with my life. But does she?

Of course not.

Instead, she starts ringing my doorbell over and over like a damn five-year-old. *Ring-ring, ring-ring.*

I snarl in frustration, turning around halfway down my hallway, and stalk back, yanking the door open. "What?"

In her defense, she doesn't look cowed by my grumpy assholeness, instead lifting her chin up defiantly. "You're right, Mr. Perkins. I am the one who reported that you seem to have some interesting things happening in your life. That's my job . . . to report on things our readers find interesting. And now it seems our jobs align. Mine to interview you and you to be interviewed . . . by me. Or perhaps there was some misunderstanding with your record label? Maybe you should call them? Or I could, if you'd rather."

I narrow my eyes, taking her measure. She's bluffing, but somehow, she hit on the one thing I don't want to do—call the label and tell them I'm not doing this. That happy bunch of assholes would probably just put out a fucking press release saying I'm off the market and probably start selling tickets to some fake engagement party they set up for PR. Instead, Todd's voice echoes in my ear. Charm her, tell some stories, get on with life. *I can do this. I can wrap her around my little finger, no problem. It's gonna suck big hairy balls, but I can do this.*

"Fine. Come on in."

I leave the door standing open and walk to the living room, not even checking to see if she follows. But she does, of course, closing the door with a soft click, and then her wedge heels swish on the tile floor until quieted by the rug.

She gestures to the chair opposite where I've claimed the expanse of couch, and I simply raise one eyebrow, but she takes it as permission and sits down daintily before taking out her phone, a small notebook, and a pink sparkly pen. Seriously?

"Okay, Mr. Perkins, I'd like to go over my thoughts for the interview series first so we can make sure we're on the same page. Is that okay?"

She smiles like she's trying to soothe an angry bear, and hell, I guess she kinda is. I lean back, letting my arm stretch out over the back of my couch, relaxing a bit.

"Keith."

Elise, who's checking her notes, looks up. "Excuse me?"

I chuckle, rubbing at my head. "For the love of fuck, call me Keith. Not Mr. Perkins. That was my dad."

I see her mouth twitch a bit and she mouths, 'for the love of fuck' before shaking her head, seemingly amused at my random turn of phrase. Still, she blushes just slightly, and I find it . . . well, she looks even hotter now. "Okay, Keith. And please call me Elise. Does that sound like a plan?"

I nod as graciously as I can muster, which is basically not at all. Hot or not, she's in my private territory, and I'm doing my best to just be polite. "Sure."

"So, I'm thinking that you're obviously an enigma and your fans want to know more about you, especially since you tend to shun the spotlight. That's really rare in this day and age, when most stars can't seem to hog the spotlight enough."

"I like having my privacy, that's all. Always have."

Elise nods, leaning forward. "And I think a series of interviews will give us a nice peek into your life. I understand your point of view."

"Is that so?"

Elise gives me a heartstopping smile, nodding. "I know you don't believe me, but yes. So maybe a past, present, future setup or something more along the lines of your professional life and personal life mixed in with tidbits about your history in each? All in all, just a bigger, better picture of who you are. It'll satisfy the fans and keep reporters like me, but with a lot less morals, off your doorstep. I'll know about the structure as we see where the interviews naturally lead. Anything you want to add or that's off limits?"

My first thought is that everything is off limits, but I know I can't say that, so I simply nod in agreement before I think better of it. "Actually, Elise . . ."

The name sounds sweet on my tongue, making me remember just how damn sexy she looked all fired up, standing in my doorway and calling me on my shit. Her cheeks are still a bit flushed from the fiery exchange, and now that she's leaning toward me, I can see her voluptuous breasts pressing fully against her dress.

It helps, and the idea that was hatching in my head a moment ago suddenly seems a lot more possible. I turn on the charm, dropping my voice a bit. "Elise . . . this is obviously not by my choice. I'm very much a private person, and I like to be in control . . . of my image, of my music, of what I do and don't do . . . honestly, I like to be in control of everything. So these interviews chafe against that by their very nature. How about we make a deal, you and me?"

I don't miss the way her breath hitches when I mention being in control. Deliciously interesting. She licks her lips, her little pink tongue darting out, and I have a flash of her tongue licking me all over. My cock twitches, and I realize . . . maybe this won't be as bad as I thought.

"What kind of deal did you have in mind?" she asks, her voice a bit breathy. I smile, knowing I've got her on the hook.

"Let's make a deal that for every question you ask me, I get to ask one back. You want to know me, but that's very one-sided. Of course, I won't be writing a tell-all expose of your private life like you seem to want to do about me. So the least you can do is make this a little easier, a little more conversational and less of an interrogation. What do you say?"

She bites her lip, thinking about it, and I want to soothe the bite with my tongue. Or shit, maybe bite her lip myself while she fucks herself on my fingers. "I don't know—"

"I'll keep it just between us," I reassure her. "Just think of it as a little pain to go with the pleasure. What do you say?"

Part of me hopes she says yes to the deal so that I have an upper hand. Part of me wants her to say no, and then I can show her out the front door and not do the interviews at all. But the biggest part of me, or maybe just the *hardest* part, wants her to say yes because I want to push her, see what she'll share, how honest she'll be when I poke and prod at her deepest secrets.

Honestly, if she left right now, I'd be jacking off to thoughts of her on her knees sucking me off within seconds, not sending up praise at the lack of interviews.

Curious for her answer, I wait silently, eyes locked on hers.

Let's see who wins.

# CHAPTER 5

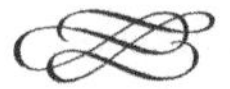

## ELISE

This is not going how I thought it would at all. I was expecting a bit of country boy charm, some hospitality, and maybe some pat interview answers. I figured I'd have to work to get deeper, tease out Keith's personality for the articles. I was prepared to dig, to have to wiggle my way into his trust so he'd relax and be real with me.

What I didn't expect was his huge body, clad in jeans and a white button-down shirt that seems to be molded to his bulk, looking so damn sexy when he opened the door. I guess I should have. I ogled his ass for an entire week to get that scoop.

For some reason, the bare head and feet made him seem casual, comfortable until he'd realized who I am. He definitely lit up then, anger flashing in his eyes, and I got a hint of the cold fire in his core.

It's that cold fire that seems to draw me in. I don't feel like I'm in control, but instead, we're jockeying, wrestling for who gets to take charge.

He's clearly doing these interviews begrudgingly, which makes his deal all the more unusual. I don't think for one second that he wants to know a damn thing about me, some annoying reporter digging into his private life when he wants desperately to keep it private.

And so we're in this little silent war, my body saying one thing while my professionalism says another. After all, why would he want to ask me questions?

I realize the answer. He told me as plain as day. It's a control move. His way of showing that even in a situation beyond his control, he's in power here. So we keep wrestling, doing our little dance and seeing who gets to be on top.

But really, is that so bad? To let him demonstrate some semblance of being the boss here, if it gets me what I want . . . him to answer my questions. Right, that's why I'm thinking of sweaty bodies pinning each other to the floor, or a bed, or . . .

Fuck it. It's not like I have anything to hide with my boring life, so he can fire away with his questions.

Decision made, I meet his dark eyes to see fire flashing there. So much anger . . . at me or at the situation, maybe both? Or is what I'm seeing as anger just passion?

I straighten my back, keeping the stare contest going. "Tell you what, Keith. I'll agree to your deal . . . *If* you answer honestly and fully any question I ask and help me write an interesting, exciting story about you. You do that, and I'll return the favor. Complete and full honesty to any question."

He studies me, and I can feel him visually taking my measure as an opponent before he gets up, towering over me as he offers a hand. I shake it, noticing that his large hand engulfs mine. "Deal. Fair warning, Elise. You just made a deal with the devil for your soul."

I grin at his dramatics, but there's a little swarm of bees in my belly concerned that maybe there's more truth to what he's saying than I'm expecting. I expected Keith Perkins to be a little bit of a bumpkin, a good ol' country boy who might be a little hostile but still stunned by the chic city girl with smooth verbal skills. Instead, he's controlled, and he's obviously a damn sight smarter than I've given him credit for . . . and that makes him all the more attractive. And a hell of a lot more dangerous.

We settle back more comfortably in our seats, and I pick up my phone, starting the voice recorder before setting it on the table in front of me as he sits back down with the grace of a tiger in his lair. He doesn't react to my recorder, but I explain anyway, covering my ass. "I hope you don't mind. Recording the sessions is just part of the deal, to make sure I'm correct with any quotes." I give him a slight death glare, remembering how his label wanted a retraction and correction as if I'd been incorrect about my reporting.

He doesn't say anything but gives me a look of tortured pain. I figure since he's not arguing, I might as well run with it and charge ahead. "So first, let's get the basics out of the way . . . the Wikipedia version of who Keith Perkins is. Tell me about yourself."

He sighs, rolling his eyes, and I know it's exactly the kind of question he's had to answer a million times before. But I need it direct from the source for the articles, and it helps break the ice a little, gets him talking on comfortable ground.

Finally, he starts. "My name's Keith Tiberius Perkins. I'm a musician, a singer-songwriter. I'm thirty years old, born and raised in Idaho in a tiny town nobody's ever heard of, including some of the people who lived there. As soon as I graduated high school, I left home for Boise to play in local dive bars and clubs. I even had to use a fake ID to get in because I was underage. As far as my mom was concerned, I might as well have run off to New York City or even hell, judging by her reaction. But I learned, worked hard, and after a few years, moved to Nashville to play in hole-in-the-wall dives there with every other dreamer. Got discovered one night, signed a contract with my label, and now here I am, years later, hit songs and awards later, doing interviews I hate."

I grin. He'd been doing so well until the end there. I do wonder, though—why leave Nashville? They'd worship him around there. What brought him to this area of the country, not exactly New York but still, not quite the center of country music?

"Sounds like you're living the dream, huh?"

Keith smirks, then remembers where he is and grows serious again. "Yeah, I worked hard for a lot of years on my music. Still do. That's all I want to do . . . write songs, sing them for people, and go home. Alone."

"Damn, dude, like a dog with a bone. Let it go. I get it. I'm in your man cave that's the size of a McMansion, but I'm really not trying to be a bitch here."

He shoots forward in his chair, giving me a fierce look, and I realize I said that out loud, not in my head. "Excuse me?"

*Shit.*

Backpedaling, I try to smooth over the accidental out-loud monologue. "Sorry for saying that out loud, but not for thinking it."

I smirk at him, virtually daring him to puff all up in anger again.

Instead, he sits back in the couch, pointing a finger at me and dropping his voice to a sexy commanding growl. "My turn. Tell me about yourself, Elise Warner."

I smile, liking this game. If a bullet point list of all things me is what you want, I'll give it to you, asshole. You're not in control of things yet.

"I'm Elise Warner, twenty-six, grew up here in East Robinsville, and went to school at State where I got my journalism degree. Did some small-time reporting for the local paper before getting hired by *The Daily Spot*, where I write celebrity tabloid crap but get to keep my investigative skills fresh. And this interview series is a big deal for me, so don't fuck it up. Please."

He huffs out a surprised laugh. I don't think he was expecting me to be so honest or so confrontational with him. By his smile, I think he likes it, too. He quickly asks the same follow-up question I did. "So, living the dream? Is this what little Elise wanted to do when she grew up?"

I shake my head, letting the 'little' comment slide. I'm all grown up, buddy, and you damn well know it. "No, not really. I like investigative reporting, but I wish I could do something more . . ."

Unexpectedly, I stumble for words, searching for something big enough to explain my heart while Keith looks on, interested. "Go on."

"Just, I want something more impactful," I admit. "Fight for the little guy, expose the bad guys, that kind of thing. But that's a hard gig to come by, so I'm working my way up. If I was in your story, I guess I'm still in the dive bars in Boise but working on that big move to better things, chasing the dream."

He hums, seemingly thinking about what I've said. I want to keep the ball rolling, to capitalize on the bit of sympathy I seem to be getting from him, so I decide to address the elephant in the room, the main reason I'm here.

"So, your professional life is golden, all you could've dreamed of. What about your personal life, Keith? What's happening on the dating front? Who are you buying maxis for? Who's the milk for, Keith?" I ask with a conspiratorial tone.

He growls, literally growls at me like an animal. It's like nothing I've ever heard, and on some primitive level, I'm scared and know I should run for cover from the apex predator with his sights on me. But on a deeper, instinctive level, my blood just started singing through my body, pulsing at a focal point behind my clit.

Holy shit. Maybe it's a little caveman-ish, but it's fucking sexy as hell too. Unconsciously, I squeeze my crossed legs tighter, needing some pressure for relief. But he notices. I expect him to start yelling, but instead he just smirks and leans forward again.

His voice is quiet, gravel as he answers, seemingly puzzled by me. "You're forward, aren't you? No finesse or foreplay. Just jumping into the question you know is most likely to set me off. No, I'm not dating anyone, nor am I looking to. Maybe the supplies were just so I can be a gracious host. Need a tampon, Elise?"

I can't help but defend myself a bit. He's somehow getting to me despite my best attempts to get under *his* skin. The score is definitely in his favor right now. Needing to get back in the battle for control, I fume. "No, fuck you very much. It's the reason this all started, that speculation, so why not address it from the start? Besides, foreplay is for people who don't know what they want, who need to warm up to the idea. I get the feeling that neither of us is like that. I know what I want . . . your secrets. And you know what you want . . . to not tell me. I'm not going to trick them out of you. Just bold honesty."

He tilts his head, searching my face for something. "Okay. But there's one thing you're wrong about."

I raise an eyebrow in question. "What's that?"

Keith smiles, but it's a predatory full baring of his teeth, more threatening and conquering than humorous. "Foreplay isn't for people who need a warm-up. Foreplay can be the best part if it's done right."

He pauses, and I know I'm breathing faster than I should be, considering I'm just sitting on a couch talking, but damn, can he talk. Every word is measured for effect, and I feel more bare than if I'd even answered a question.

The answer is written all over my face, my body. "And are you good at foreplay?"

Keith nods, his smile changing slightly, becoming as seductive as it is confrontational. "Bold honesty, huh? Very. Okay, Elise . . . tell me about *your* dating life."

It's not a question, it's an order.

I want to be bratty back, call him on his bossiness, but I realize that would be counter to my mission here, so I give in and willingly share. "No, I'm not dating either. I work too damn much, and my last boyfriend was an ass. I'm not hung up on him or anything. It's been months ago and was casual at best, more like fuck buddies than a real relationship. But I'm just . . . no, not dating."

He grins, a real one this time. "Point proven. Fuck buddies don't need foreplay. Just get in, get off, and get out. You're just not used to getting more. So much more that it becomes a necessity, an integral piece of the bigger action, not something to be rushed through or skipped." Every word he says is seduction, meant to make me squirm for him and I'm fighting the urge, forcing myself to be still.

I bite my lip, considering his words, my body screaming that it wants more, too. "Well, you may be right. But tell me, Keith. For someone who's not dating anyone, you sure do have some insight into the inner workings of the human mind and body. How'd you get so . . . smart?"

I stumble at the last second because I almost said sexy, and I'll be damned if I'm giving him that kind of ammunition, but he seems to know that 'smart' wasn't my first word choice judging by his cocked eyebrow. "I said I'm not dating. Never said I was a saint."

Before I can ask a follow-up question, the doorbell rings and

Keith rises from his seat to go answer it. I can't help but watch him as he moves with graceful power toward the hallway, returning a moment later leading a guy wearing black pants and a white chef jacket toward what I can only assume is the kitchen. I follow, drawn by both professional and personal curiosity.

As the cook tells Keith about the menu and warming times, I hang in the doorway, taking in Keith's no-muss appearance. His jeans have ridden down low on his lean hips, showing the waistband of his underwear as he reaches up and his shirt hem raises with his arms.

Wondering if he's a boxer brief kind of guy, I let my eyes dip down to his crotch and see a nice bulge that makes me picture him dropping those pants and taking his cock out for me. As my eyes drift back up, I see that his arms are crossed over his chest, showing off biceps that strain against the white cotton of his shirt and make his shirt ride up to expose a tiny sliver of his stomach. I have to admit to myself that want to run my hands over his abs, feel and caress each ridge.

When the cook takes his leave, Keith turns to meet my eyes. "Hungry?"

There's an undertone to his voice, an awareness of the fact that I was just checking him out. But I see a gleam in his eyes. He's checking me out too, which just increases my desire. Before I can tell myself not to say it, I answer him honestly. "Starving."

There's a rumble in his chest, but he seems to remember his game plan before I remember mine, still lost in some fantasy of him bending me over the kitchen counter and licking his dessert out of my soaking wet pussy. He opens a cabinet door, grabbing plates, then glasses and silverware. "Follow me."

After serving up healthy portions onto the plates and a quick warming in the microwave, we sit at the table in the kitchen nook. There's tension between us now, but it's not awkward. If anything, it feels good, flavored with the little intimate touches like using a microwave. It's like Keith's saying I know you find me sexy. I don't need to bend over backward to impress you more than I do naturally.

It's natural and heady, like I'm a stick of dynamite and he's waving a lit match around, and I'm dangerously close to begging him to light me up because everything in me says that he damn sure could.

I try to get my head back in the game, reminding myself that no matter how fucking sexy Keith may be or how horny I am, that's not happening. I'm a reporter, and my name isn't Francesca, goddammit!

I need to be professional, get him to answer some fresh questions, dig a little deeper into who he is. Discovering his secrets, writing a great article series . . . that's the goal here. Not getting my pussy licked before getting a creamy ending to my fantasies.

Keith seems to read all of my dirty, naughty thoughts, but he chooses to let me simmer in my need and goes over to the fridge. "Wine?"

I nod, curious that he didn't offer me a beer. "Just a half glass. Still on the clock, you know."

I wish I hadn't said it the moment it leaves my mouth. It's a reminder that regardless of any flirting we might have been doing, and how fucking hot Keith makes me, being here is my job. My job to tell all the things he'd rather keep private.

It's like a bucket of cold water has been dumped on our whole interaction, and I can see it in the sudden increased tension across Keith's jawline.

Dinner and the rest of our evening proceed with conversational questions and answers, but not nearly as personal and telling as our earlier talk. There's none of the burning taunting now, just a polite aloofness.

It feels colder, robotic even as he answers in what amounts to one word, sometimes one-syllable answers. And though I could write a whole book about how hot Keith is in person, how commanding his presence is, I'm not sure that's exactly where this all-access story needs to go.

That fact feels like . . . my secret.

# CHAPTER 6

## KEITH

Ten minutes.

I was totally right.

Fuck. I'm amazed I lasted this long.

Our evening of interviewing is barely over. I'd shut the door behind Elise no fewer than ten minutes ago, and here I am, in my shower, jacking off. I run a soapy hand down my stomach, grabbing my already thick cock in a tight grip, moving slowly up and down.

*Foreplay,* I tell myself, and moan at her denial of needing it. Shit, she doesn't know it but we've already started our foreplay. All evening has been an exercise in seduction and denial on my part, and she's gonna love every hot minute of it. Every moment, from the instant that I knew she was into me and I wanted her too, it's been a slow, tortuously seductive dance, half with our bodies, half with our words.

The way she challenged me . . . delicious. Her inquisitive and prying nature . . . sublime. And her body . . . I couldn't write a song good enough to describe how perfect she looked, the twinkle in her eye, the flush on her cheeks, the way her breath caught at times, and how she'd pressed her thighs together when I growled at her.

I picture Elise slipping her cotton dress over her head and letting it puddle to floor as she stands in my foyer in just her bra and panties and those ridiculous wedge heels that still made her calves look scrumptious.

In my mind, she drops to her knees in front of me, eyes begging for my cock, but she waits for my nod of permission before taking me out. I tease the head of my cock with the ball of my thumb, imagining it's her hot tongue licking me like a lollipop and then begin to pump in and out of my fist in earnest as I visualize taking her mouth, her throat.

I place my other hand on the wall, leaning into the thrusts, wanting more, wanting her. She's the sexiest fucking thing I've seen in months and she knows it. But she wants me to take control too, even though she's worried about being so vulnerable. It's so fucking sexy. I need to show her how foreplay can be dirty and satisfying at the same time.

Raw need pulses through me as I talk to the empty shower, my voice a whispered rasp in the steamy air. "That's it, take it, Elise. Suck my cock down your pretty little throat and make me come. You're gonna swallow every drop like a good girl, aren't you?"

I can see her nodding around my mouthful of cock, hungry for it, and with a few more strokes, I'm a goner, crying out harshly as I come all over my hand and the shower wall violently, jet after jet shooting from my cock as I spasm in ecstasy.

As I come back down from the high, I'm panting, my knees shaky as I lean my head against the shower wall to steady myself. Fuck. I haven't come that hard in a long time. I'm not sure that's a good thing though, considering I just mind-fucked the one person who could and would royally fuck me over, exposing my secret to the media.

But I want her. Fuck, do I want her, and reading her eyes, she wants me too.

I need to get myself in control. *Control?* I ask myself, laughing as I spray down the shower wall and make sure everything is washed down the drain. I'm such a control freak. I just need to remember that with her tomorrow during the interviews.

Except I know, on some level, she wants me to take control, to fight her for it until she has no choice but to give in to me. With her, I'll have to earn the power position, but once I have it, I'll give her just what she needs . . . a hard fucking with her at my mercy. Hell, that's what I need too.

The thought makes me shiver, and I feel another thrum down my spine to my balls. No, she's too dangerous. I have to make sure I don't get sucked back into a teasing flirtatious conversation because no good can come of that. I groan out loud, the thought of getting sucked back in making the pictures I'd just used to jack off flash across my mind, and my cock thickens again.

Already.

---

It's noon the next day, and I'm jittery with anticipation of Elise's visit. I've done the best I can to prepare, taking Carsen to school before putting myself through a brutal workout that has hopefully left me too exhausted to get a fucking hard-on.

Honestly, I'm not sure if I'm nervous or excited—maybe both? I'm still dreading her asking me questions, knowing that I'll have to carefully avoid too much honesty about my life, but another side of me is ready to demand it of her. I'll ask her everything I want to know, and somewhere in that interrogation, maybe she'll decide I really am an ass and will leave me alone.

A tiny voice in the back of my head whispers *that's not true,* and I know my conscience is at least partially right. I don't want to know everything to scare her off. A small part of me just wants to know everything about her, period. The gentleman side of my mind wants to know what she needs in a man, wondering if I'm man enough to give it to her. The dirty side, though . . . it wonders if she'd be just as sassy with my cock stuffed in her mouth.

When the doorbell rings, I instinctively look upstairs, mentally reminding myself that Sarah picked Carsen up after school to go to the mall and then out for sushi, knowing that she couldn't be here for this.

I open the door, and all I want to do is gawk at the sight in front of me, but I force my face to remain stoic as I take her in from head to toe. Her blonde hair is lightly curled today, soft waves that I want to gather in my fist and use to guide her where I want.

She's wearing a t-shirt with a logo I don't recognize stretched across her tits, a slim cotton skirt, and a pair of low-top Chuck Taylors that are cute as fuck on her. She looks young, bite-able like a fresh cherry, and curvier than a mountain road.

Thank God I wore tight jeans today because I need that pressure to keep my cock from growing too big in their stretched confines. Even my workout isn't helping. I can feel the tingle already.

My body's immediate and fierce reaction to her presence pisses me off. It makes me feel wild and out of control, and I don't like it. I'm the one in control. Always.

So I take out my body's betrayal on her, barely grunting before turning and walking, not to the living room, but deeper into the house this time. We didn't get through the whole house. She might as well see some more this time.

I hear her sigh of frustration behind me. I can virtually hear the eye roll too, but she closes the door and follows me without complaining. It gives me an ounce of satisfaction that even if my body's out of control, she's still doing what I want her to do.

That slight lift is broken when I hear her behind me, her shoes squeaking quietly on the tile flooring of my hallway. "So, we're back to grumpy and asshole-y? I'd hoped we'd made some progress yesterday."

I don't answer, just head into my music room. I have an office as well, but this room is where I've done some of my best recent work. As she walks through the door, I close it behind her, locking us inside these four walls without ever turning the actual lock.

Elise looks around, eyes jumping from the art on the dark-paneled walls, to the awards in a case in the corner, to the bar, to my collection of old vinyl and their record player. "You jam in here? Or is this where you come to brood about how you want your girl back, your dog back, and your truck back?"

I hold back the chuckle, not wanting to give in an inch, not even for an old joke about country music. "This is my cave, basically," I admit, letting my voice be honest, slightly soft, and in reverence for what this place means to me. "It's a warm and cozy place that I can hole up and do my music away from everyone and everything. I write all the time these days, in little notebooks I always carry with me, but this is where it all comes together. This is where scribbled notes turn into songs, where melodies that play on repeat in my head become harmonies between instruments and voices. This room is my music. The recording studio's just . . . production. This is where the magic happens."

Elise looks taken aback at the openness in my voice, in what I'm telling her. And it's hard, so fucking hard to let her into this room, this place in my soul, but somehow, talking about my music feels safer, easier than anything else she might ask about me, my history, or this supposed mystery woman I'm hiding. Music. I can always take it back to the music because I can talk about that for hours.

"It feels sacred in here. Thank you for sharing it with me."

There's no insincerity to her voice, no note of teasing, just truth, and it makes me feel better for sharing something so personal. She's right. The music has always been pure, even when sometimes performing hasn't always felt pure. But that's not the music's fault. Here, I can tell the truth. I can take my soul out for inspection, see where it's tattered and frayed, and see if I can somehow stitch it all back together long enough to make it through the next day.

And Elise seems to understand this. It's because of that, more than anything else, that lets me gesture to the couch. She plops down on the end, pulling her recorder out of her bag before slipping her shoes off.

Once she's satisfied with the recorder setup on the table, she curls up in the corner of the couch like a kitten, ready to ask me questions. But I have one for her first as I sit on the opposite end.

"Do you listen to my music?" I ask, maybe a bit more harshly than I intended. "To country at all? Or are you into like electronica dance shit?"

I gesture at her shirt, taking in the logo and the lushness of her tits all at once. She looks down at her shirt, then back to me. "Actually, I do listen to country some. It's not always my first choice, although that's definitely not EDM either. If I'm jamming on my own, I'll usually pick rock . . . Highly Suspect, which is who this t-shirt depicts, or Cage the Elephant, stuff like that. But if a song is good, the beat hits you in your chest and the lyrics make you feel, I'll listen to any genre. Even country."

She says the last part teasingly, and I'm a little relieved to hear she's not some super-fan who's just trying to get closer to me with these interviews. I've been lucky to not have any obsessively dangerous fans like some artists have. My fans seem to be mostly down-to-earth folks who just like to two-step a bit, maybe get a little rowdy for a party anthem, or have something to keep the dusty roads a little more tolerable as they get to work. But I'll admit that I wanted her to at least be familiar with my music. It's integral to my soul, and I'm curious to know what she thinks about my music, even if that makes me vulnerable.

Elise takes my question and turns it around smoothly, not like an interview but . . . almost like a date or something. "What about your musical tastes? What do you listen to?"

Been there, done this question before, so I answer using my usual country charm story. "My mom used to sing Patsy Cline to us, played us all the classics . . . Johnny Cash, Hank Williams One and Two, Reba McIntyre, George Strait, and more, so I always have a soft spot for those. She also played a lot of that sixties rock, when country and rock were sort of walking hand in hand some. The Doors, CCR, and of course, Lynyrd Skynyrd."

Elise smiles, humming a few bars. "I've jammed a little CCR. *Run Through The Jungle* is a damn good tune."

I nod, impressed. Most people who only pretend to like Creedence use one of their more famous songs, but Elise somehow plucked my favorite right out of her head. "But I like newer country too . . . Jason Aldean, Dierks Bentley, even Blake Shelton, but don't tell him I said that. Can barely get a hat to fit on that melon of his already."

She grins, but I'd bet my favorite guitar she doesn't even know who Blake Shelton is beyond his TV show fame or maybe his famous blonde girlfriend.

"You said you write all the time. What inspires you to write a song?"

I think for a moment, then shrug. "Everything. You ever go about your day, see a mom sitting on a park bench with a baby in a stroller and then a guy in a suit walks up? That's a song . . . about love, responsibility, doing whatever it takes to make your woman light up when she sees you at the end of a long day. Or the guy on the side of the road, lost in his own mind and missing the life he once had. His story is a song. Watching the news and seeing a tragedy, that's a song too. Even a party, letting loose and having a great time with friends. That's a song. Every experience, every emotion . . . they're worth having, worth feeling, worth sharing. It's addicting, that ability to connect through words and notes, transform something surreal and hazy into something palpable and visceral."

Elise is biting her lip, looking at me with delight, and I realize I think I just gave her a good quote for her article even though I was talking off the top of my head. Guess I can talk smoothly without even trying.

My attention is drawn to Elise's mouth, watching the small white flash as her teeth press into her bottom lip before her pink tongue darts out, licking her lips to soothe the bite and leaving them shiny.

I want to taste her mouth, to abandon myself to my inner desires and let loose the reins of my lust. Before I can move from the other end of the couch, though, she asks another question, saving me. Or maybe saving her, I don't know. "So once inspiration strikes, how do you get it to song . . . music first, lyrics first, both simultaneously?"

There's a dirty joke in there if ever I heard one, but I try to refrain, sticking to the safer topic of music, especially since it's why she's here. It'll help me just enough to stay in control of myself.

Although I can't help riling her up. It's just so damn fun. "The short answer is yes, all of those. Depends on the song. I've had melodies that I couldn't find words to, or lyrics all laid out that just needed a tune, or sometimes, I just sit and pick at a guitar and see what happens. I had one set of lyrics that sat in the drawer for three years before I got the music right, and another that hit full on, both coming hard at once."

Elise looks around the room again, her voice a little shaky at my last words. "And this is where the magic happens?"

I wonder what she sees when she sees this space, my private place. Does she feel the music in every molecule the way I do? Does she see the awards, the lineup of guitars, the pictures of me with favorite artists I've met, or does she see the hours I've spent in here with my eyes closed or staring at the guitar in my hands, sweating bullets as I try to combine inspiration with perspiration? I wonder what she would say if I told her about that side of things, but that's not what I ask her.

"So that was a bunch of questions in a row. Seems like it's my turn now, according to our deal."

She laughs, a soft acquiescence in her nod. "Hit me. What do you want to know?"

God, woman . . . so much. Everything. What's her favorite flavor of ice cream? Does she like candlelit dinners or fun nights out? Has she ever had eight and a half inches of thick cock up her ass?

But I try to focus, or at least to keep my horniness in check. What do I really want to know about her?

I eyeball her, curled up in the corner of the couch with her arms wrapped around her knees, perfectly at home in my room, my presence, her cheeks flushed as she waits to see what I'm going to ask.

Finally, I know. "Tell me a secret."

It's not a question but a demand, and I want to see what she shares when given an open-ended opportunity. She's demanding all of my deepest, darkest secrets, so it seems only fair to own hers too. And I want to see . . . she's filling my head with all these dirty thoughts and desires. Just how dirty is that mind of hers?

Her puffy lips frown, but it seems to be in thought as she searches her mind for what she wants to say.

Finally, she narrows her eyes, looking at me defensively. "Okay, this might not seem like a big deal at first, but let me tell the whole thing before you judge."

I nod, and she takes a steadying breath, which makes me curious what exactly she's about to spill. "I like to . . . knit. Scarves, sweaters, socks, hats, anything I can get a pattern for. I knit."

I can feel my face scrunch up in confusion. "Knit? Sweaters? This is your big secret?"

I know I just said I wouldn't judge, but come on. She's gotta be fucking with me, especially after all the emotional shit I just shared about my music. She wants my deepest secret, wants my daughter exposed even if she doesn't realize that's what she's doing, and she tells me that she knits? Seriously?

I can feel the flames of anger licking at me from inside, and I shake my head, poison dropping from every word. "I thought we had a deal, Elise. But if you want to shit on the arrangement, fine. We'll go back to pat PR answers. Get up, get out of my room. Let's go back to the living room, the kitchen . . . somewhere less personal to me."

She stands, breath heaving as her tits rise and fall, pointing a maroon-tipped finger at me as she speaks just short of a yell, her eyes sparkling with anger. "I said to wait to judge, you asshole! But by all means, jump to conclusions that I'm giving you a superficial answer. FYI . . . I've literally never told anyone that."

She grabs her bag and shoes, stomping barefooted toward the

door. I can hear the truth in her vehemence, and it surprises me. I jump to my feet, reaching out but not stepping toward her. "Wait."

Again with the orders, but she doesn't seem to mind given that she stops immediately, looking back at me over her shoulder but not saying a word.

I sigh, gesturing toward the end of the couch. "You're right, I shouldn't jump to conclusions. Sit back down. Please."

The nicety feels foreign on my tongue. I'm used to telling people what to do and they do it, no please or thank you required, except maybe to Carsen or Sarah since I try to be less of an ass to them.

Elise returns to the couch but perches on the edge, ready to rage again at any second as I stand in front of her, looming. It feels telling, symbolic. She's wild chaos, on the edge, and I'm ordered control, caging her in.

I keep my voice steady and look her directly in the eye. "So you knit."

She lifts her chin, and the posture suddenly feels very heated with her lips mere inches from my crotch, looking up at me with fire in her eyes. I feel my cock twitch in my jeans, thickening and straining to be closer to her. My fingers dance over my thighs, playing invisible chords to keep from grabbing her by the hair and taking what I already know I want so desperately.

Needing to stop that freight train from crashing into us for both of our sakes, I sit on the coffee table, my knees wide on either side of hers, my eyes waiting impatiently for her to continue. Finally, she sighs and nods, relenting to my unspoken request for her to continue.

"Yes, I knit. So the story is two-sided, I guess. When I was a kid, my parents would ship me off to my Gran's house every summer. It was awesome and occasionally boring as hell, especially for an active kid. I couldn't run through the house. She had all of these really fragile things that I swear only old people or people with too much money have."

I chuckle. I know just what she means. My grandmother had a carnival glass lampshade in her dining room. God help anyone who even stomped through that room and made the shade even twitch.

"So Gran taught me to knit, probably to keep her doll collection in one piece," Elise says before I can interrupt. "Every night after dinner, we'd sit on the porch and listen to the cicadas buzz, and we'd knit. That first summer, I made my first scarf. I was so damn proud of that ugly thing that I wore it to school every day, no matter the weather."

I'm trying to picture a miniature Elise, blonde hair sticking up every which way and wearing a scarf with shorts and a tank top. It's cute and makes me smile a little. "What color?"

She tilts her head at the question. "It was yellow, like the sunflowers in Gran's yard." She smiles too, but I can see she's not really here with me. Instead, her mind's far away, long ago in this moment.

Blinking, she continues. "So I kept at it, making stuff all through school and eventually nobody even wanted the things I made any more, so I started shipping them off to charities. That's one side, that I honor this gift of a skill my Gran gave me by helping as much as I can, anonymously of course. And the other side of the story? Why the big secret?" Elise grins saucily. "Well, I have an image to maintain. Part of my work is going to clubs, the whole party scene . . . seeing who's there and what's happening and reporting on it. I'm spontaneous, a fly by the seat of my pants kinda girl most of the time and that's what everyone expects of me. But knitting is my time to recharge, just me in the silence of my apartment."

I can see that she's telling the truth. Never would've seen that coming, and maybe that's the point. "Okay, so you knit. I promise not to tell." I make a zipper motion across my lips and she grins. My eyes focus in on that smile, her lush lips pulled wide and I want to devour her. She must feel the pull she has on me because her smile falters, her lips parting slightly to invite me in. I meet her gaze, knowing my lust must be written all over my face, but I'm surprised to see the need so plainly on hers too. It's all I can do to stop from moving closer, but I restrain myself by sheer will. My voice is gravel as I try to force lightness into the heavy moment.

"I think I'd like to see that. Think you could model some for me?"

She giggles a feather-soft baby's breath of a laugh, which suddenly becomes vibrant and bubbly as she plants her palms on my chest and pushes me. I'm aware of her touch on an animal level, wanting to push her back, down on the couch, pinned underneath me as I ravish those lips and neck along the way to tying up her wrists with her old yellow scarf.

She keeps laughing, shaking her head. "Asshole, just for that, I might actually do it! I'll expect pictures of you in it to go along with the story in return though."

She thinks I'm kidding, but in this moment, I'd probably do that . . . for her.

# CHAPTER 7

## ELISE

Settling into my desk at the office, I'm already sipping on a huge coffee knowing I'm going to need the caffeine hit today. I've barely even turned my laptop on when Maggie stops by, perching daintily on the corner of my desk, her feet swinging.

"So, what's he like?" she asks, almost vibrating. "Tell me everything!"

Her excitement is infectious, especially since she's truly excited for me, not just pumping me for info to steal my story. Well, maybe a little jealous too. She is the office's self-proclaimed biggest country fan.

I grin, teasing her with a long, dramatic pause. "Why, Maggie," I finally say after taking a long sip of my coffee and setting the mug down, "you're an eager little beaver, aren't you?"

Maggie laughs, tugging at a lock of her hair. "Of course! This is like the assignment of the year, and we're all curious about what you're going to write up on the elusive Mr. Perkins."

We? Yeah, right. I know quite a few people who don't really care, but for Maggie, Keith Perkins is right up her alley. I look up, trying to collect my thoughts, both for the first article in the series and to explain our encounters, knowing that I can't possibly explain how he makes me feel . . . how his powerful presence makes me want to climb him like a tree or maybe kneel at his feet.

For my own safety, I'm definitely leaving out the bit where I swore he was going to lean in to kiss me yesterday after I pushed him in the chest, and definitely how fucking bad I wanted him to.

"He's actually a lot different than I thought he'd be," I finally reply. "I was expecting a good ol' boy vibe, even with the awkwardness of the forced interviews, but he's . . ." I pause, searching for the word I want before continuing, "intense. He was definitely pissed when he figured out that I was the one who wrote the original article and that I would be the one interviewing him. He slammed the door in my face."

Maggie, whose idea of rude is to not offer you a cookie when you stop by her desk, gasps. "Oh, my gosh, he did not!"

"Oh yes, he did. But we seem to have worked it out," I reply, leaving out the arrangement I made on answering questions tit-for-tat with him. "The interviews have been going really well since then. I haven't got any real dirt, no hidden secrets, but he's letting me in. I feel like he's at least being honest and not totally PR with me. I think I'll be able to show a real and deeper picture of who Keith Perkins is. Not just the image he portrays on stage."

Maggie looks like she's about to swoon, and I'd bet fifty bucks she's got one of those huge Keith Perkins posters at home. "Speaking of stage, didn't I hear on the radio that he's doing a local private show this weekend?"

I nod. It was something we went over right at the end of last night's talk . . . it's hard to call something as intimate as what we're doing an interview. "Yeah, he is. That's actually our next interview date. He said that we could do a field trip and he would get me a front-row seat for the show. I'm hoping to get backstage access before and after too so I can see his whole process for a show. I think that'll be a slam dunk for the article . . . him in his element, doing what he does."

"So you're going to his private show with a front-row seat and backstage access?" she asks, blushing as she clutches at her chest and sighs dreamily. "That sounds like heaven! Surely, you'll get some juicy details there?"

I smile. Maggie's too cute not to. "Honestly, I haven't found any dirt . . . really, none at all. He's a bit of a controlling jerk, but no deep, dark secret that I've been able to find yet."

Maggie pouts. I don't think she likes the idea of Keith being controlling as much as I secretly do. "Well, you know Donnie won't be happy with that. You're going to need to find something."

I wave it off. "I know, but I swear he's basically boring . . . he writes, he does shows. I don't know what else he does with his time."

Maggie taps the tip of her nose, smiling as if she's got the perfect idea. "And there's your story. What's he do in his free time, because you know he doesn't write and sing all the time. That's what he's hiding."

I purse my lips, mulling that over. Maggie looks young and innocent, and many a mark have taken her to be naive, and well, she is cute in a way that makes you want to pat her head like a sweet puppy sometimes. But she's also a shrewd and brilliant investigator who uses her gifts to her benefit without getting jaded or down from the dirt she digs up. "Hmm, maybe you're right. I'll have to stick my nose into that area . . . carefully. But this weekend, I'm staying with the performance aspect because I know that'll be interesting. Trying to dig up what else he does in his free time could be a dud, and it's risky. But thanks, Mags."

She smiles, planting her hands on the corner of my desk and transforms back to looking cute enough I want to stick her in my backpack and take her home. "No problem! I'm just as curious as you are. Lord knows, there's a whole lot of women who'd love to know what makes that man tick, and I bet you'd be up for a promotion if you can figure it out and let us all know."

With a hop, Maggie is off my desk and off to do her own thing, leaving me tapping at my keyboard. I'm not sure what I want to say yet, and her comment about wanting to know what makes Keith tick rings a bit true and close to home.

He's been angry, dismissive, and downright rude to me in some moments, the perfect target for one of those bloodletting exposes that can get a shitload of website traffic. I'd have no problem with ripping him apart if that's all he was.

But it's the other moments where he's attentive, open, and intriguing. Not to mention, he's just so damn sexy when he gets all bossy and gruff. I've always gone for confident men, but Keith is on a whole different level. It's not confidence. It's raw power over his domain. And fuck, do I want to be in his domain.

That means I'm not being objective, and that makes me hesitate before I start to write. The words come slowly, slow clicks of my old-fashioned keyboard that start to string together, slowly becoming like machine gun spurts of words, long pauses shortening until I find my stride.

This first article, it's going to be mostly surface, about a country star who cherishes his privacy but is allowing his fans a peek into his private life. I'm careful to paint an accurate picture, including his gruffness and larger than life presence along with his passion for his music.

By the time I hit my two-thousand-word goal for the first feature, I think I've managed to hit all the points I need to, both the basics and giving hints at a deeper picture. There are no groundbreaking dirty secrets, but even if I had any, I wouldn't want to spill too soon anyway. But I've got a solid, intriguing hook so readers feel a more intimate connection with Keith and to the series for follow-up feature reads.

After some edits, I hit *Send* and submit it to Donnie with a smile.

Now . . . what am I going to wear to Keith's concert?

# CHAPTER 8

## KEITH

Pulling up in the service's rented Lincoln Town Car, I tell my driver to let the engine idle for a moment as I take in Elise's apartment building. It's pretty standard for East Robinsville, far enough from the downtown center to be needing a coat of paint, but probably close to work for her and has rent that fits her paycheck. Seems safe enough, I guess, although the homeless guy lounging up against the corner seems a bit out of place. I'm about to hop out to ring the bell when the bodyguard in the front seat does it for me.

*Fuck.*

I swear sometimes I forget that I can't just do shit like that, even if it should be no big deal. But since I topped the charts for the first time, the label keeps putting in new rules on their 'investment.' Number one, I can't do shit when I'm dressed in my usual boots and hat, making me more recognizable. Chances are, it'd be fine. But just in case, that's what the bodyguard is here for. I sigh, leaning back in the seat . . . until I see her come out.

Behind the dark tint of the car window, I can look my fill as she comes closer. And what a fill it is. She's strutting, but not in an overt way, just a subtle natural feminine roll of her hips. And oh, sweet mercy, her legs, just thick enough to make them sensual, covered in slightly torn white denim that looks painted on. She's got on slouched black cowgirl boots, and I wonder vaguely if they're new, but when I scan up . . . my breath catches in my chest.

She's the epitome of country sexy, with her hair curled and fluffy, makeup that looks sultry and sexy, not too dark but not too bright either. She's got a face that could sell about ten million pickup trucks back home right now, and that might be a conservative guess.

But what grabs ahold of my attention is the fullness of her breasts, pushed up high in the simple black tank she has on. I can see the outline of a bra, but that makes it even sexier, like she's dressed down but dressed up at the same time. She's somehow managed to be both girl-next-door and femme fatale all at once, and my cock surges in my jeans. I press my palm against the fullness, willing it down by sheer mental force.

I clear my throat, needing to get my head on straight before the door opens. I wish I could step out, greet her like a lady, but I can't. Security rule number two . . . stay in the vehicle unless instructed by the guard.

Sigh. All it took was for one dickhead to threaten one guy, and now the label's gone apeshit whenever I have to be 'the artist' Keith Perkins. Sometimes, I miss the days when I showed up by pulling around back in my pickup and grabbing my guitar case out of the truck bed.

But as she ducks in, climbing in beside me, I forget about my first world problems and try to make up for my apparent lack of manners.

"Holy fuck, Elise. You look gorgeous."

Okay, so maybe my manners aren't quite up to snuff after all. I can't help my mouth, except around Carsen, and even then, I slip up every now and then. I am human.

She doesn't seem to mind, though, judging by the smile that breaks across her face. She's checking me out too, and I swear her gaze lingers on my crotch for just a split second longer. Or maybe that's wishful thinking on my part and she's checking out my belt buckle.

"You too, Keith. You look ready to rock . . . I mean, ready to country?" she teases.

She laughs at her own joke, but I chuckle, dropping a wink for her. "Definitely ready to rock. Just don't ask me to dance."

She laughs, and it's comfortable for a moment, just sitting next to each other on the leather seat, two people just . . . I don't really know. The feeling is broken, though when my phone rings shrilly, shattering the silence.

I stifle a curse and fish it out of my pocket. Glancing at the screen, I answer. "Hey, Todd."

Todd, who's in either LA or New York, I'm not sure and don't really care to find out, sounds energetic. "You good to go tonight, man?"

"Yeah, I'm good. Thanks for checking in. Security and driver were right on time. I'll do a gear check when I get to the venue."

"Good, good . . . what else?"

I roll my eyes at his usual pop quiz, glad he can't see me. For fuck's sake, I'm a pro. "KCTY radio sponsor, promote the summer tour and the new single."

"Perfect. You've got this, man. What about the reporter? She's coming to the show tonight, right? It'd be a good image for her to highlight. Maybe some pics of you onstage or with fans to help kick the grocery store ones down the image search on Google?"

The reminder pisses me off, and I know the grit is in my voice because Elise flinches beside me. "Yeah, she's right here. I'll tell her what you said."

Todd sounds apologetic, and I can understand why. He knows the interviews are a pain in my ass. "I know you can't say much with her right there, but are the interviews going okay? Tell me if you need a rescue or if we're going to need some spin doctoring."

I glance over at Elise, who is pointedly staring out the window, but I know she's hanging on every word. "It's fine. A bit rough at first when I slammed the door in her face . . ."

I see Elise crack a tiny smile, confirming my suspicion as Todd sounds like he's about to have a coronary. "No you fucking didn't!"

I chuckle, reaching over and patting Elise on the knee. "Actually, I did. But we came to an agreement and it's been fine since. She's . . . she's good."

Todd laughs, while I can see Elise blush lightly at my compliment. Or maybe it's my hand on her knee, which I still haven't lifted yet. "I can't imagine what your agreement is, and I probably don't want to know, do I?"

"Nope, you don't." I'm not even sure what our arrangement should be called. I'm just wondering if she could stretch across the backseat so I could touch every inch of her silky skin.

Todd lowers his voice, virtually whispering in the phone as though Elise could hear him, and I smirk over at Elise, who's smiling back, her eyes gleaming as she stretches out a leg for my perusal. "Any suspicions on the you know what front?"

I think for a second how to answer in a way that won't make Elise suspicious, and part of me is reminded again why I have to be careful around her. I've got miles to go and secrets to keep. "So far, so good."

Todd sighs in relief, and in the background, I hear someone holler out his name. "All right then, man . . . listen, I gotta cover some fires on this end. Have a great show. I'll be in touch."

"Sure thing," I answer easily, glad I don't have his career. "'Bye, Todd."

I hang up, turning to Elise, who's still not taken my hand from her leg. "Sorry about that. Manager always checks in before a show to make sure I'm not gonna screw something up."

Elise looks thoughtful for a second, then gives me a raised eyebrow. "So, you're here alone, basically. No big crew, no manager clearing the way, no team of stylists getting you primped and teased up for stage. That seems . . . unusual."

There's not a question in there, but I treat it like one anyway. A part of me wonders if Elise sort of likes it that it's just me and her. It's more intimate this way.

"For tour, there's a bigger crew and a whole team of folks that travel with us. I mean, I don't need a huge backup band, but I do like to have a consistent crew for that. But for shows like this, I try to keep it simple. I've done bar gigs my whole life, so I don't need a bunch of guys telling me how to tune my guitar or what to wear. Damn sure don't need a hair stylist," I say, taking my hat off to run a hand across my bare head. "Although I should get Gillette to sponsor my next tour."

Elise laughs, moving her leg but scooting a little closer. "Holy shit. Did you just make a joke? I didn't think you knew how."

I smile, leaning a little closer to stage whisper in her ear. "It's been known to happen . . . on rare occasions. So consider yourself lucky to witness one."

I turn my head, and Elise locks eyes with me, the magnetic

pull between us shimmering in the air. "Oh, I definitely feel lucky."

There's another one of the increasingly frequent moments where I'm this close to grabbing her by the neck and kissing her, but the car stops with a slight jerk, bringing my attention to the front seat, where the bodyguard is already moving to our door.

Without thinking about it, I grab Elise's hand, her soft warmth immediately sinking into my skin and forming some sort of bond between us. She looks down, then up, where I catch her gaze with my own.

"I'll get out first. Follow behind me and we both follow the guard," I explain quickly. "Things shouldn't be bad, not many people out here right now, but don't stop and don't look scared. Smile and look friendly."

Elise nods her head, but her eyes give away the panic she feels.

A tiny part of me thinks evilly, 'Not so great on the other side of the paparazzi lens, is it?' But another, maybe more nobler side of me wants to protect her from the fear and the pain. Mostly, though, I just want to get us in the backdoor of the bar as quickly and safely as possible.

We step out of the car, and the flashes immediately go off. I basically drag a stiff Elise to the door, a smile frozen on her face as I smile and wave, and I only stop once to sign one autograph for a little girl holding a sign that says *Keith, I'm too young to see the show tonight so will you sign my poster?*

I know I really shouldn't, but the kid's cute, and just a little younger than Carsen. The beaming smile she gives me as I ruffle her hair is worth the delay, even if my bodyguard is a little abrupt, shoving us inside and slamming the door behind us. We're thrust from the light to being alone in the dark. We're not really, because I can hear people onstage setting up, and there are no doubt radio people already out in the bar, but backstage in this little alcove hallway, it's just the two of us.

I can feel Elise's body pressed tightly against me, her hand still grasped in mine. She's so close I can feel her heart hammering in her chest, and her breasts heave as she catches her breath.

"Wow, that was insane," she whispers, our eyes adjusting enough that I can just start to see her face. "How can you do that all the time?"

I shake my head, wanting to brush a lock of hair out of her face but not wanting to let go of her hand. "That was nothing. When I'm on tour, it takes four guys to get me in the building because there are hundreds of people yelling your name, grabbing at you, and shoving Sharpies and more in your face."

She's hisses, obviously imagining what that'd be like. "Shit, no way could I do that."

In the sub-twilight dimness, I cup her face, tracing her cheekbone with my thumb, marveling at the texture. "You okay, Elise?"

I feel her nod, but I can sense the tension in her body, and even though I damn well know I shouldn't, I dip down, catching her mouth with mine, needing to make sure she's okay. It's soft, tender as our lips press together for the first time for real and move against each other.

I feel her free hand move up, and she lays a flat palm against my chest, but she's not pressing me away. She's using it as leverage to get closer to me, wanting more.

My hand moves from her cheek to grip the back of her neck, encouraging her and taking that touch of control I need. She responds to it with a moan of enjoyment and desire, opening to let me take the kiss deeper.

Our tongues tangle, and it's like getting hit by white-hot lightning. Her body galvanizes and she lunges into me, the softness disappearing into almost a thrashing battle for dominance. It's just for show though. We both know I'm going to win this. She wants me to—she just wants me to work for it.

And I do, overpowering her even as she grabs my belt loops, pulling me in tighter, and when she feels the hard ridge of my cock against her belly, she moans. I grind against her, letting her feel what she does to me.

Vaguely, from seemingly far away, I hear my name being called, and it's like a bucket of cold water. I pull back, wiping at my mouth. "Fuck. I'm sorry, Elise. That can't . . ." I curse, not believing that just happened.

Elise understands my muttering, nodding. "Me neither . . . conflict of interest. For work, I mean."

I know it's the right thing to do, step away from the woman who has the power to ruin me, but goddamn, do I want to press her up against the wall and take her raw, hot, and fast right now. I think if we'd met under different circumstances, I'd fucking do it.

I haven't dated in . . . well, ever since I got custody of Carsen, but I'm not sure I could date Elise anyway, even though she is the most interesting woman I've met in a long time.

What I really want right now is to fuck her mercilessly until her eyes roll up and she's fuck-stunned from being pounded over and over. But with a steadying breath, I grab her hand again, loosely this time, and lead her through the dark corridor backstage to my green room. As we approach, a busy looking guy with a clipboard claps at me as he proclaims to the heavens like his redemption just emerged from the dimness. "Oh good, you're here. I'll be happy to get you anything you need tonight, Mr. Perkins. Anything now?"

I growl, still on edge. What I need . . . is what I can't have. "No. Just give me fifteen, ten, and five-minute warnings. That's it."

He nods, smiling broadly. "You got it." With that, he hustles out to the next thing on his list, leaving us alone again.

Shit.

I can still feel my cock throbbing in my jeans, and I know Elise can see it, the way she's looking down at my jeans.

And we both know that if we rush . . . yeah, we could get it done before I go on stage.

# CHAPTER 9

## ELISE

*What the fuck, Elise? You can't be doing shit like that, no matter how irresistible Keith is. Work . . . remember work? The interview series that is going to jump start your career, maybe get you a gig with a real magazine, not celebrity trash fodder. Get your shit together. You don't get paid to feel that thick, throbbing cock pumping in and out . . .*

Wait. Okay, start over.

*Stop thinking with your hormones and think with your head! Get your shit together and do your fucking job!*

Better. Mental pep talk complete, I move around the room, feeling Keith's gaze follow me, burning into my neck, my back, my pussy and my . . . well, everything. My words aren't helping. The power in his eyes is breaking me down.

I need to reset us, calm down the flames still licking at my insides, the need pulsing in my clit. Taking a deep breath, I dive back into reporter mode, locking the door on my inner sex-starved bitch for now.

"Green room, huh?" I ask with forced sarcasm. "Seems pretty . . . standard. No bowls of just blue M&Ms, buckets of

Popeye's chicken legs, or fancy champagne. What's in your rider for requirements?"

Keith hasn't moved, standing stock-still as he watches me, making me feel like prey that he could pounce on at any moment, or not, solely at his discretion. Even if I wanted to, I couldn't resist him.

"No rider," Keith says in a low, sexy purr. "The venue always comps my beer and some bar food after the show and supplies water bottles before and during. But I'm not some asshole who needs caviar and Cristal. I'm just here to sing songs, shake hands, and go home."

I nod, taking it in. He's so much a dichotomy. On one hand, he's commanding, on the other easygoing. It's . . . unique. "Seems easy. Maybe even too easy."

Keith chuckles, his eyes flashing again with humor, desire, and power. "Definitely nothing easy about me."

Before I can question that statement, there's a knock at the door, and Keith turns his head, breaking our eye contact for the first time since we entered. "It's open."

The door opens slowly before a herd of guys comes barreling in, loud and big and . . . loud.

Really, it's just three guys, but it's a small room, so their appearance and energy make the room feel claustrophobic. Keith moves to greet the group, a big grin on his face as he bro-hugs and back-pats each one. "Hey, Slim, you're not going to have that nickname much longer."

"Man, fuck you," *Slim*, a slightly chubby guy who's wearing a jean jacket, says with a laugh. "Good to see you. You don't want to know what the other offer I had for the weekend was."

"What?" another of the guys asks. "I turned down playing backbeat for a folk-opera fusion. Let that sink in . . . Folk. Opera."

"Try a studio session for a Prince tribute band," Slim replies with a shudder. "I mean, I can play bass to anything but . . . fuck me, a slow-dance version of *When Doves Cry*? Fuck my life. And Prince would be pissed as hell at the hatchet job they're doing."

After a round of laughter, Keith turns to me. "Elise, these are the guys. We've been playing gigs together for years. Guys, this is Elise. She's a reporter, doing a couple of articles about me."

One of the newcomers, a lean guy with long, shaggy blonde hair makes a whooping noise, grinning widely to show off perfect, square teeth that are almost a little too big, giving him almost a feral look. "Ooh, writing an article about our Country Star? Want me to tell you all of his dirty little secrets? I'm Jim, by the way. In my day job, I'm the lead singer in a blues band."

I grin, my eyes jumping from Jim to Keith as I shake Jim's offered hand, teasing. "Actually, that'd be great. Maybe you can give me all of his juicy secrets?"

Keith jumps in, his voice amused but still brooking no argument. "Shut your mouth, Jim. You too, guys."

He looks at the other two. Slim, whatever his real name is, nods, and Keith continues. "She's interviewing *me*. Got it?"

There's a hint of possessiveness to Keith's tone, and something else I can't quite place . . . a warning, maybe?

But the three guys seem to catch Keith's meaning loud and clear, whatever it is. They nod in unison, and Jim speaks up. "Got it, boss man. But maybe I could share some gig stories? Tell her about the time that chick crowd-surfed up to the stage and damn-near jumped your bones before security could snatch her off the stage?"

I'm grinning, already visualizing how that snippet is going to add some flair to my next article about Keith's performances. "God, yes . . . tell me more about that!"

He glances to Keith, obviously silently asking permission, and Keith gives the approval, shrugging. "Well, you damn-near already told it, so you might as well go ahead."

The next thirty minutes are spent listening to Keith and the guys banter, joke, and reminisce about past tours and shows. I finally figure out that Slim and Eric are one and the same, and it's interesting to hear about their time on the road together as they obviously have a long history and a deep friendship.

"Wait, let me ask you one thing," I interrupt Eric as he goes on about a time he was painted up on stage. "You guys talk about lots of different music. You're not just country?"

"I prefer country," Eric says, "but with us mainly working in the summers, we can pick up other gigs that sound interesting . . . or pay well. Besides, while Keith won't admit it, he can do a pretty stellar *Sweet Child O'Mine* if you get him drunk, or sometimes if you just beg hard enough."

I blush, thinking about begging Keith for anything, and say nothing. As I listen to another tale, Shane asks Keith, "Hey, remember that time Sarah brought us all chili dogs and we ended up puking ten minutes before the show? God, that show sucked."

I wouldn't have even caught the namedrop if the temperature in the room hadn't just plummeted at the same time the tension in Keith's entire body sprang tight. Shane cuts his eyes to me, wide and panicked. He looks like he wants to crawl into a hole and make sure someone's hidden all the pointy things nearby.

I look at Keith, questioning. "Obviously, a story there?"

Keith glowers but finally relents, although her voice is ice. "Sarah is my sister. She comes on the road with us in the summer sometimes, kinda acts like my assistant. She's not to be included in the article. She has her own life and doesn't need mine fucking hers up."

He gives me a hard look, daring me to disagree with his

decree. I give him a tiny smile, acquiescing for now but knowing I'll need to do a bit of digging to make sure there's nothing hinky about the sister he was obviously hiding. I mean, if there's nothing there, why not just say up it up front? "Fine."

Before the tension in the room can settle, the kid with the clipboard pops back in without knocking. "Fifteen minutes."

Keith hops up before the kid can leave, calling out to him. "Hey, can you take my guest out to her table? It's reserved up front."

The kid actually looks at his clipboard for a moment, and I have a split second where I kinda want him to say no, just to see what Keith will do.

But eventually, the kid waves at me with his board. "Follow me," he blurts out before muttering something under his breath.

I glance at Keith, who is searching my eyes for something, his eyes narrowed like he's analyzing me. I'm not sure what telltale sign of my possible dishonesty he's looking for, so I smile warmly. "Have a great show! Break a leg . . . that's what you say, right?"

Finally, he relaxes slightly and speaks dryly. "I'll see you in a few. I'll be the cowboy on stage in the hat."

I shake my head, rolling my eyes. "I'll be the girl in the front row, yelling 'yee-haw' louder than everyone."

Keith actually smiles as the guys laugh. "Good lord, woman. Do *not* do that. Or you're likely to get kicked out for being drunk."

I grin, considering doing it just to mess with him.

As the kid sets me up at my table, a fresh bottle of beer magically appears from a passing waitress. I yell out 'thanks' but she's already gone.

A few minutes later, I've taken some notes on the show attendees. Most are fans wearing t-shirts from Keith's last tour, with a pair of radio djs wearing polos with their KCTY call letters on the chest and a slew of half-naked women all giggly and girly as they wait impatiently for Keith's appearance on stage. I try not to feel catty about them, but I can't help it . . . some of these bitches need a muzzle and a tranq dart.

*Shit, maybe I'm the one feeling possessive.*

When Keith finally emerges, it's a riot of noisy yells and clapping. As he greets the crowd, I can see just how comfortable he is on stage, his energy creating a buzzing sort of high among the crowd. He starts singing and it's magical. I didn't tell him this, but once I got this assignment, I did my homework like any good reporter.

I've listened to all his biggest hits, both the ones that sold millions and the ones the critics raved about, which ironically aren't usually the same songs. I've heard him sing about parties, about women, about dads, about long drives home, and more. But none of those hours spent with Keith blasting through my earbuds prepared me for this. His deep tenor is amplified until it vibrates my chest, making me feel his words, both physically and metaphorically in my heart.

I can see how the emotions of every song resonate for him, both upbeat and subdued. It's amazing how in this entire room full of people clamoring for a piece of him, it feels like he's singing just to me, and I'm sure if I asked every person in the crowd, they'd feel the same way.

It's in the tilt of his head, the way his eyes slowly move across the space, connecting with people, how he even winks at a couple of those giggly women with a sign proclaiming *Keith, we love you!*

As he sings his latest hit about the girl he wants but can't have yet, he bends down low, right in front of me, reaching out a hand. Even though I held his hand earlier, when I touch him on stage like this, larger than life, I swear I light up just like a teenybopper at a Justin Beiber concert.

And I don't care. I'm swept away because he really is singing to me right now. *Baby, take my hand; we'll buy a little piece of land; it'll be just me and you; forever, if you say, 'I do'.*

Okay, obviously not singing to me like he means what he's saying, but his eyes are locked on me until the end of the song, and then he kisses the back of my hand like the gentleman he's decidedly not. With a wink, he tears off across the stage as the band changes tune and Keith starts belting out his most famous party anthem.

I'm still swooning a bit, plopping back in my chair when I feel a tap on my shoulder.

I look up to see a young guy in a button-up and jeans standing there, and he smiles and leans in, whisper-yelling in my ear. "I'm Ethan. I'm with the bar crew. Mind if I sit with you for sound checks?"

I nod, mouthing "Sure" as I gesture to the chair. He sits down and I go back to watching Keith rock the crowd for a few songs. My legs are still shaky, knees knocking under the table as I catch my breath from singing along. Keith is strutting his stuff, grinning and playing his heart out over to the right side of the stage, but I notice a tight look on his face when he looks back at me, eyes bouncing from me to Ethan.

I shrug in an attempt to let Keith know it's no big deal, because I really don't mind sharing the primo table, but he seems stiffer than he was just a moment ago. He finishes out the song but keeps playing a guitar riff as he resets the microphone center-stage right in front of me.

When he stops, he takes the microphone, his eyes radiating power that takes over the room. "Thanks so much, everyone. I have to tell y'all a secret if you think you can keep it quiet."

He looks straight at me, daring me to say no as the audience responds en-masse with a resounding 'yeah'.

Keith nods, adjusting his hat a little to pull it down, making him look like an old-time gunfighter or something. "I love playing shows just like this one . . . small venue, tight-knit crowd, with everyone singing along. It's closer, intimate when I can hear you singing and see your smiling faces. So I just wanted to say . . . Hello."

Without even pausing, he rolls right into one of his older and lesser-known songs, but somehow one of my favorites. *Hellooo, girl; C'mon over here and let me get to know you; Hellooo, girl; gimme five and you won't believe what I can show you . . .*

As Keith hits the chorus, Ethan leans over, whisper-yelling in my ear again. "Was the transition from music to speaking to music okay for you? I think it sounded a bit tinny on the right."

I nod at him, smiling and mouthing 'it's good' and returning my attention to an obviously scowling Keith. Shit, what's wrong with him?

After a few more songs, which feel forced and not quite as casually comfortable as the vibe had been earlier, Keith wraps up and takes a bow. I rise with everyone else, clapping like a maniac and sticking my fingers in my mouth to let out a piercing wolf-whistle instead of the yee-haw I threatened.

Keith smiles at the crowd but doesn't even glance at me as he struts off stage. Piped-in music begins playing as people get up and take to the dance floor, building on Keith's energy to get their groove on.

Ethan nods and gives a little wave as he heads off to talk to a guy behind the soundboard at the back of the floor. Honestly, I don't know what to do. Should I go backstage the same way I came out? Wait here for clipboard kid?

I drain the last of my beer, now hot from being ignored while I focused on the show, and I decide to find my way back. After all, I'm supposed to have all-access to Keith, so surely, they'll let me backstage?

When I get to the edge of the floor, I see Keith's bodyguard and make my way over. "Hey, I'm Elise . . . from earlier. Can I go meet up with Keith now?"

He doesn't even answer. Hell, I'm not sure if he looks at me since his eyes are covered in sunglasses, but he bumps his head to the left so I take that as a yes and quickly scoot on through to the curtained backstage area.

I'm a little fuzzy on how to get to the green room, but I'm shuffling along in the dark when two hands reach around from behind me, one grabbing loosely at my neck and tilting my jaw up and the other firmly around my belly, pulling me back against a hard body.

I'm frozen in fear for an instant before I hear Keith's voice growling quietly in my ear, "What the fuck was that, Elise? What kind of games are you playing?"

Before I can speak, he moves his hand over my mouth, muffling my questions . . . my explanation of whatever has set him off. Keith grinds against me, and I can feel his cock, thick and hard, even more so than during our stolen kiss before the show, and I'm instantly on fire for him. All the flirting and eyeballing we've been doing is coming to a fever pitch between my legs, my pussy thrumming like a guitar string.

I arch my back, circling my hips, wanting to feel him, wanting to make him lose control the way I am. I whimper, trying to beg if that's what it takes, but before I can, he continues.

"Leaving me with your taste still on my lips, and you're already sitting with some asshole for my show? Think you can cock tease me and make me jealous? Guess what? It worked."

I try to shake my head, wanting to tell him that it was just a sound guy, but he doesn't give me a chance, and I can barely form a coherent thought anyway because he's licking and nibbling my neck.

"You've been wanting me since the first second we saw each other," he whispers as he works his way up to my ear. "You've been dreaming about it, haven't you? And I'll let you in on one of those juicy secrets you always want—I've been wanting to fuck you since that first night too."

The words explode in my brain, and I moan against his hand as Keith's lips move lower, to the curve between my neck and shoulder. His hand on my waist fumbles with my button, but he gets it undone.

"Shove your jeans down," he growls. "You were naughty, so take your punishment like a good girl, Elise."

I don't know what punishment he has in mind, but *fuck, yes* to whatever it is. He can fuck me right here in the middle of the backstage area if he wants. Hell, he could shove me down on the dirty stage in front of the crowd and I'd happily take him. I'm that gone.

I push my jeans down, leaving my lace thong because he didn't tell me to take my panties off, and on some instinctual level, I want to do what he says. Exactly what he says.

I feel his hand, broad and rough, caressing the cheek of my ass, and it makes me shiver in anticipation.

Before I realize what he has in mind, he lifts his hand, popping it back down on my cheek with a loud smack. I cry out, but the sound is muffled as he presses his hand tighter across my mouth. And then he does it again, and again . . . three times total, and I'm a quivering mess.

I've never felt this on fire before. My pussy's quivering, almost dripping down my inner thigh as I give him total control. Keith is undeniable, a force of sexual nature that I don't want to resist. I just want him to fuck me, hard and pounding and mind-blowingly . . . and make me his dirty secret.

Keith grabs the strip of lace, pulling it tight against my soaking pussy and whispering hotly in my ear. "Are you gonna come for me? Just from me smacking your delectable ass?"

I shake my head. As on the edge as I obviously am, I need more, my hips bucking as I look for relief. Keith laughs darkly. He knows I'm lying. "Need me to rub your hot little clit? Make you come all over my fingers?"

Whimpering, I look over my shoulder, meeting his eyes in the dark, begging silently. He grabs a handful of my tender ass in his calloused fingers, squeezing hard, and I know—hell, I hope—I'll have his fingerprints there later.

When he lets go, his fingers dive around my hip, tapping little smacks right over my lace-covered clit. I'm so on fire it only takes a few, and I detonate, my body shaking and convulsing as I press his hand tighter on my mouth, muffling myself so I'm not too loud.

As I come back down from the high, I pull his hand down, gasping for air as I still writhe against him. I feel him bend down, grabbing my jeans and trying to pull them up, and it's like a wakeup call.

Holy fuck . . . I just *fucked* my assignment. Well, not fucked, but I might as well have. And I've never had anything blow me up like that. I can't imagine what he could do to me pounding that thick fucking cock into me, but I damn sure want to find out.

I can't get my racing thoughts corralled, so I start to button my jeans back up. "That guy . . ." Keith growls, and I turn, placing a hand on his cheek.

"That guy . . . was the sound tech. You had me in the palm of your hand all night."

I can hear Keith's teeth grinding before he gives in, his voice velvet over gravel. "Fuck. Get in the damn car. Let's go."

# CHAPTER 10

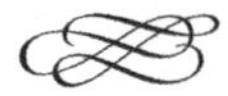

## KEITH

Stupid.

So fucking stupid.

I was so on edge, but that . . . I can't believe how I exploded when I saw her. It wasn't like she was eye fucking the guy. Sure, he was some young stud, whispering in her ear, getting her smiles. Fuck that. I felt played and pissed, but apparently it was only my mind playing tricks on me, not Elise.

But I basically attacked her when I saw her uncertainly stumbling backstage, even if she didn't seem to mind. Instead, she went with it, giving me all the sexual energy that I knew she kept inside her. The feeling of her body writhing against me, the sound of her ass smacking under my hand . . . my God, she's perfect.

As long as I live, I'll never forget the moment she pressed my hand tighter on her own mouth as she vibrated through her orgasm, covering my hand in her sweet cream.

I wanted to taste her, to drop to my knees behind her and bury my face in her ass as I feasted on her. I wanted to shove her up against the wall and fuck her so hard they'd have heard her screams over the music on the dance floor. She'd have let me, too. I fucking know it.

At least I didn't lose that much control of myself. But I've damn sure done enough to screw myself up in a big way. Because as hot as that was, and as much as we both wanted it, she's still the reporter digging into my private life.

As we sit in the car, speeding back to her apartment, it's hard to focus on that when my fingers are tingling with the desire to grab her again. It doesn't help my cock any when Elise puts her pink-nailed manicured hand on my thigh, making me turn to look at her. "The show was awesome."

She's trying so hard to settle me, the tension obvious. I stare at her hand for a moment, trying to decide on the best course of action. Cold professional or hot lover? Inside, I feel like I'm both right now. I want to push her away, to keep my secrets safe . . . but the other side of me wants to make Elise mine, to show her what it really feels like to have a man take her completely and fully.

What keeps Carsen safest? Finally, I decide that's the only real result I need, regardless of what my throbbing cock wants. I can't push her away. She's so smart she'd just keep digging. And I can't trust her either.

Decision made, I play somewhere in the middle, taking her hand loosely in my own . . . not quite professional, but decidedly not the guy who just spanked her ass and made her come.

Giving her my best attempt at a 'fan-friendly' smile, I answer her evenly. "Thanks. Those really are my favorite types of performances, even better than the huge arenas stuffed with fans. Those are great too, the roar and energy of the crowd, but the smaller shows where I get to shake hands with folks, see their faces as they sing along . . . it's more intimate and more satisfying."

Shit, ten seconds in and I've already fucked up and betrayed what I'm thinking. That's definitely not what I meant to say because 'intimate' and 'satisfying' do not have me thinking of the show anymore.

Apparently, Elise's thoughts track the same way, and she lowers her voice just in case the driver and bodyguard up front can hear. "He really was the sound tech, Keith. Not that I'm at all upset about the misunderstanding."

I cut my eyes over at her, and she's smiling broadly, her whole face lit up, but there's a flash of uncertainty in her eyes. I know what she's saying, and I guess she's got the same fears running around in her head. I can't be a *total* asshole about this.

I sigh, running a hand across my head, and turn to face her fully. "There's obviously something between us, chemistry for damn sure. But—"

She interrupts, placing a hand on my forearm, giving me that pitying look that I know but so rarely get. "It's inappropriate while I'm interviewing you," she says, sighing softly and making this hurt a little. "I agree. Maybe later, we can see where this goes, or maybe not? But I need to be as impartial as possible while I'm writing this series."

I nod, relieved knowing she's at least partially right. "Elise, I told you the first time we met . . . I'm not dating and not looking. I have my reasons that are not up for discussion or for reporting. But they won't change, not even when the job's done."

She bites her lip, nodding, and all I want to do is lick the sting away where she's worrying it between her teeth. It hurts. It hurts a lot. So many years, sleeping alone in an oversized king bed for no reason other than my bedroom would look ridiculous with a twin-sized mattress in it. So many nights sitting up alone after Carsen's gone to sleep, wishing I had someone I could share those things with that I can't even share with Sarah. Too many years, but I have to protect my daughter, and that means I can't let Elise in further.

"I understand. Won't say I'm not disappointed, but I get it," she says bravely, trying to keep her voice light but not really quite making it. "You've got a lot at stake here. You're a big country music star and I'm a tabloid reporter."

I nod, and she smirks, but it feels sadly ironic. "Funny thing is, I've shared more with you, stories and connection, not just chemistry, than I have with anyone in a long time. Maybe ever. I know your original arrangement was just to even the playing field a bit, but I have to tell you, I like you. I like talking with you, hanging out. You hide it in a lot of ways, but you're a good guy, Keith. Not too many of those out there."

I smile, genuinely shocked by her words. "I don't know that anyone's ever called me good . . . good for nothing, maybe?" I joke. "And I didn't feel good backstage."

Elise smirks. "That wasn't good. That was bad. But in that case, bad was fucking awesome."

Her words draw me in, and I can't stop my fingers from gently grabbing a curl of hair that's hanging by the side of her face, twirling it around my finger. "I like you, too. Definitely made this whole interview thing a hell of a lot better than I thought it'd be."

All too soon, the car stops at the curb in front of her apartment. It's late, after two in the morning, and the street is dark and deserted. When the guard opens the door, I get out too. "Gonna walk her up."

The guard takes another look around, then dips his chin once. I chuckle. I've already ditched the hat and changed shirts. The most noticeable thing about me right now is the Town Car with a muscle-bound man in black in the front seat.

As we get a few feet away, Elise whispers. "That is so weird. That's one scary ass dude."

I laugh. Our thoughts are so similar. "He's just doing his job, and I appreciate that. I try not to be an annoying asshole that makes the security team's life hard, but I couldn't sit in the car and watch you walk to the door alone. Better say good night at the door though. If I try to go up, he'll shit a brick."

Elise stops on the steps by the door, turning to face me, and puts her hands on my chest. "Probably best if you don't come up anyway. I'm not sure I have the willpower to not . . ." She stops, and fuck, do I wish she'd finish that sentence, tell me what she'd do if we weren't fighting this thing between us.

Before I can ask, she leans in, kissing my cheek with her velvety soft lips before moaning lightly.

She lingers, and I can't take it, groaning. "Fuck it, Elise."

I pull her closer, encircling her waist in my arms, and turn to take her mouth once again. She's right there with me, kissing me back as she wraps her arms around my neck.

I squeeze her ass, knowing she's likely sore from the earlier spanking, and she cries out softly, opening her mouth, and I take advantage, invading her with my tongue to taste her.

Easing the sting, I rub her cheeks through the denim, cupping her and pressing her against my raging cock. From behind us, I hear a polite interrupting cough.

Shit, the bodyguard and the driver. I forgot about them, lost in Elise . . . again. Literally minutes after agreeing that we can't do this, and I'm holding her, the two of us making out like horny teenagers at the end of prom night. I take a big breath, pressing my forehead to hers and firmly cupping her face.

"I have to go. Now. Or I'm gonna throw you over my shoulder, run to your apartment, and bury my cock in your pussy so deep, so hard, you'll feel empty without me there."

She shudders, placing her hands over mine and squeezing. "You do have to go. Because if you do that, I'm sure as fuck gonna let you. Hell, I'd beg for it. But . . . we can't."

Grinding my teeth, I agree. "We can't."

"We have a dinner interview tomorrow. That still okay?"

I laugh softly, inhaling the scent of her hair, the innate purity underneath the scent of beer and sweat from the bar. "I'll probably still be jacking off from the raging blue balls you've given me tonight . . . repeatedly."

Elise leans in and whispers in my ear. "If it'll help . . . my vibrator might need new batteries by morning."

I moan, knowing exactly what she'll be doing and wishing I were the one doing it to her. "Fuck. I'll see you tomorrow, and I promise to behave if you do."

She's quiet, not promising me back but still with that little smile on her face. "Elise?" I question. "Do we have a deal?"

She grins, but sassy as fuck and not apologetic at all. "Sorry, yeah. Behave. I was just picturing you stroking that thick cock I felt in your jeans, coming all over your hand but still not stopping because you're still rock-hard . . . for me."

I growl, but instead of grabbing her like I want to, I step back. It's the hardest thing I've ever done. "Watch it, woman. Don't poke the bear. You just might get attacked. See you tomorrow night."

She doesn't answer, just nods and smiles, but as I turn toward the car, I hear her hushed whisper. "I fucking hope so."

---

By lunchtime, I've already made up my mind about Elise and our situation. That is, before changing it at least twenty times.

Maybe we could have a little fun after the interviews are done and with a clear understanding that whatever things we get up to are not to be written about. There's a chance we could be . . . well, I don't know, fuck buddies? Friends with *very* good benefits? More? the little voice in my head whispers to me in my weaker moments.

But that's playing with fire and I know it. Elise is an investigator at heart, curious and wanting to know things. I saw that when she was just chatting with the guys.

And the one most likely to get burned there is Carsen.

I promised myself years ago after what happened that I wouldn't do anything to jeopardize her ability to have a normal childhood, and fucking a tabloid reporter damn sure isn't the brightest idea I've ever had.

I'm still flip-flopping when Sarah comes in the kitchen, cautiously giving my grumpy ass a wide berth. She's come over to pick up Carsen again so I can keep up the façade of a publicity-shy loner bachelor. "So, did the show suck last night or something?"

Caught off-guard, I give her a confused look, realizing I've been dipping a cookie into some milk for so long the poor damn thing has dissolved and I've got nothing but a chocolate chip between my fingers. "Huh? Not that I know of. Why?"

"Well, usually, the day after a show, you're buzzing a bit, ready to tackle the day," she says, coming over and rescuing my plate of cookies, grabbing one and munching on it contentedly. One of the ways I reassure myself when things are tough . . . eat cookies with Sarah and Carsen. "But you're wearing a cloak of 'fuck off' right now. Ergo, did the show suck?"

I laugh at her, loving that she knows my routine to a T. "No, the show was great, as usual. They loved the songs, even did an old one I haven't performed in years. *Hello Girl*."

Sarah nods, doing some more chocolate chip deduction with another cookie. "That's not in your usual set list. Anything in particular make you feel like singing that?'

I shake my head, not wanting to let her in on the truth. "I dunno, just felt it."

She hums, and when I look at her, her eyebrow is raised as she dunks her cookie, obviously seeing through my bullshit. "So, wasn't the reporter going to the show last night? That wouldn't happen to be her favorite song or something, is it?"

I laugh. Close, but no cigar. "Hell if I know. Elise isn't even a country fan, really. More of a rock person she says, good taste in rock at least. But she went to the show last night. Must've done her homework too because she sang along with almost every song." I say, thinking back to how she looked as she belted out my words, my songs. Everyone was singing along, but somehow her doing it felt like winning a prize.

Sarah snaps her fingers, grinning impishly. "That's it. It's the reporter. Spill it, Keith."

I know my eyes are wide, panic showing, because Sarah continues, her smile dimming but her voice becoming more intense. "It's all over your face when you talk about her. And no woman just memorizes a bunch of songs for an assignment like hers. What's her deal?"

I force my emotions back under control, schooling my face into a calm dismissal despite her comment about Elise dropping a bomb into my emotional calm. "She's fine. We've had a few interviews now. The first article is already published, mostly just basics. Record company was happy."

Sarah shakes her head and downs the rest of my milk, including the soggy cookie bits in the bottom. "Nice try at diversion, big guy. You forget I grew up with you and know all your tells. That's what Todd and the record company want to hear. Tell me about her."

I swallow, trying to speak in a way that won't show my hand too much, even though Sarah has always been able to read me like a book. "She's a tabloid reporter. The one who printed the first article that started this whole mess, actually. But she's good, seems to want a real story, not a made-up melodramatic one, which is better than I can say for most of the vultures."

Sarah interrupts, not interested in Elise's resume. "Yeah, yeah, yeah . . . work, work, work. Tell me what *she's* like."

"Fuck, Sarah . . . what do you want to know? Her damn cup size and favorite food?"

Sarah smirks, hopping up on the kitchen island and swinging her legs back and forth. "Funny that's where your mind goes. Question is, do you *know* her cup size and favorite food?"

I duck my head, busted and pissed as fuck about it. "Maybe."

Sarah claps like this a good thing. "Finally! Hallelujah and pass the peanut butter, my prayers have been answered!"

I growl, glaring at her pure . . . glee. "What the fuck are you so damn happy about? This is bad, Sarah. Really fucking bad."

Sarah shakes her head, not clapping but still smiling. "No, it's not. You took this vow of being alone like some martyr, sacrificing your own happiness for Carsen in a misguided notion that it's somehow better for her. But she doesn't need that. She's a happy little girl who has everything she could ever want . . . but one thing. She needs you to be happy with her, with your work, and with a partner. Show her what love can look like."

I sigh, wishing it were that easy. I love my sister, but sometimes she can be a bit idyllic. "What? I don't love Elise. How could I? We just met, for all intents and purposes. I just . . . want her."

Sarah puts her hand on my shoulder, patting it gently. "Fine. So you don't introduce her to Carsen. But you take a little joy in life for yourself. She's the only woman who's even intrigued you in all these years. I never said anything before because I could see that about you. And I can see that you're fighting this now. But maybe . . . don't?"

"What about the articles? It's not exactly professional for either of us to be fucking while she's writing a tell-all expose on me," I exclaim. "And it gets her closer to the truth."

Sarah smirks, shaking her head. "Uhm, I'm sure more than one article has been 'researched' that way, especially in show-biz. At least you two can go into it with eyes wide open. Talk to her, see if you can figure out how to tell her what she needs to know for the articles without putting Carsen at risk. It could work. And judging by the way you're behaving, it's gonna happen sooner or later anyway, so best to get in front of it. Control the outcome, Mr. Control Freak. You can't tell me you haven't been going over every possible scenario already. Just pick the one where you get to have a little fun for a change."

Fun. My own sister, telling me to have fun, which of course means get my fucking freak on. "I can't believe you're telling me to fuck the reporter. This has bad written all over it."

Sarah grins and punches me in the arm. "Well, a little bad can be a good thing sometimes, little brother."

I groan, remembering how Elise said something similar just last night. And now, my sister. "Ugh, don't. For the love of fuck, do not. You're my sister, Sarah. Just hush."

She laughs, miming locking her lips as she gives me a sassy look and walks out of the kitchen, calling for Carsen. "Carsen, c'mon, honey. Grab your gear and let's roll. Don't forget to think of a chick flick for us to watch. Something romantic . . . maybe Enchanted?

Quieter, I hear her mutter under her breath. "Mmm, McDreamy . . ."

I shake my head, definitely not wanting to know who my sister fantasizes about.

Carsen runs through, bag tossed over her shoulder, grinning. "Bye, Dad, we're leaving."

"Hey, wait a second, young lady," I declare, holding up a hand. "I at least need a hug bye."

She grins, wrapping her arms around my shoulders, and I pick her up, giving her a big hug. She's still so young, so fragile, and if I were a stronger man, maybe I'd be able to keep the promise I gave her. But I'm weak, I'll admit it.

Elise lights me up like no woman ever has, and I can't hold out much longer against my desire. I've got to figure out a way to keep Carsen a secret, keep her safe, but give in to this thing with Elise, at least a little to let the pressure off.

Giving Carsen one more squeeze, I give her a kiss on the cheek. "I love you, baby girl. You know I'd do anything for you, right?"

She looks at me weird, like I've lost my damn mind. "Of course, Dad. I love you, too."

I set her down, and she's off with Sarah, already talking about ordering pizza. "And popcorn too! Okay?"

Sarah laughs, nodding at Carsen before looking at me, giving me a little wink. Before I know it, they're driving away in Sarah's SUV and I'm alone.

Elise won't be here for hours, not until dinner time. But I'm already craving her, her breathy moans as I picture fucking her like I have every time I've jacked off since last night.

If I'm honest with myself, it's not just the sex I'm after though. I want her smiles, her laugh, for her to tell me about her day.

I want to know her. That's the scariest part of all.

# CHAPTER 11

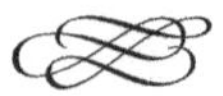

## ELISE

My fingers are flying across the keyboard for this second article. It really is some of the easiest writing I've ever done. It's like I'm just pouring myself out on the pages, and I know the hardest part will be keeping myself under the word limit.

*"So tell me about your first performance."*

Keith's recorded voice is deep and casual, sending warm ripples through my body as he chuckles in my earphones. *"Wow, that takes me back. It was . . . fourth grade. My school's talent contest, and I knew that I wanted to sing my ass off. I couldn't play well enough yet, but I got my hands on the instrumentals to some Garth Brooks."*

*"Garth Brooks?"* I asked, laughing. *"You didn't."*

*"Oh, I had the whole getup, from that solid black colored shirt to a black cowboy hat. The only other song I could get the chords to was Shania Twain, and I looked like hell in a dress."*

I smile at our mutual laughter. *"So, what happened?"*

*"Well, I was nervous as hell when I got up there, even though I'd practiced for a month straight. But I closed my eyes and started singing. The*

*response was good, and so I kept going. Everything was good up until the bridge."*

*"What happened?"*

*"Let's just say I'm a better singer than dancer,"* Keith says with a laugh. *"There's a reason I don't do dance numbers in my shows now. A whole month of practice in front of the mirror at home . . . not enough. Still, I got a standing ovation, which I guess set the bar pretty fucking high for future performances."*

I snicker to myself and work in some backstory of his years perfecting his craft on small stages in dive bars before I segue into my experience with Keith's local show, the way he kept it pretty low-key and wasn't some hard-to-work-with diva star but instead was easygoing and casual with the small backstage crew and band.

I add in how he talked about his fans with sweeping compliments and appreciation, making sure to highlight the little girl he'd stopped and signed an autograph for. The guys' stories from the green room add a bit of a rock 'n roll element and tour absurdity that makes Keith feel like a perfect blend of country good ol' boy and rock star god that I know will tickle the fancy of even the non-country fan readers.

It's hard to stay objective, though, when I talk about the concert itself. More than once, I find myself deleting whole passages as I gush like a fangirl about his command of the room, the way his voice vibrated through my body to enflame my desires, or the sexy swagger and the way his ass looked in his jeans as he strutted back and forth across the stage. Sure, some of it can be in my final cut. I need to entice the readers and maybe make a few panties wet, but I can't come off like some newbie with a total crush on him . . . even if I'm starting to feel that way.

I most definitely leave out the moments in the dark backstage. Those are ours, whatever they were. Even now, with his voice talking though the recorder, my body heats as I remember the feel of his hand smacking down on my bare cheek, the taps on my clit. I can feel the blush in my cheeks as I remember our agreeing that we can't pursue anything and then seconds later, going at each other again.

It's like we've crossed a line, and no matter what, it can't be uncrossed. The pull between us is too damn strong.

I've never felt anything like this before. Even though we haven't seen each other that many times, the time we've spent together has been intense, full of deep conversations and sharing about ourselves over long hours. I've had whole relationships that lasted months that haven't been as deep as the sharing that Keith and I have done. Add in the explosive chemistry, and we're so fucked.

Well, I am.

If something happens and people found out, Keith comes out like a famous music star. The worst someone might accuse him of is slumming it with a reporter to try and get a better angle. A little naughty, but nothing all that bad.

I'm the one who's compromising her professional morals. Even if I'm not doing it for the story, which I'm definitely not, no one would believe that. They'll think I'm just as bad as Francesca, using my body to get ahead professionally. And quite frankly, too many girls get chewed up and spat out by the industry once it gets out that they fuck their way around. There'd be no chance in hell of my ever getting out of the sleazy tabloid circuit. No chance of getting the job that I really do want.

As much as that should give me pause, and normally it would, I know that if Keith had come upstairs last night, there's no way I could've said no. Underneath my desk, I have to cross and uncross my legs just to relieve some of the pressure as I think about the ridge I felt in Keith's jeans, the jealous possessiveness as he punished me in the dark.

My hands drop from my keyboard to press against the top of my shorts just over my pussy. My mind is back to picturing him stroking himself, imagining his groans as he cries out my name when he comes, thick spurts of cum coating his hand.

Fuck it . . . professional morals be damned.

I want Keith.

I want him in a way I've never wanted a man before. Something about the way he's both soft and rough unexpectedly does it for me, and if I have a chance, I'm going for it. If I get burned . . . well, I can try starting over writing books. They say every reporter has their own version of the Great American Novel kicking around in their heads. Might as well put mine out there.

Decision made, I shake my head with a smile and take a deep breath, attempting to refocus on my article.

As I read back over it, I know it's good. Really good, maybe the best I've ever written. I know for sure it'll make our readers feel like they've actually experienced what backstage with Keith is really like. Donnie will like this one without a doubt. It paints Keith in a positive light but has just enough exciting dirt from the tour stories to be intriguing. It teases, and while it doesn't say anything bad about Keith, it does let the reader fantasize just a little.

It's more than a usual 'man on the stage' piece, delving into Keith's performances from day one to now, along with his thoughts on the whole journey he's been on. I've even got a lead for the next story . . . where does Keith go from here?

With a flourish, I hit *Send* and lean back in my chair. Two down, at least another couple to go, but Donnie is going to expect some dirt now that I've set up Keith as the hero in this tale. He needs a dark moment, but I really don't know if there is one. I'm beginning to think that Keith really is just who he says, a guy who wants to write, sing, and be left alone.

There's a tiny voice in the back of my head reminding me of what Maggie said about finding out what he does in his free time, and I make a note to ask some questions about that tonight. Selfishly, I want to ask about his 'why no dating, now or later' rule, and as I get dressed, I try to decide if I can do that without sounding like a whiny cling-on.

Realizing the time, I decide casual is the order for the day and grab black leggings and a soft pale blue sweater I knit last winter. The neckline is wide and hangs off my shoulder. I'm still not as good as Grandma ever hoped, so I slip on a lacy purple bralette underneath. I change panties too, into a matching purple thong that nestles softly between my cheeks, making me bite my lip thoughtfully.

Yeah, I'm going in with all thoughts of being professional tonight, but if something happens, I don't want to be wearing ugly granny lingerie.

I drive quickly to Keith's place, my mind whirling as I try and think of questions to ask . . . but really, all I want to do is hang out with him, to see where this evening takes us.

I knock on the door, expecting to have to wait, but instead I hear a voice from inside. "It's open."

I swing the door open, and my first thought is that Keith seems to have had the same thought of casual comfort. He looks downright edible, grey sweatpants hung low on his hips and a tank top stretched across his chest. I can see tattoos peeking out along the neckline and twisting down his arms in thick bands of design that I've never seen before. They're intricate, they're detailed, and I want to trace them with my tongue.

My eyes are running across his chest, down his thick arms to his clenched fists. He's here not to talk, not to have a casual dinner. He's here to conquer, to take what he wants. And fuck, do I want to give it to him.

"Elise."

It's not a question, it's an order, and I look up as a shudder races through me. I can see the lust he's holding back, the control he's using just to stand in front of me. I want to test it, push him and see where his limit is, if for no other reason than my own sanity, which is mind-numbingly lost in his presence. "Keith, what are you thinking right now?"

He doesn't step toward me, but his whole body seems to vibrate as he growls quietly, his eyes blazing with need. "Right now, I'm thinking that I want to bite that bare shoulder, leave a mark while I hold you in place and pound into you from behind. I want to make you scream my name and fill you with my cock and come until we're both satisfied."

And I'm done.

I haven't even made it in the door yet, not a single interview question asked, but I can't hold myself back like he is. I don't have the iron will he does.

Instead of answering, I drop my bag inside the door and jump into his arms.

In a testament to his strength, Keith doesn't even flinch when he catches me, his large hands easily cupping my ass and holding me high as I wrap my legs and arms around him, hanging on. He presses into me, taking my mouth in a heated kiss. I hear the door shut behind me and vaguely realize he must've kicked it shut because his hands are squeezing me, kneading my cheeks roughly.

He slams my back against the door, using it as leverage to get one hand free. He dips his free hand under my sweater, tracing my hip, up my side, and finally grabbing a handful of my breast. His thumb swipes across my lace-covered nipple, already hard for him, and I arch for more. "Fuck . . . Keith . . . fuck, I can't—"

He pulls me to him and holds me against the door, leaning his head back to meet my eyes.

"Tell me no, Elise," he grates out, control and choice battling in his eyes and his voice. "Tell me to put you down and stop this. Because if you don't, I'm gonna fuck you. This is my point of no return. I fucking need you."

The last part is nearly a whisper, and I'm not sure he meant to say it, but as much as he needs me, I need him more . . . need him to fuck me, make me come apart under his hands. His tongue. His cock.

I cup his face and try to insert some steel into my voice to show that I'm doing this of my own free will. "Put me down."

I can feel the power it takes him to do it, how much he doesn't want to, but he does, letting my pussy slide down every inch of his rock-hard abs and cock. His fists are on either side of my head, knuckles pressed to the door, his breathing so heavy I can feel it on my cheeks. "I need . . . an answer."

That's the sweet with the rough I want, that edge where he's in control but just barely, hanging on by a thread.

Once my feet touch the floor, I push him back just a half-step, giving me enough space to grab the hem of my sweater, pulling it up and off before dropping it to the floor next to us.

I meet his eyes again, my fingers fidgeting with the hem of his tank top. "Didn't want you to ruin my sweater. Keith, yes. I need you, too."

I see the instant he recognizes what I said, his feral grin hot for a split second before he growls. "Fuck!"

Grabbing me and tossing me over his shoulder, he strides further into the house, an area I haven't seen before, but now, it's upside down and my attention is mostly caught by the way Keith's back and ass are flexing under my weight as he moves.

I get a sense of a dark blue bedroom before he tosses me unceremoniously onto the bed, and I bounce. If I wasn't so turned on, I'd be giggling and yelling, but right now, what I want is to be fucked as hard as Keith can give me.

"Pants. Off," he orders, his voice iron-hard. I hear the undertone. He asked, I gave him control, and now . . . I'm *his* to do with as *he* wishes. My choices are over for now.

I'm already hurrying to do what he says, but as he rips his tank over his head, I freeze, taking in the picture in front of me.

His chest is broad, covered in tattoos that would take my tongue hours to trace, and I make a note to do just that. His stomach ripples with muscles, lines and ridges that all flow together before dipping down to a V on the lower half. The lines disappear into his sweats, which are tented with obvious evidence of his arousal.

Keith cups his cock through his pants, blocking my sight for a moment, and I look up, knowing my desire is all over my face. But it's all over his face too, his blue eyes intense and focused on my still legging-covered pussy.

"Take them off," he warns me, his jaw clenching. "Or I'm gonna rip them off and tie you up with them. I need to see your pussy, taste you, feel you come on my tongue. Last warning."

I wiggle, trying to slip the leggings off gracefully, but I'm distracted by Keith's hand rubbing up and down his cock through his pants.

When I finally get my leggings down to my knees, Keith gives in and grabs them, pulling them the rest of the way off before grabbing my knees. He spreads me wide, leaning in close enough that I feel the brush of his nose through the lace as he inhales my scent.

His face is buried in me, and I feel his hot breath dance over the small holes in the lace and against my burning skin. "They match. Your pretty purple panties match your lacy bra. Did you do that for me, Elise?"

I bite my lip, not sure if I should tell the truth, but when he traces a finger along the fabric at my hip, I gasp, unable to hold back from him any longer. "Yes, for you."

"Mmm, naughty girl," he moans, pulling the hem of my panties to the side, exposing my pussy to his gaze. "Fuck, you're soaked for me. This tight, little pink pussy wants my throbbing cock, doesn't it?"

I don't answer this time because I can't, but I lift my hips toward Keith's mouth, and he takes my invitation, licking a long line up to my clit, circling it with the tip of his tongue before sucking on it hard. I cry out, balling the comforter in my fists as I buck my hips, desperate for him to do it again. "Please."

My wavering plea triggers him even more, and he yanks my panties off, immediately diving back in. Switching targets, he strokes his tongue over my outer lips, tasting my softness before using both hands to spread me wide.

With a jolt, his tongue pierces into me, and he finds a rhythm, fucking me with quick, stabbing licks as he moves a thumb up to tease my clit in small circles that drive me wild.

My body is thrashing back and forth on the soft bed, my head whipping from side to side as I rise higher and higher, but I need more. It's so damn good, but I'm greedy and I want more.

"More . . . Keith . . . please."

Keith hums, the vibration shooting sparks through my pussy, but he complies, pressing one thick finger into my pussy and licking at my clit lazily. He strokes his finger in and out, looking up into my eyes, his voice deep, water over gravel. "This what you need, Elise? Want me to fill your pussy with my fingers and suck your hard little clit?"

I reach for his head, trying to direct him where I need as I give in to begging. "Fuck. Yes, Keith."

Finally, he gives me what I desperately need, slipping in another finger to fill me and pumping them in and out, curling up to my front wall to hit that spot that makes me see stars. He takes my clit in his mouth, sucking hard and flicking the tip of his tongue across it so fast it feels like butterfly wings.

I curl up, my shoulders lifting off the mattress as every muscle in my body goes tight with how good it feels. I linger on the edge, feeling trapped in bliss before Keith hums and I'm rocketed over the edge, screaming out as I come. I shudder and shake helplessly, chanting his name and reaching for him, not sure if it's to make him stay between my legs or to make him move. Everything feels so good, but it's too much, overwhelming me with pleasure.

Everything unhinges, and I collapse back on the comforter, tears leaking from the corners of my eyes at the intensity. Keith kisses up my belly, dropping one wet kiss to each breast before kissing me hard, his fingers still softly thrusting deep inside me. I whimper, cupping his face as he pulls back, confidence and sex appeal radiating from every pore of his body.

"That was fucking delicious," he says softly, his fingers slowing. "Taste."

He takes his fingers out of my pussy, bringing them to my mouth. I don't even think. I just suck his fingers, licking and nibbling on the calloused pads.

Keith watches my mouth, licking his lips in anticipation. "Fuck, Elise. I want you to do that to my cock. Suck me down just like that, but if you do, I'm gonna come down your pretty throat. And I don't want that right now. I want to come deep in your pussy. It's all I've been thinking about."

I nod, writhing under him, but he wants more. "Tell me."

I moan, reluctantly taking his fingers out of my mouth to give him my plea. "Fuck me, Keith. God, please, fuck me. No mercy, no questions. Fuck me hard. Use me. Make me yours."

He stands, yanking me to the edge of the bed by my ankles and throwing my legs up high on his shoulders. Grabbing his waistband, Keith pulls his sweats over and down his cock, which springs out hard and already oozing precum like jewels from his tip. Just like I imagined, he's huge and gorgeous, thick veins running along the shaft that I know are going to light my nerves on icy delicious fire.

He grabs his cock in his hand, reaching beside him to the bedside table for a condom. I'm sad when he's covered, the beauty of him encased where I can't marvel at it. I want to foolishly plead for him to take it off, to take me raw, but then he teases my opening with his head and I completely forget. I don't need to see him. I need to feel him deep inside me.

I drive forward with my hips, my pussy trying to suck him in as I try to wrap my legs around him. Before I do, though, he reads my need and obliges in one deep thrust, going balls-deep and forcing every breath of air out of me in a gasp.

He stretches me just on the good side of pain, my eyes rolling up because it's so overwhelming. He doesn't give me a minute to adjust to his girth, immediately retreating and pumping back with force, his balls slapping against my ass. I can feel my inner walls clenching against him, desperate to feel every nerve turned on in ways they've never been before.

Keith grunts, his eyes never leaving my face as he thrusts harder and harder. "Squeeze me just like that. Fuck, Elise. You're so damn tight."

I try to do as he says, clutching at him, both with my hands on his forearms as he holds my hips and with the muscles deep inside me. He strokes into me, filling me with every thrust.

As he leans forward, pressing his body against me more and taking me fully, I bend my legs, folding myself in half as my knees roll next to my shoulders. I say a little prayer of thanks for my yoga habit as he pounds me even harder at the new angle, the head of his cock rubbing that spot inside again. A deep whine of hunger starts in my chest, and I stare up at him, my mouth dropping open as I feel myself caught helpless again, swept up in another orgasmic wave that'll shatter me when it finally crests . . . but I don't care as long as I feel him come first.

He grabs my hands, forcing them to the bed with our fingers entwined, and I realize I'm his total prisoner. This powerful man is pinning me to his bed, both with his hands and with his body as he speeds up, his strokes getting harder and more intense with each slap of our hips.

All I can do is take him, enjoy the sensation of every inch filling me up and the control he has over me.

"Oh, fuck," I force out between deep breaths that ripple through my entire body. "Keith, I'm gonna come."

His eyes are hard as he meets my heated gaze with a commanding shake of his head. "No, not yet. You come with me, when I say."

His voice is tight, so I know he's close, but I don't know if I can hang on as I thrash below him. "I— "

Keith lets go of one hand and grabs my jaw, just above my throat but still cutting off my words like a switch. "Look at me, Elise. Do not come yet. I want you to come all over my cock, squeezing me in your perfect little pussy. I want to ride out our pleasure together."

His words aren't helping me wait. He's teasing me on the edge even more. His hands tighten in mine, and his hips hammer me even harder, and as I cry out, unable to wait any longer, he roars as I feel him jerk inside me.

"Fuck, yes . . . Elise!"

I clench and squeeze as much as I can, lifting my hips to meet his as he slams against my thighs, working to prolong our orgasms together. Our eyes are locked, never leaving each other as we both pant our way through the pleasure and the return to earth.

A smile is already breaking across my face when I see the stern look on Keith's and I sober.

He grinds against me as he scolds me, his eyes still burning with desire. "Mmm, that was so damn good. But you came before I said to."

For a moment, I think he's kidding, and I tease back. "What are you gonna do? Punish me?"

He smiles back, but it's predatory, and a little chill mixes with the heat of his cock still pulsing inside me. "Yes. Yes, I am."

If this were any other man, I'd be pissed. As if he's in charge of me? I'll come when I damn well feel like it, and just count yourself lucky you got to be here for it.

But the tiny voice deep in the back of my mind reminds me about his punishment before and surprisingly, how much I liked it. He talks as if he wants me to be a good girl, but being bad sounds so much more delicious, so I consider playing a bit coy.

I let that voice win, smirking. "So should I turn over for my spanking then?"

Keith shakes his head, pulling his cock out of me, and I immediately want him back, feeling empty without him inside me. He slips the condom off, tying it off and tossing it to the trash, where it drops in like a jump shot.

"No," he says, turning his attention back to me. "I think I'm ready to come down your pretty little throat now. Don't flip over, Elise. Get on your knees."

So help me, I do. And eagerly, at that. Both because he told me to and because I really do want to taste him the way he tasted me.

He's already thickening again by the time I get on my knees, his gorgeous cock bobbing in front of me. Keith gathers my hair in his fist, and I look up at him through my lashes.

I stick the tip of my tongue out, teasing his head with the faintest touch and moan at his taste. "Mmm, you taste good too."

But Keith is done with teasing, all pretense gone as he pulls my head back, bending my neck so that I'm forced to look him in the eye. "Put your hands behind your back, Elise. Suck my cock down your throat and make me come. Take your punishment like a good girl."

I have a flashback to him saying that last night and how good that made me feel, and I know for Keith, I do want to be his good girl. I do as he instructed, clasping my hands behind my back and opening wide as Keith presses his cock into my mouth. He stretches my mouth too, my lips as wide as they can go, but I don't stop.

I hollow my cheeks, sucking him deeper and letting him direct my pace with his hold on my hair. He pushes into my throat, and I gag slightly, but Keith doesn't pull out. Instead, he retreats into my mouth just enough to let me breathe while he strokes my hair. "Shh, just relax. Breathe and let me fuck that sweet little mouth."

He doesn't ask, but he looks at me questioningly, so I blink, humming my agreement. Keith moans as his cock jumps in my mouth, making me feel . . . good. He starts slow, thrusting further with every stroke until he's deep in my throat. He holds me there for a split second, and I work to relax, wanting this, wanting to make him lose control. He pulls back with a shudder and then does it again, and again. I open up more, amazed at how much of him I can take, letting him invade my throat and take me fully.

The next time he holds me, pressed so close to his body that I'm forced to hold my breath, I swallow and hum again.

He loses it, that sexy control snapping like a rubber band as he grips my hair tighter and pistons wildly in and out of my mouth, growling. "Fuck. Swallow it, Elise. Swallow my cum like a good girl."

I gulp and suck as Keith roars his release, trying to catch every bit as he shoots his salty-sweet cum down my throat, but it's so much I lose some and it runs down my chin, dripping onto my chest. And he's still coming, holding himself deep in my throat again as he jerks. When he's depleted, he leans back, looking down at me with wonder in his eyes.

"God damn. That was . . ." I can tell he's searching for words, and then his mind settles and he smiles. "Mmm, good girl."

I grin, pleased that I've made him brainless. "Thank you. I aim to please."

As he watches, I use my thumb to gather the bit of seed on my chin, slipping it into my mouth with a moan of delight at his taste on my tongue. Then I rub the drops on my chest into my skin.

He groans at the sight and scoops me up from the floor, raising me to my feet and taking my mouth in a deep kiss. "Very good girl."

# CHAPTER 12

## KEITH

It feels strange yet appropriate to do the interview in bed, although I'm not sure if that was my idea or Elise's. Either way, it's a brilliant one.

As we curl up naked over delivered pizza, Elise turns to me, putting her voice recorder in the space between us. "So, we've done the history of Keith Perkins in article one. Article two is all performance-related, with an emphasis on the show experience I had at your local venue gig."

I raise an eyebrow at her, and she laughs, stretching out with one pink-tipped foot to kick me. "My entire performance?"

"I didn't include any of *that,* of course. Despite our current situation, I do know where the lines need to be drawn. And yes, none of what we've done tonight is ever going to see the light of day. I promise you."

There's a hint of something in her voice that I can't place. I grasp her chin in my hand, gentle but not letting her look away and hide from me. "Are you okay with where we are right now?"

She sighs, her eyes dropping, but she answers, scratching at her lovely hip as she does. "Personally, yes. Professionally, no."

I narrow my eyes, needing to understand. This is maybe even more important than even the interview itself. "Explain."

She drops her pizza to the box, climbing up to her knees and sitting back on her heels. I refuse to be enticed by the sight of her breasts pressed between her arms, but she's still so sexy and beautiful, it's hard not to notice.

"Okay, so look, there's this woman at my office, Francesca. She's ambitious, always wants the best assignments, and if I'm honest, she's a pretty good writer. But she gets the cherry assignments because she's sleeping with the boss. Our gross, older boss."

I'm looking at her, still not sure where she's going.

"And because she slept her way to those assignments, it doesn't matter how well she writes them. She could be Mark fucking Twain, and everyone will discount her because of the way she got there. I don't want to be that girl. I'm a good writer, and this series means something to me. It's my first shot at something real and not just . . . well, rumor mill tabloid fodder. And I think it means something to your fans and is good for your image. But I'm not the woman who trades for inside information on her knees."

My gut tightens as my blood boils. "Have I done anything to make you think this is a quid-pro-quo situation? That I'm going to tell you my deepest, darkest secrets because I fucked you?" I know my voice is too loud by the way she winces at my reply.

Elise's head drops, her chin almost touching her chest as she shakes her head.

My voice is hard, even as I work to quiet my volume. "Is that why you fucked me?"

I'm holding my breath as I wait for her to answer. She doesn't realize that it may be the most important question I've asked her the whole time I've known her.

Elise's eyes snap to mine, her cheeks flushing with anger as she squares her shoulders, glaring at me as she yells. "No! Of course not. That's why I'm so fucking torn up. I wanted this. Hell, I want to do it again right now. But I shouldn't when it could mess up everything I've worked so damn hard for. But you're just so damn . . . irresistible. You drive me fucking crazy."

I pounce on her in reply, slamming her to the bed underneath me and covering her mouth with a kiss, demanding entry and tangling my tongue with hers. Our bodies press together, and even though I've come twice in the past two hours, I can feel a tingle in my cock as it starts to raise its head again.

Once she's breathless and I know she'll be quiet for a second, I pull back, looking into her sapphire eyes. "You drive me fucking crazy too. No, we shouldn't be doing this. For more reasons than you know, but someone I consider pretty smart told me that if I fight this, I'll regret it. So I'll take what I can get with you, Elise. We do the interviews, you do the stories, and whatever this is . . . it's between us, not a thing to do with your work. Can you handle that?"

She bites her lip like she's actually considering what I've proposed, and at first, it pisses me off. I'm laying it all out there and she's fucking hesitating. But then I realize I'm not laying it all out there. And as much as I'm holding back, she's making a pretty ballsy career move by agreeing to be with me outside of the interviews, and suddenly, I appreciate that she's considering so carefully.

While she thinks, I decide to tilt the odds in my favor and I move in, suckling a spot in the curve of her neck I found that she likes, and she leans to the side, giving me more access. It's all I need. I know I've won. I give her tender skin a little more, biting gently, just enough to leave a mark, but I know it'll fade in minutes as I lick over the spot, soothing the sting.

Elise sighs happily, stroking her fingers down my back. "I can handle it."

I grin into her shoulder before pulling her back up to sit opposite me, and I sit back, recognizing that my cock is half-hard . . . guess I do need at least a little bit of time before I'm ready for full action again.

"Fine. You've got thirty minutes before I take over again . . . so hit me. What questions do you have?"

She looks flustered, my move from seduction to business making her spin. "What?"

I raise my eyebrows at her, teasing as I set a timer on my phone. "Thirty minutes. Twenty-nine and fifty seconds now. Better get some questions done or article three is gonna be a hard write." I scold her teasingly.

Elise laughs, going along with me, but not before teasing me back. "And what happens in thirty—twenty-nine—minutes?"

I let the smile drop off my face, the dark need shining through. "In twenty-nine minutes, I'm shoving you face down in this bed, grabbing your arms behind your back, and taking you again, banging your hips so hard your ass will be bright pink when you leave. Next question?"

I see her shudder, the heat rising between us already, but she rallies, pulling herself together. With a quick reset of the recorder between us, she starts.

"Okay, history . . . check. Performance . . . check. What about your personal life? What do you do when you're not on stage and not driving me crazy with want?"

I stutter, trying to figure out how I'm getting out of this when she's hitting too close to topics I'd rather leave alone. "What do you mean? Are you already turning stalkery on me?"

She laughs, shaking her head and pushing at my chest playfully. "No, but like, take me through a typical day, a typical week in the life of Keith Perkins. What do you do all day, all night?"

I hesitate, quickly trying to edit my day to leave out any mention of Carsen. "Well, I get up, get coffee, and run errands like everyone else. I normally work out just before lunch, and I spend a big chunk of the afternoon writing songs, playing music. I don't know, just usual stuff, I guess."

Elise is scouring my face, and I wonder if she can see through me. It has to be the biggest gap-filled schedule in history. I mean, seriously? I gotta figure out a hobby to throw in or something.

"Wow, that's really . . . boring," she says before laughing self-consciously. "What do you do that your fans would be surprised about or would like to read about? Hobbies, activities? Any secret fetishes?"

Whew, I guess I dodged that one a little. "If there was, I'm pretty sure that'd fall under our previous agreement about *not* being in the article," I say with a wink.

Elise grins, biting her lip even as her nipples crinkle at the meaning of my words. "Fair enough . . . thought I'd just slip that in there for my own curiosity. But really . . . hobbies, activities?"

I try to think of something. In the few seconds that I have to consider, I throw out a lot of ideas. Star Wars? Too nerdy. Pro wrestling? Please. Baseball cards? Where's my collection? I'm stumped and stumble for anything. "Well, not really a hobby, I guess, but I like being outside. I try to go camping, hiking, fishing, and hunting occasionally, that sort of thing. I've got a couple of ATVs and a parcel of land out in the mountains. I like to escape out there. No TV, phones, or Wi-Fi. It's just nature, clean air, and waking up with either the sun or my own body's needs. It helps me recharge away from everything. I always do that before and after summer tours, catch the spring blooms and the fall leaves turning colors. Makes everything else seem a little less impressive when you see the things Mother Nature can do."

I see her eyes soften as her mouth silently repeats what I just said, and I know she's mentally making a note for another quote. I like that she hears something important in the things I say. I work for days, sometimes weeks to make a song say just what I want to convey, but I rarely do that on the fly while talking to someone.

But somehow with her, it comes easily. I just open up, and what comes out seems to be right.

"Okay, my turn," I say, picking up a pepperoni and chewing it thoughtfully. "Why aren't you seeing someone?"

Her jaw drops, and she glowers at me, mock-outraged. Okay, maybe not quite mock. "That's not fair! I asked you an easy one and you're coming back with the big guns."

I flex my biceps at her, deadpanning. "Damn right, they're big guns."

She groans at the cheesy joke but turns thoughtful as she ponders her reply. "Okay, if I want honesty, I've got to give honesty. Just know that I'm already ready with my next question, Mr. Perkins."

I smile but gulp, glad that I've got a few moments to figure out how I'm going to get out of answering what she wants to know. I knew it was a risk, but I really do want to know the answer. Elise is so gorgeous, smart, and funny, I don't understand how someone hasn't snatched her up and slapped a ring on her finger.

"Well, I grew up an only child," she starts, looking shy again, "so initially, I was a little socially awkward. I had a good family, I told you about Grandma, but still, I was a little awkward at first. By high school, I'd figured out how to fit in, but I suspect that had a lot more to do with how I developed physically than emotionally."

She gestures to her bust and I make a low wolf-whistle. "Mmmhmm, I can see how you might be distracting for a teenage boy because you're damn well distracting a fully-grown man."

I'm teasing a little, but I feel my cock as it jumps in response to my eyeful of her lush tits.

Elise laughs, her eyes darting down to my rising third leg. "Yeah, well . . . high school was fine, and then I went away to college. I was . . . serious. At least more serious than people expected me to be. I guess because I'm blonde and a bit bubbly, people expect me to be an airhead or an easy lay. So I had to work twice as hard for professors to give me the grades I deserved, and I avoided guys for the most part because every time I'd try to date someone, I'd instantly get treated like brainless arm candy. I dated a bit after college, thinking it'd be easier once the frat boy mentality ended, and I did find a few guys who'd grown out of that. Including Trevor."

I try to hold in a growl when she says his name. I don't even know him, but I already hate him because his name is on her tongue. "Trevor?"

She smiles, seeing right through my question with a hint of amusement. "He's a chef, a really good one, actually. We met at a club. I was there for work . . . seeing who was out, what they were doing, and who with. He'd been there for a nightcap after a late closing. We hit it off, dated for a few months. But mostly, we just met at the club and hung out afterward."

I hear the code for 'fucking all night' and it riles me up even more. I know I'm not exactly planting a flag on new territory, but I know how I feel about the thought of her with other men. "What happened?"

She smiles sadly, fidgeting with the sheet. "He had an investor dinner. Invited me as his girlfriend, asked me to entertain the wife of the investor. Be the little lady for him. And I was happy. I was fucking proud to do that for him. Until the dinner." She shakes her head, remembering. "It was just the four of us. I thought it was going well. Everyone was talking, laughing, and when Trevor and the investor started talking figures, I was trying to help him, talking up the success he'd had, but he basically told me to shut up. Not in those words, but degrading enough. I sat there at that dinner and realized he didn't respect me at all. Just wanted me to sit still and look pretty, just another piece of arm candy. And so I got up, excused myself to the restroom, and walked out. When he called later, yelling about how I'd embarrassed him, I just told him goodbye and hung up. I still think I should've yelled, fought with him about it, but really . . . what would be the point in that? I'd already seen who he was inside, what he thought of me, and I was done. Better to just move on, right? That was about a year ago, and I just haven't found anyone who interests me since then." Her eyes meet mine, and she blushes. "Until now, I thought maybe I'd just missed the boat on good guys."

The silence that drops over us seems to press me toward Elise, enveloping me and urging me to take her in my arms and ignore the so-called 'professional' side of what we're supposed to be doing. My phone dings, the thirty minutes up, and with a breath of relief, I cup her chin in my hand, leaning in for a sweet kiss.

"You deserve so much more than that, Elise," I whisper when the kiss breaks and I pull back, just enough to look into her eyes. "I want to hear all the things you have to say. Truly."

She smiles, cupping the back of my neck and scratching lightly. "And you will . . . after. If I recall, you made me a promise?"

She purses her lips, daring me to renege on the words I spoke earlier. If it were anyone but Elise, I'd think there's no way they could go from such an emotionally revealing conversation to thinking about sex so quickly, but I can see the truth in her eyes. For her, everything was part of the foreplay that I teased her with during that first interview.

The vulnerability she shared, she needs to close it back off. We're seeing each other in a different light, accepting the complexities, but it's time to be vulnerable in a different way.

I kiss her softly one more time, a smacking sound as our lips caress each other, and I make sure she's good before pulling back, my voice hardening just the way we both need. "Elise. Lie on the bed, face down, and stick that perfect ass up in the air for me."

She grins hugely and immediately moves as I instructed, going even further and placing her crossed hands at her lower back for me. She remembers, and that sends another little thrill up my spine. She remembers exactly what I told her I was going to do to her sweet body, and if she's going to be this good then she deserves that I be just as good in return.

I line up behind her on my knees, running a fingertip down her spine and watch as she arches so prettily, her ass spreading a little, showing me a hint of her little pucker. I wonder if she's ever had her ass kissed before. If not, she's about to find out what it feels like.

I scratch my fingernails up her thighs to the globes of her ass, the skin smooth and unblemished, making me want to watch it pink up under my hand. Instead, I spread her ass wide, exposing her tight little asshole again and already wet pussy to my eyes. I dip down, kissing her cheeks, getting closer and closer to her asshole as she circles her hips, chasing my kisses, wanting my licks. "Oh fuck, Keith, what are you doing?"

"I'm going to make you feel amazing before fucking you as hard as your body can take," I promise. "Now . . . tell me if you want this."

Elise's breath catches, and she looks back. "I . . . yes. First time for everything, and you . . . yes."

My chest warms as I give her what she wants, licking a long line from her clit to her ass with the flat of my tongue, and Elise cries out, a shockwave wracking her body.

I rest my cheek on the fullness of one globe, watching as I use a finger to dip into her wet pussy, spreading her honey up to her asshole and circling it slowly.

"Have you ever been taken here, Elise?" I can feel her tensing underneath me, but she's lifting her hips toward my teasing finger and she whimpers softly.

"No, just . . . a finger once."

I groan, making up my mind. "Mmm, good girl. I'm gonna take this ass, Elise. Be the first one to fill you up, come deep inside you as you cry out at how good it feels. But not tonight. You need some prep before I can fuck you like that. Do you want that?"

She nods against the bed, and I can see her juices dripping down her thighs.

"Good. Now don't move."

I leave her there, face down, ass up in anticipation as I hop off the bed to reach the nightstand. I watch her eyes follow me, but to her credit, she doesn't move at all, ready for me to take her as I promised. I quickly roll the condom on, assuming my position behind her once again.

Moving behind Elise, I slip a finger deep inside her pussy, coating it and moving up to tease her ass. She shivers, whimpering again as I line up my cock with her pussy and slowly, oh, so slowly, slip my cock inch by inch into her, and my finger millimeter by millimeter into her ass. Her ass clenches, and she whines deep in her chest.

"Relax. Breathe and push against me. I won't hurt you."

I can feel her tensing, convulsing against the intrusion, and then with a big exhalation, she relaxes some. I go slowly again, slipping my finger in and out of her ass as I pump my cock in time until I'm seated fully in her, cock and finger. I stay still, letting her adjust to the fullness.

She cries out again, but it's in pleasure. "Yes."

"You okay?" I tease, wiggling my hips a little. "Think you can take it all?"

She grunts, turning to look back at me with all the sassiness that I'm already coming to appreciate. "I need you to move. Fuck, Keith . . . move."

I grab her crossed wrists with my other hand, pinning them to her back and giving me leverage as I piston my hips, slow and easy. I can feel her clenching around me, pushing her hips in time to fuck me back, and her pussy gets even wetter.

As I pump into her pussy, I start to move my finger in her ass, just little thrusts in and out, but she notices and arches even more. "You like that? You like my cock in your pussy and my finger in your ass? Filling you up. You want that? You ready for more?"

Her voice is hoarse as she begs, surrendering herself to me. "Fuck, yes. More."

I give it to her, thrusting faster and rougher, slamming into her pussy with everything I have, timing my thrusts in her ass to fill her completely and then leave her empty and wanting. "I'm going to let go of your hands, Elise," I grunt between deep breaths to keep up with my frantic, powerful fucking. "I want you to rub your clit, pinch your nipples for me. I'm going to overload your body, but you can take it. You can take it all, and hold on until I tell you to come. Can you do that for me?"

She nods, and I let go, watching with pleased delight as her hands move exactly where I told her. I can feel her fingers blurring across her clit, the pulses immediate around my cock and my finger. I speed up, slamming into her as I push her into the mattress, pounding her body with all of my strength.

"That's it. Your nipples, your clit, your pussy, your ass . . . all mine."

She cries out, and I know she's almost at the point of no return. I'm throbbing just as much, holding on with only the strongest of wills as I give her a couple more thrusts before I'm unable to hold out any more. I growl, my voice rough as I order her. "Come for me, Elise. Do it now."

I rain a handful of smacks on her ass cheek, feeling the gush as she comes, covering me down to my balls in her juices. Her muffled scream fills my ears, making me come too, shouting out my release as I bury myself as deep as I can go, pulse after pulse shooting from my cock.

The only thing that would make this even more perfect was if I was busting deep inside her, feeling her body taking all of me deep inside her.

In the almost reverent silence that follows, I pull out of her ass slowly, pressing my body forward to lie on top of her, still inside her sweet pussy.

I kiss her shoulder, her neck, her cheek as she recovers from the onslaught before she turns toward me, reaching up for a kiss on her swollen lips. I soothe them with a lick before nibbling her earlobe and tugging on it between my teeth. "Mmm, your thirty minutes starts now."

She laughs, sighing happily. "I'm renegotiating terms. Five-minute grace period between transitions. I . . . I can't even breathe right yet."

I lay another kiss to her shoulder before pushing up to take care of the condom and get a warm, wet washcloth, which I use to gently, carefully clean her. "I think we can do that. Deal."

We spend the whole night like that . . . talking about nothing and everything, then devouring each other again and again. Somewhere in the early morning, we fall asleep tangled in each other, her head pressed to my chest. But when we wake up, we do it all over again.

It's not always the same, but that doesn't matter. Whether it's me going down on her, her sucking my soul out through my cock, or any of the positions we end up in, it's all delectably perfect.

Eventually, after a particularly intense mid-morning session, I need a shower, but Elise elects to stay in bed, passed out from all the times I've taken her. I'm smiling as I shower, overjoyed at how good last night went. Elise is amazing . . . responsive, open, brilliant, funny, sweet. And most of all, her sass. She's everything I could ever want.

If only the timing were better and she wasn't a reporter who could crash my whole life to ashes. But as long as we keep this what it is, we should be fine. More than fine, judging by last night. I come out of the bathroom, releasing steam to the bedroom as I towel dry my hair.

I see the empty bed and grab a pair of sweats, thinking to track Elise down for a late breakfast.

As I walk down the hall, I hear it. Voices. Not just Elise. She's talking to someone. As I step into the kitchen, I see Elise, wearing one of my black workout t-shirts, so huge it drops down to her thighs, her obviously freshly-fucked hair pulled up in a messy knot on top of her head.

And she's smiling, talking to . . . Sarah.

Before I can say or do a single thing, the back door opens and Carsen comes barreling in like always, her voice announcing her long before her head pops around the corner.

"Daddy! Guess what I did on my girls' night with Aunt Sarah?"

She freezes when she sees Elise, and I see everyone's eyes cut to me, Elise's jaw dropping as Carsen covers her mouth with her hands.

*Fuck.*

# CHAPTER 13

## ELISE

The frozen silence stretches out for a seeming eternity, the four of us caught in some sort of crystalline pattern that binds us immobile but just needs a single tap in the right direction to shatter and set us free . . . if only we could.

I can see the fear on the little girl's face as she looks at me like I'm a monster, and Keith is looking at me with barely-contained fury. I'm not sure what's going on here, but I do know that the girl just called Keith 'Daddy.'

That changes everything in more ways than one. Before I can even let my mind roll through the possibilities, both professional and personal, Keith takes control of the situation.

He kneels to gather the girl in his arms, giving her a hug that seems to make her more nervous at first, judging by the way she's stiffens, her voice pleading as she hugs him. "Sorry, Dad. I'm so sorry."

Keith pats her back and then meets her eyes, stroking her hair with a feather-soft caress that tells me that no matter what, he loves this girl . . . his daughter. He. Has. A. Daughter. My mind races, jumping from question to question . . . *holy shit, how? I mean, I know the logistics. But with who? And why didn't he tell me?*

"It's okay, honey. It's fine. I'll take care of everything."

And I realize . . . *this* is the big secret.

With a frown that I can tell is as much fear as it is his being upset, he stands and introduces us. "Elise, this is Carsen and Sarah. Ladies, this is Elise."

I move forward to shake Sarah's hand first, figuring it's the safe move for right now. Things are in a very precarious balance, that crystal lattice I felt earlier starting to strain . . . if I don't want a disaster on my hands, I have to do things very carefully. "Keith's sister, right? Shane mentioned you backstage, told a funny story about some chili dogs on tour."

She smiles at me, but it's tentative, especially as I move closer to Carsen and offer the girl my hand too. "Hi, Carsen. Nice to meet you."

She looks at Keith, but at his nod of approval, she takes my hand and shakes. "Nice to meet you, too," she says in a quiet voice. "Are you . . . the writer?"

I've never felt like this before, like everyone in the room is terrified . . . of me.

The girl who came barreling in, loud and vibrant, is now almost shivering as she clutches at Keith's waist.

Keith looks at Sarah but talks to Carsen, the siblings communicating through some form of telepathy that only they share. "Honey, Aunt Sarah is going to take you out for a bit of lunch. Let me finish talking with Elise here. And when you get back, I can't wait to hear all about your night out. Okay?"

She nods, silently moving over to Sarah and they walk back out the door, but as she goes, Carsen looks back once more. "Sorry, Dad."

Sarah looks between Keith and me, and I can feel the threat in her eyes, warning me not to fuck with her family. Seems alphaness runs in the DNA around here.

The door closes, and Keith rubs at his head, growling softly, looking like he's about to start head-butting the nearest hard surface to make the pain go away. "Fuck. Fuck. Fuck."

He walks out of the kitchen to the living room, and I follow, perching on the edge of the couch as he paces back and forth in front of me. He pauses as he identifies the path he's tracing in the plush rug and locks a stern gaze on me.

"Let's get this clear up front. What you just saw, what you just heard . . . that is not for public consumption. You can't include anything about it, not even a hint, in your articles."

It's an order, hard and fierce, but underneath the harsh tone, I can hear the pleading. It cuts me to the core, and I shiver. For a man like Keith to be reduced to begging for his daughter . . . she must mean the whole world to him. I know that no matter what, I can never do anything to hurt her. "I completely understand that, but . . . what the hell is going on? How does no one know that you're a dad? You have a daughter, Keith."

He starts pacing again, his right hand waving as if he's trying to pluck the words he needs out of the air. "It's a long story and not many people know it. But all of them are loyal to me. And they know that I would burn the world to ashes before I let anything happen to her. Promise me you won't write about her."

I'm torn because this is the dirt I've been tasked to find. This is my ticket to a ground-breaking interview series that could launch my career. But I know I didn't come by it the way I should have, and whatever Keith's story is, he has every right to keep Carsen a secret if he wants to. It's not moral—hell, it's not even right to expose Carsen. She's just a little girl, and judging by the way he's reacting, he definitely wants to keep her existence unknown.

I also hear the threat about burning the world, and I have no doubt that he'd do it in a heartbeat, me included in the flames.

"I promise," I solemnly say, holding my hand over my heart. "I won't write about her if you don't want me to. But I don't understand why she's such a secret. Tell me, Keith. Please. All the things we've already shared? Articles be damned, tell me."

Keith stops, seeing I'm being very serious, and turns to face me, his hands clasped behind his back. Probably to keep them from shaking as I see his shoulders twitching. "She's the secret I always keep. I don't let the world know about her because I want Carsen to have as normal a childhood as she possibly can. She goes to a regular school . . . without bodyguards. She can go to the park or the mall with her aunt and nobody knows who she is. Carsen comes on tour with me and can walk around in the crowd without a second glance. I want that for her . . . the gift of being just a normal kid. If people find out she's my daughter, all of that would change. Paparazzi would chase her, take pictures of her, and fans could approach her. I won't let that happen. I won't let my daughter be turned into some fucked up tabloid fodder celebutante."

I flinch, knowing that's why the vibe in the kitchen was so chilly. They'd all assumed that as a tabloid reporter, I would throw them under the bus and cash in on the big scoop, drastically changing their whole world with one broad sweep of my pen, exposing Keith's deepest secret.

I'll admit there was a tiny piece of me that considered it, but it's that deep, ugly part inside us all that plays devil's advocate, tempting the part that dreams of bigger and better things.

The larger piece of my conscience knows I would never reveal something like this if Keith doesn't want me to. I've been silent too long, my thoughts ping-ponging as I study all the angles of the problem, and Keith comes to stand in front of me, looming over me but somehow feeling as though he's begging on his knees.

I look up at him, and I can see it in his eyes . . . the pain, the fear, the confusion. I reach out, putting my hand on his stomach. "Keith, I won't write about her. I won't say a word. I promise. Will you tell me everything though? I feel like we've shared so much, our bodies and our souls naked as we've talked about everything. But this is huge. I feel like you've been hiding this big piece of who you are, even as I was telling you everything with nothing held back. This is about trust."

He sighs, sitting down in a chair next to me with his elbows on his knees, head hanging low. "All of this is a hundred percent off-the-record. I'm not kidding, Elise."

I nod, putting my hand over my heart. "As God is my witness, I promise you Carsen's name will never see the light of day."

Keith nods and begins. At first, his voice is slightly tentative, filled with pauses, and I'm reminded of how I sometimes type. "When I was a kid, I had a girlfriend, Janie. She was my high-school sweetheart. We wanted different things. She wanted to settle in our small hometown, and by then, I was already dreaming of Nashville and being a musician. When I left after graduation for Boise, it was amicable enough, I thought. We didn't know it at the time, but she was pregnant."

"How'd she . . .?" I ask, feeling stupid as soon as it leaves my mouth.

Keith shrugs. "I was a teenager, in love, and stupid. Anyway, shortly after I left, she moved away to live with her grandmother, keeping the pregnancy a secret. That sort of town, you understand. Only her parents knew and they were disappointed, wanted her to go away to her grandmother's too. She gave birth to Carsen and then stayed with her grandmother for almost two years after having her. The two of them did a great job raising Carsen. She was a lucky baby, loved and well cared for."

"She didn't tell you?"

Keith shakes his head. "But when Janie's grandmother passed away unexpectedly, Janie couldn't do it alone and didn't want to go back to her parents. She showed up on the doorstep of my crappy, rundown hovel of a studio apartment with an almost two-year-old toddler on her hip. I hadn't seen her in years by then.

"She begged for forgiveness, and it wasn't like I could turn her away. She had my daughter with her. She moved in that day. It was awkward at first. We didn't really have feelings for each other anymore, but we'd made this amazing little person together."

I can't help but give Keith a sad smile. In one short statement, he told me so many things about himself and the sort of person he is. It doesn't even matter about the rest. But still, I need to listen, to know the details. "What happened?"

"I did," Keith says softly. "I would go back and forth from being mad at Janie for taking those two years of Carsen's life away from me to thankful she'd done this selfless thing to let me chase my dreams unencumbered, even if she thought it was because I wouldn't be able to support them, financially or emotionally. I mean, I'd left her . . . them, even if I didn't know it . . . for what? To play in smoky bars for drunks for all hours of the night? But she gave me this incredible gift. Carsen stole my heart the moment I laid eyes on her.

"We'd been living together for about six months when Janie didn't come home after work one day. I was scared something had happened to her, but I had a gig at a new club, the biggest one I'd ever played. I had to leave Carsen with a neighbor, and I called Janie over and over between sets."

"No answer," I say, reading where this is going.

Keith shakes his head again, his voice hitching as I see tears well up in the corners of his eyes. "The next morning, her parents called me. Janie had been walking home, crossing the street, and a drunk driver hit her before running into a pole.

Janie didn't make it. She died instantly. The driver died too. The police had called Janie's next of kin, her parents. Not me, because I wasn't her husband. I was just the father of her child whom she lived with."

I can see the hurt in his eyes, and my heart aches to soothe Keith's pain. So much pain, more than any one man should have by himself. "Keith, I'm sorry."

He nods, plunging ahead because he has to unburden himself of this weight. "It messed me up bad for a while. Luckily, Janie's parents were fine with Carsen staying with me. They could've fought me for custody, especially since I was barely scraping by back then. But they agreed that Carsen needed to be with her father. I think they felt guilty over what happened with Janie before she left home, and having that reminder wasn't something they could handle. That's when Sarah came to Boise to help me. She stayed with me in that shack of a room, taking care of Carsen. Hell, taking care of *me*. And that's when I got another call.

"That night, the same night Janie had been hit . . . there'd been an A&R at the new club and he'd liked my sets. He told me to get my ass to Nashville, that I was good, had potential but had some growing to do."

A&R . . . industry term for a talent scout. "What did you do?"

Keith laughs bitterly. "I was in bad shape, but Sarah knocked some sense into me, literally and figuratively. So we moved to Nashville, the three of us. I played there for a while, learning as much as I could, and one night, that same guy came in. That's when I got a contract and the machine of my 'career' started really turning. At first, it wasn't really a conscious decision to keep quiet about her. But when things started happening fast, I realized how quickly my life was changing and was scared what that would do to her. I wanted her to have as normal a life as possible."

"How many people know about Carsen?" I ask curiously. "The record company has to know."

"Their lawyer does. It's part of the whole copyright estate thing," Keith says, "but not too many people, actually. Only those I truly trust."

He doesn't have to say it, but I'm obviously not one of those people, but now I know too. He's quiet, the weight of everything he just said heavy in the room as I digest it all.

"So? What do you think?" he asks. "Devoted father? Misguided fuckup?"

I stand, moving in front of him, and kneel down between his legs to bring myself to the same level and look him directly in the eyes. "I think you sound like a wonderful father who loves his daughter very much."

"Thank you." I can feel his relief at my positive judgment. "I haven't told anyone this in a very long time. Elise, can I trust you with this?"

There's no doubt in my mind or my heart as I nod, taking his hands. "I know that even though I'm saying yes, you'll have doubts. That it'll take time for you to trust me. But Keith . . . yes. I will never tell, and if I can, I'd like to get to know you more, and Carsen too, if you're okay with that?"

He scans my face, looking for any trace of lie, but I'm telling the truth. I may not quite understand Keith's vehemence at keeping Carsen a secret, but if that's what he wants, I can support him and not be the weapon of destruction that obliterates the normal life he's built for his daughter over the last decade.

He leans forward, kissing me softly but holding my chin firmly in his palm. After a moment, he pulls back. "Thank you."

I press my lips to his once more, relief and joy filling my heart. "Thank you for telling me. I know you're scared."

A thought occurs to me, and I smile as I lean back. "Is this why? I mean, why you don't date?"

He dips his head once, smirking a little. "Carsen has already had it so tough. Too many deaths, and then she's forced to keep this big secret so that her life can stay the way it is. That's heavy for a kid. She's happy the way things are, so I want to keep it that way. I promised to keep my focus on her and my music, make things as simple and easy for her as I can."

I sit back on my heels, putting my hands on top of my thighs and tilting my head questioningly. "But what about you? Don't you deserve to be happy too? It's good for kids to see their parents loved and in love. That's how they learn what a relationship can be. Did it ever occur to you that by locking yourselves away, you're taking away both of your opportunities to have that? You're teaching her that to be a good parent, you have to be a martyr."

"No, I never thought about that until recently," he admits, looking a bit shell-shocked by what I've said. "Giving Carsen a normal life has just always been the priority. But it seems you and Sarah share the same point of view. She said something very similar to me. Let's say it pushed me over the edge toward us . . . you know." He lets out a huff. "This is all just a bit overwhelming."

"Points for your sister. I owe her a box of chocolates or something," I reply. "You're not the only one feeling overwhelmed. Because I just found out that the guy I'm head over heels for is not only majorly out of my league, but he's a fucking awesome dad who takes great care of his daughter."

He smirks at me, leaning forward, and his aura of confident command slips back into place like a familiar glove. "Head over heels?"

I bite my lip, again blushing furiously. "Uhm, can we pretend like you didn't hear that? I feel like we've maybe done enough expose for the moment. Oh, speaking of expose . . ."

He looks at me, his eyes narrowing, but I at least seem to have distracted him from my slip of the tongue. "Two things. One, on the article front . . . we really are going to have to come up with something more exciting than fishing as a hobby. I don't know, maybe like you're into bows and arrows or something?"

"I've shot a bow three times in my life," Keith says but shrugs.

I grin, figuring we can come up with something. "And two, can you maybe tell Carsen I'm not the boogieman? She looked terrified of me."

He laughs a bit, and it sounds foreign after the deep conversation we've just had. He pulls me into his lap, my legs hanging off the side of the chair as he wraps his arms around me, his hands resting lightly on top of my ass.

"What's wrong with fishing? I like to fish. And yeah, I can talk to Carsen about you. She knows to avoid questions, so I think she felt bad that she accidentally spilled the beans."

I smile, feeling something pressed against my panties that certainly tells me Keith's accepting this more and more. "Well, she probably wasn't expecting to find me in your kitchen in the middle of the morning."

Keith growls, nuzzling into my neck. "I think I like you in my kitchen. And in the living room. And in my bedroom. Shit, definitely in my bedroom."

He nibbles at me, tickling my neck, and I squeal, squirming as I playfully fight back even though I love it. He pauses, looking at me intensely. "Are we okay, Elise? Really?"

I scratch my fingers through the morning scruff on his face and over the slight prickle of hairs on top of his head as I meet his eyes. "Yes, Keith. We're okay. Except that Sarah and Carsen are going to be back soon and I'm still wearing just your t-shirt and nothing else. Awkward. Especially since you're making my panties wet again."

Keith hums, squeezing my ass tightly. "Can't have that, now can we?"

With a single exhilarating swoop, he stands, holding me with one arm under my knees and one behind my back. "Seems like a quick shower is in order. Maybe I can help with your back?"

I purr, scratching the back of his neck lightly. "You can help everywhere."

# CHAPTER 14

## KEITH

Even though Elise is dressed again, in the same leggings and pale blue sweater she wore here yesterday, it's still awkward when Sarah and Carsen pull up out front as I'm kissing Elise good-bye.

Apparently, the shower wasn't fast enough even though we really did just wash up. Our bodies spent from the night and morning and our minds racing with all the revelations, we just soaped up and rinsed off. Although I did take my time helping Elise dry off. Thoroughly.

With one more soft kiss, she bounds down the front steps toward her car, waving shyly at Sarah and Carsen, but the truth is in her eyes, which are shining bright. Her words come back to me . . . *head over heels*.

There's still a lurch in my gut, a moment of worry rearing its dark head. What if she's bounding off to go tell her boss she just got the best story ever and that's why she's so damn happy? I shake my head, letting the thought go. I need to trust her. She said she would keep this secret, and everything about her said she was telling the truth. The look in her eyes . . . if

I'm to ever become the man I want to be, the father I want to be, I need to trust those eyes.

Sarah gives me an appraising look as they come inside, her face neutral even as she looks at me hopefully. "Well, how'd it go?"

For some reason, I decide to be playful. "Well . . . I hear that they've got good land for sale in Costa Rica, and we can live there for the rest of our lives quite well."

Sarah sticks out her tongue and punches me in the shoulder. "Come on, I'm being serious!"

I grin, putting an arm around her shoulders. "Better than expected, for damn sure. She says she'll stay quiet about the whole thing. I want to believe her, but I might've also been a bit threatening."

Sarah grins, elbowing me in the side. "Threatened her? I'm thinking that didn't go over too well."

*Actually, she climbed into my lap and told me her panties were wet . . .* "Well, okay . . .maybe I didn't exactly threaten *her*. Just told her that I'd burn the world to ash to protect Carsen if need be."

Sarah pats my chest, smiling. "That's not a threat. That's a promise, because I'd be there with the matches to help you light the flamethrower."

We walk in the kitchen, where Carsen is already sitting, a pen and piece of paper in front of her on the table. She's all business. "Again, I'm so sorry. I didn't expect that you'd have, uhm, company when I came in."

She's blushing, but she continues, looking more like the world's smallest lawyer or politician than a little girl. "What's the fallout? Whatever needs to happen, I understand. But please, please do not make me change schools."

She's poised like she's going to take notes on some new security protocol, and it makes me grin, but it also makes my heart ache. Most of the time, I still see her as the little thing that used to curl up in my lap and fall asleep to cartoons.

But she's growing up, too. And she needs to know that life is more than sneaking around to avoid the media. In that, maybe I do need to change, while still figuring out how to protect her. And I thought learning how to play guitar and sing at the same time was hard. "Carson, baby. It's okay," I tell her, cupping her face. "This is your home and you did what you have every right to do. I'm sorry that I've put you and Sarah in a tough spot, but I talked with Elise. She's agreed to not write or say anything about you."

Carsen's frown softens, and she looks like she might actually smile. "Really? That means I can stay at my school, right?"

I nod, taking her hand and giving it a squeeze. "Yes, we'll ride it out for now. I trust Elise and I think we should have faith that it's all gonna be fine." Maybe that's not entirely true yet, but I'm hopeful and I think parents are allowed to paint an optimistic picture for their kids. At least I hope so, because I'm trying hard to be positive here and not freak out now that Elise is gone, maybe putting my family on the news.

Carson nods, grinning. "Okay, if you say so. Is Elise like . . . your girlfriend now or something? Do you love her?"

Wow, what a lot of stuff to dump on my head at once. The little girl who's had my heart her entire life, asking all this stuff about Elise . . . how the fuck do I answer this?

I need to reassure her that nothing has changed, that she's still my priority, but the things Elise said about being a good example, not a martyr, come back to me. Besides, I do need to be honest . . . I know I feel something for Elise, I just don't know what yet.

"Baby, it's still soon to say I love her, but I like her a lot. And that's new for me, maybe enough for now. I don't think I could fall in love with a woman unless you got along with her too. You're the most important thing to me, Carsen."

She smiles, giving me that look that I'm sure all parents get when their children think we're talking like a silly, senile idiot. "I know that. But if you like her a lot, and you want me to get along with her too, don't you think I should meet her? I mean, more than just a freak-out in the kitchen where I froze like a dork? I want to meet her."

I look up to Sarah for her opinion but she shrugs her shoulders. I think back to what Sarah told me before about living a little, having a bit of fun, and what Elise told me about showing Carsen what a relationship should look like, and my decision is easy.

"Okay, baby. Elise said she wanted to meet you too, and to let you know something."

"What's that?"

I lean in, whispering in her ear. "She says she's not the boogieman. So . . . is dinner good?"

Carsen looks like she's thinking for a minute, and I kick myself a little. For fuck's sake, the kid just caught Elise half-naked in our kitchen two hours ago. Even if she's asking to meet her, I need to slow my roll here and not move too fast. But my daughter surprises me every time. "Yeah, but we're gonna need the supplies to make s'mores out back if she's coming for dinner. Oh, and Aunt Sarah? You need to make those chipotle chicken wraps you kick butt with."

I laugh. She's not reconsidering. She's making the damn menu. I smile at her, ruffling her hair. "All right, kiddo. We'll get the supplies. But also, let me call Elise, see if she's available for dinner tonight, okay?"

Carsen rolls her eyes. "She's your *girlfriend*, Dad. Of course she's available."

Sarah snickers, and I can read her face clearly. *If only things were that easy.*

---

When the doorbell rings as dinner approaches, I'm nervous. I've never done this, introduced someone I'm interested in to my daughter. Hell, I never thought I would do this, at least not while she's still a kid.

But fate intervened, I guess, and here I am. I'm excited for Carsen to get to know Elise though. I think they'll like each other.

At least I hope they do or I'm fucked. Elise looks stunning. Her hair is pulled up, but curls cascade down her back and her cheeks are flushed. She's wearing a pink tank top that shows a hint of her cleavage, but she's thrown on a sheer jacket with a floral design all over it that dips long in the back over her jean-covered ass and a pair of white Chuck Taylors.

It's more 'city chic' than what I've seen her in before . . . but it's cute and I like it. She looks sweet and sexy, all rolled up into one tempting package. "Come in," I greet her, taking her in my arms. "You look beautiful."

I kiss her lips lightly, aware that we probably have an audience spying from the kitchen. So I keep the kiss quick, and Elise hums. She probably understands. "Thank you. And thanks for actually greeting me instead of stomping off like Conan the Barbarian."

I chuckle. I have been a bit of a grumpy ass. I look down at her, lowering my voice just in case. "You ready for this?"

She smiles, her lips wavering a bit, but she nods. "Yes. I'm ready."

I take her hand, holding it between us for a split second before turning and leading her into the kitchen, where Carsen and

Sarah both scuttle back from the edge of the doorway. Busted, you little spies.

Sarah recovers first, offering a hand again but with a decidedly warmer tone than earlier. "Nice to meet you, Elise. I'm Sarah, this big oaf's sister."

I can feel the tension in Elise's hand lighten at the casual comment, and I make a mental note to thank Sarah later for making this easier. She's always known how to help make things easier for me.

Elise shakes, then offers her hand to Carsen. "Hi, Carsen. Your dad said it was your idea to invite me over for dinner, so thank you for the invitation. And I heard something about s'mores?" she asks, looking around the kitchen. "Mmm, I love s'mores."

It's perfect. She's not treating Carsen like a little kid but is being genuine and treating her like the young lady she is, as much as I forget that sometimes. We head outside to the backyard. It's one of my favorite family places around the house, a large flagstone patio with a fire pit and loungers that opens up to a green yard, blue pool, and a hot tub. "Whatcha think?"

"Can I live in your hot tub?" Elise jokes. "That thing's bigger than my bathroom."

"No peeing in the pool!" Carsen declares somberly before grinning. "But sure!"

I assume my place at the grill to get the chicken going, Sarah having already made her chipotle rub. "Hope you like things hot and spicy."

Elise smirks and glances over at Sarah. "Does he know what he's doing?"

Sarah laughs, nodding. "With the grill? Yes, he's a total pro. With teasing you? Well, I'm just going to pretend he's innocent."

They laugh, and I'm glad to see they are starting to bridge the gap between them. Carsen brings me the chicken, and I pat her on the back before letting her get to know Elise.

"Elise?"

"Yeah, Carsen?"

"So you love my dad?"

I'm surprised and glad I haven't had a drink yet or else I'd choke. I know I should jump in to save Elise, but I'm kinda curious what she'll say. Instead, I just lay out another chicken breast and adjust the fire to the right level.

Obviously, she doesn't love me, despite her earlier slip of tongue. It's too soon for that, but we've definitely got something here, I think. Whatever the original reason we met, whatever the excuses we've used to start talking, we've left the idea of it being just an 'interview expose' long behind. So I'm interested to see what she'll say.

I can feel Elise's eyes on my back, but I'm not letting on for a second that I'm eavesdropping and instead pretend to mess around with one of the chicken breasts. Still, I'm holding my breath for her answer.

"We haven't known each other that long, but I definitely like him," Elise says with frank and open honesty that warms my stomach. "I want to get to know him better. You too, if that's okay?"

I hear Carsen hum, and the smile in her voice is evident when she replies. "I'd like that too. I asked him the same question."

"Oh, and what did he say?"

Carsen laughs. "I can't tell," she replies sassily. "I can keep a secret."

Elise laughs back, obviously 'served.' "You got me. I can keep a secret too, though. I promise, Carsen."

The last bit is solemn, truth in her every word. I hear it, and Carsen must too. She lowers her voice some, but she's like me, she's got a terrible whisper than tends to carry. "He said he likes you too . . . a lot."

I can't help it. I have to know Elise's reaction, so I look over my shoulder, ignoring the grill temporarily. My tongs clatter, and Elise hears me, so I see her looking at me like I just caught the moon, a wide smile on her face and her eyes glittering.

"Is that so?" she says. "Well . . . let's see how he cooks before I say anything else. I'm a liberated woman. I want a man who can at least cook for me once in awhile."

Conversation continues, with me mostly butting out to let the ladies get to know each other. Maybe, just maybe, I put a little extra attention into the chicken so that by the time we sit down at the big table, dinner looks scrumptious.

"Well, what's the verdict?" I ask after two minutes of silence.

Elise looks up, wiping the corner of her mouth. "I'd say . . . I like it a lot."

Carsen giggles and forks some sliced and grilled corn. "Just wait until Dad makes s'mores. He does them just right, browned and not flamethrowers."

"What if I like flamethrowers?"

"Everyone likes a good flamethrower," Sarah jokes, inserting herself. "Useful for . . . difficult ex-boyfriends."

"Oh, I'd love to hear that story sometime," Elise says with a wink. "Just in case."

I swallow, getting up. "I think I'll go get the marshmallows and stuff."

The only regret I have as the four of us toast and prepare our s'mores is that I'm not using a real wood fire. Maybe another time, I could take Elise out camping, do it right.

Nobody complains about the lack of smoky hints though, and I notice after she's finished that Elise has just a little smear of chocolate and marshmallow on the corner of her mouth.

"Hold still," I growl, leaning in close. Elise smiles as I kiss her, licking the sticky mess before tasting her even more delicious mouth.

Carsen groans, pretending not to gag. "Ugh, LD moment."

Elise laughs, pulling back a little. "Uh, what's a LD moment?"

"Lovey-dovey," Carsen explains in that *adults are so ignorant* voice. "It means get a room. Some of us are innocent. Like Aunt Sarah."

We all burst out, but I have to know something. "Carsen, do you know what 'get a room' means?"

She smirks, nodding. "Yep, it means you're grossing everyone out with your kissy faces, so go kiss somewhere else. I have watched Netflix, you know."

"Yep, that's exactly what it means, little daughter of mine. And yes, your aunt is totally innocent."

Sarah, Elise, and I stifle giggles at her innocence, and I'm reminded again just how sweet this age is, on the cusp of teenage drama but still young and naïve. With her Netflix comment, though, I make a mental note to double-check the parental control settings. A dad can't be too safe with his little girl.

I know it's impossible, but I want to preserve this time for Carsen as long as I can. It's sweeter and better that way.

After the mess of s'mores, we clean up and Carsen heads upstairs for a shower.

"What do you think?" I ask Sarah as we clean up the dishes, Elise outside wiping down the table.

"I think . . . good job, baby brother," Sarah says. "I like her so far."

I tell Sarah goodnight and watch with joy as she gives Elise a hug. "He's a good one," she says when they part. "Stubborn as a damn mule, but good. Don't break his heart."

Elise shakes her head, not letting go of Sarah yet. "I won't. I know he's a good man."

Sarah heads home, and as soon as the front door closes, I grab Elise to my chest, hugging her tight.

"Think it went okay? Did they like me?" she asks as I run my hands down her back.

I kiss the top of her head, nodding. "It went better than okay. They loved you. I think Carsen is gonna hold you to that promise to teach her to knit though."

I can feel her smile as she lays her head on my chest, humming happily. "I hope so. I meant it. I haven't done a single stitch with anyone since my grandmother died. It'd be nice to share it with someone else, even if only for a minute. I think Grandma would like that."

We're quiet for a minute, just swaying in the foyer as we hold each other tight. I feel a little torn. I want to invite her to stay . . . but at the same time, it's so fast. Maybe taking a few hours' break might do some good, let this all settle in. For Elise, for me, and mostly for Carsen. I definitely don't think she's ready for her dad to have sleepovers.

"Thank you, Elise," I say, my voice gravel as I resist letting her go. "This was better than I ever would've dared dream. And right now, even though I know you should go home and have a good night's sleep in your own bed, the only thing I can think of is taking you upstairs and burying myself inside you, telling you thank you over and over again."

Elise pulls back, looking up at me and placing her hands

behind my neck. "Thank you. You let me into your story, your family, your world tonight. And I know that's not something you do lightly. And as much as I'd love for you take me upstairs right now, we shouldn't. It was a big night for Carsen too. Be with her tonight. Make sure she's okay with all of this."

One statement, and it sums up how she's breaking down my every wall, every defense. Whatever fucked up gossipy rag story brought us together, Elise is good at her core. She cares about people, about my daughter and how she's doing after a good but pretty risky night.

"Good idea . . . but still," I growl, backing her up against the door, taking her mouth in a passionate kiss. I gather her hands in mine, pressing them to the door above her head, forcing her to arch. I hold her there with one hand, the other moving down to cup her throat, lifting her chin up to meet me, kiss for kiss, breath for breath.

I'm not even sure whose air I'm breathing anymore. It's ours, mixed between the two of us in panting gasps as we fight for more from each other.

I press against her, grinding my cock against her softness, and she gasps. I take advantage and dip my tongue in to taste her. It's hot, heavy, and heady and I want more.

But we can't, not tonight.

Not with Carsen here, especially when I need to check in with her and make sure she's okay with all of this. With a groan of unsatisfied frustration, I pull back and press my forehead to Elise's.

"When can I see you again?" I groan, my control wavering. "Because it's stupid, but I need you soon. I can't imagine going to sleep without us coming together."

Elise's eyes are still locked on my mouth as she licks her lips, and I know exactly what she's thinking. With a blink and shake of her head, her eyes clear. "Huh? Oh, I should go into the office tomorrow. Write the next article, and I need time to work in your 'dirt' without exposing your real side. How about the day after?"

I think for a second, knowing it's probably for the best. "That works. What about if we go out to my little piece of land, ride ATVs or hike? We could get you a bit of 'behind-the-scenes with Keith Perkins, Country Star' out there for the next article. And then, there's a little cabin. It's rough, but we could stay overnight."

Elise smiles like she just won the lottery. "That sounds like the best plan I've heard in ages. Except . . . by rough, you do have plumbing, right? And heat?"

I laugh, letting go of her hands. "So high-maintenance. Yes, there's plumbing and electric. Heat is handled by a wood stove, but it's a small cabin so it's enough. Besides, if you get cold, I can probably come up with some ways to warm you up."

# CHAPTER 15

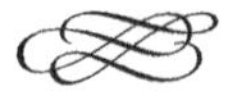

## ELISE

*And so, in an ironic twist, the story that brought us into contact with Keith Perkins was easily explained.*

I pause, pondering before highlighting the whole paragraph and deleting it. "Nope, just won't do."

"What won't do?" Maggie asks, making me jerk my head up. "Let me guess, Keith's got a girlfriend?"

Ouch, close to the bone. "No, it's not that," I reply, lying my ass off while trying to distract my friend. "I just . . . I have a lot of information, and it's been harder trying to figure out what's supposed to go in this one and what goes in the next one."

Maggie nods, taking a seat on the edge of my desk, a familiar spot for her. "So what's his big secret then?"

I smirk, knowing I'm lying, but it's the lie that Keith said was okay when I texted him. "He was out running errands, and if you can believe it, his maid was having a bit of a situation and he was just doing her a favor."

"Uh, by buying half the aisle?" Maggie asks, lifting an eyebrow. "Nice boss. I think if I had that problem, Donnie's response would be to ball up a copy of *The Times* and chuck it at me." She doesn't sound remotely convinced.

I shrug, wanting to change the subject as quickly as possible because the more I think about it, the more ridiculous it sounds. "Keith's just boring, really. His only unusual hobby is archery. Next time, I'm going to get some shots of him practicing. But other than that, he's just a normal guy. So . . . what's with your face?"

"My face?" Maggie asks, rubbing at her cheeks. "What's with my face?"

I look closer, squinting as I confirm my suspicions. "You're . . . glittering. What the hell have you been up to?"

"Oh, well . . ." Maggie says, blushing. "That undercover at the senator's office didn't pan out, so Donnie has me following another angle. There's this club out by the airport, Petals of Heaven—"

"Oh my god, Donnie has you, of all people, at a strip club?" I ask, gleefully shocked. "I mean, not that you don't look the part but . . . well . . ."

"Don't worry, I'm not stripping," Maggie reassures me. "I'm a cocktail waitress, so the glitter's more for showing up under the blacklights."

"What does Donnie have you out there doing then?" I ask, worried. I've heard of Petals. It's one of those places where you don't ask questions most of the time. You don't want to piss off the owners.

"They get a lot of celebrity patrons, apparently," Maggie says, waving her hand. "One of Hollywood's big *family* men, in particular, has been in three nights in a row now, having himself a particularly good time in the private rooms in the back. I don't have pics yet, but I think I'll be able to. Someone's going to have some explaining to do!"

"Wait, what is this?" I ask, surprised. "You're liking this assignment, aren't you? Our innocent little librarian has a naughty streak to her? What happened to the Maggie who was scandalized when someone told her that her ass looked good in a dress?"

Maggie blushes and shrugs. "She's still there. I guess I get caught up in the fun of the bust, that's all. Speaking of busts, tell me how the interviews with Keith are going. I need boring and nice right now, honestly."

I lean back in my office chair, humming. "He is nice, actually. Still sometimes a bit of a commanding asshole, but . . . well, it's the good kind of commanding asshole. I'm feeling good about the interviews."

"Feeling good, huh?" Maggie asks, lifting an eyebrow. "Sounds like you're feeling good about *him*. You starting to like him?"

"No!" I protest, maybe a bit too strongly. There's no way I'm going to let anyone, even sweet little Maggie, think that I'm getting this story Francesca-style. I can't even let them think that I'm interested in Keith. "I just . . . it's nice to be pleasantly surprised, that's all. He's hot but boring."

"I see. Well, I think—" Maggie starts, but before she can finish, I hear a yell from down the hall.

"ELISE!"

"Oh, great, what's he want?" I mutter, looking at Maggie. "Any ideas?"

"Maybe Donnie wants to say great job and give you a raise?" Maggie asks, then grins. "It'd be a first, but hey, miracles *do* happen."

"We'll see," I answer as I get up. "See you later."

I head down the hall to Donnie's office, where I find him behind his desk, popping jellybeans into his mouth. "What can I do for you, Donnie?"

"Have a seat," he says, pointing as if I don't know where the chair is. "I wanted to talk about your third article."

"What?" I ask, surprised. "Donnie, I barely got the outline done and sent in to you."

It's company policy that all articles other than editorials need to be outlined and sent in to Donnie after the website got burned to the tune of a half-million dollars for not verifying a claim. It could have been worse.

"I know, I checked it over," Donnie says, popping another jellybean, this one black licorice by the looks of it. "And while I normally let you just run with your gut, you always back up your shit. I'm worried this time."

A compliment and a concern in one sentence. That's a first. "What're you worried about? There's nothing that'll get us a lawsuit in there."

"That's exactly it!" Donnie exclaims. "Elise, we won't get sued, but we won't get read either! This article . . . it's boring as fuck. My God, a story about the Pope's diet would have more sizzle than this! This is just . . . listen, if I wanted to read this type of fawning bullshit, I'd buy *People!*"

"What can I say, Donnie?" I ask, ignoring his dig. "This series is different. It's good, I think. More in-depth and driving readers with a real insight into Keith. His music, his life, let them really get to know the man. I've included some interview snippets from some calls I made to his manager and some of the club owners from Boise and Nashville that he used to play in, to give the readers a sense of how much he's grown."

"Growth . . . now you sound like *Reader's Digest,*" Donnie gripes. "Come on, Elise! We run on dirt, smut, and knowing who's fucking who! Not how Keith Perkins learned to play guitar at the age of six and what might be next for him with this summer's tour!"

I'm trying to keep my cool. I'm walking into deep waters now with Donnie, and while I'm not technically lying yet . . . I'm not being honest and frank either. "I've gone through everything in his background, online searches, criminal record, everything available. And when I talk to Keith, he seems to be real. He was pissed about the record company springing the all-access interviews on him initially, but he's been forthcoming. I'm telling you, Donnie, there's just nothing salacious. The man's just an All-American sort of dude."

I hope it's enough, that he believes me and doesn't pry any further. Donnie may have questionable morals when it comes to Francesca, but he's a crack reporter and can smell a story long before anyone else does.

"Dammit, Elise. There's something!" he yells, slamming his hand down on his desk and sending jellybeans rolling everywhere. "Nobody is this fucking whitebread. Nobody can become as famous as he is without having at least a fucking parking ticket in his background. There has to be *something*. I don't want this to be a big waste of fucking time. Find me something, or I'll get someone who can."

"What?" I gasp, my face paling. "Donnie, this is my story—"

"I know it is! So do your damn job!" he yells, his face getting redder as his voice carries. I know the people out in the office can hear him reaming me out. "Even Pollyanna Maggie out there has more dirt in her life than you've written about Keith. Now, I'll let you write part three the way you want, but end it with a teaser about some *legit* dirt for part four." His voice drops dangerously. "And you'd *better* get it, one way or another. Am I clear?"

"Clear. I'll find something." I say as I nod, but my gut churns.

"Then get the fuck out of here and finish up part three. What are you going to do for the next interview?"

"I convinced him to get out of his house. I'm hoping that the change of scenery will get him to open up more. If I thought there was anything worth reporting on in the house, I'd have stayed, but he's shown me every room . . . the only person who'd find it interesting might be the Style section."

Slightly placated, Donnie starts scooping up his jellybeans and putting them back in his bowl. "Where are you doing the interview?"

"His land outside town," I reply honestly. "Get to know his country boy roots. I'm hoping it'll let me in past his image, getting back to who he used to be. You know what I mean?"

Donnie nods, his eyes pinching slyly. "Okay. Get a thread with the unvarnished Keith, and then tease that out. Even if it's just innuendo, I want something, Elise. Now get the hell out of here. You owe me part three by the end of the day."

"On it," I reply, getting up. Going back to my desk, my head aches and my heart twists.

Dirt . . . well, I know dirt. I know some life-changing, bomb in the middle of the room sort of dirt. But I promised two people that I wouldn't disclose it. And I won't.

But what sort of dirt on Keith can I come up with that'll be okay and still keep Donnie off my ass?

I've got a lot of work to do.

# CHAPTER 16

## KEITH

The weather is perfect, late enough in the spring that my t-shirt and jeans are all I need for the days while the nights are going to be cool enough that Elise and I are going to have no problems snuggling up next to the fireplace in my cabin.

"It's been too long since I've been up here," I admit as we pull off the deserted dirt road onto the grassy shoulder at the trail-head, shifting my truck into park. "Guess I got too caught up with stuff this past winter. By the way, are you sure about those clothes?"

"What about them?" Elise asks, turning and sticking out her chest. "Don't think I'm covered enough?"

I take a look at her tight blue tank top, the valley between her breasts deep and proudly displayed before clinging to her stomach and hips. Her legs are just as displayed, as Elise showed up wearing a pair of tights that show every curve of her body.

"You look amazing," I tell her honestly, "but I'm just worried. It's a five-mile hike to my cabin. Are you sure those tights are what you want to wear in the woods?"

Elise grins, shifting her knees and giving my eyes a little treat that sends a warning twinge down to my cock. "I'll have you know, Mr. Country Music Star, that these are top of the line trail runner's tights, and the person who sold them to me at the store told me they're better for me than those old ass Levis you're wearing. They support and compress my leg muscles, giving me just what I need."

"And I thought I had what you needed," I joke, making her blush. "Just one thing."

"What's that?"

"Stay behind me on the trail because if I have to spend five miles looking at your ass in those tights for the whole walk . . . well, we won't last five miles before we scare the local wildlife."

Elise grins, biting her lip. "Maybe I'll want to take a break from walking . . . we'll see. Come on, let's get the packs."

I could have come up here yesterday and brought the ATVs down, or there is an old fire trail that I could take if Elise and I wanted to bounce and jolt our way for ten miles going around the backside of the mountain, but hiking up for a weekend just felt more real.

I help her with her pack before grabbing mine. "Come on, and if your pack gets too heavy, tell me."

"I'll have you know, I was a Girl Scout. I did go camping . . . once or twice," Elise says, grinning. We start off, and as we take the trail, a comfortable silence drops around us. It's not totally quiet, of course. There's plenty of natural forest sounds, but there are no cars, no traffic. Just us.

"Wow, it feels like another world," Elise says quietly as we hike. "It's . . . it's kinda like you."

"How's that?" I ask, thinking how she nailed it in one single sentence. She's got a gift for it, that's for sure.

"Well, on the surface, it's a little intimidating, beautiful but imposing at the same time," Elise replies, her eyes still in the trees as we walk. "Then you get this sense of nothing going on, like it's just boring and calm . . . but if you really look, there's a lot going on. You just have to be quiet and let it unveil itself to you. You're a lot like this place, I guess."

I smile, reaching over and taking her hand. "And they say *I'm* the songwriter. Come on, if you think this is nice, wait'll you get a view of the cabin."

It takes us about ninety minutes to make the hike, taking our time because there's really no need to rush. Elise does tease me a little as we go up one hill, pushing past me to give me a very inspiring view of her ass flexing as she makes her way up the trail. I probably could've made the climb quicker on my own, but I'll admit to being more than happy with my slow, distracted pace since it gives me more time to admire Elise's assets as we reach the crest and start down the other side.

"Just up this side trail," I tell Elise as I unlock my gate and hold it open for her. "Don't worry about the signs. They're mostly to scare off hunters."

"Do you get hunters out here?" Elise asks as she eyes the *Private Property, Trespassers Will Be Prosecuted* signs. "Or at least, have you had to prosecute anyone?"

"Once I found the water tank a little low. Someone had obviously refilled their water bags, but I've never had a break in," I tell her, taking her hand. "Don't worry, we're perfectly safe." I lock the gate behind us as we resume the final stretch of our hike.

"Is that what you call it when we're alone together? Doesn't feel safe to me," Elise jokes. "To be honest, it feels . . . thrillingly dangerous, like the world's sexiest rollercoaster."

Conversation trickles off as we climb the last hill, the hardest one, actually, and we have to lean into the slope. It's not that bad, but I am carrying three days' worth of food and supplies for a weekend on my back.

I'm curious what she'll think of the cabin. It's definitely different from my house in the city, but as we crest the hill, I feel relieved. Her eyes widen and her hands pop up to cover her exclaimed, "Oh, my gosh!"

"You like it?"

She looks at me, a smile stretching over her beautiful flushed and glistening face. "It's perfect! It looks like something out of a painting."

I like that she can appreciate a rustic log cabin, even one as small as this. It's one of the things that sold me on the property too. I don't need glitz and glam. I bought this place as a getaway because of the privacy and rustic charm.

"Well, come on then," I reply with a grin. "Let's get down there, get the fire going so we can have some hot water for later, and get things going!"

We go inside and drop our gear, and Elise seems enamored with the small space. The main room is a square with a bed to the left, a couch area to the right around the woodstove, and a working kitchen along the back wall. The bathroom is through a door off the kitchen. Bare-boned and simple, like I am at my core. The only concession to simplicity is the large hammock on the all-weather back porch, where Carsen and I have watched sunsets on numerous occasions.

"This is perfect," Elise purrs, setting her bag down on the kitchen table-slash-food prep space. "And it's ours all weekend?"

"Until we either have to go back or run out of food," I joke, watching her. I like seeing her here. It feels right somehow. Watching her stretch out and wiggle on the couch, my cock thickens in my jeans and I know what I need.

"Come here," I half-growl, feeling in touch with my inner wild nature. Elise's lips are twisted in a little smirk that says she already knows what I want, and her hips are doing a tantalizingly sexy sashay as she comes closer.

"What for?" she asks, laughing happily when she's in arm's reach and I grab her, kissing her deeply. Our bodies twist and tangle as I lift her up, walking her back to the couch and forcing her to clutch me tightly as I bend her backward.

There's no worry, though. I've got her securely in my arms, and as she moans when she feels my cock press up against her thigh, I set her back upright, my heart hammering in my chest. "We need to get out of here," I growl, "because I really want to show you some things . . . and if I don't get you outside in the next ten seconds, I'm going to rip those tights off and devour your body until you can't walk anymore."

"Sounds good. I do want to see what you have to show me," she purrs, running a hand over my chest. "I have some things I want to show you too."

I groan, pressing into her touch for a moment before getting under control. "No, really. I have every plan to fuck you until we collapse of exhaustion tonight, but I want to show you the land out here first. And if we don't leave right now, there won't be hot water, and I'd like to help you wash up after I get done burying myself inside that tight little pussy of yours."

She shudders in my arms, nodding. "God, I love how you talk to me. And I like that plan, but maybe I don't need hot water when I've got you."

She's pouting, but it's playful and I can see she's teasing me. She's been just as excited as I am about exploring the area. I pull her close one last time, grinding against her belly, and give her ass a good smack.

"Out, woman. Let's go."

She pulls away to walk toward the door, and I smack the other cheek for good measure. She looks back over her shoulder, sass and brattiness in her eyes, and I shrug. "I'm all about equal treatment, so the right had to get what the left got."

"I'll remember that later," she says. "Your ass is mine, country boy."

Outside, it's still picture-perfect beautiful, and after showing Elise how to fire up the small generator I have and starting the water pumps, I lead her to the parking shed for my ATV. "Hop on."

"And if I want to do the driving?"

I grin, mounting the ATV and firing it up. "After you know the local trails, I'll be happy to let you. Safety first, though."

Elise gets on behind me, pressing her breasts to my back and wrapping her arms around my waist, her hands dangerously close to my crotch. We ride, and I goof a bit, having fun and stopping to show her bits about the trail and property. Reaching the top of a ridge, I come to a stop at the beginning of a small trail. "Here's a nice spot. Can't take the ATV up though."

Elise gives me an amused look but says nothing, which I appreciate. I'd hate to ruin the surprise. "So how'd you get into the outdoors?" Elise asks as we go. "You seem totally at home here."

"Guess being country's always been in my blood," I explain, smiling. "My dad would take me out, sometimes into the mountains. We'd go fishing, camping . . . Dad wasn't a hunter, but we had fun. There was this lake up at Lucky Peak that I loved to go swimming in. We had some good times there." I fall quiet, not really wanting to talk about my parents and their reaction to my 'damn-fool' career, so I decide to turn the questions back on her. "What about you?"

"Other than those six months with the Girl Scouts, I've never really spent a lot of time outdoors," she admits, grinning. "I did a few nature walks when I was in college, but those were more parks than real nature. I mean, you could hear the cars if you listened hard enough. Not at all like this."

"Well, check this out then," I tell her as the path ends in the clearing. I found this place on my first trip up here, and as Elise takes it in, I can tell she's just as enchanted as I was. "It's the biggest reason I bought the cabin."

"It's . . . you've got a fairy forest," Elise says, looking around. The trees here are all pines, shooting high into the sky and shadowing a lot of the clearing, and for just a moment, I can imagine sparkly little creatures fluttering between the branches, intent on making magic.

"I never thought of fairies before, but it is magical," I agree. Taking her hand, I lead her on. "And up here is the best part."

I don't know how a creek this high up in the hills is able to form a pool, but it does, with a soft grass bank and half of the pool in the shade, the other half in the sun. "Have a seat. I'd say swim, but it's a bit cold except in July and August."

Elise sits down, letting me gather her in my arms as we lean back, my leg cocked to the side to let her press her body against me. "And you don't live here all the time why?"

I laugh softly, brushing a lock of her hair away from her cheek and inhaling the soft aroma that is naturally Elise. "If I thought I could, I might. But Carsen needs good schools, and besides, if I were up here all the time, I'd have to have visitors, all that shit. Ruin the scene. So I save it . . . for special people and for special occasions."

Elise turns, looking up at me and taking my hand. "Thank you. I know this is a crazy way to meet someone, but . . . I really am glad I followed you that day."

"So that *was* you," I confirm, chuckling. "Took me a while. Those sunglasses and wig are a hell of a disguise. So, how's the story coming?"

Elise sighs, leaning back and I can hear the worry in her voice. "Good and bad. Part three is done, but Donnie insists on dirt for part four. I don't think posing some archery shots is going to be enough." She spits out in disgust. "Hell, I wouldn't put it past Donnie to make up some random shit and publish it, and that's exactly what you don't want to happen, so we've got to come up with something. Got any ideas on a scandal I can give you that is juicy but won't be too embarrassing?"

I look up to the blue sky, trying to think and hoping to find an answer in the clouds. Partying on tour? Too hard to keep up appearances this summer. Drinking and drugs? I don't need that sort of attention. "Hey, what if I had a girlfriend? I just keep her locked up in my love dungeon and never let her out." I wrap Elise up tight in my arms, growling into the soft skin of her neck.

Elise giggles, wiggling away from the tickles of my nibbles. "I don't think that's the kind of thing you want getting out. Women would be lined up around the block for the *Yes, Mr. Perkins* experience."

"Well shit, I don't know, but we have all weekend to figure something out. For now, I have an idea." I hold her tight again, nuzzling in her hair and taking in her sweet girl-sweat and sunshine scent.

But she twists in my arms, surprising me with a smack of a kiss before scurrying towards the pool. I know the first few feet are shallow and mostly sandy bank, and likely freezing, so when she drops down and dips her hands in with a glint in her eyes, I can fully read her intentions.

"You'd better not, Elise. That water's fucking ice cold. You wouldn't dare." I warn her.

"Hell yes, I dare." and with a whoop of delight, she throws handfuls of water to splash at me.

I hop up, charging at her like she waved a red flag in front of a bull, and she retreats into the knee-deep water, where I follow her, splashing her with my stomping steps. "You've done it now..." And I grab her, splashing her with the frigid water as we both laugh and shiver.

"Holy shitballs!" Elise yells. "It's fucking cold!" But even as she complains about the water, she's reaching down, tossing more my way.

I laugh, and for the next few minutes, it's a water war of freezing proportions, both of us getting soaked but not caring in the least. Our calves and toes quickly numb, but the warm sun on our bodies helps. When we're both breathless, dripping, and smiling, I help her back on the bank, laughing as I stroke her wet hair. "Truce, I won't splash you anymore."

"How about you let me drive back as a peace offering?" she asks. "Do that, and maybe I'll let you join me for the warm-up shower."

"Deal," I reply, kissing her softly. This kiss feels different, like we're not getting ready to fuck but just . . . foreplay. Her lips are tender and soft, and when her tongue touches my lip, I caress her tenderly, holding her close before pulling back. "Thank you for letting me share this with you."

Elise takes it nice and slow, controlling the ATV on the ride back down, listening as I give her clues and point out where to turn. By the time we get back, the sun is getting low, which is great because we'll have plenty of hot water for our showers.

Elise brakes and turns off the ATV, pulling off her helmet as she looks out at the golden valley below the cabin. "I keep getting my breath taken away. It's beautiful," she whispers.

"Not as beautiful as you," I murmur, hugging her from behind. We watch the sun disappear behind the mountain, then push the ATV into the shed. I turn back to Elise in the fading light. "It'll get chilly up here quickly now. I'll grab some firewood, get that started for some heat while you wash up."

"And what if I don't *want* to wash up?" she asks, sassy again. In response, I come over and pull her close, growling lightly.

"I might just have to spank you," I threaten. "Hard."

Elise hums, pressing her breasts against my chest and squeezing me close. "I don't know if you understand what punishment means . . . because that sounds exactly like what I wanted anyway."

I hum, reaching down and cupping her ass, squeezing it as I whisper in her ear. "So you like it when I spank you? Hold you down and make your ass pink up so pretty for me?"

She bites back a moan, but I hear it even as she nods, grinding her hips forward to brush against my cock. Turning her around, I wrap a fistful of her hair around my hand, splaying my other on her belly as I lean down, nipping and sucking on her neck. Elise cups my head, holding me still. "Harder. Please . . . God, you make dirty feel so fucking good."

I nip her again, licking her skin and making her jump, pressing her ass against my now raging cock. "You want me to mark this pretty neck, leave bruises to show how well you've been fucked?"

She nods, and I have to give my lady what she wants, sucking harder and licking lines to find the next treasure spot to mark with my kiss. As I do, I grind my cock against her ass harder, finding a rhythm as I ride her through our clothes. Needing more . . . more skin, more contact, more of Elise surrounding me, I use my hold on her to walk toward the cabin, leading her inside.

"Sit," I order as soon as we're inside. "I wasn't joking about how cold it'll get. Once I'm in your pussy, I'm not going anywhere."

She sits, breathless and blushing, and I love that she looks like she's ready for me to take her, claim her any way I want. I quickly start a fire before turning to face her.

"Forget the shower. Show me your tits, Elise."

I expect her to pull her tank off, but instead, she stretches the neckline low, letting her tits pop up, the tank pushing them up like they're being cradled on a serving platter for me to feast on. I pull my shirt off in response, showing her that while I might be in charge, we're still equals. "Now touch your nipples, pinch them for me."

She looks at me from under her lashes, mouth already parted as she pants, wanting more. She reaches up and pinches her right nipple, rolling it between her finger and thumb and whimpering in desire.

I reach down, unbuttoning my jeans and sliding them down my hips a bit, my already hard cock tenting my boxer briefs. I slip my hand down, cupping myself through the thin fabric to show her the outline of my thickness. "Is this what you want?"

Elise whimpers again, the firelight starting to dance in her eyes as she nods. "Yes."

"Then say it. I want to hear it from those sweet lips of yours."

Elise's knees spread on their own, and I can see the contours of her pussy lips against the wet fabric, her eyes dark with desire. "Please . . . I need to see your cock."

"And what do you want to do with it?" I tease, toeing my boots off. "Do you want to suck it into that sassy mouth of yours?"

She nods, licking her lips. "I want to suck it, to choke on it . . . I want to feel it in my pussy . . . I want to feel you in my ass. I want you . . . everywhere."

"Do you, now?" I ask, letting my jeans drop the rest of the way to the ground before stepping out of them. "Has anyone ever fucked your ass, Elise?" She shakes her head, but her eyes never leave my cock, her desire for me to claim her in every way written across her face. "And do you think your tight little virgin ass is ready for my thick, pulsing cock?"

Elise pinches her other nipple, gasping and replying breathlessly, "No . . . but I want it anyway."

"I promise you . . . when you're ready, I'm going to fill your ass and make you scream my name," I rasp, hooking my thumbs in the waistband of my shorts. "But first, you need to get down to your panties. Fair's fair."

Elise scrambles to comply, nearly ripping her boots off to yank her tights down her long, sexy legs. My cock throbs watching her breasts bounce as she tumbles off the couch, kneeling in front of me before sitting back on her heels, looking up. "I can be very good," she winks.

"I know," I reply, teasing my underwear down some before stopping. "You do it. Suck my cock, baby."

Elise's eager hands pull my underpants down, my cock springing out to almost slap her in the tip of the nose. She's so hungry for me. Grabbing a handful of her hair, I take control. "Open."

As soon as her lips part, I feed my cock to her, deeper and deeper into her warm mouth. Elise moans, looking up at me as I start pumping my cock in and out of her lips, grinning. "I can see it in your eyes, Elise. Don't try and fool me . . . you want to show me you're the real boss here, don't you? That you can make me lose control and come down your throat."

"Mmm-hmm." Elise vibrates around my shaft, reaching up and fondling my balls.

I growl, shoving my cock down her throat. Elise swallows, taking it all but gagging as I hold my cock buried in her throat. "Is this what you want? Want me to fuck your pretty lips, let your throat work me every time you swallow?"

She nods slightly, her movement inhibited by my hold on her hair. I pull back, pausing to let her breathe for a moment, but she's already going back for more, so I fuck her mouth harder, pumping in and out as she tries her best to take me balls-deep with every stroke.

Still, I hold back, not hurting her but watching as she moans around me, her hands slipping down between her legs to start rubbing her panty-covered pussy.

"That's it, baby . . . rub that sweet pussy for me and get it nice and wet, because I'm gonna fuck you all weekend long." She cries out around my cock, and I see her hand move even faster, matching my punishing pace as I fuck her mouth. I'm already so damn close. "Elise . . ."

She looks up at me, and I hold her in place, tracing her pink lips with my head. "Do you want my cum inside you?"

Her tongue darts out to lick up the drop of precum already beading, her eyes answering my question. "Fuck, I want that too." Pulling my cock away, I tug her to her feet, half dragging her to the couch before I bend her over the arm, letting go of her hair.

"Grab that cushion, and if you let go, I'm *not* going to spank your ass, and I know how much you want me to spank you, baby," I tell her, getting behind her perfect, peach-shaped upturned ass. "God, you look fucking gorgeous, you know that?"

Before Elise can reply, I smack her right ass cheek, watching it pink up as I kneel behind her. She gasps, her legs spreading, and I get a great view of her panty-covered pussy. Reaching up with both hands, I pull them down and toss them across the room, already forgotten as I bury my stiff tongue in her pussy.

"Fuck!" Elise screams as I lick her wet folds, sucking and slurping hungrily. She's sweet and delicious, just what I need to quench the thirst inside me. "Keith, oh, fuck . . ."

I find the glistening jewel of her clit and lap at it with rapid little licks that leave her wiggling her hips as she chases me, desperate for release. Growling, I reach up and smack her ass, harder this time. "Don't move or I stop."

Elise freezes. I don't think she even breathes as I tease her opening with first one finger, then two. I slowly slide the length of my fingers in and out, feeling her pussy squeeze around them as I go as deep as I can. "Hands. Elise, hold yourself open for me. Fuck, I need to see you taking my fingers in your tight little pussy."

She does as I ask, pressing her cheek to the cushion and grabbing her ass to spread herself wide for my feasting. "Fuck, so pretty and wet for me . . . taking my fingers like you're gonna take my cock."

Slowly but powerfully, I finger fuck her pussy, letting the tip of my tongue skate across her clit, her lips, and up to her asshole. She whimpers, and I bite the fullness of her cheek before soothing it with my tongue. "It's mine, Elise. And I'm going to lick and suck and fuck you anyway I want."

I can't see her face pressed down to the cushion, but I see her body relax as she presses herself to my tongue, ready for whatever I give her.

I curl my fingers inside her, pressing along the front wall and sucking hard on her clit. I feel vibrations start to course through her body, and its only seconds before she comes. "Keith!" she squeals, trying to stay still for me but overwhelmed. "Oh, fuck!"

She's still convulsing around my fingers when I stand up, my cock pulsing with my racing heartbeat. Precum is oozing out, and I can't wait to slam inside her, but I stroke myself a few times, coating my cock with the juices from my fingers as I memorize the sight before me. She's so fucking gorgeous, waiting for me to fill her up. I can feel her soft lips pulsing, trying to suck me inside. "This is what you need, isn't it? Take it, take my hard fucking cock balls-deep."

I bury myself all the way in, our hips slapping together, and I grind inside her, feeling her pussy clench and relax as she adjusts to the fullness. "Fuck, Keith . . . I feel so full."

I reach back and smack her ass again, seeing the pink handprint I leave behind. "Mmm . . . your ass looks so good when it's red like this."

Elise moans, her pussy squeezing even tighter around my cock in response to the smack. I pull back, slamming into her again and making her back arch up. Reaching around, I cup her breasts with one hand while grabbing her neck with the other. She freezes, looking back over her shoulder but not resisting as my fingers close around her throat.

"Trust me," I whisper as I start pumping in and out of her. Elise shudders, her eyes never leaving mine as I stroke my cock faster and faster, our hips smacking together. Elise's eyes sparkle, and I can feel her pulse all around me . . . in her pussy, under my thumb along her neck, and under my palm at her breast. With every beat, it urges me to go harder and give her more.

"Your pussy is fucking choking my cock," I grit through clenched teeth. "This tight little pussy that's mine now, isn't it?"

"Yes," Elise cries out. "It's yours. I'm yours. Give it to me, fuck me and give me everything you've got," she says as her pussy gets impossibly tighter with every filthy word.

She reaches up to grab my wrist. For a moment, I think she's going to try and pull away, but she instead pulls me tighter, urging me on.

I speed up, feeling her body start to quiver again, and I look in her eyes. "I can feel you're close, Elise. Tell me."

She shudders, her voice and body both begging "Please, Keith . . . I need to come. Can I?"

I growl. "Come for me, baby. All over my fat cock. Cover me with your sweet cream."

My words are all Elise needs, and her fingernails tighten on my wrist, breaking the skin as she marks me too. Her eyes flutter as she pushes back, her pussy spasming around me as she starts to come again. I can't hold out, and I barely pull out in time to spurt all over her beautiful ass, covering her in thick streams that gleam in the firelight. I collapse, rolling us to the floor with Elise in my arms.

We lie on the floor, the soft light from the stove illuminating the cabin, until a strange sound breaks the silence. "What was that?"

Elise giggles, blushing a bit. "Uhm . . . my tummy. I'm hungry."

I laugh and sit up, helping her to sit with me. "Well then, I have plenty to feed you with. To start, how about some Dinty Moore beef stew?"

"Dinty Moore?" Elise asks, smirking. "And here I was thinking I was going to get three-star quality meals."

"Hey, it reminds me of the better times with my dad," I explain, helping her up. "And besides, it's quick and filling because you're gonna need your energy later. I'm just getting started."

# CHAPTER 17

## ELISE

We spend nearly all of the next thirty-six hours entangled in each other over and over, and it feels like my every sex fantasy come to life, but somehow, there's more than just sex between us now. In the mid-morning hours, after another round of him taking me, claiming me, pounding me into the mattress until I screamed out my release and he growled in my ear, we're still and relaxed. Finally exhausted, but I can't control the warmth that spreads through my body.

Lying on his chest, scratching and petting at the tattoos that traverse his skin, it feels comfortable. Especially as he twines a section of my hair around his finger and then releases the curl. We're naked, but maybe more so emotionally than physically.

There's been a change forged between us. There's still a bossy gruffness to Keith that is all him, but the defensive asshole seems to be mostly gone now that there's no big secret to tell.

Sometimes when he looks at me, I can still tell that there's a hint of doubt in his eyes, a constant demand for me to keep my mouth shut. But that's understandable when he's had this looming secret for so long and hasn't shared it with anyone new in years. I'm a risk, and we both know it.

Good thing I don't intend on tattling his story to the public, not at all. In fact, I feel special that he chose to share it with me. Granted, it was initially by force with Carsen barging in like that, but Keith could've shut down completely. He could've stopped the interviews, sent me away, and called in lawyers to force me to keep my mouth shut. But he didn't. And I think it's because he wants this . . . whatever this is between us, just as much as I do.

So I've spent the weekend reassuring him with my words, with my body, with everything I have that he can totally trust me and that I'm feeling this thing inside that would never let me hurt him. I wasn't looking for it, and I certainly didn't think I was gonna feel this way about the jerk who slammed a door in my face. But now that I know why, I understand. And that protective streak is damn sexy.

A man who will go to the lengths he has so his daughter can grow up safe and happy? Every girl should be so lucky. And lying here in Keith's arms, I feel like I'm a lucky girl too. Safe, peaceful, cherished . . . and I want to return those feelings to Keith, be his strength when he needs it, and most importantly, protect him and Carsen at all costs.

"What are you thinking?"

I blink, looking into Keith's eyes as I snuggle up to him more, pressing against him gently. "I'm thinking that I wish we could just stay here like this, in this perfect little bubble, away from reality and responsibilities. Just sleep and hike and fuck, and then do it all again."

He chuckles, tracing his thick thumb across my lips, and I pucker, kissing the pad and darting my tongue out for a quick taste of his skin. He presses into my mouth, and I suck his thumb like I've sucked his cock so many times already as he swirls across my tongue. "And when we run out of food?"

"There's some old wisdom . . . country boys can survive?" I joke, licking his skin again. He tastes like sweat and sex, and I bite my teeth down gently, holding him there so I can circle my tongue around him. "Mmm."

He groans, and I feel his cock jump, responding jealously and wanting my attention lower. Keith moves unexpectedly, pulling me beneath him and pressing my hands to the bed above me. "I think I like your plan," he purrs, touching his forehead to mine. "I could stay inside your tight little body, your hot silky walls caressing me all day."

I smile, writhing against him, pressing my wrists against his restraint even though I don't want him to let me go. I just want to test him, make him press against me harder, force him to dominate me a bit rougher because we both know I can take it.

It's a new awakening for me. I've never really experienced anything like it before. But in giving in to Keith, I've found my body responding more to every touch, every stroke of his fingers on my skin. He drives me wild, and I feel like a different woman from when we first met . . . stronger and more satisfied than I've ever been.

He leans down, kissing me fiercely before biting at my lower lip, hard enough to make me whimper. "There's just one thing. I promised you pancakes on the way home, and if we stay for another round, I'm gonna wear you out so much that we'll have to go straight home so I can be there when Carsen gets home from school."

I pout, puffing out my bitten lip. "I don't want pancakes. I want you. One more time before the real world intrudes?"

But even as I curl my hips, searching for his touch, my traitorous body responds to his promise of pancakes and my stomach growls loudly. I guess cans of chili and stew aren't enough.

Keith smirks down at me, pushing up a little. "See? I need to feed you. I promise we'll get another chance, but you've got to be sore."

He moves one hand down my body, soft caresses meant to soothe as he traces my breasts, my belly, and across my hipbone. Sweet, but oh, so tantalizing, and as he brushes across my mound, I quiver, whimpering again.

He's right, I am sore from our repeated rough couplings, but I'm still hungry for more. I'm addicted to Keith, fully head over heels even if I've never said that to him again, and I want every caress and every orgasm he can give me. I arch my back, but my stomach growls again, betraying me. "Dammit."

Keith laughs, cupping my pussy and making me hiss, both in heat and a little ache before he bends down and kisses me just above my belly button. "Don't worry, Elise. I know what you need. Food and maybe a little recovery time, then I'll make you cream all over my cock again."

I sigh, knowing he's right. He stands, pulling me up with him, his thick cock sandwiched between us.

Keith hisses at the contact, pulling back reluctantly. "Get dressed before I change my mind," he growls mock threateningly. I'm not scared. Hell, I want to push him a little further just to find that line of control he skates on the edge of every minute of every day, and then shove him past the boundary.

So I do as he says and get dressed, but I do it with every bit of sexiness I can muster. I find my panties on the floor and bend over, exposing myself to him as I pick them up. I can feel his eyes blazing on my skin and I look over my shoulder, delighted to see his gazed fixed on me. I can see his cock hard, throbbing, wanting him to change his mind.

Loving that my tease is working, I flick my panties, getting them turned right side out before inhaling, and holding them out to him. "These are dirty from yesterday. They smell like sex. I need fresh ones from my bag."

I walk past Keith, who is as still as a statue, and lay the panties against his chest where he grabs them in one fist. "What?"

"Souvenir," I reply as I dig in my bag, again exposing myself to him as I grab a tiny scrap of satin and pull it out, holding it up where I know he can see it from his position behind me. I dip even lower, slipping first one then the other pointed toe into the undies and pulling them slowly up my calves and to my knees.

When I get mid-thigh, Keith growls. "Stop."

I look back, a smirk already on my face. But when I see him, it vanishes, my mouth dropping open as I see Keith with my sexed underwear wrapped around his cock as he jerks himself.

"You think you're in charge here? Your little pussy is what needs a break. My hard cock needs a release, you little tease."

I bite my lip, eyes focused on his hand slipping up and down his length, rubbing the silkiness of my panties against the velvet of his skin.

I try to explain my bratty behavior, knowing it's already useless. "I wasn't teasing you. I want you. I want you to fuck me . . ."

Keith's face is hard, feral, and sexy as fuck as he speeds up, shaking his head. "Oh, no, I already told you. Pancakes. But now . . . look what you've done."

I glance down again and whimper, wanting him, and I move closer but he stops me. "No. Leave those panties wrapped around your thighs so you can't move. Bend over again and show me that wet pussy."

I do as he says, spreading my legs as wide as I can with the confines of the satin at my thighs. "Put your hands behind your back. No touching."

Again, I obey, leaning to one side so I can see him behind me. "That's right. Watch me. I'm gonna jack my cock off with your sexy little panties, come all over them. And you're not gonna move. Stay right there and show me how soaked your pussy gets from watching me come."

I cry out, desperate for his touch, my touch, needing to come. "Tell me. Tell me what you feel, Elise."

"I need . . . God, I can feel my heartbeat in my clit, begging for release."

His eyes leave mine, locking on my pussy, and he groans, squeezing his cock tighter. "I can see your cream coating your thighs. Your pussy is so hungry for my cock that I can see your lips pulsing, searching to pull me inside."

I buck my hips a bit instinctively, opening wider to his fierce gaze. God, I never thought someone could come from not even touching, from just words, but watching Keith, I'm about to come and I haven't even pinched a nipple.

"Mmm, so pretty. I'm fucking close. You want me to come?"

I nod. He's driving me so insane with lust, I know I could come just from seeing him erupt. "Fuck yes, Keith. Fuck my sexy panties. Come all over them. Show me how you jerk yourself, thinking of my pussy surrounding you. I want to see you explode while you look at my needy pussy."

I'm getting dizzy from standing slightly upside down and from panting with lust, but I'm not moving. Not until I see what I want. Thankfully, only a few hard strokes later, Keith comes with a roar, jets of white pulsing out of his cock and ruining my panties. Well, not ruining them . . . making them better.

I'm gasping as I watch him, forcing myself to stay still even though the need to touch myself is overwhelming.

Keith's breathing is labored as he finishes, a few last jerks as he gets every drop out. He smiles, taking in my body with his adoring eyes. "Such a good girl, Elise. Not moving even though I know your pussy must be begging for release."

He stands there just like that, watching me, eyes moving from mine to my soaked slit. "How close are you? Are you about to come from watching me? From standing here with your dripping pussy on display for me to jack off to?"

I whine, mad at myself because I couldn't hold myself back even if I tried. "Fuck, Keith. I'm so close. So fucking close."

He moves closer and stuffs the cum-covered panties in my mouth, and the flavor of his essence coats my tongue, making me moan at the deliciousness.

He gives me a hard look. "One lick, Elise. That's all you get, you naughty cock tease. Come on my tongue or you'll have to wait until we get home for some relief. It's a long, hard drive home, baby. You don't want to wait, do you?"

I shake my head, my thighs quivering, so close to the edge I think his breath might be enough to send me over.

He leans closer, inhaling my scent like it's the finest of wines and making me wait even longer. Oh, my God, do it already! "You smell so sweet. I know you're gonna taste like honey on my tongue, coating me as I lick you down while you taste my cum on your gag. Don't drop it, Elise. Bite down and taste me while I give you your one . . . good . . . lick."

He leans forward, his hands spreading me wide, and the flat of his tongue presses against my clit, tracing through my soaked lips, up to my asshole before fluttering there, never breaking contact but still . . .

I detonate. From just one lick, shudders wrack my body as I see stars. I cry into the makeshift gag, his flavor bursting on my tongue sending me spiraling again. My knees buckle, and I start to pitch forward but he grabs me with one arm, supporting me as I lose all control, futilely trying to breathe oxygen into my blackened vision when Keith grabs a gentle handful of my hair, pulling me up to stand in front of him.

Supporting me from behind, he reaches around, taking the

panties from my mouth and letting a rush of sweet, cool oxygen flood my body. Placing his lips by my ear, his breath is warm as he holds me tenderly. "Such a naughty girl, but you took your punishment fucking beautifully."

I grin, finding the strength to stand up on my own. Keith reaches down, grabbing my still pristine panties that are twisted and stretched around my thighs and pulls them up, smoothing the stretch of material between the cheeks of my ass. “Keith . . . I have so much to say.”

“Over pancakes,” he promises me, stepping back. He takes my panties and inhales deeply, savoring their scent. “You’re right, these are mine now.”

He puts them in his backpack, cinching the top closed. "Get dressed. I'm feeding you some fucking pancakes on the way home."

Fuck yes, pancakes sound like heaven now, my body on empty after the intensity of what we just did. With one lick.

That's all it took.

We take the ATV down, Keith using some ramps in the back of his truck to put the vehicle inside before he ratchet-straps it in place. “Just one thing,” I tell him as we sit in the cab, finally finding words. “You have to promise me something.”

“What’s that?” he asks, smiling as he sees me regain my equilibrium and a little bit of my sassiness.

“Promise that if you start wearing my panties, I have your permission to include that dirty secret in the articles. And maybe take a picture . . . but I’ll keep that to myself,” I say with a saucy wink, the imaginary image of a big, rough country boy like Keith even getting one tree-trunk of a thigh in my tiny panties quite laughable.

He laughs, twisting the key in the ignition before pointing a finger at me. "Not happening . . . the wearing, the story, and most definitely, not the picture."

We start back toward the city, stopping at a restaurant known for its weekend brunches, and my thoughts return to the promise of pancakes and coffee. God, coffee . . . I need a thermos full considering how blissfully worn out Keith has made me.

"Just a moment," Keith says, getting a hat from the back and pulling it over his head. "There."

"You just going in here, thinking you won't be recognized?" I ask, laughing.

He chuckles, shaking his head. "Actually, if I don't have a cowboy hat and tight jeans on, most folks don't even give me a second look. Especially when I pull out the *fancy* disguise."

He pops open the console, pulling out a pair of thick black-framed glasses, slipping them on. He looks like a sexy nerd, and I'm reminded of my earlier thoughts that Clark Kent could learn a lot from this guy. Then again, maybe Keith is from Krypton . . . he certainly is the cock of steel, at least.

"So, what do you think?"

"I think if you throw on a fake Boston accent, you could pull that off in the middle of Kentucky and nobody'd bat an eye," I say, impressed that the glasses actually do a decent job of disguising him. I should know since I've had some pretty stellar disguises in my investigations. "So does that mean I get to hold my boyfriend's hand and not have to worry?"

"Damn right," Keith says, and he's true to his word as we go inside. Also true to his word, the hostess doesn't even give Keith a second look before leading us to a table by the window. The waitress gives us an appraising double-take as she takes our orders of orange juice, coffee, and pancakes, and worry starts to twist in my stomach. Despite what's growing between us. We absolutely *can't* be public.

As she walks off, I lean over, trying to keep my voice low. "She knows."

He grins as he wiggles the glasses at me, totally assured. "You don't know that. Maybe she just thinks I'm hot."

My fears are confirmed, though, when she returns a moment later with the steaming cups of caffeine nectar. She leans forward, her voice careful. "Uhm, excuse me, but are you Keith Perkins?"

I freeze, curious how he's going to handle this, and admittedly, my journalist gene kicks in a bit. He gives her a confused look and tweaks his voice a little to make it sound totally un-Keith-like as he replies. "Who? My name's Adam. You must have me confused with someone else. Sorry."

He flashes her an innocent smile and shrugs his shoulder. She looks at him for a second longer before sighing wistfully. "Sorry, sir. You just kinda look like him. You've never been mistaken for him before? He's a country singer."

Keith smiles wider. "Not that I recall. And I'm more of a rock guy myself. Ever heard of Highly Suspect?"

She smiles back, and if this girl starts flirting any more openly, I'm going to know right where to stuff my first handful of pancakes. "Nope, can't say that I have."

Keith nods, adjusting his glasses. "Good band. You should look them up."

Seemingly appeased, she heads off to check on our pancakes. I'm grinning behind my coffee cup, damn proud of myself for not laughing and blowing Keith's cover.

"Have you even heard a single song by Highly Suspect or did you say the first rock band I mentioned in a desperate attempt to distract her?" I ask. "And by the way, she was flirting with you."

"Maybe both," Keith admits with a chuckle. "The distraction

worked, but I gave them a listen after you mentioned them. They do have a good sound. And even if she was flirting . . . I'm taken."

I smile, my heart melting at the simple statement. "You surprise me, Adam. Just when I think you're a gruff asshole, you're sweet too. Keep it up."

We're halfway through our stacks of pancakes when I see someone I never expected to see working her way through the tables. Her eyes cut my way and lock, the surprise obvious on her face even if her eyebrows don't move because of all the Botox. She turns, bee-lining straight for us. "Shit. Incoming."

Before Keith can even question me, Francesca stops by our table, all airs and elegance. "Elise, darling! What a surprise to see you! Out for a bite of brunch? They do have the best mimosas here." She says it like she's sharing national secrets, whispering slightly and gesturing to my non-champagne orange juice like we're besties.

I force a smile, knowing it's fake, but Francesca can't tell the difference anyway. I don't know if it's because I've given her so many dishonest smiles or if she just doesn't care. Not bothering to correct her assumption about my juice, I tell her neutrally, "Good to see you too."

Francesca dips her chin demurely, her eyes zeroing on Keith. "Ooh, aren't you going to introduce me to your friend?"

She knows who Keith is, I'm certain of it. Hell, Donnie and she have probably had some gross form of pillow talk about my article series, but she's playing coy. Fuck that.

"Of course. Francesca, this is Keith. Keith, this is a coworker of mine, Francesca. She works with red carpets, galas, award ceremonies, that type of thing mostly."

Keith is polite as he shakes her hand, and I can see on her face that she's thinking he'll be impressed by what I said and by her good looks.

But what Frannie doesn't know is that Keith knows about her too, and her hopes are quickly dashed. "Oh, yeah, those are all events I mostly avoid like the plague if I can help it. The vampires and vultures are out in force there."

I smile, keeping my giggles inside, as Francesca seems a bit miffed at his dislike of her favorite arenas to see and be seen. "Well, yes . . . I'm sure they're not for everyone. So, Elise," she says, directing her focus on me. "How're the interviews going?"

"Oh, great," I reply, jittery until I feel Keith's foot touch mine under the table. *Keep it together, girl.* "Keith was showing me some of his hobbies, like hiking and archery. A bit of outdoorsy stuff for the next article."

Francesca sniffs, literally sniffs like she's smelled something distasteful. "Outdoorsy? Sounds . . . interesting." Her tone says she obviously finds it anything but interesting.

Keith interjects, saving me. "Elise was a natural out there. I'm sure some reporters wouldn't be willing to get dirty . . . hiking, riding an ATV, shooting a few arrows. But she jumped right in. Anything for a story, right?" He says it with a true smile, but I can see by the flint in his eyes that he remembers what I'd told him about Francesca.

"Oh," Francesca replies, giving me a worried look like everyone doesn't already know how she gets her assignments. "Uhm, well . . . sounds like you've got some good scoop, so I'll let you two finish brunch. I'm off for a hair appointment. See you Monday."

After Francesca leaves, I freak a bit, gasping. "God, do you think she suspected anything?" I whisper, trying and failing at not looking guilty. "I'm pretty sure we were just eating when she came up, nothing suspicious. Right?"

Keith smiles, patting my hand. "I think we're fine, nothing sketchy. Am I *your* dirty little secret now?"

He's teasing, but there's a hint of truth to it, and a bit of hurt too. I try to corral my thoughts. "Honestly, there's a piece of me that wouldn't mind shouting from the rooftops. But that wouldn't be great for either of us right now. Professionally, it'd be career suicide for me, and you would have those vultures flocking around so fast your head would spin. And that's dangerous . . . for Carsen. Neither of us can afford for suspicions about a flirty breakfast to get out."

"Touché, you're right. There's a part of me that'd be right there next to you on the rooftop, but . . . Carsen is first, always." Keith responds, picking up a piece of bacon and munching on it as the gravity of the situation sinks in. "I will say, Francesca has barracuda written all over her. She's the one giving favors to your boss, right?"

I shudder, nodding. "Yes. Ugh, so gross. I just imagine . . . jellybeans."

"Huh?" Keith asks. "Jellybeans?"

I explain about Donnie and his crystal bowl of jellybeans, and he nods, trying to chuckle, but I can see it. The spell's broken and there's a dullness to everything now that reality has crept back in, the risk of what we're doing more real.

We finish brunch, but as we walk back out, we don't hold hands.

It feels too dangerous.

# CHAPTER 18

## KEITH

"So, here we are," I muse as I drop Elise off at her place. "Thank you for a wonderful weekend."

Elise gives me a ghost of her normally megawatt smile, still worried about running into her co-worker at the pancake joint. "I should thank you. Keith, about the restaurant . . ."

"There's nothing we can change about it now. She'll either suspect something's up between us or not," I reply evenly. "The best thing you can do is make sure your story is a knockout and you drop enough hints of dirt that your editor's going to be happy. Just make sure of one thing."

"What's that?" Elise asks, brightening a little.

"When you tell the world how much you're addicted to my big, fat cock . . . don't skimp on the size," I joke. I'm trying to lighten the mood, ease her mind, but I know her career is serious to her. And as much as we're both enjoying this growing thing between us, I don't think either of us is ready for the fallout of everyone knowing. But I don't want to end our amazing weekend on a suspicious, fearful note, so some prodding to get Elise to smile seems warranted, even if it's a bit less bright than her usual megawatt grin.

Elise finally laughs, shaking her head. “What, are you kidding? That’s my *big* lead-in! I mean, it’ll *hook* them in for sure!” She holds up her finger, bent at the knuckle into a hook shape.

I laugh but grab her hand. "Don't even joke about that, woman. Or I'll have to remind you just how big and *straight* it is when I'm bottoming out in that tight little pussy."

Elise laughs, blushing a little. "I’ve already told you, you're the worst at punishing my brattiness. That sounds like a reward."

I look around to make sure we’re alone on the street, and I lean forward, sipping at her lips, driving her crazy wanting more. I pull back and she chases my kiss. “That’s enough for now. You’ve got work to do.”

She sits back in her seat, full bottom lip protruding in a pout. "You want to come inside?"

I smirk, knowing that if we do, work just won’t get done. "Maybe next time. Right now, you're gonna go in, work your magic on another story, and I'll call you later. And Elise, don't you dare come without me. Save it for me."

She nibbles at her lip, then nods. "I take it back. You're better at punishment than I give you credit for."

I smile, hitting the unlock button for her door. "I know."

I grab her chin and give her one more kiss, fiery hot and powerful to stoke her fire one last time before she goes inside. As she closes the door behind her, walking to her apartment building, I take a deep breath and adjust myself in my pants. I might be able to keep my control when she’s with me . . . but she pushes me to the limits. I wouldn't have it any other way.

Driving home, I sing to myself a few bars of something that’s been floating through my head. I don’t quite know what the song is yet, just one of those little ditties that float through my head from time to time . . . but this one feels like it could be one of those that turns into something.

Getting out of my truck at home, I'm barely in the door before Carsen's hounding me, a hundred questions pouring out of her ever-curious mouth.

"So what did you do? Did you take her to the creek? What about the ATVs? Did you see any deer?"

I laugh at the way Carsen is bouncing and dragging me inside by my hand. Carsen's always enjoyed going to the cabin, but I think she was even more excited for someone new to experience the beauty and fun we always share there.

"Slow down, honey. Let me at least get my pack in the door and get these boots off, and I'll answer your questions. Think I can do that?"

Carsen nods, stepping back before coming closer again to hug me tightly. "I missed you."

I hug her back, kissing the top of her head before looking up to see Sarah watching us with a smile on her face. "How was it?"

"Good," I reply, letting go of Carsen and putting my backpack down. "I'll get that later. Let's see, my weekend . . ."

I give Carsen and Sarah a rundown of what's happened the past forty-eight hours, a heavily edited version, of course. "And after the pancakes, I dropped Elise off at her place so she could start work on her story," I finish, leaning back and sipping the Coke Sarah got me while I was telling Carsen about cooking chili. "Like I said, it was fun."

"So, do you like her? Is she your girlfriend now?" Carsen asks.

I take another sip of Coke and lean forward, watching Carsen carefully. "Do *you* like her? Because yes, I like her a lot."

Carsen smiles, nodding. "She's cool, Dad."

"Remember, baby, that no matter how much I like Elise, you're always my number one girl, right?"

Carsen rolls her eyes, and I feel like sometimes she thinks I'm about fifty years older than I actually am. "I know that! But I want you to have more than just me and Aunt Sarah."

I reach out, and Carsen comes over, plopping into my lap. She used to fit on one thigh, snuggling up to my side to watch cartoons. Now, she's tall and all gangly limbs, but I'll happily hold my little girl anytime she'll let me, knowing it's getting more and more rare as she gets older. She's wise beyond her years sometimes, and it strikes me just how fast she's growing up. "I love you, Carsen."

She looks at me, no doubt in her mind. "I know, Dad. I love you too."

Behind her, I see Sarah give us a nod and get up. "Think I'll start dinner for tonight. How's my famous biscuits and gravy sound?"

"Awesome!" Carsen says. "Uhh . . . so does that mean I have to go do my homework now?"

"You'd better," I mock growl, making Carsen bounce up and run off with a laugh. I laugh too and watch her disappear before looking at Sarah.

"So you were fine taking care of her this weekend?" I ask her as soon as Carsen's out of earshot.

"You know I adore that girl. Don't you even think about that. Carsen's right. Elise is good for you." Her tone takes a more serious note. "If she's it, you need to circle the wagons, make sure she fits with you and Carsen. Dinner went well, but you need more time together. Both you and her, and the three of you."

"The four of us, you mean. You're a huge part of this too, Sarah. Carsen has only had you as a mother figure. I don't want to ever replace that, but I want to see if this can go somewhere. Who knows, maybe add to our ragtag motley crew."

Sarah reaches up to hug me, lightly kissing my cheek. "I like that plan. Let's see if we can do dinner this week . . . the four of us."

# CHAPTER 19

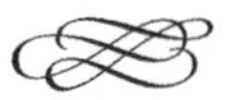

## ELISE

Checking my dress, I realize that I'm even more nervous than when I came to interview Keith the first time.

I know why. I feel like this is a test. Dinner before was to make sure I'd keep my mouth shut. Then, this thing between Keith and I was . . . physical, primal, but not emotional.

This is more personal. This is to see if my edges fit in with Keith's family and their edges. Figuring out if it's an easy, smooth fit or a forced one that leads to friction and fraying. I'm praying it's the former, because I really like Keith. It is emotional now.

Hell, I'm pretty sure I more than "like" him, even if I'm not ready to put a label that big on it yet. But I will admit, to myself, at least, that I want to see where this goes . . . beyond the interviews, beyond casual hookups. I want to see him as a father and get to know Carsen and Sarah more, because they're important to Keith and that means they're important to me.

And hence the nerves. We're not doing anything fancy, just a casual dinner at a restaurant near downtown. But I want this to go well. Really well.

Walking in, I'm suddenly unsure whether Keith would've given his real name. "Uh, hi, I'm supposed to meet someone here at seven?" I tell the bored looking hostess. "I don't know what name it's under though."

"You can check," the hostess replies, waving a hand vaguely behind her. I look around, and after two passes, I see Keith sitting in a back corner, facing the wall. I'd know that bald head and set of wide shoulders anywhere. Plus, the fact that Carsen is waving wildly at me is a sure tip-off. But I don't see Sarah. I hope she's here.

Heading over, I'm not sure what to do. Should I kiss him in front of Carsen or just sit down like it's no big deal that I'm invading a family dinner as a trial run? "Uh, hi."

Keith stands up to greet me with a hug and a quick kiss, and I see he has on his Clark Kent glasses disguise again and an oversized polo shirt that amps up the nerd effect.

It's cute, but still sexy as he gives me a smirk. "So glad you could make it."

I smile, taking the seat Keith motions to, next to him and across from Carsen. "Of course. I wouldn't miss this. I've been excited and nervous about it all day!"

He smiles, leaning in to whisper in my ear. "Don't be nervous. They both already like you."

Just like that, the swarm of nervous butterflies is gone and instead I'm filled with warmth, reassured that this is going to be okay. "Where's Sarah?"

"Right here," Sarah says behind me. "Sorry, had to use the ladies' room."

We sit down, chatting about our day, and I quickly realize that Carsen and Sarah are raptly watching every exchange between

Keith and me and have matching wide grins plastered across their faces.

"What?" I ask, feeling heat rush to my face after we place our orders. "You guys don't like fish?"

Carsen giggles a little girl laugh but leans towards Sarah, talking low even though we can all hear her. "Check out her eyes. They're sparking like fireworks. Think that's Dad or makeup?"

Sarah hums, obviously used to Carsen's sense of humor. "Ask her." she tells Carsen as she gives me a wink.

Carsen leans back to me. "Do you wear makeup?"

I grin, catching on. "I do, just a little to bring out my features. But you know the trick to looking your absolute best?" Carsen tilts her head, eager for the answer. "Being happy. Always makes you glow from within." I wait a half a beat and then we all giggle like only females can do and I feel a knot unfurl in my belly even more.

"I was too nervous to say anything last time, but I really love your hair. It's much cuter than your dad's."

Carsen grins, her eyes shooting to Keith as he rubs at his head, which is covered with a few days worth of stubble on top. "Think I'll grow it out until the next show. Helps with the anonymity."

"Brother, was that a five-syllable word? Elise, I think you've worked miracles! He's doing more than grunting like a grumpy ass," Sarah teases.

"Hey, I do more than that." Keith protests, "I talk. Sometimes."

"Ugh, man speak, woman understand," Sarah jokes, grunting as Keith glowers at her, but I can see the twitch of laughter at the corners of his mouth as he fights to keep a straight, stern face.

We eat for a few minutes, comfortable and chatty with each other when Carsen pipes up. "Hey, got any plans tomorrow?"

I wipe my mouth with my napkin. "Nothing really. What's up?"

Carsen looks at Sarah, who nods. "Aunt Sarah is taking me shopping so I can find a dress for the school dance. It's going to be epic . . . the dance and then it's my best friend Kaitlyn's birthday, so I get to sleep over at her house after. You wanna go shopping with us?"

She's speaking so quickly and animatedly. It takes my brain a moment to catch up to my ears. "Shopping sounds like something I might know a thing or two about," I say carefully, looking at Sarah, not wanting her to think I'm stepping on her toes with Carsen. But she's smiling and seems excited about the idea too. "Sounds fun! What time?"

Keith gawks, looking around the table. "Are you sure?"

Carsen bounces excitedly while Sarah smiles. "We'll pick you up at four? Then we can grab some dinner to bring home while we're out."

I smile back at them both. "It's a date!"

Keith mock growls. "I don't know whether to be happy you are all getting along, or scared you're going out without me."

Sarah laughs. "Oh, you'll be there with us . . . in cash form, Daddy Big Bucks." We all laugh as dessert is served and Sarah promises to tell me all Keith's embarrassing childhood stories.

Dessert is wonderful, caramel cheesecake for me, and after we pay—I notice Sarah uses her credit card, probably another layer of protection—we walk outside. "Thank you," I tell Carsen. "You were right, the cheesecake was to die for."

"Anytime," Carsen says, giving me a quick little hug. "I can't wait until tomorrow. Can I get some heels too?"

"Let's talk about that in the truck," Sarah says with a knowing grin, taking Carsen by the shoulders and steering her away. "We'll be waiting."

The two of them walk away, and I'm left with Keith, who's been quiet through most of dessert. "You okay? You've been a little quiet."

"This was the best family dinner out we've had in years," Keith says quietly, taking my hand as I lead him toward my car. "Carsen really likes you. I was just taking it all in."

"She's a great little girl," I answer honestly. "Sarah's done a good job being a mother figure for her. But . . . do you think she'll be worried if Carsen and I become friends?"

"Not at all, we talked about that already," Keith says. We reach my car, and he pulls me in close. "You're a wonderful person, and I'm glad you're getting to know my daughter."

I put my arms around Keith's neck, looking up into his eyes. "I'm happy to know my nerdy boyfriend has such a sweet family."

Keith chuckles and pulls me in close for a kiss. It's tender, and while there's a little bit of fire underneath his touch, it's restrained for now. Still, I moan, slipping my tongue over his once before pulling back. "Just in case they're spying on us again."

"I have no doubt they are," Keith says, smirking. "Carsen because she's curious, Sarah because she wants to make sure I behave."

"I happen to like when you don't behave," I purr, pressing my body against his. "I missed you."

"I know. I missed you too," Keith rumbles. "And if you can be a good girl for just a couple more days, you and I can have plenty of time together to make sure you get a heaping dose of—"

“You’d better stop,” I warn him, my heartbeat speeding up. “Or else we’re going to have a not-family-friendly moment in this parking lot.”

Keith smirks, stepping back to create a small space between us but leaving his hands on my hips, and I leave mine wrapped around his neck. “I never thought I’d be doing this, but it feels right with you.”

I nod, feeling my heart swell in my chest. “It does feel right. This feels big, Keith.” The last part is almost a whisper, feeling like a confession as I wait with bated breath to see what he says.

“I know. I didn’t think things could happen like this, so fast and with a less than friendly start. But there’s something about you, about us . . .” He says as his eyes are searching mine.

“I feel like that too. Keith, I never thought it was real . . . but I really think I’m—”

"Not here,” Keith says, putting a finger to my lips. “I feel it too, but when we say it, I want to be able to take you, claim you and have you claim me back. And I can't do that in this parking lot with my kid a few cars away.”

I nod, the warm assurance of Keith’s feelings sinking in. Suddenly, I pull him to me, kissing him hard, claiming his mouth in a turnaround that leaves him stunned for a moment before he kisses me back, cupping my ass with his hidden hand to give it a squeeze. I can feel him swell, and when I pull back, Keith’s breath is fast and deep, his eyes glowing with desire.

Keith nods, breathing deeply as he regains his control. "I need to go. Are you sure about taking Carsen shopping?"

I nod, smiling. "Absolutely. Girls’ shopping trip sounds like fun, and I want to get to know her."

"You're amazing," Keith says before lifting my hand to his lips and kissing my fingertips sweetly. “Goodnight, Elise.”

"Goodnight," I answer, watching him go as my fingertips tingle from his kiss. Despite the oversized polo, he is still an amazing figure as he walks away, his ass perfectly filling his jeans and flexing enough to give me good dreams tonight.

Very good dreams.

# CHAPTER 20

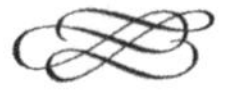

## ELISE

"So, what do you think?"

It's only the third time Carsen's asked me, and I'm happier than ever that she's asking. It was a little awkward at first, despite the good dinner we all had yesterday. I can understand this isn't about Keith and me. This is about how I fit with Carsen and Sarah . . . and that's going to take a little longer to adjust to.

But Carsen has loved having our undivided attention, giving a fashion show-worthy walk and twirl with each dress she's tried on. It's helped us relax, the giggles taking us over more than once, and making the conversations with Sarah more comfortable as Carsen changes into another possible dress selection.

"I think it looks great, Carsen . . . but I'm not sure it's my favorite," I admit. "What about the black one?"

"No way, that looked so old lady," Carsen replies, making me wince inside. I thought it looked beautiful and classic, but then again, to Carsen, twenty-one is middle aged. "What about the red one?"

"NO!" Sarah and I say simultaneously, making me grin. Sarah smirks too and explains. "Honey, I know you want to look grown up, but that's just not something a twelve-year-old should be wearing. What about the blue one?"

"I think that's my favorite style, but I like it in green better," Carson says. She looks at us both and we give her double thumbs up, all in agreement on her choice.

With the dress decided on, we move on to accessory shopping. "So, are you looking forward to the dance?" I ask.

"Well . . ." Carsen says before blushing. "I think Max will be there. I hope he asks me to dance."

"Max?" I ask, catching Sarah's shrug out of the corner of my eye. "A boy from school? Does your Dad know about this Max?"

"Of course not!" Carsen says. "Daddy would freak out if he knew Max gave me a card for my birthday. He said I'm cute. And he's like, the cutest guy in my class. And it's not like Dad can come to the dance and do the whole intimidating dad thing anyway." She raises a finger to her lips, "Ssssh, it's a secret."

I smile. "Who's a secret? Your dad or Max?" Carsen smirks, and I can read her answer all over her face. "Ah, so *both* of them are top secret."

Sarah smiles, but shows that she's heard every word. "I'd just like to point out, you shouldn't use your dad's desire for secrecy against him, you know?"

Carsen nods, trying not to look guilty. "I know. I know that if everyone knew, we couldn't do stuff like this . . . walk the mall and shop. Unless the big scary guys came with us."

I'm struck by how mature Carsen really is because most kids would be shouting about their famous dad all over Instagram and demanding special treatment. Hell, I know some adult children who act that way. I've written stories about some of them. Instead, Carsen is chill, understands the risks of fame, and seems content to be exactly who she is, secrets and all.

Accessory shopping is quick and easy. Carsen might be on the budding cusp of womanhood but her tastes are simple and elegant. A thin necklace and set of earrings later, and we decide on an afternoon snack at the food court.

I'm about halfway through my ice cream cone when I get a prickle on the back of my neck. Wiping my mouth with a napkin, I glance around discretely.

"You okay?" Sarah asks, sipping a Coke. "You look like you've seen the boogeyman."

"No . . . but I do feel like I'm being watched," I reply. Across the food court, I see why. Francesca is sitting near one of the pillars, a wide, floppy hat on her head but still, I know her too well to be put off by a simple hat. "Shhh-oot." I manage to correct myself. "We should go."

"What's wrong?" Carsen asks, instantly on alert.

"My co-worker," I reply, giving Sarah a pointed look.

Sarah catches my meaning. "Alright, honey. Grab your stuff and we'll go shoe shopping somewhere else."

Carsen doesn't dilly-dally, but Francesca seems to be faster. Just as I'm grabbing my purse, she comes over, a big, fake smile on her face. "Elise, it's so good to see you again!"

I glower, annoyed at her intrusion . . . again. "Francesca, figured you'd still be at the office today. Cut out early?"

Francesca laughs, an obviously fake tinkle like a bell. "Oh, I'm just out shopping for a gown for the premiere next weekend. Thought I might treat myself, you know. I was just grabbing a half-caff frappe when I saw you out with . . . sorry, I don't remember your names."

"Sarah and Car," I answer, praying I can keep this short and not have to give Francesca any more information than I have to. She might cut corners to get ahead, but she's got good instincts.

Shit, I should have used fake names. At least Francesca will likely assume Carsen is Sarah's daughter.

"So, what's got you out?" Francesca asks, her eyes clicking from bag to bag on the table like she's taking mental notes. Fuck my life, she probably is.

"Just out for some girl time with my friends," I reply. "Listen, I'd love to stay and chat, but we really need to roll."

As we walk away, Carsen doesn't seem to realize the significance, but Sarah gives me a worried glance. "Is everything okay?" she asks quietly while we close the trunk of her car and Carsen's getting into her seat. "Should I tell Keith?"

"No . . . no, I don't think he needs to worry," I answer softly. I give her a nod, attempting to convey that I think we're clear and that I understand how important this is . . . to Carsen, to Keith, to Sarah, and now, to me. There's a wiggle in the back of my mind that finds it odd that I've seen Francesca twice recently, considering we never run into each other, but I let it go considering the place is popular and is near some of the busiest streets in town. Francesca could have been legit dosing on caffeine and shopping, just like us. "I'll handle it."

"Okay," Sarah says, her voice still a little tense. She's probably kicking herself as much as I am for coming to a popular shopping center.

I should've had a better plan for that. Hell, I can do disguises that'll fool people all the time . . . yet I forgot to even come up with some fake names for Sarah and Carsen, a cover story, anything. I do it all the time when I'm working a story, but it hadn't occurred to me to do it for a simple shopping trip.

That's a mistake I won't make again.

"Listen, Sarah?" I ask as we're still outside the car. "I promise, I'll handle this. I'll do my best to keep Carsen and Keith safe."

Sarah studies me for a moment, then nods. "I hope so. I believe you."

# CHAPTER 21

## KEITH

For the past a week and a half, it feels like a new routine has established itself in my life. I wake up, make sure Carsen's good for school before Sarah drops her off, then grab a workout before spending a few hours putting together tunes. That little ditty in my head keeps developing, and as I work on it, I'm more and more convinced it can be a good song . . . maybe even my best.

Sometime during the day, Elise either calls or comes over to talk about this and that for articles, showing me rough drafts on what she's got. More often than not, she stays for dinner, and on those nights, the whole evening is a heady mix of professional and personal as we talk about music and tours and then roll into deep late-night conversations about everything and nothing. One night, she'll hang with Carsen and we'll be all about what's on TV. The next, Elise and I damn-near have ripped the headboard off my bed as we fucked ourselves into a near coma just from an intense quickie before Carsen got home from school.

It's been amazing to watch how Carsen, Sarah, and Elise have bonded so quickly and easily, although I'm even further outnumbered now, but I wouldn't change it for anything. I'd worried so much for so long, assuming that I'd be alone until Carsen was grown, turning off that part of my heart, my soul.

But Elise makes it possible to have a connection with my daughter and still have a safe haven where Carsen knows she's my priority. That takes a special woman, and I'm glad that it's Elise.

We haven't retraced those steps we were taking in the parking lot, saying how we feel. We haven't had a night alone to address those feelings the way I want to. But looking over at her, I smile.

She's at home in my house, washing up the dinner dishes from our date night-slash-interview and loading the dishwasher the way I like. It's a small thing, really, just a nuance of daily life, but the simple fact that she's comfortable doing it here, in my home, makes all the difference.

It resonates deep inside me, a fiery ball of joy singing out at her presence in my life, completing a puzzle at my core that I didn't even know was missing a piece. I feel solid with her here, and I need her to know that.

Standing in the doorway with my arms crossed over my chest, I watch for one more second before I interrupt her, "Elise." There's already gravel and heat in my voice, but I can't and don't want to control it.

She looks over at me, a question in her eyes. "Keith?"

"Leave the dishes for later. I need you now. Come with me." I can see the moment of hesitation on her face, the way she weighs whether she should sass me back, but she must sense the weight in my words. I'm glad. I don't want to punish her tonight. I want to love her, fuck her, be inside her body so deep she feels my imprint there forever more.

Tonight, I don't just want her body. I want her soul and her heart. It's only fair because she has mine.

I press off the doorframe, turning to walk down the hall, feeling her presence behind me as she follows me to the bedroom. As soon as she passes the threshold, I turn, closing the door behind her.

Her eyes track me, her breath already shallow and fast as I slip my shirt over my head and toss it to the floor. I stand in front of her, and I can feel her gaze as she traces the tattoos along my chest and arms. "Strip for me, Elise. I want you naked."

She doesn't rush to do as I command. Instead, she takes advantage, knowing her own power even as she submits to what I want. Slowly, she slips the straps of her dress off her shoulders, looking up at me through the fringe of her lashes, a flirtatious faux-innocence on her face as she holds it to her chest.

With a dramatic flair, she lets go and it drops to the floor, puddled at her feet in a whoosh. She steps out, kicking it out of the way and standing before me in her bra and panties.

I take a mental snapshot. "So fucking beautiful, Elise. Take it all off. Show me everything."

She reaches to unclasp her bra and slips her panties down her legs. She stands still, hands at her sides, confident in herself as she should be. She's a work of art and I'm a lucky fucker to get to see her this way. No falsity, no pretense, just bare and exposed and vulnerable.

It's a gift she's bestowing on me and I know it. I walk around her, memorizing her full beauty, trailing a finger along her arm, across the back of her shoulders, around to her collarbone, down between her cleavage, and along her hips.

"Michelangelo himself could not have created a creature more beautiful than you," I murmur as I trace my finger across her stomach, dipping into her shallow belly button and continuing across to the other side.

She is virtually vibrating with need by the time I stand in front of her again. I undo my belt, dropping my jeans and then my boxer briefs to stand nude in front of her too, letting her see me just as bare, just as vulnerable. "Keith . . ."

My cock is rock-hard, straining to get closer to Elise as I hold back, needing to do this right, wanting more than just the gift of her body. I take a half step back and speak from the depths of my soul.

"Elise, there's nothing to hide behind right now," I reply softly, my voice intense with emotion that fuels every syllable. "Just you and me, naked physically and emotionally. I told you before that I felt it too, but that I wanted to be able to claim you, mark you as mine when I said it."

Her eyes, which had been roving over my form, are now locked on mine, her lips parted in anticipation. "I didn't think this was ever going to happen to me, but you came in and crashed my world in more ways than one. You challenge me, you make me wish for things I never thought I would. Elise . . . I love you."

I can see the glitter of tears in the corners of her eyes, but she doesn't let them fall. Instead, she takes a deep breath and puts her hands behind her back, not only offering herself to me but making her look even more beautiful. "I didn't see this coming either . . . any of it. I want more with you, with Carsen, than I have any right to want. I love you too, Keith."

It feels like vows, like we're making promises beyond this moment, the gravity of the situation pulling us together. I close the distance between us, wrapping my arms around Elise and taking her wrists in my hand as our lips meet in a passionate kiss, sealing our words with our actions.

Our tongues tangle, the fire burning hotter, brighter as we press against each other, moans and skin melding into one being.

"Take me, Keith," Elise begs breathlessly when our lips part. "Claim me, mark me as yours."

My whole body starts to tremble at her request, knowing this is more than we've done before, physically, emotionally and spiritually, because she is giving herself up to me all the way to her soul, the way I am hers.

Turning, I lead her over to the bed, still keeping my hands on her wrists, as if by encircling them I'm closing the circle that's between us, forging our bond stronger even though I don't have to 'command' her at all. "I need to worship you. Every inch of your fucking delicious body is mine. Lie down."

I release her and she lies down, her arms and legs splayed out like she's making a snow angel in the white sheets, and it gives me a dirty idea.

Stepping into the closet, I grab a few of my rarely used ties and make my way over to her. Slowly, methodically, I tie her to the bedposts, forcing her to spread even wider, her body open and available.

"You okay?" I ask, running a finger down one silk tie to her wrist, tracing her skin all the way to the inside of her elbow. "Not too tight?"

Elise smiles, but she's writhing, trying but unable to get more contact between us. "No, I need you. Fuck, Keith . . ."

"No, my love," I rumble, leaning down and kissing her lips softly. "Not fucking. Loving."

Elise mewls as our lips brush against each other so softly that only the electricity between us guarantees that we're actually making contact. "Mmm . . ." I murmur against her skin as I kiss down her neck to nibble at the hollow of her throat. "You look fucking stunning like this, all tied up for me, your eyes just as open as your long legs are. Is this what you want, Elise?"

"Oh, God, yes. Yes," Elise groans as I lick her collarbones. I perch on the edge of the bed, wanting to touch her but knowing if I do, I'll abandon all self-control, and I don't want that.

"Your body . . . so sexy and smooth," I purr before running my tongue over her skin between her breasts, nibbling on the soft skin. I kiss over, watching Elise's eyes as I grow closer and closer to her nipple. I can feel the stiff pink nub drag over my throat and chin before I take it between my lips, sucking hard before biting down just enough to make Elise arch her back, moaning in pleasure.

"Keith . . . yes."

"Sex with you is like nothing I've ever had," I add, kissing down her body. I finally climb onto the bed between her stretched out legs, running my palms up her inner thighs as I look at the soft, delectable lips of her pussy. "You're smooth all over . . . and delicious."

"If you—" Elise tries to say, but her words are cut off as I lean down, covering her pussy with my mouth and kissing it lovingly, tracing my tongue from base to clit while my lips caress hers. Elise's breath catches, her words dissolving into a long, guttural moan that's deeper than I've ever heard her make before.

Guided by her sounds, I make love to her body with my mouth and tongue, sucking on her pussy lips before stroking her clit with my tongue in quick, soft little flicks that have Elise arching her back and trying to press her pussy against my mouth.

"Oh, God . . . I'm so going to make you come when you untie me," Elise groans, showing me her strength and sassiness. It's what I love and what makes her so special. She can take all I have and not wilt but come back wanting more. I nip at her thigh for her comment though, knowing that even though it's meant to be punishing, it only fuels her higher.

But all of my focus is on her as I lower my mouth again and devour her. I'm unrelenting, cupping her ass and lifting her to my eager tongue as I stroke and suck on her clit, my ears listening for the moment when she's about to come. "That's it, Elise. Let me hear what you like. Tell me."

Elise's breathing deepens, her chest heaving as she grunts out. "Keith . . . lick me, suck me . . . please . . ." before she's lost for words, one keening cry escaping with her air. She's almost vibrating on the bed as I lap at her clit, and I know the moment's here. Raising my head, I look into her beautiful eyes. "I love you."

Elise's breathing deepens, her chest heaving as she starts to quiver, almost vibrating on the bed as I lap at her clit, and I know the moment's here. Raising my head, I look into her beautiful eyes. "I love you."

Elise's answer is torn from her lips as I bite down lightly on her clit, ripping the orgasm from her body in a tidal wave that makes her throw her head back, screaming in pleasure as she covers my face in her delectable juices. I suck, taking everything she has, letting her ride it out slowly until she's limp, unable to even look down at me as I raise up from between her legs.

I come around, kneeling over her and tapping her cheek with my cock. "Open for me, Elise. Suck my cock down that amazing throat of yours. I'm gonna fuck your face, baby. Can you take it like this?"

She opens wide, her tongue poking out to lick at my tip as she nods. Slipping into the wet warmth of her mouth, we both moan at the sensation. "You like that? You like my thick cock in your sweet mouth while you're tied down at my mercy?"

Elise nods again, hollowing her cheeks and sucking hard. Her eyes tell me everything I need to know as she uses what little range of motion she has to bob up and down on my cock, getting it wet and throbbing for her.

"That's my good girl. Suck that cock, baby. Suck me hard."

I lean forward, grasping at the headboard with one hand and tangling the other in Elise's blonde locks. I'm getting deeper with every thrust until she's taking me fully into her throat as I fuck her face.

My eyes are locked on her, watching as my cock disappears into her puffy pink lips, her eyes gleaming with need. I'm so close, but not this time. Not now.

Elise moans in disappointment when I pull out, gasping as she looks at me with lust. "I wanted to taste your cum."

"I know, but I want to seal this moment inside you," I promise her. Moving down, I kneel between her spread legs, grabbing her inner thighs as I stare at her. "I need your pussy. Are you ready?"

"Oh, my God, Keith. Inside me, please. Fill me." Her hips are bucking, trying to get closer to my cock, but she's limited by the ties, unable to get what she desperately needs.

I move my hands higher, spreading her lips and lining up my cock with her entrance, teasing her. "Whose pussy is this?"

She cries out, "It's yours. My pussy, my heart, my fucking soul, Keith."

An even better answer than I'd dreamed of. I reward her with a sharp thrust, going balls-deep in one motion, forcing a satisfied cry from her throat. I hold her hips up, her back arching as I pound her mercilessly, the pleasure overwhelming my shredded control.

"Fuck, Elise. You too . . . my heart, my soul." I grunt, accentuating every word with another powerful stroke of my cock. "I love you."

Elise's eyes fill with tears, but she's smiling so I know they're happy tears, and I feel her pussy quiver. "That's it, come all over my cock," I encourage her. "Squeeze me so tight with that little pussy. I can take it, and I'll fill you so full you can't even hold it all."

With a final thrust, she shatters in my arms, writhing and pulling hard on her arm restraints, but I don't lose rhythm, keeping the driving force hard and deep as she cries out my name over and over like a prayer.

Her voice rises as her pussy clamps around me, and the pressure is too much. I come hard, my balls pulling up tight and my spine tingling before I crash over and shudder my pleasure, emptying into her.

Pulling out, I jerk my cock a few last times, covering her pussy lips with the last few spurts of my essence, needing to mark her inside and out.

I shake my cock a few times, wanting every drop on her, and then use the head to smear it around on her. It's primal, probably something that would turn some women off, but that doesn't matter in this moment.

What matters is that I need to mark her and that Elise wants to be marked by me. Her pride at being covered in my cum is just as palpable as my delight in seeing her dirty like this. *Mine.*

I untie the restraints, gently rubbing her wrists and ankles to get the circulation back as I kiss each one delicately.

"You okay?"

She smiles, stretching and squirming around like a pleased kitten as she curls up into a ball. "So much better than okay. Only one thing could make it perfect."

"What's that?" I ask before realizing what Elise needs. Sliding behind her, I gather her in my arms, my finally sated cock nestling against her ass as I wrap myself around her as much as possible. "That's perfect."

## CHAPTER 22

### KEITH

I look at Carsen, unable to tell her exactly how I feel. Part of it, I guess, is that seeing her twirling in her dress, looking more mature than I've ever imagined possible scares the shit out of me. What happened to the little girl in pigtails who'd wake up in the middle of the night and beg to climb into bed with me so that I could keep the monsters away?

There's no evidence of that little girl now as she struts and twirls, looking comfortable in the short one-inch wedge heels that Sarah and Elise talked me into letting her wear. The other part of me is so damn proud of my little girl and the young woman she's growing up to become. It's an oddly oppositional pull to want to see who she can be while at the same time wanting to force her to stay my baby forever.

Carsen comes over to me, wrapping her arms around me in a hug. I look down, seeing just the hint of mascara and blush that Elise did for her, and when she smiles, she looks so much like the woman she's going to become it makes my heart ache. "I love you, Daddy. I'm sorry you can't take me to the dance."

"It's okay honey," I promise, rubbing my freshly shaved head.

The label wants me to get some new photos done for the next album and summer tour, and that means 'Keith Perkins' needs to be in full effect. "You look beautiful, baby. More like your mother every day. Did I ever tell you about the time I took her to our first high school dance?"

Carsen shakes her head, making me sigh. I know I don't talk about Janie much, but Carsen should hear these stories. Her mother loved her so much, and it certainly wasn't Carsen's fault that we fell out of love or what happened in the end.

"Come over here and sit down," I reply, noticing Sarah and Elise quietly moving toward the exit. I can see they understand. This is our time. "Over the years, Janie and I went to a few dances together. But the very first one was a winter formal. I wore what had to be the ugliest suit in existence. But she looked gorgeous in a white dress with little blue flowers on it. It actually looked a lot like what you're wearing now."

Carsen looks down, delight obvious on her face as she runs her hands along the skirt of her dress. "Really?"

I nod, smiling a little at the memory. "I was so nervous I didn't know how to dance at all. But your mom helped me, just swayed back and forth with me. It was a great night, the first of many. And that's what tonight will be for you too. The first of many greats as you grow up. I know she'd be real proud of the young lady you're becoming."

Carsen's eyes are shining, and when I open my arms, she runs into them, giving me a big hug and laying her head on my shoulder, climbing into my lap a little. She barely fits, but that's okay. I hold her tight, knowing that my little girl is growing up so damn fast. Too fast, and I want to freeze time right here, where she's on the cusp of leaving her innocent childhood behind and becoming a teenager.

A teenage daughter? What the hell am I going to do?

I don't know how to raise a teenage daughter. Hell, I barely survived my teen years with my sanity intact. I know I'll have my hands full when she starts being interested in boys, that's for sure.

But as I look around, I know I'm not alone. Sarah and Elise are still in the doorway, holding hands and watching the scene between Carsen and me with watery smiles. They're so different, yet so vital and similar.

Sarah has been there for me almost since the very beginning, sacrificing so much to make our lives work as I chase my music dreams. She's been essential to my becoming a true man, and she's never complained.

And Elise has fit in nearly seamlessly to our little family, bringing with her sass and joyfulness, and a love of life that's reignited the passion in my own heart. It's not what some would call a picture-perfect life, but it's perfect for me, and I'm so damn thankful for it.

Sarah glances at her watch. "All right, young lady. Go grab your purse and let's go."

Carsen runs off to her room and Sarah pats my shoulder. "Good job, Keith. I was scared you'd end up locking her in her room and not let her go."

I smile, knowing that I'd considered it, but I also know I can't stop my little girl from growing up. "It definitely crossed my mind, but I figured you two would stop me."

Elise chuckles and comes over, sitting on my knee and putting her arms around my shoulders. "Well, I'm the bad influence here, so the plan was for Sarah to distract you while I showed Carsen how to sneak out a window. I figure it's a life skill that'll serve her well."

I growl at her. "You'll teach her no such thing."

There's a moment where the unsaid threat hangs in the air, tension coiled around us, then it breaks as we all bust up laughing. Elise leans into me and gives me a smack on the cheek. "Okay, we talked about it but I wouldn't have actually shown her how to sneak out. Probably. Maybe."

I love her brattiness, knowing that she's joking and wouldn't actually lead Carsen astray, but to tease me about it is enough to warrant a bit of a spanking later, the kind that leaves us both more than satisfied, and that makes my smile more than a bit predatory and we both know it.

Sarah clears her throat, turning toward the hallway. "Well, on that note, I'll be leaving now. I'll pick up Carsen and bring her home tomorrow mid-morning. Maybe be dressed this time?"

I grin, but Elise blushes. It's a pretty sight and makes me want her round ass the same flushed pink color.

As Carsen jets back into the room, I call out some last-minute reminders. "You've got your phone to call if you need anything. Have fun, baby. Sarah will pick you up at Kaitlyn's tomorrow after your sleepover, and then you can tell us all about the dance. Behave, young lady!"

Carsen runs back, a knowing look on her face as she kisses my cheek. "I love you too, Dad."

And then she's gone in a flash, so much sooner than I expected. I sit in my chair, stunned at how fast it happened. Sarah gives me one more smile as she follows Carsen out to the car, and they're gone. To my baby's first dance.

The silence is deafening but slowly becomes filled with promise and potential as I realize we're alone all night. I meet Elise's mouth in a soft kiss, pulling her body flush to mine. "Thank you for being here tonight. I know Carsen liked that we were all here to celebrate her first dance, and she was thrilled with the dress you found."

Elise smiles, snuggling tighter against me and melting into my arms. "I'm glad I was here too. She looked beautiful and I think she liked the story about her mom."

I apprise her carefully, running my hand up and down Elise's arm, knowing I'd have to talk with her about this but hopeful there isn't a problem. "That didn't bother you, did it?"

"Of course not!" Elise says, sitting up and smiling. "A girl needs her mother, even if it's only through stories. She's lucky to have had a mother who loved her and a dad who can tell her those stories. Plus, Sarah is a great role model for her. She's a loved girl."

"She is. And so are you."

Elise smiles at me, obviously pleased. "I know it's fast, but I'm hoping that I can be . . . well, not a mom—I think Sarah's got that role covered—but at least a good friend and role model for her too."

"I think it's not too early to think about that," I reassure her, giving her another kiss, already getting lost in her sweetness. Suddenly, there's a shrill beeping from the nearby kitchen. Sitting back, I laugh a little sorrowfully. "Goddamn phone. I'd better check it anyway in case it's Carsen."

Elise lets me up, and I go into the kitchen, where it's sitting on the counter, still ringing away. I check the screen, but it says unknown number. Normally, I'd let it go to voicemail considering not many people have this number, but it could be Carsen calling from a friend's mom's phone or something, so I pick up. "Hello."

There's a moment of silence, then a man's voice comes on, sounding muffled but still distinctly male. "Keith Perkins?"

"Who's asking?" I reply, the hairs on the back of my neck standing up.

"Mr. Perkins, we need to meet," a voice says, more clear now and almost . . . snooty sounding. "I've come into some information I think you'd be rather interested in. Write this address down. 3489 Johnson Boulevard, right off Main. Be here in one hour."

"What?" I ask, wondering if this asshole is drunk or something. "What are you talking about? Meet for what?"

Elise steps in my field of view, a concerned look on her face. "Everything okay?" she mouths silently. I shrug, and she lifts an eyebrow.

I hold up one finger, asking her to wait a second to fire off the questions I can see in her eyes, and focus on listening to the man on the phone. "One hour. 3489 Johnson Boulevard," he repeats. "Do not be late, Mr. Perkins. I'm certain you won't like the consequences if someone else were to get this information before you do."

There's a click and the line goes dead as the man hangs up. I stare at my phone for a moment, feeling like I've just been punched in the gut.

"Who was that?" Elise asks as I set my phone down. "What's wrong, Keith? You look pale as a ghost."

"I don't know," I reply, trying to keep my voice level. "A guy said that he has information I'd be interested in. Gave me an address and said to be there in an hour."

"What?" Elise asks, shocked. "What are you going to do?"

I shake my head, running my hands over my smooth dome. "I don't know."

I search my memories, replaying the conversation again, looking for clues what this could be about, a sinking feeling in my stomach. He said I wouldn't like it if someone else got the information. That sounds like a threat, whatever it is. Of course, my brain leapfrogs to Carsen first, since she's always my greatest secret, but there's no reason for anyone to know about her.

Elise, ever the investigator, stays calm, trying to be helpful. "What's the address? Maybe we can look it up and get a clue?"

"3489 Johnson," I recite for her, and her jaw drops.

"Oh, my God!" she gasps, her voice trailing off into a whisper. "No way."

"What? Do you know the address?"

She nods, her face frozen in horror. "That's my office, Keith. That's the address of *The Daily Spot*."

Elise's office. Okay, keep it cool . . . "We should go. Maybe it's just about the articles?" I say hopefully, knowing I'm full of shit even as I say it. The man didn't introduce himself like it was a professional call, and he specifically said he had information I wouldn't like.

The truck ride into town is silent, both of us considering a million possibilities for what we're walking into.

Pulling in, it looks like a normal office building on a weekend, empty and just waiting, recovering after a busy week before it gets swarmed again on Monday with worker ants trying to hustle a buck.

The main parking lot is empty except for one Mercedes parked up front. "Guess that's the mystery man."

Elise's voice shakes, and her hand comes to cover her mouth. "That's Donnie's car."

My phone buzzes again, and I look to see I've got a text message. *Upstairs, sixth floor. Front's unlocked.*

Elise reaches out, and I take her hand as we go inside, the empty, nearly dark lobby making things even more foreboding. We take the elevator up to the sixth floor, stepping off and following the only light visible, a dim glow that brightens as we approach. "Is this . . .?"

"My office," Elise whispers in reply, pointing at the etched glass. "At least, the lobby."

We open the door and follow the glow to another office, where inside, we find a round weasel-looking man sitting behind a large desk. Even before he speaks, the crystal bowl of jelly-beans on the corner of his desk tells me exactly who he is. "Donnie."

Donnie doesn't look surprised, but instead his ruddy face glows, obviously pleased. "Keith! You don't mind if I call you Keith, do you? That whole Mr. Perkins shit is for people who aren't friends, and I think you and I are going to be very good friends. Elise . . . so good to see you too. I wasn't sure I'd be seeing you tonight." He pauses, a comical sneer on his face. "Oh, who am I kidding? Of course, I knew you were at Keith's tonight!" He claps his hands twice, like he's overjoyed at our being here, as if this is some twisted fucking social call.

I don't respond, keeping my gaze on the man. I don't trust him. He's too at ease here, delighted at calling the shots as we come running to his territory when he beckoned. I sit in one of the chairs in front of his desk, wanting to show that I don't perceive him as a threat. Elise follows my lead, sitting in the other chair, but she looks scared and disgusted at the same time.

As we sit, there's a sound behind us and Francesca walks in, shutting the door behind her and going over to Donnie's side to perch on the narrow built-in bookshelf behind him. Putting a well-manicured hand on Donnie's shoulder, she sneers at Elise, smug satisfaction rolling off her in waves.

Donnie looks over his shoulder for a moment, patting Francesca's bare knee like you'd pat a strange dog on the head. "Thank you, Fran. We're just getting started."

She smiles wanly at him, but I catch the flash of disgust in her eyes at his touch. His eyes stay locked on her leg so Donnie doesn't notice her reaction.

Donnie turns back to Elise and me. "So, Elise. I have to say, I've been mostly pleased with your work. It's well-written and if I was running *Country Music Weekly*, you'd probably be getting a raise. However, this is the goddamn *Daily Spot*, and your articles are decidedly lacking on . . . juiciness."

He says the word juiciness with emphasis, spittle pooling at the corners of his mouth. Reaching over, he picks up a small handful of jellybeans and pops a few in his mouth.

Elise starts to speak, but Donnie waves her off. "Don't bother telling me there's nothing again. You've already said it enough, and I'm well aware that you're lying. After all . . . you've given me all the dirt I need."

Elise's eyes snap to me, but I keep my eyes locked on Donnie, trying to get a read on him. Looking at Elise, he smirks, chewing his jellybeans like a cow with its cud as he grins smugly. "I suspected there was more, that you were holding out on me. So I assigned my favorite reporter to investigate."

I let my eyes tick up to Francesca, remembering how we'd run into her at brunch. I'd dismissed it to reassure Elise, but it hadn't been a coincidence at all.

For her part, Francesca adjusts herself self-righteously, like the cat who just got the cream. She even seems to preen a bit as she re-crosses her legs, an obviously practiced move designed to look sexy.

I look back to find Donnie still eyeing Elise with a leering appraisal. "You're quite good at following a mark, Elise," he continues, his jaws never stopping as he smacks his way through another candy. "Seems you're quite a bit less adept at being followed. Usually, you never even noticed."

Donnie smiles at Elise like she's prey he's preparing to devour, but even though he's insulting her, I'm the real target here. I know that with every bit of dread running through my blood right now. My fingers tighten on the arms of the chair, and it's only thirty years of self-control that prevent me from grabbing him and jacking him up right now.

Francesca interrupts, puffing up even more as she giggles, but the sound is more mean-girl than sweet. "You really should be more aware. I followed you for days . . . to Keith's, to the cabin, to dinner, to the mall. The cabin was a little hard, but nothing a good telephoto lens couldn't fix. And you never suspected a thing!"

"You backstabbing, dirty little bitch—" Elise says, starting to get up, but Donnie claps, getting our attention again.

"So, as Francesca was following you, looking for the dirt *you* were supposed to be finding, we discovered something rather interesting. It didn't take long to figure out that you two are sleeping together. A bit salacious to fuck the talent, Elise, and definitely a bit of slumming on your part, Keith."

"Fuck you, you fucking dirt-peddling slimeball," I growl. "So what if two consenting adults are having sex? Is this what passes as shocking news these days?"

Donnie laughs, looking at me like I'm dense. "Well, it could be a good story. Trust me, as they say, sex sells. But more important is what it led us to discover. It seems that in addition to fucking a tabloid reporter, you seem to be doing it to buy her silence . . . about your twelve-year-old daughter."

I can't stop the growl that tears from the depths of my chest, and I hear Elise gasp next to me. I'd known walking into this tonight that this was probably what was coming, but hearing it straight from this asshole's mouth is more than I can take. I'm going to tear his heart out and shove a crystal bowl of jelly-beans in its place.

"Whatever you think you know, you'd best keep your fucking mouth shut about it," I threaten, my lip curling.

Donnie steeples his fingers, regarding me coolly as he opens a file folder on his desk, spreading out picture after picture, along with detailed reports of our outings. "If I had a dollar for every person who's threatened to kick my ass over what I find out, I'd be rich enough to get out of this gig and retire," he says, pushing the photos toward me.

They're sharp, hi-def, and show a variety of things. Sure, there are a few of me and Elise getting romantic . . . but what's even more hurtful is me hugging Carsen. Of us at the restaurant. Of me with my little girl. There are others too . . . of Carsen by herself, or with Sarah when she's getting picked up. "There are a couple of possibilities here, but what happens is totally up to you."

"What do you want?" I snarl, only the thought of ending up in jail and Child Services taking Carsen away from me keeping me in my chair.

"Well, this can go one of two ways, and I'm being gracious enough to let you choose," Donnie says greasily. "Option one, you will pay me a half-mil each year that you want this secret to stay quiet. My understanding is that Carsen's twelve. So probably, you'll want to wait until she's at least eighteen. So let's say $3.5million to make it easy?"

"You son of a bitch," Elise rasps, but Donnie plunges on.

"Option two, I'll publish an exclusive story breaking the news of your secret child and the relationship you had to keep it quiet. Either way, I win. I get money from you directly or I get notoriety for breaking a huge story and make money on clicks and sales. Win-win either way for me."

I'm furious, and it's taking every bit of my control to keep from jumping over this desk and pounding this weasel's face. Elise is mad too, but not nearly as controlled as I am.

She's like a screeching wildcat, vaulting out of her chair to slam her hands down on the desk, sending Donnie's jellybean bowl tumbling to the carpet where it bounces. "What the fuck, Donnie? You can't go around blackmailing people! You cannot publish this story. She's just a little girl!"

Donnie laughs mockingly, his voice pitching high into a screeching falsetto that's clearly a mockery of Elise's voice. "You can't blackmail people! She's just a little girl!" He laughs again, leaning back in his chair. "Of course I can. You think this is the first story to get squashed this way? If only you knew the celebs and their secrets in my little black book of dirt. So many juicy stories, all ready to be hung out like dirty laundry for everyone to consume. Or, for the right price, washed and sanitized and never to see the light of day. Why the fuck do you think I stick around this shitrag of a 'news source' with the shit pay and bennies? I get ten times that off the books. You can help the Save the Donnie Foundation . . . or the world can find out about you. Your choice."

I clench my hands in my lap, trying to get ahold of myself. "I'll sue you and this piece of shit tabloid you're running. I'll burn this place to the ground and piss on the ashes."

Donnie shrugs, unconcerned. "Go ahead. But since what I'm reporting is the truth, you'll lose. It won't matter by then anyway, because I'll have already published the story and gotten the sales and the money off your secrets. You'll just add fuel to the fire by suing."

"And in the meantime, I'll make sure every sleazy paparazzi I know is at your house. They'll follow Sarah, try to get interviews and pictures with Carsen. What she's wearing, which boy in school she thinks is cute. Do I need to continue?"

He's right, and I hate that he's thought of this from every fucking angle, obviously experienced at doing this while I'm stumbling. Like he said, this isn't his first round of blackmail, and I bet he's got a basketball team of lawyers ready to cover his ass.

I feel outplayed. He's planned ahead, and I'm still reeling, hoping this is a nightmare I'll wake up from any minute. All I can think of is kicking Donnie's ass, and while that might be worth it for a few short seconds, it'll just land me in a lawsuit. Seeing the resolve on my face, Donnie offers a consolation.

"You don't have to decide right now. I suspect getting those kinds of funds prepped is time-consuming, even for someone like you. I'll give you some time to decide. The article is already written, ready to be public with one click if you don't have the money ready to transfer to my account . . . oh, let's see. Today's Saturday . . . so how about by five o'clock Monday? Understood?"

I dip my chin once, knowing I'll need to evaluate the risks of this proposition carefully. I've got roughly forty-eight hours to figure out what the fuck to do, and I figure I'll need every minute. "Fine. Elise, let's go."

"See you at work Monday morning!" Francesca calls out nastily as we leave the office. We say nothing as we get in the elevator and leave the office.

The truck ride is awkward until Elise breaks the silence, rating. "I can't believe this! I knew Donnie was a sleazeball, but this is beyond what I'd ever imagined."

She's pissed, which helps, but I'm furious, and my mouth is running away from my brain. "Just like a paparazzi, always looking for juicy gossip even it ruins people's lives."

I see Elise flinch, knowing my comment about Donnie likely hit a little close to home for her too. I clench my teeth, biting back the rest of what I wanted to say as she looks down into her lap, cringing. "I never ruin people's lives," she says, so quietly I can barely hear her over the noise of my engine. "Just report stupid shit about them. Nothing like this."

"But even that stupid shit hurts people, Elise," I growl, watching the road ahead. "Even what you think is stupid can be important to others. All of this started because you reported something seemingly inconsequential, but look what's happened. My buying some fucking maxi pads for my little girl's first period has turned into a $3.5 million blackmail proposition."

She makes a small sound, hurt by my words, but I'm angry, lashing out. "I should've fucking known better," I mutter, shaking my head as I get off the freeway and head toward my house. "Should've done the fucking articles and sent you on your merry way and you wouldn't have found out shit. I told myself I wasn't going to get involved while Carsen was young. She's my number-one priority and I let myself get caught up." I bang a fist to the steering wheel, frustration and anger bubbling past the boiling point in my veins. "I knew better, I fucking knew better."

"Keith, I'm sorry!" Elise cries out, her voice choked with anguish. "Really, I am. But this isn't my fault. Maybe we should've been more careful, but it was bound to come out eventually. You can't keep her a secret forever!"

"Like hell I can't! I've kept her hidden for ten fucking years!" I half yell, pulling over and glaring at Elise. "We were doing just fine until I thought I could have more, and look what's happened! I hurt the one person I'm supposed to protect!"

Elise blinks, her eyes looking like I just slapped her. Her eyes brim with tears, but she's too strong to cry, and instead, her face hardens. "I think you should take me home."

"Fine."

Neither of us says anything as I turn at the next light, pulling up to the curb by Elise's apartment five minutes later. She's out before I even put it in park, stomping toward the door, her hurt morphing into fury.

I'm so angry I don't even watch her go inside, just peeling out from the curb to get away from this nightmare that's become real. The ride home is maddening, my mind replaying everything Donnie said about my options and then hearing everything Elise and I said when we fought.

Yeah, I know I was in the wrong to say she started it. But I'm not exactly in my right mind. I'm not pissed at her. I'm a grown ass man and it was my decision to let Elise in. I'm just pissed about the situation and that I can't rewind time and figure out a way out of this.

Getting home, I walk inside and am instantly surrounded by silence. Sarah's at home, Carsen's at her sleepover, and Elise . . . isn't here. I have a momentary thought to have Sarah pick up Carsen early, just to be safe, but I hold off knowing that if her world is about to implode, she deserves one more night of innocent fun.

Sitting on the couch, I put my head in my hands. The quiet void surrounding me echoes the emptiness in my heart, which is quickly filling with anger. Not at Elise, not at myself even, but where it should be directed . . . at Donnie and his scheming. How did this get so fucked up?

# CHAPTER 23

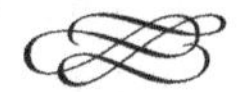

## ELISE

What the fuck just happened?

In the thirty minutes I've been home, I feel like that question keeps coming back into my head, like I'm stupid drunk or something and the world just isn't making any damn sense.

Donnie wants to blackmail Keith. And according to what I heard from the slimy, jellybean scarfing son of a bitch, he's done this before. Maybe lots of times. I always knew Donnie was an asshole, but every good editor has a strong streak of that in them. Can't get to that job without it.

But there's being an asshole . . . and there's this. And while I'm so disgusted with Donnie that I'm not even thinking of going to work on Monday, I'm hurt most by Keith.

He blames me for this shitstorm, or at least for starting the snowball down the hill. And from a certain point of view, he's right. But I've done nothing but help him hide Carsen since I found out about her, actively lying to Donnie and putting my job in jeopardy by not reporting it in the articles. Hell, I went to him with ideas for out and out lies to use that he could live with so that he could keep Carsen a secret!

It doesn't matter. Even if he's mad at me, I'm going to help him. I *have* to. I love him and Carsen, and I'll do whatever it takes to help them. That's what love's supposed to be, doing the right thing and taking care of those you love, even if it hurts you.

So that means I'm going to step up and do anything. Except pay the money, obviously. I don't have that kind of cash. I never really even considered whether Keith did either.

His fame, his wealth hasn't been a factor in our relationship at all. I love him for the bossy, intense, protective way he loves me and Carsen, not because of some sordid angle he's manipulating like Donnie insinuated.

I spend hours lying on the couch, not sleeping but just tossing and turning as I think, testing and discarding every idea my brain comes up with, my frustration growing as I think through the whole situation from every angle.

I flip-flop between anger, raging at the empty room around me, to crying in frustration, hot tears slipping down my face. It's just not right, it's not fair. Somewhere around midnight, I have an epiphany.

I need help, someone to bounce ideas off. And Keith doesn't want to talk to me right now. But right and fair . . . innocent ideas in a sadly dark world. I know someone brilliant who might be able to work some magic for me. Someone right, a little innocent, and whose sense of justice and fairness will make sure I might actually have a chance to conjure up righteous justice out of thin fucking air.

With crossed fingers, I call Maggie. She picks up after three rings, the background of her call telling me what's up even before her falsely abrasive voice comes on.

"This better be good because it's the middle of the night and I'm at work."

"Maggie, I need your help. Can you come over?"

Maggie's voice immediately changes, going back to the kind, open voice that I know and adore. "Elise, are you okay?"

"Yeah," I reply, glad I didn't take a left turn into Crazy World where Maggie's a jaded bitch like she sounded at first. "I just need your brain. Can you come?"

Maggie sighs, and I know the answer. "Not for a while. Closing's at two and then I have to clean up. Want to come to the club? It might actually help my cover, if you don't mind. Otherwise, I won't be able to get there until three thirty at the earliest."

I look down at myself, already schlubbing in sweats and knowing my face is red and splotchy from the tears. What the hell, it's not like anyone'd expect me to be going to see Maggie . . . not where she's undercover. "Yeah, it'll take me a bit to get presentable. But I'll meet you there. I've never been to a strip club, Maggie. What should I wear?"

Maggie sounds happy, and she probably is. "Nothing flashy. You're better off if you don't take attention from the working girls. They're . . . touchy. Just jeans, something casual and comfortable. Tell them you're looking for Megan."

I nod, then remember she can't see me. "Okay, I'll be there in a few."

After I hang up, I take her advice and keep it simple, just jeans and a t-shirt, not dumpy but not flashy. My hair and face are a lost cause, though. Five minutes of scrubbing only makes my cheeks and eyes look like I'm tweaking out or something. I pull my hair into a poufy messy bun that takes advantage of a freshly fucked look and slick on little bit of lip gloss. Looking in the mirror, I know it's barely passable, but fuck it. It's all I've got in me right now, and I head down to catch a ride over to the club.

The Uber driver gives me an odd look when he pulls up, verifying the address. I smile. Guess he doesn't drop off many single women to a female strip club at one in the morning.

The bouncer at the door looks like a monster, muscled and tattooed and looking more like an MMA fighter than a late-night doorman. His biceps are bulging against the crisp white button-down shirt he has on, his black jeans are slung low on narrow hips, and his boots look heavy enough to crack a skull with a solid kick. He's intimidating. Every pore of his body exudes a dangerous coolness that lets you know up front that he could fuck you up and walk away without a scratch. Oddly, it reassures me. There's no way shit goes down in this club without Mr. Chill here taking care of it. Maggie couldn't be safer, and in re-evaluating him, I guess you could call him handsome in his own way. Kinda the way a lion is pretty . . . from afar, and when it's not looking at you like dinner. I'm not sure how this guy is looking at me though. His eyes are hidden behind mirrored shades, probably for the intimidation factor.

He obviously notices me though, raising an eyebrow just enough that I can see it over the rim of his glasses as I approach. "You here hunting your man?" he rumbles in a voice that promises violence if someone pushes him too far. "We don't want any old ladies causing problems."

I shake my head, giving him the most reassuring smile I can muster right now. "No, just meeting a friend. She works here . . . Megan? Short, pretty, and sweet as pie?"

The smile he gives is so fleeting that if I wasn't watching his face intently, I'd never know his mouth had even twitched a quarter-inch at the edges or that his chin dipped maybe a half-inch. "Meg's here, all right. I'll waive the cover for you since you're her friend."

I nod my thanks and step inside, uncertain about this but desperate for help. Inside, it's dark and smells like a mixture of stale beer and floral perfume with an undercurrent of cigarette smoke that immediately scratches at the back of my throat.

When Maggie told me she was working at a strip club, the first thought that came to my mind was sleazy, but the tasteful decorations and the women I can see are way too high-quality for that label. Maybe . . . erotic? I'd need my thesaurus at home to really get it right.

The music is thumping, the heavy bass pulsing through my chest as a stunning woman wearing black heels, lingerie that basically consists of a few skinny strings, and a seductive smile is twirling and working up and down a pole on stage. It's an amazing display of strength and grace, and the acrobatics momentarily stun me, but when someone bumps me from behind, I remember to move and work my way toward an empty table off to the side.

There's no way I'd want to be close to the action here, looking at the leering faces of the jackals surrounding the stage. It's a shame too, because for all of the sexual arousal hanging in the air, the dancer's routine is as beautiful and elegant as it is sexy.

Randomly, a thought pops in my head to check out a pole fitness class, but before it can solidify, Maggie struts up. She's glittery still, but at least she's wearing a top and clothes, although I don't think I've ever imagined Mags in a black bustier top and miniskirt before. "Hey, honey! You made it, you must *really* need some help. Want me to grab you a beer, or do you need something a little stronger?"

I consider asking for a shot, but I know I need to keep my head straight to figure a way out of this. "Just a beer. Gotta keep my head straight. Anything good on tap?"

Maggie nods, adjusting her glasses. "Sure thing, let me grab one of the local brews and I'll see if I can take my break in a few."

"That's fine. I know I'm intruding on your work, so whenever you have a minute is fine. At least there's a show," I reply, indicating the girl on stage, who's currently hanging upside down with her legs so splayed she sort of looks like the letter

T. I'm jealous. I don't think I could get my legs that wide apart even if Keith were . . . nope, don't need to go there right now.

Maggie grins and bounces off, and I'm struck by how even in this club with her tits popped up and her ass hanging out, Maggie comes across as cute and sweet. Sexiest Girl Scout candy striper in the whole world, and she's working undercover in a strip club.

Maggie has an innocence about her even when I see her banging on her tray as she claps for a particularly difficult trick the woman on stage is performing. I follow her sightline and see the buxom brunette flashing her panty-covered pussy to the audience as she stands on one foot and raises the other leg high, splitting vertically in the air like a gymnast as she leans way far back. It's almost a ballet-like position, minus the leotard and tutu. And then when she grabs the pole, flipping herself up onto it again, the audience goes wild, clapping and whistling.

Holy crap! I *definitely* need a pole fitness class if it can teach me how to do that.

Maggie brings me a beer, and I lean back, sipping it as another girl makes her way on stage.

"Hey, baby, you enjoying the show?" a guy asks, coming up. He's a little tipsy but not drunk, and while he's not hideous, he wouldn't be my type even if I wasn't seeing Keith.

"Sorry, just waiting for my girlfriend to take a break," I reply, letting him draw his own conclusions. Thankfully, *girlfriend* has so many different meanings. The guy looks intrigued for a moment, and I wonder if he's going to press his luck, and I cut my eyes toward the door for the bouncer just in case. The guy immediately chills out and shrugs in defeat when he sees the bouncer look this direction, and he takes a step back, tossing back the rest of his drink.

"Have a nice night," he says simply before disappearing back toward the stage.

For the next hour, the scenery turns into a blur of sweat, stale smoke, glitter, and thumping music between two slowly-sipped beers. Maggie never does get a chance to take a break, but when the sound guy gets on and says that Tina Tempest is the last act and they need to clear out, the patrons comply quickly.

"I need to change and I'll sit down with you," Maggie says, looking tired but still concerned about me. "More privacy out here than in a back room."

When Maggie comes out a few minutes later, clad in a tank top, baggy sweats, and Ugg boots, I can't help but crack a big smile. She's wiped all the makeup off her face and pulled her hair up into a cute off-center ponytail, looking more like an eighteen-year-old girl on any college campus in the US than a strip club waitress. Or more importantly, a reporter. All traces of her night in the strip club are wiped clean.

Well, except for the glitter sparkling in her cleavage. "You look great. How do you do that . . . sexy sweetheart to girl next door in two minutes flat?"

She looks pleased at my compliment and sits down, pulling her knees up to her chest and curling up like a tiny spitfire ball of cuteness. "Just how I was made, I guess. I'm totally not a femme fatale type for sure."

"Speaking of femme fatales, you won't believe what Francesca has been doing," I growl, glad I've got the two beers in me or else I'd be throwing shit, I'm still so fucking angry.

"What?" Maggie asks, sensing my displeasure. "She didn't . . . stab you in the back, did she?"

I laugh bitterly, nodding. "Like it's nobody's fucking business. She's been following me, on Donnie's orders! Me! Like I'm a target."

"And?" Maggie asks, not getting upset yet, "What did she find?"

I stop, immediately defensive. "How do you know she found something?"

"Because you've been sitting in a strip club for over an hour waiting to talk to me, ergo, she found something," Maggie explains matter-of-factly. "If she hadn't, you'd have just told me the story and called her a stupid bitch on Monday. Am I right? So what did she find?"

"Well, I can't exactly say everything she found," I reply before taking a deep breath. Fuck it, right now I need to trust someone with some secrets, or else I'm going to be spinning my wheels and going nowhere. "But she figured out pretty quickly that Keith and I are dating."

Maggie reaches out, putting a hand on my arm. "You two are . . . dating?"

I nod, pushing on. "There's more, but that's not my secret to tell and I promised I wouldn't. Suffice it to say, Donnie made it sound like Keith is just fucking me to keep me quiet. But that's not it. I love him, and he loves me."

Maggie smiles, leaning back in her chair and giving a little fist pump to the stale sky. "That's awesome, Elise! I mean, I hate you too—you got the hunkiest guy in country music and you held out on me . . . but I understand why you didn't spill that around the coffee pot at the office. So, what's the problem?"

"Donnie gave Keith an ultimatum," I reply, loving Maggie totally in that instant as she cheers for me. "He said Keith either has to pay him three and a half million dollars to keep quiet or Donnie will publish a story with the secret Keith doesn't want to get out and get his money that way. Donnie set it up pretty well. Apparently, he's blackmailed other celebrities too so he's got experience. Keith has until Monday night to decide."

Maggie looks pissed, slamming her tiny little fist on the table and making my two beer glasses rattle. "Donnie is such a creep. I'm honestly not surprised he's pulling something like this, nor that he's good at it, considering how long he's been in this business. He's manipulative and a great strategist. But there's always a weak point to every plan. We just have to find it and exploit it," she declares, holding up first one finger and then another like she's making a to-do list.

I sigh, hope lighting bright for a second before I crash back down. I look at the last dregs of beer in the nearest glass and realize it looks a lot like my life right now, a room temperature puddle of piss. "There's no weak point. I've been thinking for hours now. The only way to keep Donnie quiet is to pay him off, and I don't trust that he wouldn't get the money and then publish the story anyway. We both know he's fine with double-dipping considering that he slept around on his ex-wife with Francesca."

Instead of joining me in my misery, I can see Maggie's brain turning. I quiet down, watching the wheels spin as she talks silently to herself, until suddenly, her face breaks wide in a huge ear-to-ear smile. "I know what the weak point is, but you're not gonna like it."

"What? Anything, God. Help me!"

"The weak point is Donnie. He literally gives zero fucks about keeping his life private, flaunting things most people would hide—like sleeping with Francesca—so that he's untouchable. And in doing so, he assumes most folks do actually give a shit and want to keep their secrets just that . . . secret. He targets people he thinks will do anything, pay anything, and he's set his sights on Keith."

I see where she's going, and I nod, feeling a light at the end of the tunnel as she continues.

"Donnie's entire plan hinges on that initial supposition that Keith will want to keep this quiet, and that he'll do anything, and that will be enough to get the millions. I think he'll likely take the money and publish too. That's just the sort of snake he is. Probably not even give Francesca a decent cut of it either. He'll just keep stringing her along until she's too deep in to ever go anywhere else, then cut her free when he finds his next fresh-faced girl willing to sleep her way to the top."

Maggie nods sadly, sparing a bit of sympathy for Francesca. I guess I can understand why. That, and Maggie's the reincarnated spirit of Marsha Brady. "That's right up his alley. So, based on that, the secret is coming out . . . whatever it is. Keith just needs to get in front of it. It's the only way. Go on the morning talk show racket and apologize for the drug use and check into rehab . . ."

I give her a severe look, my inner feelings flaring up. "He's not on drugs."

Maggie smirks, knowing she's been caught. "Had to try. Maybe apologize for the . . . red room of pain and explain that you're into it too?"

I laugh, wondering if Maggie's brain is really as innocent as she seems. "Nope, not it either. Really, I can't say. But I know Keith isn't going to want to publicize it. He's worked his whole life to keep this secret."

"Well, I have to say, I don't think he's going to have a choice about whether it gets out," Maggie says, shrugging reluctantly. "But he can decide *how* it gets out."

My jaw drops as something comes back to me. Donnie said the record company's initial push to have Keith do the interviews with me was so that they could . . . control the narrative.

Quietly, I murmur the phrase to myself, like a magic incantation that can change the very fabric of the universe. "Control the narrative."

"What?"

Maybe . . . maybe it can. Getting excited, I reach across the table and grab Maggie's hand. "We have to control the narrative. Donnie's power is in that he's the only one with the information, but what if he wasn't? Keith could do the morning show racket and tell it himself. Then Donnie won't get the blackmail money and he won't be able to publish it and get the exclusive breaking news. It takes away his power and lets Keith control the narrative! Control the narrative! You're a fucking genius!"

Maggie laughs, cute and self-conscious now. "Well, sometimes yes and sometimes no. Just glad this seems to be a yes-time for your sake. So, you're really not going to tell me the secret?"

"Nope, but I'm gonna need your help getting Keith on TV the day after tomorrow *without* telling the shows why and keeping the whole appearance *Top Secret* so Donnie doesn't find out and try and jump out in front of the whole thing. Can you do that?"

"Yeah, I can make a call or two and make that happen for a top name like Keith," Maggie says. "I know a few people down at the local station, and if it's Keith, they can probably get him on the national circuit if we promise them a big enough prize. But shouldn't his manager do that though?"

"Well, that's my next problem. I have to get Keith on board with this plan because he's not going to like it," I reply, sighing a little. "He's not going to like it at all. We kinda had a fight about the whole thing. He didn't really blame me, exactly, but he was mad at himself for dating me because it's led to this whole drama. He's got some definite anger toward the media and paparazzi, and I've got this huge glaring neon sign on my forehead, blinking 'REPORTER' in big capital letters right now, and it's got his shields up."

"Well, this isn't really your fault, exactly, but maybe it is time for you to do something a little different if you're pursuing something a bit longer term with Keith," Maggie counsels me. "Not saying you're not good, Elise. I mean, you've taught me a few things in the time we've worked together, but a gossip reporter and a country music star don't exactly sound like a match made in heaven. And we both know you're too good for this job anyway. Maybe you really could parlay this series into something with one of the legit music industry magazines? Or do some investigative journalism that's not so, I don't know . . . gossipy? Not like you can go to an award ceremony after-party on Keith's arm and be trusted if you're publishing all the drunk hookups on Monday morning," she says jokingly, but she's on target.

I sigh, knowing Maggie's right, but there are so many variables up in the air. "I know, and I'll have to figure that out. But right now, I just want to figure out this thing with Keith. Thanks so much . . . Megan."

I give her a little smile as I use her cover name, glad that our conversation has been private even in this club and trusting that she will help me. Giving the bouncer a nod of thanks as he *ushers* out a few overindulged guests, I leave, stepping into one of the waiting Ubers.

I've got a lot of shit to do, and not a lot of time to do it in. So the only question I have is . . . do I wait until sunrise to talk to Keith about this . . . or wake him up at three in the morning to deal with it?

# CHAPTER 24

## KEITH

I stare at the walls of my kitchen bleakly, my mind constantly replaying that smug asshole telling me that I'm going to pay him or he'll expose Carsen to public scrutiny. Like any teenage girl needs that! I'm furious at Donnie, but maybe even more at myself.

I couldn't sleep at all last night, racked by anger and punishing myself for being a total dumbass. I was so worked up by what Donnie said, and my anger at the situation, that I took it out on Elise. I know that was a really shitty thing to do. She didn't deserve to have me give her shit, especially since she never intended for this to happen.

But I have to push that to the back burner and figure out what the fuck I'm going to do about Donnie's threat. The problem is, I've drawn a blank as to any course of action.

I can't sue him. He's right that it wouldn't do any good because it would be too slow-moving to stop him, and he is telling the truth.

I can't go beat his ass into a pulp. That'd get the cops involved and only get Donnie what he wants, a fat payout in the form of a civil suit.

I even had a dark few minutes late last night, well, early this morning, where I thought about hiring a hitman and taking Donnie out. Problem solved. But that's not who I am, nor is it the legacy I want to leave to my daughter. And as much as it sounds like a solution, I know it's just one for a TV show ending where the good guy gets away scot-free every time. Reality is a lot different, and as the hours go on, I'm still trying to figure out my way past the harshness of that reality.

I'm still stumped, slamming my fourth coffee at eleven in the morning when Sarah and Carsen come blowing in, all girly giggles and excitement. "Daddy, oh, God, I had the best time! You wanna hear about it?"

My head is pounding and I'm worried as shit, but I can see the swoony hearts in her eyes like some old-school cartoon.

Still, it's hard to find the will to be happy for her. All I can think about is that my baby's first dance was probably going to be her last because by the next one, she'll need security guards and won't know whether to trust people's friendship because of who she is or because of who I am.

It makes my blood boil, and I realize it's carrying over as Carsen and Sarah have stopped giggling, looking at me worriedly.

"Daddy?" Carsen asks, her smile disappearing and breaking my heart. "What's wrong?"

I thought about telling Sarah during one of my more desperate moments of trying to sort this all out, but I held off, hoping I'd be able to find a solution before scaring her with all of this. But she can see things aren't right. "What happened?"

I try to school my face into a calm mask and shake my head. "Nothing, everything's fine. Hey, Carsen, can you go hang out upstairs for a few minutes? I need to talk to Aunt Sarah about something, and then you can tell me all about the dance, okay?"

She nods, but I can see that she's not fooled by my forced calmness. "Sure, Dad. Holler when you're done and I'll tell you about it."

"I can't wait, baby," I reply, giving her a hug as she passes me to head upstairs. It hurts, because I know even as she hugs me that her world's about to shatter, and that like Humpty Dumpty, it can't be put back together again.

"So tell me what's going on," Sarah says, going over to the cabinet next to the plates where she gets out the Tylenol she keeps there. "And take these. I can see you wincing every time the sunlight sparkles in the window, and you kept wincing every time Carsen laughed. Guess you didn't sleep?"

I shake my head slowly, taking three Tylenol along with a glass of water, which somehow tastes a lot better than it should. "That fucking bastard is trying to blackmail me."

"What?" Sarah asks, shocked but trying to keep her voice down. "Back up, start slow, and omit nothing."

I actually don't tell her everything, just giving her the basics because I just don't have it in me right now. "And in the end, that jellybean loving motherfucker said if I don't pay up by five tomorrow, he's going to publish."

Sarah nods, biting her lip as she thinks. "And Elise? What does she say about this?"

Fuck. I thought my headache was doing better after telling the story, but Sarah's reminder brings back the pain around my temples. "Well, I was so fucking furious that I might've said some things . . ."

"Keith, you stupid son of a bitch," Sarah says softly, reprovingly. She sighs, waving her hand. "What did you do?"

"I might've blamed her for starting this whole mess with her first article and told her that if I'd just done the damn articles and kept her at arm's length, I wouldn't be in this mess now . . . and that I knew better than to date her," I reply. "It hurt her, and I dropped her off at her place. I haven't heard from her since then."

"This isn't her fault and you know it!" Sarah says, still trying to keep her voice down but managing to yell at me all the same. "From what you just said, she's been putting her own career at risk to keep this secret. She's done everything she can. It's not her fault a coworker got suspicious when she saw us at the mall."

I rage. "I didn't even know about that! Until I saw the pictures of the three of you out shopping. Why didn't you tell me?"

Sarah grimaces. "We thought it was just bad luck. It's a mall, Keith. We thought the woman was shopping."

"That wasn't a coincidence. She followed Elise there and Elise didn't know it. Hell, she followed us all, and none of us caught her. She had pictures of us all." I huff, fuming as I remember the stack of photos.

Sarah snorts, shaking her head. "So you're mad at Elise because she should've recognized something you didn't even notice. How many times has she been followed before? What about *you*?"

I rub across my head, the calluses on my hands scratching on the smooth skin up there. "I know! I fucked up. I know that, and I spent most of the night divided between wanting to tear this Donnie asshole's head off and wanting to tear my own off for hurting Elise. What am I going to do?"

Sarah studies me for a moment, then comes over, putting a hand on my shoulder. "You're going to man up, like you always do. Call her, have her come over, and the three of us are going to figure out what to do . . . together. That's what family does, Keith. We'll stick together, through the good times and the fucking bad times."

I nod, knowing she's right, and I grab my phone, dialing Elise's number. It rings and rings, my hand drumming on the countertop in frustration as my mind runs in a hundred different exhaustion-and-caffeine-fueled directions before switching over to her voicemail. *"Hey, this is Elise. Leave me a message or send me a text. Check ya later!"*

"Uh, hey, Elise," I say, clearing my throat before I can continue. "I just wanted to say that I'm sorry. Can you call me back, please? We need to figure this out . . . and I need you."

I hang up, looking at Sarah, knowing my face shows my disappointment, my anger, and my sadness. She pats my shoulder again before giving me a little side hug. "She'll call back. She loves you, brother."

The reassurance feels empty even as it gives me a little whisper of useless hope. "But what if—"

Before I can finish my sentence, the doorbell rings. Sarah and I look at each other, and she gives me a nod. "I'll get it in case it's reporters."

There's a brief silence as she walks to the door, but when it opens, she laughs before calling out. "Hey, Keith? It is a reporter, but I think you'll want to see this one."

My heart speeds up and my jaw drops as Elise walks into the kitchen. She looks stressed, dark smudges under her eyes and her skin pale. Honestly, it looks like she had just as rough of a night as I did, and I know I look like hell too.

Still, I've never seen anything more beautiful in my life as I get up, crossing the kitchen to stand in front of her, wanting to embrace her but knowing there's something I need to do first. But I have to touch her, reassure myself that she's really here and not some insomnia-induced hallucination. Holding her upper arms gently, I wait for her to look up at me, needing her to see the truth in my words as I speak. "Elise, I'm so fucking sorry. I was scared and mad and I took it out on you. I shouldn't have. I love you."

I lift my head to look her in the eyes, and she's smiling a little, but it's tremulous and her eyes are a little sad. "I know, Keith. I'm sorry too. For starting this whole mess. If I hadn't put you on Donnie's radar, you wouldn't be in this situation now."

"We," I correct her, reaching out and taking her hands.

"Huh?" she asks, looking confused.

For the first time in what feels like a year but has only been less than twenty-four hours, a smile that isn't one of bitterness comes to my face. "*We* are in this situation. You, me, Sarah, and Carsen. You've made a place in this family, and I want to work with you to figure out what to do. This affects us all."

Elise stutters, a single tear rolling down her cheek as I gather her in, and she hugs me hard before stepping back. Wiping at her face, she takes a big breath and I can see her putting her emotions away, at least for now, and getting down to business. "Okay, good. Good, because I've got a plan and it'll work. But you're going to hate it. Can we sit down?"

I nod, gesturing to the living room, and we all sit down. I make sure to guide Elise to my side on the couch, needing to be in contact with her. Sarah sits across from us in one of her favorite easy chairs, leaning forward, her eyes darting between the two of us. "Judging by appearances, you two look like you got about thirty minutes of sleep last night . . . combined."

"Actually, I got about an hour," Elise admits. "But it sorta sucked. I was too busy trying to think and working some angles. I wanted to come over here to talk about it with you . . . but I wanted a full plan in place before I did. I was just worried you'd say no outright if I didn't have a full plan."

"Why do I feel like I'm repeating myself?" Sarah asks the sky, then sighs. "Start at the beginning, omit nothing."

Elise starts, telling us about visiting her friend at a strip club. "You told your friend about us? At a strip club?" I ask incredulously. "But . . . why?"

"Maggie's one of the smartest people I know," Elise replies. "I edited things and didn't say a thing about Carsen, and Maggie's someone who will respect that. And she gave me the idea that we've got to get out in front of this."

"What do you mean?" Sarah asks. "Get in front of it how?"

"Right now, Donnie's power lies in one thing only," Elise explains. "He thinks you're only going to consider one of two options. Let it blow up in your face and maybe try and deny . . . or pay up. But there's a third option."

"What?" I ask, even though I see Sarah's face dawning in realization. "Okay, guys, little words, haven't slept."

"We go public first," Sarah says, nodding. "Then we're in control."

Elise nods. "Keith, Carsen's going to become public knowledge one way or another. I don't trust Donnie not to take the money and then publish anyway. He's got zero fucks to give and nothing to lose. Hell, he'll come out way ahead that way and I'm sure that's his idea already. But if you go first, get out there and tell the story, then Donnie's going to have nothing. And you get to control the narrative."

"But . . ." I answer, taking a deep breath, trying to get my brain to line the fuck up and think straight. "It means going public."

"And we do it the right way . . . talking about Donnie's blackmail attempt," Elise explains. "Don't you see? This isn't just about you and Carsen. He's done this before and he'll do it again. You have a chance to control your narrative, but you also have a chance to control Donnie's narrative too. Let everyone know what a sleazeball he is, blackmailing and threatening people to create tabloid gossip headlines for cash. Get in front of both stories. It's the only way."

I shake my head, feeling desperate as my whole world seems to be turning to quicksand that's slipping through my fingers before sucking me down to my doom. "No. That defeats the whole purpose. The only thing I care about is keeping Carsen's life how she's used to. I'll just pay the money and pray that he keeps his word about not publishing the story. He's gotta have at least a little honor among thieves. If he's done this before and breaks his word now, nobody'll trust him in the future when he pulls the same shit, don't you see? It's the only scenario where she has any chance at being left alone."

Suddenly, Carsen steps in from the hallway, where she's obviously been eavesdropping. Part of me wonders for how long, and I'm too exhausted to be upset. "No, Dad. This guy's a bully, and the only way to stop him from hurting other people is if we stop him. Just tell people about me. That's what he's holding over your head? Who cares if people know you're my dad? I'm proud of being your daughter and I don't care if everyone knows."

If only it were that easy. "Carsen, you don't understand, baby. If everyone knows you're my daughter, it'll change your whole life. You might have to get security, change schools, always be on the watch, and never know who your real friends are. It'll change everything."

"I know, Dad. I understand, really, I do," Carsen says, coming over and sitting on the other side of me and Elise. "But, it's the right thing to do. Don't let a bully win. You're stronger than he is, and I'll be okay with whatever we have to do."

I'm torn. Carsen looks so certain, sitting next to me so tall and proud. I know she's strong, but she's still just a little girl and I wanted her to make this decision when she was a little older. I look at Sarah and Elise, and they're both nodding, agreeing with Carsen.

"Keith, she's right. It's the right thing to do. And you said we're a family, so we can do this together, support each other through whatever this storm brings," Elise says.

I look at Carsen, searching her eyes. Keeping her a secret has been my main focus for so long, and that's coming to an end, apparently. I'm terrified. Most of my instincts are telling me to just grab her up and go hide, leave music and everything behind. But she's right, I'm stronger than that.

And I don't want to leave.

I want to have a life with my daughter, my woman, and my sister, this crazy family unit we've created where we all fit together somehow, bringing happiness and growth and love into each of our lives in a way I never expected.

"Okay, I'll do it," I reply, leaning forward and putting my face in my hands, exhausted and knowing I can't wait. "Elise, set it up."

I thought she'd be happy, but she knows what this is costing me. Not in terms of money like Donnie wants, but it's costing me all the same in my peace of mind, which is going to be sorely lacking for a long time, I suspect.

Elise's eyes are somber, serious as she reaches into her purse and pulls out her phone, dialing quickly. "Maggie, it's a go," she says simply when the line's picked up. "Work your magic."

I hug Carsen to me tightly, hating that her world is about to change but knowing it's the only way.

Donnie needs to be stopped, and I can do that.

# CHAPTER 25

## ELISE

Sitting in the 'green room,' waiting as the makeup people do last-minute adjustments to Carsen's wardrobe and makeup next door, I'm struck by last-second indecision. "Keith, are you sure about this? I mean, I know it's my idea, but it's your decision. Nothing has been done that we can't undo. We can stop this train if you're uncertain."

Keith glances out the door at Carsen, who looks like she's having the time of her life as a makeup artist and hair stylist give her the full celeb treatment, then he shakes his head. Crossing the room, he grabs my waist, pulling me to him. "No, I'm not sure, but this is what we're doing. My manager agreed with the plan too. And though you're right, as much as I wish I could turn back time and not have to disrupt Carsen's life, that would mean not having you. And this, us . . . I've got to believe it'll be worth it in the end."

I bite my lip, trying to stop the words I've already said so many times from spilling out again, but I can't help it. I might be forced to say it another ten thousand times, but I mean each one. "I really am sorry, Keith. I never meant for any of this to happen. I can't believe Donnie is such an asshole, and if I could take it all back, I would. Except for you, of course."

Keith's hands move down to cup my ass in a firm grip that gets my attention, and I'm glad the green room is only us for the moment. "Stop apologizing. I think we've both apologized enough. We haven't done anything wrong. It's Donnie and he's forced my hand. He expected me to roll over and give in, but he's threatening my family, and I'm more of a bite than bark kind of guy."

I feel a warmth spread throughout my body and my nipples tighten in my sensible, professional bra that I'm wearing. "I've noticed that . . . the biting, that is. I happen to like it sometimes. Although your bark is pretty loud too."

I'm intentionally trying to lighten the mood, even if I am starting to get massively turned on. But Keith needs this. He's been a growling beast of a reluctant man all morning. But I love him for it because I know it comes from a good place. He loves Carsen, and he wants the best for her. This is just one of those situations where the best path forward isn't the one he planned. But he's still doing it, and that's why I love him.

"I just hope the hosts go easy on us," he says, raising his hands enough that he's not quite making me want to dry hump his leg in the middle of a TV studio but still making his point. "You know, with Carsen and everything."

"Really, Keith. I know this is the exact opposite of what you've wanted for Carsen, but I think it'll be for the best," I reassure him, running my hands over his broad chest. He looks handsome in his button-down shirt. "You won't have this constant threat hanging over your head. I just hope the fallout isn't too bad."

"It'll be whatever it is, and we'll handle it," Keith says, gaining confidence. "I promise."

Sarah and Carsen come in from make-up, and Carsen looks like she's actually having fun. She's not too made up, which I know Keith was worried about.

"Wow. So this is a green room?" Carsen asks, coming over and grabbing a bottle of water. "I thought it'd be green, but the walls are just blah wallpaper. And they said there'd be cookies!"

Her nerves are obvious, even if she is pretty awed by the whole production of a morning television show. Keith walks over and kneels down in front of her.

"Carsen, honey . . . are you sure about this? Of all of us, this mostly impacts you. I'll happily pay the money and we won't have to do this. Everything can stay just as is. Say the word, and I'll make that happen."

Carsen looks thoughtful for a moment, and I'm glad she's taking this seriously because this really is going to impact her life in a major way.

"I know, Dad. It'll be okay. You can't let this guy bully us around though. It's not right. But maybe being the daughter of the world's best country music star won't be so bad. Maybe you can even take me to school every once in a while?"

There's a knock on the door and a production assistant pokes her head in, looking slightly bored by all of this, as if changing people's lives is just part of her normal Monday. Then again, I guess it is. "Time, everyone. Follow me, please. We'll get you over to set."

Walking across the TV studio, it's interesting to watch the quiet chaos going on behind the cameras while the two hosts gab on about the latest political scandal getting headlines. We reach the 'on deck' spot, and Keith reaches out, holding my hand on one side and Carsen's on the other. Sarah places a stabilizing hand on his shoulder.

I can feel him take a deep, fortifying breath, knowing he's about to go to war . . . against Donnie, against the paparazzi, against his own secrets. "Hey."

"Huh?" he asks, looking over. I give his hand a squeeze and a small smile.

"You're not doing this alone. We've got your back."

Keith nods and gives my hand a squeeze back. "Thanks. I love you."

The show kicks to commercial, and a flurry of activity erupts. Keith is herded over to a couch in the middle of a set made up to look like one of those 'in-your-house' style living rooms. A quick sound check makes a tech adjust Keith's microphone, and the host comes over, shaking hands with Keith before sitting down and assuming her perfectly trained chair pose that looks ridiculously uncomfortable.

"Ten seconds!" a producer calls, and Keith gives us a thumbs-up, but I can see him forcing his emotions in check and prepping mentally for what he's about to say.

"Three . . . two . . . one!"

The overly perky morning host immediately starts up, grinning nearly orgasmically. "Welcome back to *Good Morning*! We have a special surprise guest for you, an exclusive you'll only see here on KTSR-TV this morning. I have to tell you, this was a surprise for me too. When I got the call from my friend, I said she had to be pulling my leg . . . but I've known her for years, so I was able to convince my producers to give this a shot. You see, we don't even know why this guest is visiting today, it's all top-secret, hush-hush. But I can tell you he's one of my favorites, so forgive any fan-girling I might do in the next five minutes."

I think the host's actually telling the truth and is a fan. The professional side of me knows that definitely works in our favor, although the personal side of me will want to rip her extensions out if she starts eye-fucking my man.

Crossing my arms over my chest, I watch as she gestures to the side. "Please welcome one of the hottest country music artists today . . . Keith Perkins!"

There's a bit of silence, and I guess that in the production booth, they're mixing in a few clips of Keith performing as the host starts up again. "Breaking onto the charts five years ago with his first big hit, *Gonna Do It The Country Way,* Keith Perkins has, over the past three records, consistently been one of the top ten artists in country today. With enough party to draw in new listeners and enough roots to have even old-schoolers impressed, Keith's star just keeps rising. Keith, welcome."

The host reaches over and shakes Keith's hand for the cameras, eyes starry as she looks at Keith, and I have to giggle a little bit. I'm pretty sure that's what I look like too, but I'm the lucky girl going home with him tonight. Not her, so she can suck it.

"So, Keith, we're thrilled to have you with us this morning. According to what I was told yesterday, you have some type of announcement you'd like to make? Are we talking your usual summer tour already? If so, put me down for two VIP tickets!"

"I'll remember that when tickets go on sale," Keith says on stage, "but unfortunately, tour info isn't why I'm here this morning."

"Okay, what brought you here this morning then?"

"Well, if you're a fan, you know I'm pretty quiet about my personal life. I always have been, just keeping that line between my professional life and my day-to-day stuff, you know? And recently, there were reports speculating that I may have a woman in my life."

Even from here, I can see the host's eyes light up, and you can virtually see her salivating for the story even though she must be reading between the lines since Carsen's already made up and in the wings just off camera behind Keith.

"Are you saying there is someone in your life? You're gonna break some hearts if that's the case!"

Keith nods, his smile widening before dimming by half. "Well, yes . . . but there's more to it. You see, when that story broke, I did have a young woman in my life, but not the way everyone thought. I'm not much for dating. It's kind of hard to do when you're . . . a single father."

The host plays it well. She can't have been that stupid to not see the similarity between Keith and Carsen, but to anyone at home, you'd think she'd just been kicked in the gut she's so shocked. Her mouth gapes open and closed a few times like a fish before she speaks. "A father? Oh, my."

Keith nods, his voice gaining strength as he gets into his tale. "You see, for a long time, my daughter, Carsen, and I have been a team, along with my sister, who's the biggest help ever. Carsen has been my number-one priority, and part of that responsibility was keeping her safe. I felt that the best way to do that was to keep her out of the public eye. She's a twelve-year-old girl. She deserves to have a normal childhood, and that's what I've worked damn hard to give her."

The host nods supportively, her eyes cutting to Carsen as I see a production assistant tap Carsen on the elbow. "So your daughter, Carsen. Is that the young lady I see off-set here? Carsen, would you like to join us?"

Keith nods, turning to look at us, and Carsen bravely walks to Keith, sitting down next to him on the couch as the host looks on with a smile.

"Wow, so very nice to meet you, Carsen! It must be awesome to have the one and only Keith Perkins as your dad."

Carsen smiles, looking at Keith and taking his hand. "I guess. To me, he's just Dad though. He makes me do my homework, clean up my room, all that stuff."

The host laughs, turning her attention to Keith. "So, you've kept Carsen a secret for all these years. What's changed now?"

Keith smiles, but it's bittersweet. "Well, after that article came out, my record label got the brilliant idea that I should do a series of interviews so a reporter could write an all-access story about me. Maybe you've seen them?"

The host nods, totally engrossed in every word of Keith's story. "Of course I have. Actually, I have printed copies of them backstage in my dressing room. Maybe you can sign them later?"

Keith chuckles. "Sure. I'd be happy to do that for you. So, the interviews were going well, but the real news wasn't what was in the articles. It was the reporter, Elise Warner. During the process of the interviews, I fell in love with her, and she fell in love with me. We've been dating for a little while now. Carsen and she get along well, and we're just trying to find our way."

For the first time, the host looks genuinely shocked, and she looks over at me, her eyes a mix of *go, girl!* and *I hate you, bitch!* She looks back at Keith, her grin still mostly professional but at the same time, she's eating this news scoop right up. "Wow! A daughter and a new love interest! Can Elise come out too?"

I squeeze Sarah's hand, wishing I could take her with me, but we'd decided that it'd be best for her to stay off-camera. It's not her style, and besides, it's good for at least one of us to stay unrecognizable.

With a shiver of nerves, I head over to sit beside Carsen. Keith stands up and gives me a hug, which eases my nerves a little bit. And when we all sit down, he stretches a long arm out along the couch back, marking us both as his.

"Welcome, Elise! I must admit, I'm a bit jealous and I imagine there must be thousands . . . I take that back, millions of women with shattered dreams right now. Tell us, how'd you claim this one?" She smiles as she points at Keith with a thumb.

She laughs a bit, but as far as I'm concerned, she's right. Keith doesn't give me a chance, though, leaning forward and shaking his head. "I'm the one who needed to claim her. Elise is a great woman, and I'm lucky she puts up with my grumpy ass."

Carsen giggles and looks over. "Dad, you can't say ass on TV!"

We all laugh a little, and the host jumps in. "Don't worry, we're on a ten-second delay. So . . . wow! What an announcement! We appreciate your sharing with our viewers this morning. What prompted you to come forward and not stay mum like usual?"

Keith's smile falls, and his face clouds as he lets a hint of his anger pierce the happy buzz of this morning's announcements. "Well, that's the bad side of this business. Most people have been nothing but positive and are happy to read stories about my background and music. I've tried when I do go out to perform to give back to them, because I know if it wasn't for them, I'd be still working honky tonks out in Boise. But there are others out for blood and dirt and any juicy tidbit they can find. Vultures, that's what I call them. And they take that information and exploit it, looking for a way to make a buck off someone else's life. I was recently given an ultimatum to either pay three point five million dollars hush money to one of these people, or he would publish a story exposing Carsen's existence. Total blackmail."

The host gasps, and I can see the crew members' shock and disgust. These people might like a little titillation themselves, but they're legit journalists, not tabloid bottom-feeders. "Oh, my gosh, that's awful! I'm so sorry."

One of the camera guys adjusts his angle to get what I assume is a full-frame close-up of Keith as he continues. "This man had his mistress, who is also a reporter, follow us . . . me, Elise, Carsen, and my sister. She took pictures of all of us, both in public and in private, using a telephoto lens, which is illegal and feels like such a personal violation. He was counting on his belief that he had all the power because he knew about my desire to keep Carsen out of the public eye." Keith pauses, his eyes meeting Carsen's with an apology obvious in the stress on his face. "So my choices were to pay him off or let him publish the story, which would let him get richer from clicks and sales. I couldn't let that happen. Schemers like that shouldn't be rewarded for their misdeeds."

The host nods. "So, by coming forward on your own, you preemptively cut him off at the knees?"

Keith nods. "I just want the opportunity to tell the truth of my story. I have a daughter, who is an amazing young woman, and I'm in love with Elise Warner, who through some stroke of luck is actually in love with me too. And as much of a bombshell as I know this is, I hope everyone will be respectful in their handling of this news and not overwhelm my family."

Keith looks at Carsen, then me, and I can feel his gaze like a physical touch, knowing that he'll protect us no matter what. The host is obviously trying to think of a next question, and when she touches her ear, I know that someone in the booth is feeding her words because she's so stunned.

Finally, she gets it together. "Wow, Keith. That's horrifying, and I'm so sorry that's happened, but I'm glad you came to *Good Morning!* to dispel any rumors before they got started." Her voice takes on a more serious tone as she asks, "Can you tell us who attempted to blackmail you?"

There's a sense of breath-holding suspense as I see more than one person lean forward, eager to see if Keith is going to name names. While all of them show some signs of disgust at the idea of blackmail, they've all got the secret shame that they're just as gossipy as the next person, wanting to feed on someone's secrets. To some degree, it's human nature to be nosy, but this is well beyond curiosity.

"Yes, the man who tried to blackmail me is Donnie Jardine, the editor-in-chief at *The Daily Spot*. The reporter who took the illegal photos and was complicit in his plan is Francesca Knauss, also of the *The Daily Spot*."

The host's eyes snap to me, her eyes widening. "Elise, isn't that the online magazine you work for? The one who's published your articles about Keith?"

I nod, knowing this was something we'd have to answer. "Yes, it is. Donnie Jardine is my boss." I look directly into the camera. "However, effectively immediately, I quit."

## CHAPTER 26

### KEITH

My strength holds out until we get backstage, where in the dressing room, I've had enough. I sag into the couch, too exhausted to even unbutton my shirt.

"Enough . . . no more," I say, leaning back. "Tell the whole world to piss off."

"Once we get home," Elise says, kneeling next to me. "You can let us take care of you . . . family."

I nod, leaning back and attempting to relax for a second. I shouldn't be so tired, but that was the hardest thing I've ever done. I've spent so long keeping quiet about Carsen, and serving her up on a fucking platter for the morning news went against every code of honor I have. But I have to trust that it's the right call.

Carsen's privacy is a fucking impossibility now, though, because as we're leaving the studio garage, the driver and bodyguard are talking up front in code. But I know what they're saying.

There are paparazzi right outside the garage waiting for us.

How the hell did they get over here so damn fast? After the interview, we whisked through the back halls and were out in minutes.

But they're already here like vultures, waiting to snap and pick at the remains of our privacy even after I've literally given them everything I have and more than I ever wanted to.

"Just get us home safely," I call up front, leaning back into the leather seats. "I can't do any more publicity today."

"Of course, sir. Make sure everyone's buckled up back there . . . sometimes, I have to punch it."

Carsen seems to be handling it well so far, still smiling, and it brightens my mood just a little.

As we drive out of the garage, the paparazzi swarm the SUV with their cameras and phones and faces pressed up against the glass. They're knocking and slapping at the windows, their yells a jumble of noise I can't understand except for my name over and over. Carsen cringes, the fun of being a 'celebrity' temporarily snuffed out, and she gets her first scary lesson in the price of her new identity.

Donnie, if I do see you again, I'd love to shove my fist so far up your ass people would think you're a puppet. *Damn you for doing this to my little girl,* I think in anger toward Donnie, even as a wave of guilt washes over me at the part I might've played in this mess too.

I realize the driver is barely rolling and look out the front window, seeing a group of daredevil cameramen standing in front of the vehicle, their lenses zooming through the untinted front windshield to try and get a shot of us in the back.

"Mother truckers," I growl, censoring myself at the last second. I'd say run them over but that's probably not a good idea. "Should we just keep rolling or do we need to stop?"

The driver and guard don't even respond to me. They're too busy doing their thing. It makes me glad that they're here and that they're well-trained for these situations.

Deciding I'd be better served by not distracting them, I turn my attention to my family sitting around me. Carsen and Elise both look horrified while Sarah just looks disgusted, but all of their heads are whipping back and forth, taking in the swarm still calling out and banging on the vehicle. Hearing a particularly hard slap behind me, I whirl around to see several reporters behind us too. We're completely surrounded on all four sides, barely inching forward as the horde moves step by step with us.

"Oh my God, Keith! I had no idea. I'm so sorry . . . is it always like this?" Elise asks, her voice small, but there's an undercurrent of anger. *That's my girl.*

I can feel Carsen's eyes on me, wide with fear, and I try to reassure them. "No, it's not usually like this at all. Maybe at some kind of awards show, where there's lots of media coverage and cameras flashing, but even then, it's nothing like this. Especially not in my daily life. No one usually follows me around, desperate to get pics. Still, might be a good idea to lie low for a bit until this whole thing dies down. Guess it's a good thing the house is stocked with everything we need for a few days."

Elise finally tears her eyes away from the chaos surrounding us and looks at me. "Right. I guess that Plan W-T-F is going into play?" she deadpans, but there's still a touch of fear even as she tries to joke.

A small smile plays at the corners of my mouth, even though we're still in a rather precarious situation. I reach over and hold Carsen's hand, giving it a little squeeze.

"It'll be fine, honey. I promise."

After a few more minutes of tension-filled progress, we make our way into the street and the driver is able to find a hole in the human shield surrounding us, speeding up and getting us out of the area by punching it through a yellow light. Once we hit the highway, we all breathe a sigh of relief, the pressure ratcheting down as we put miles between us and the studio.

There are several idiots gathered around the house as we approach, but they're outside the gate and they move out of the way as we go on through. As bad as it was, I know it could've been much worse, but thankfully, we're home safe and sound now.

Heading inside, I see Elise and Sarah already getting out the coffee for us and hot chocolate for Carsen. Carsen is pulling off her 'fancy' clothes as soon as she steps inside, eager to get comfortable.

"I don't know if I want to be a celebrity," she says, looking out the window. "Guess there won't be too many girls-only shopping sprees in the future."

"Oh, I don't know about that. If we need to, maybe we can get a cool female bodyguard, like our own personal Wonder Woman," Elise says thoughtfully, giving Carsen a comforting smile. She turns the stove on, pouring milk in a pot to warm it. "Come on. Hot cocoa with marshmallows always make everything seem better." I appreciate the calm and sweet way Elise is handling this with Carsen, helping her find a moment of lightness even as we're all freaked out.

Carsen smiles back, but it's weak and I know she's pretty shaken up by what happened. There's a big piece of me that wants to just gather her in my arms and run away where no one would be the wiser, keep her safe and secret forever. But that ship has sailed and now, we adapt, grow stronger. It's going to be tough, but looking around the kitchen, I know that Carsen has the best support system a little girl could ask for. Still, I go over and hug her tight.

"You did great today, honey. Did you know the first time I had to go on live TV for an interview, I got so nervous I puked all over the green room?"

"No way!" Carsen exclaims. "But you did it?"

"I did. And you were a pro today in comparison. You've already got me beat."

She laughs a bit more fully at that, which soothes the anger still coursing through my veins like a salve. We look up as Sarah sets a cup of coffee in front of me and hot chocolate in front of Carsen.

The four of us sip at our cups, sitting quietly on each side of the table as our minds replay the morning's events in a comfortable few minutes of silence. We're all just taking the day in.

Always the planner, Sarah finally jumps in, setting her mug down and breaking the silence.

"So, now what? We can't just hide out here forever. We got as far as the morning show interview, but we haven't really made a plan for what happens now. Keith, what are you thinking?"

I hum, still wishing I could wake up and this all be a nightmare. For it to not be real. I drain the rest of my coffee, promising myself that after yesterday's overload, I'm not going to have another cup, and think for a moment before answering.

"Well, I need to check in with Todd. I told him I'd do that the second we got back here. Just taking a moment. I'm sure he was watching, but he needs to know about every detail and the ride home after." I intentionally don't say the word paparazzi, not wanting to bring it up any more than I have to in front of Carsen.

"After that, I do think we'll need to be a bit scarce for a bit. No coffee runs or errands for me. And Carsen, you're going to have to take a few days off school. I'll call the school. I'm sure they understand and can have your homework sent here."

"Aww, Da-ad," Carsen says, then stops when she sees my face. "How long, though? I wanna talk to my friends."

"You can, honey. We'll just be a little more reserved until all of this dies down. It won't be long. There will be something else they'll be buzzing over soon enough. Maybe after a few days, we can see if any of your friends want to come over."

Carsen's eyes twinkle. She's never had her friends here. She always has to go to them. "Really?"

"Really . . . but let's not rush things. First, we need to see what we can do. Elise . . ."

I look at her as I say her name, and I see that she'd been staring at Carsen with a sad look on her face as I told her no school.

"I'm sorry, Carsen," she whispers. "Really, I am."

Carsen, who's probably already in her head planning a sleep-over with her best friend, smiles at Elise. "No apology needed. This isn't because of you. It's that jerk boss's fault."

Carsen gets up from her spot at the table, hugging Elise around the neck. I can see the shock on Elise's face as she pats Carsen's back. Elise's eyes are bright with unshed tears as she whispers into Carsen's hair. "Thank you, honey."

It's a heart-warming sight, and even though the situation sucks ass, I'm glad that Elise and Carsen are bonding so much. It eases the knot in my gut about bringing a woman into my life while my little girl is still so young.

As Carsen sits back down, she ducks into her hot cocoa, obviously not wanting any more attention right now. I smile, knowing she's going to be okay. She's a tough cookie, that girl of mine.

"Elise," I say, waiting for her eyes to meet mine. "We need to stay together, not be spread out across the city. You should stay here for a bit while this dies down, not just overnight."

"Oh, Keith, that's not necessary. I don't want to intrude," she says, looking pointedly at Carsen. I know she's trying to say she shouldn't stay over if Carsen is here, but fuck that. I want her here with me, where I can keep her safe . . . and fuck her whenever I want.

"No arguments. You're staying here," I reply in a more commanding tone.

Carsen chuckles. She's probably never heard me use it with anyone but her before. "Don't bother arguing. Once he uses that drill sergeant voice, just forget it."

"Oh, his 'drill sergeant voice'? Is that what you call it?" Elise asks, giving in, but in her way. She's going to stay . . . but she'll give me plenty of sass while she does it, too. Lowering her voice, she mock-whispers to Carsen loud enough for everyone to still hear her. "I usually call it his caveman voice . . . but I'm no dummy and I only say that in my head so as not to poke the bear."

Carsen laughs, her eyes twinkling as she glances at me and mock-whispers back. "Poke the bear? Is that when he gets all growly and grumpy?"

I keep my voice deep, but the amusement is obvious as I interrupt them before they can go further. "That's enough, you two. I'm right here and can hear you making fun of me. Next commentary outta either one of you gets punished."

Carsen smirks, giving me a raised eyebrow. "I'm basically grounded already. What else you gonna do, Dad? Spank me? I'm too big for that now."

I laugh at her joke, thankful she seems to be moving on from the trauma of the morning. I harrumph at them both, crossing my arms over my chest and looking down at them mock-threateningly.

Elise laughs too. "I know . . . he's the worst at punishments, isn't he?"

Elise's eyes are flashing fire as she teases, and I silently promise her with my eyes that she'll definitely be getting a punishment later. Maybe exactly the spanking she obviously wants.

Sarah interrupts us before things go on, probably for the better. "So Elise, for tonight, we're good, but do you need me to pick up anything from your apartment? I can have someone go with me, just in case they're scoping your place, but I can get whatever you need."

"Oh, would you?" Elise asks, relieved. "Thank you! Yes, I need some clothes and bathroom stuff. But mostly, I need my laptop and my knitting bag. Maybe while we're cooped up here, I can show Carsen a few stitches?"

Carsen's face lights up as she realizes that our new family dynamic could have some benefits for her as well as me. "That'd be awesome! Thank you."

A plan in place, Carsen asks to be excused, wanting to see if her phone has blown up with texts from friends at school. As she gets up, I give her a final bit of warning. "Remember, honey. Don't say too much. Just that I'm your dad."

She rolls her eyes at me. "I know! Don't worry."

I sigh, knowing she'll do her best. "Just . . . be careful. Everyone's going to be asking you questions. And I want you to . . ." I reply before stopping, seeing Sarah's tiny shake of her head. Let her fly on her own, Keith. Even if it scares you. "Just be careful, baby."

Carsen leans over and kisses my cheek, "I will. I love you, Dad."

"I love you too, Carsen."

Sarah gets up, grabbing her keys from the board next to the door. "Well, no time like the present. I'll grab the hunkier of the guards and stop by your place. Think you can text me a list of what you want before I get to your place, or should I just ransack it and grab what I think you need?"

Elise laughs, taking out her phone. "I'll have it for you. Don't stress if you can't, though. Seriously . . . it's not like I need to meet any deadlines. I'm kind of unemployed at the moment. Be careful, okay?"

Sarah *pshaws*, waving it off. "I've spent years knowing how to look normal after leaving this place, and I'll have a cute guy with me who knows how to kick ass. He can even help me pack."

Having a caveman moment, I let out a growl. "But don't let him touch her stuff, especially not her clothes."

Sarah smirks, twirling her keys in her hand. "Oh, really? I figured he could pack up her bras and panties while I got her makeup. No?"

I growl, but I know she's messing with me. She knows better than that. I just couldn't control myself. "Get out of here . . . and thanks again, Sarah."

She sticks out her tongue and heads for the door, and I hear her calling to the driver before she gets too far away.

Once it's the two of us, Elise comes over to me and I push back from the table, spreading my legs wide to let her step between them. She sits down on my left thigh, wrapping her arms around my neck. "Are we okay? I mean, *really* okay?"

I encircle her waist with my arms, nuzzling her neck, pressing my lips to her racing heartbeat to feel the soothing arousal she brings me before answering. "Yeah, we're okay. At least, we're gonna be."

I pull back, grabbing her chin with my fingers in a firm grip so she's forced to look into my eyes. "Elise, I love you. All of this drama, that's outside of us. What I want is right here . . . you, me, Carsen, and Sarah. That's all I need."

I see her eyes soften as she sighs, letting the rest of the guilt she's been feeling slip away from her conscience. "I love you too, Keith. I still feel so bad it's all turned into this . . . this shit-storm," she says, gesturing toward the world outside before laying a hand on my chest. "But I wouldn't change this right here."

I growl, covering her hand with mine and clasping it to my chest. "Stop worrying yourself or I'm gonna have to smack your ass for it every time."

She grins, raising an eyebrow. "You are so bad at punishment." She leans in, kissing me sweetly. As our lips part, I slip my tongue into her mouth, exploring and tasting. I feel her relax into me, and I rear back and smack her cheek where she's lifted it from my lap.

"Hey!" she gasps as I grab a handful of her ass, kneading it firmly, spreading the heat from my hand and turning the outraged gasp into a deep, throaty moan. "God, yes."

I nip at her chin, licking the spot before pulling back reluctantly. "There's more where that came from, but while Carsen's distracted with her friends, I really do need to call Todd. Make sure everything is okay on the professional front."

Elise sighs in disappointment and acceptance, placing her head on my shoulder. "Do you need me to leave while you call?"

"What? No way. We're done with secrets around here. Everything in the open, at least between us. Okay?"

She hums happily but still gets up to let me get my phone. "Okay."

Grabbing my phone, I dial and Todd picks up on the second

ring. "Hey, Keith! How are you doing?" His voice is serious, not his usually chipper clip.

"Well, all things considered, I guess I'm okay. Still, I think I'd rather be in the Yukon right now. How's it looking on your end?"

"Good and bad, if I'm honest."

I freeze, not liking the sound of that. "What do you mean? Tell me."

Todd adjusts, and I can hear a *tap-tap-tap* sound that tells me he's fiddling with a pen on his desk. "The media is having a goddamn orgy with the news about your 'secret daughter,' still-frame shots of the show are already hitting online news sites, and there's lots of speculation about why you've hidden her, where her mom is, that sort of thing. We kinda expected that though, right?"

"Yeah. You got a press release ready about that, though, I assume. What else? There's obviously more, judging by your voice."

"Yeah, that's the bad news. Donnie and the tabloid already lawyered up. They contacted me within minutes of your accusations on TV. They're talking about suing you for slander."

"It's only slander if it's not true. And it's definitely true."

"Yes, I know. But we're going to have to fight it, since it's your word against his. I've already contacted the local authorities. They're sending out a detective this afternoon to talk to you and Elise. You're going to have to file a report so the paper trail starts on our end. With no real evidence, there's not much a DA can do, but at the same time, a civil suit could be a possibility."

"A civil suit? You've gotta be joking."

"Don't sweat it, man. The lawyer from the label I talked to said that there's no jury in the country that'd find against you for trying to protect your little girl. And if Donnie says one bad thing about Janie, about your past, any of it . . . I'll have his ass nailed to a board so fast he'll wonder what the fuck hit him. Just hang in there, bud. And no talking to reporters. Other than Elise, that is."

# CHAPTER 27

## ELISE

When the doorbell rings at about three in the afternoon, I jump, dropping the Ritz and cheese that I'm trying to eat to calm my nerves.

Sarah, who's been a great calming presence since coming home, gathers up a few dishes that still have food on them. "Hey, Carsen, let's go watch a movie upstairs while your dad talks to the police officer. 'Kay?"

Carsen goes without complaint, and Keith answers the door after checking that one of the guards is with him. "Hello, Officer. Please come in."

I don't know what it is, but as soon as the guy walks through the door, everything about him screams 'cop.' He's in his mid-forties, and he's got on a pretty decent suit, but I think it's his eyes that make the difference. They say he's seen some shit, and that despite Keith's celebrity status, there's a lot of other things he'd rather be doing on a Monday afternoon.

It makes me like him, relaxing some. If he'd come in starry-eyed and asking for Keith's autograph, I know I wouldn't trust his ability to handle a case like this. But his air of professional indifference and just-the-facts seriousness seems like a bigger help. He offers a hand to Keith, then me, shaking them in turn. "Detective Morrison. Nice to meet you, Mr. Perkins . . . Miss Warner."

Keith directs Detective Morrison to the living room, and we sit on the couch next to each other, holding hands.

Detective Morrison pulls out a small notepad and pen, along with a voice recorder, and begins. "I've already seen the interview you did this morning. Just for my records, I'll need you to confirm everything. You said the threat was over your daughter. Is that correct?"

Keith nods, leaning forward, his elbows on his knees. "Yes, and that I'm dating Elise. The threat was to publish both of those things."

"Can you tell me how the threat was made?"

With a large sigh, Keith starts telling Detective Morrison about the suspicious phone call and our late-night meeting with Donnie and Francesca.

Detective Morrison writes in his notebook as Keith talks, but he looks up sharply when the $3.5 million blackmail is mentioned. He seems to search Keith's face for a moment, then motions for him to proceed.

As Keith wraps up his retelling with the Monday five o'clock deadline, Morrison hums. "And what happened then? Did you approach him in any way? Touch him at all?"

"No. I was furious and I damn sure wanted to. But in that moment, I was just thinking about keeping everything quiet for Carsen's sake. As mad as I was, I needed to figure out my play, not rush in hot-headed and make things worse. So we left."

Detective Morrison turns to me. "Miss Warner, you were there to witness these events? Anything you'd like to add?"

I shake my head, wondering what Morrison's hinting at. "No,

that's exactly what happened. Maybe add in there that Francesca and Donnie are sleeping together? Not sure it's relevant, but I'm not covering up anything for them."

"Okay. Mr. Perkins, so after leaving, where did you go?"

"Why? Do I need an alibi?" Keith says, getting a little pissed. "I'm the one getting blackmailed here, for fuck's sake. No, I was here at home, and nobody was here with me. But there are cameras. The feed is recorded so there's video of me coming in. No person to really confirm, but video of the whole house for the whole night."

Detective Morrison scribbles something down and then turns to me. "So, Miss Warner, you weren't here that night? Where were you?"

Keith sighs, his anger evaporating as he looks ashamed for the first time. I squeeze his hand. "Well, we had a bit of an argument about the whole thing, so Keith dropped me off at home. Later, I went to see a friend to help me figure out what we could do. I went to the club where she waits tables, and we talked while everyone cleaned and closed up. Lots of people saw me there."

He nods his head once, his eyes skimming his notes. "Okay, I will need the video from the cameras and the names of the people who saw you that night."

Keith and I nod, still not sure what that has to do with Donnie's blackmail. "I'm feeling like I'm being charged with something here when Donnie is the one who committed a crime. What's going on?"

Detective Morrison looks at us, and it feels like he's scanning us for mistruths or misdeeds, like he's a living lie detector.

Finally, he caps his pen and puts it back in his suit pocket. "Mr. Perkins, I believe you and your accounting of what happened. That's important for you to understand because I don't think you're going to like what I say next. We received a phone call this morning, shortly after you went on-air, in fact, from Donald Jardine. He reported that you came to his office two nights ago, angry about an article he was publishing. He stated that you were violent, aggressive, pushing him against the wall and breaking things throughout his office. He said you then punched him several times, in the abdomen and across his cheek. I went to see him at the hospital this morning."

"That son of a bitch!" Keith seethes, getting to his feet. "I never laid a hand on him! I wanted to, but I didn't."

Detective Morrison doesn't even flinch. He's stone cold as he gestures back to the couch. "Please sit down, Mr. Perkins. Remember how I said I believe you?"

Keith takes a big breath, obviously steadying himself, and sits down. "Sorry. I didn't lay a hand on him," he says more calmly.

"I've been doing this a long time, learned a few things along the way. One of which is how to read people. Mr. Jardine doesn't particularly strike me as an honest character, just based on his storytelling. It was full of sensationalism that made sense with his particular profession. I took pictures of his injuries. I visited his office too, took some evidence shots there as well. My gut tells me he saw you on TV this morning, concocted this story, and went so far as to have someone punch him to give the story credibility."

I blurt out in shock and frustration. "So what do we do?"

"Stay right here at home, get me the tapes and the names of your alibi witnesses, and wait for me to write up this report."

"That's it? I'm just supposed to sit here and wait?" Keith growls. "My family's being threatened, and I'm supposed to sit on my ass?"

"Yes, exactly that. And leave your cameras on and recording just in case. I think this will be pretty quick once the alibis check out, but if Mr. Jardine is willing to blackmail you, and I suspect intentionally injure himself to make you seem violent, he might be willing to play hardball in other ways too. Just stay put and I'll be in touch."

Keith shows Detective Morrison out and comes back to sit next to me before pulling me into his lap to straddle him. He holds me tight, pressing his cheek to my breasts, breathing heavily as he calms down. "This is so fucked up. I can't believe he's saying I beat him."

I scratch my fingers along his jaw, letting the scruff tickle my fingers, letting my man know that I'm here for him. "It'll be okay. Detective Morrison seems to be on our side and will check everything out. Donnie's a media pro with strategies and manipulations at his fingertips, and this is his move in response to our going public. He wants to create drama and questions about your character to save his own skin. But we know the truth, and that's enough."

"You know as well as I do that sometimes the truth isn't what people want to hear," Keith says, pulling back and looking up into my eyes. "They want scandalous secrets and dirty laundry, told with dramatic flair. It makes them feel better about their small lives. Most folks don't get that a small life, just you and the people you love living simply, is the best thing to have. They want for more when they have the best thing a person can wish for."

I lean back, marveling at the wisdom he spouts off so easily. "You're a good man, Keith Perkins. I love you."

"I love you too, Elise," Keith rumbles, looking at me with desire as the mood changes. There's still anger, but it's against something we can't change right now . . . but we can celebrate us and what we have.

He grabs my hair and the back of my neck, and I eagerly go to him, opening up as he plunges his tongue in to twist with mine. He cups my breast through my t-shirt, letting his thumb trace back and forth across the already pebbled nub.

Gasping, I push back, even as my body betrays me and my hips grind in Keith's lap, knowing what it wants. "Keith, we can't . . . Sarah and Carsen . . ."

He grins evilly, not even glancing in the direction of where they went. "Are watching a movie upstairs. I'm in charge here, Elise. And we need this . . . something normal, something that feels right."

He waits for me to protest, but he's right. I need this as much as he does, to let the drama outside our doors disappear and get lost in each other's bodies for a moment. I nod, and his grin widens as he lifts me off his lap. "Get on your knees. Suck my cock between those pretty lips, looking in my eyes like you know I love."

As I move to the floor between his legs, unbuckling his jeans, he runs the pad of his thumb over my lips and I suck it into my mouth, teasing his pad with my tongue. "Mmm . . . like that?"

Keith's eyes are locked on my lips, watching his thumb disappear and reappear from my mouth. "Yes, just like that. Suck it like a good girl."

When I finally manage to get his jeans open and boxer briefs pulled down, his cock springs free, thick and hard. There's already a drop of precum at the tip, and I lean forward, keeping eye contact as I lick the delicious drop, moaning at his sweet masculine taste. "God, I love your fucking cock."

Keith gathers my hair in his fist, keeping it out of my face as he looks down at me like a king. "I need to see. I want to see every inch of my cock disappearing into your hot little mouth. You can take it, Elise. Show me . . ."

With every beat of love in my racing heart, I take him to the root in one motion, holding him deep in my throat as I press my nose into the soft hairs at the base of his cock. I hold my breath as long as I can, hollowing my cheeks against his shaft and massaging the head of his cock with my throat, swallowing again and again before lifting back up, gasping for air.

I do it again and again, both of us getting more aroused with every thrust. With just the head of his thick cock in my mouth, I look up at Keith through my lashes like he wants, knowing the sight of my lust, my love on my face as I suck him does wondrous things to him. "Like that?"

Keith growls, nodding slightly. I return to my task with a gusto, bobbing up and down on his cock as I keep my eyes on him, my panties getting wetter with every stroke of his cock over my tongue. I don't go deep throat every time, but I give him all I can, licking and worshipping his cock with all that I am.

Keith groans above me, running a soft hand on my cheek as our locked gazes tell me to stop. I pause, circling his head with my tongue and waiting for his command. "Your hips are bucking the whole time you're sucking me. Is your pussy nice and wet for me, baby? Are you getting off on having my cock fill your mouth?"

I nod, pulling off his cock but still pumping him with my right hand as I answer. "Fuck, yes. I'm soaked from your taste, from having you in my throat. I fucking love it."

Keith smiles down at me, his cock jumping in my fist as he hears me return his dirty words and thoughts. "That's a good girl. Slip your jeans down a bit. I want you to touch your clit while I fuck your face. You don't come until I'm splashing down your throat and over that beautiful face of yours though. You hear me?"

I nod, hurriedly shoving my jeans and panties down my thighs. Sitting back on my heels, I spread my legs as wide as I can and slip my fingers into my folds. I moan at the slickness I find there, and Keith leans forward, looking down at me. "Is this what you want?"

"Fuck, yes," Keith says, his voice rough and deep. "*Just* like that. God, your pussy is perfect."

He watches for a moment, taking his cock in his own hand and stroking himself in time to my movements against my clit. We build together slowly, his fist pumping his cock while I slip another finger into my pussy, pushing them in and out in sync with his hand until we're both moaning, my chest flushing as I feel the orgasm build within me. Suddenly, Keith reaches for me, grabbing my hair again and pulling me forward. "Give me your fingers. I want your taste on my tongue when I come."

I move my honey-coated fingers to his mouth, and he sucks them in, licking them clean before pushing them back between my legs. I'm watching his hand move up and down right in front of me, and I see him squeeze himself hard just behind the head, milking a drop of precum out.

"May I?" I beg, opening my mouth for him, sticking my tongue out, wanting that drop so badly.

Keith taps his head to my tongue, and his taste bursts across my tongue again and I can't help but lick and lap at him for more. He moans, guiding his cock back into my mouth. "Mmm, fuck. Take me in your mouth again and rub that clit. I want to feel your moans all the way to my balls."

I take him in deep again, holding him there and humming, and Keith growls as he starts to fuck my mouth, his hips jerking as he fully takes over. "Dammit, Elise. I can't hold back. You feel too fucking good. Get there, because I'm about to come down your throat. I want you choking out your orgasm around my cock as I fill you."

I moan in happiness at his compliment as I speed up my fingers, blurring across my clit, moans and gasps coming from us both as we get closer to the edge. Keith lets out a grunt, trying to be quiet but failing spectacularly. I can feel his balls tighten and his cock swell even as he chokes out his order. "Come. Now."

As soon as I feel the first hot jet of his cum splash the back of my throat, I shatter into a million pieces. I'm slurping to catch every drop as Keith keeps pumping his hips, driving his cock into my mouth, crying out in a strangled gasp as his climax overcomes him and he throws his head back, filling my throat with his cream.

My clit is pulsing as my pussy clenches around nothing, hungry for Keith's cock. I'm floating, darkness surrounding me as flashes of white spark across my vision behind my closed eyes as I feast on his sweetness, both of us so caught up that he doesn't pull out but instead stays inside me for every pulsing release.

Finally, I collapse, laying my head on Keith's hip and humming out in satisfaction. Nuzzling his cock, I lick at the softening skin, mewling in pleasure and contentment. Thinking he's laid back on the couch too, I'm surprised when he speaks up, his voice still full of heat and desire. "Elise, I need to taste that orgasm. Give it to me."

I smile, reaching down between my legs again and rubbing gently across my sensitive pussy, coating my fingers. "For you."

I look up, keeping my head on his thigh as I offer my fingers to him once again. He holds my hand, drawing the essence of my scent deep inside him, searing it into his mind and soul before sticking his tongue out for a long, lapping lick along their length. "Mmm, so fucking good. Come here. Taste . . ."

He pulls me up from under my arms, depositing me sideways in his lap, and takes my mouth in a kiss. As our tongues slowly tangle, I can taste myself on his tongue, and I know he must taste himself on mine too. Somehow, it feels filthy and dirty, but at the same time it doesn't. It's the joining of two souls, mingling as one and making something new, something better. It couldn't be more perfect.

He was right. That was just what we needed.

# CHAPTER 28

## KEITH

For weeks, the firestorm has raged, surrounding and consuming reputations like they're nothing. Between me, Elise, and Donnie, I'm not sure any of us will survive the ugly gossip and snide commentary from the tabloids, who seem to be playing the odds and supporting both sides of the story, even though ours is the truth.

Donnie and *The Daily Spot* basically wrote Francesca off, leaving her to fend for herself as they focused on their own spin-doctoring. She went the Hollywood path, and after a few too many tabloid mentions of her sleeping her way to the top and harsh speculation about basically everything she'd ever written, she checked herself into a 'health retreat' due to exhaustion rather than suffer a public mental breakdown. While she's still a bitch who had no problems trying to stab my family in the back, I can't help but feel a twinge of sympathy for her. A tiny one. But we've all got shit to bear right now.

It's been hard for both me and Elise to deal with all the craziness. The speculation was so random and out-there, I couldn't believe anyone would think it was true. One night, some stand-up comedian on late-night TV thought it'd be funny to question the magical powers of Elise's *vajayjay* to get more than just secrets spilled.

I'd been a second away from calling Todd to see if anything could be done about it, but Elise distracted me, teasing me that maybe her pussy was indeed magical and that I should probably check it for rabbits. I had to spank her ass pink for that bit of brattiness.

By the time we were exhausted and satisfied, it'd been too late to call Todd and I let the cruel joke go, realizing that Elise's distraction was probably the best idea.

But we keep watching the headlines and celebrity gossip shows when Carsen isn't around, needing to know what's being said about our interview stunt and the whole situation with Donnie. Even I can tell that the paparazzi and tabloid shows are repeating the same story now and that there have been no new developments they're aware of.

It's all a waiting game now, the police charging nobody so far and the lawyers on both sides waiting to see who blinks first. Todd tells me that the lawyers don't want to jump the gun early since a police report going against us could torpedo our case even before it begins.

So we sit and wait. Hiding out doesn't feel right. I still feel like yelling from the rooftops that Donnie is a scumbag, maybe actually punching him for good measure since he's using that claim to garner sympathy like the master manipulator that he is. But Todd assured me that that's not a good idea, and Elise and Sarah agree with him. I know I'm not thinking straight on this issue, so I'm trusting their judgment.

Other than the sneaky viewing of the shows and the drama outside our door, sitting at home has been oddly easy. We've spent long hours eating, playing board games, watching movies, and hanging out just the four of us.

I work off my stress in my home gym and in my music room,

furiously creating dark licks on my guitar that I'm not sure are country or sometimes angry metal. It's helpful, and each night as I set my guitar aside and look at my red, aching fingertips, I feel better.

It might be hostile outside these walls, but in here, we're safe, cocooned together and bonding more and more each passing minute.

Emerging from my shower following a good afternoon workout, I grab a beer and look out the window to the back porch and the setting sun. I can hear Elise and Carsen talking outside, but it seems like they're speaking in code, their backs to me so I can't see what they're doing.

"So go under, over, pull a loop, and then cast off the left."

"Okay, but what about this piece?"

Curious what they're up to, I quietly sneak out the back door, moving to the side so that I can see them better. To my heartwarming surprise, my girls are sitting face to face on the patio lounger, their legs crisscrossed, mirroring each other as Elise teaches Carsen to knit. It's a beautiful picture, tender and sweet as they giggle at the uncooperative yarn. The soft laughs feel like a balm to my soul with all the anxiety lately, and I can see Elise being maybe not a mother to Carsen, but motherly.

I never realized just how much Carsen needs that. She has Sarah, and always will, but this feels different and special. My little girl can only be happier surrounded by more love, and I realize that Sarah was right all along about my dating.

I catch movement out of the corner of my eye and look up, where I see Sarah standing in the window of her bedroom, giving me a nod. I give her a nod back, and she smiles before stepping back, giving us a moment of privacy.

I'm glad, because nothing could compare to this moment right here. The woman I love sharing one of her passions with my little girl, teaching her so much more than just skills with yarn.

Elise must feel my eyes on her because she looks over, grinning as she holds up her little patch of yellow. "Hey creeper, you just gonna stand there and watch? Come on over and see what we're working on."

Carsen looks up, delight written across her face, "Look, Dad! Elise helped me get two whole rows done."

I look at the small tangle of knots and loops she's holding up, clueless whether it's right or wrong, good or bad, but she's proud of it and that's all I need to know I'm proud too. "Great job, honey! So what are you guys trying to make?"

"Well, since we don't know how long we're in for," Elise says, "I figured this was a perfect time to learn. And we'll start with the same project I started with, a coaster. Simple, small, and it'll keep us busy. Be productive, all that good stuff."

I plop onto the lounger nearest them, sipping at my beer and watching the pink sunset light wash over their faces, thanking the fates for bringing me this moment. A little beauty with the ugly, a bit of joy with the pain. I hop up, suddenly inspired.

"Keith, you okay?" Elise hollers as I head inside.

"Fine," I yell back, not stopping. "Don't move."

I grab one of the notebooks scattered throughout the house and rush back to my perch on the chair, a song taking shape in my mind already. This is different from the angry, rage-fueled metal-country that could still make some damn good songs. This time, as I sit and watch my girls knitting and chatting, I feel peace and gratitude and love.

I watch the sun set on another blessed day.

I think about the storm raging beyond our doors and my need to keep my family safe and surrounded by love.

Before the last sun ray dips below the horizon, I'm done. It's not a ballad, it's not a party jam . . . it's something else. It's a good one too. I can feel it in my bones.

Born of pain and hardship, lit by love and appreciation, and filled with my heart and truth, it might just be the best song I've ever written. I set the notebook down, eyes taking in the progress Elise and Carsen have made on their projects and on their developing relationship.

I'm a lucky fucker. I drink the rest of my forgotten beer, not even minding the warm suds but just wanting to drain the bottle before dumping the glass in the recycle bin. Behind me, the door opens and Sarah sticks her head out. "Hey, guys. Dinner's almost ready. How about if we eat out here tonight?"

"Yay!" Carsen says, obviously giving her two cents while Elise flashes a thumbs-up. Sarah looks at me and I give her a nod.

"Sounds good."

"Okay. By the way, Keith, your phone just buzzed. Think you got a text."

I sigh, wishing I didn't have to step back into the reality of the world outside, wishing I could just stay in our safe, cozy hideaway. But reality comes calling no matter what, so I know I'd better deal with whatever has happened now.

Grabbing my phone, I see it's a text from Todd. *Call Me ASAP.*

It must be important because he picks up on the first ring.

"Holy shit, Keith. Are you watching this?"

"Watching what? What happened?"

"Turn the TV on. Do it now."

I head into the living room, snatching the remote off my couch and jabbing the power button. "So what am I looking for?"

"News. Shit, any news."

I click a couple of times as Elise, Sarah, and Carsen come in, likely hearing my raised voice even from outside. I find the news and see a blonde pseudo-pageant-looking reporter talking in dramatic tones, as if the world were hanging in the balance.

*"That's right, Joanna. What we saw here today was something I don't think anyone was expecting, especially Donnie Jardine. Police arrested him at the offices of* The Daily Spot *this afternoon, reportedly rushing in with multiple arrest warrants. Simultaneously, they raided his home, executing more search warrants. Police and crime scene investigators were seen leaving with several dozen boxes of evidence. No official word yet what the boxes contained. Speculation is that they contained evidence proving the multiple allegations of blackmail that were brought to light earlier today."*

My fingers half numb, I put the phone on speaker so we can all hear. "Todd, what the fuck is happening? What are they talking about?"

Todd's glee is evident even through the phone line. "It seems Francesca had a surge of conscience and started naming names. You'll get the list later, but there are some heavy hitters in music and media . . . and they fought back. A little late, considering most of them already paid him, but they've got lawyers that make ours seem like goddamn *Night Court*. And with Francesca now turning on Donnie . . . he's going down for sure."

"So they arrested him?" I ask, stunned. "I mean, I'm glad he's going to be prosecuted, but what does this mean for us?"

"Well, Schrodinger's cat is already out of the bag. Everyone knows about Carsen now. But you don't need to stay at home anymore. The complaint against you has been dropped. It's up to you, but we have a good case to go after the tabloid since Donnie committed these felonies under their employment umbrella using staff to do his dirty work. I'm gonna be honest, it's the only way to get money. By the time the other lawyers are done picking Donnie's financial bones, he won't have two nickels to rub together."

I look to Elise, wanting her opinion. She shakes her head,

speaking up. "The tabloid itself didn't do anything other than what it's designed to do, which is report gossip. I hate it, but it's the truth. This was all Donnie, his evil scheme and power play. Besides, I've still got a friend working there, so going after *The Daily Spot* would just hurt people like her, and she is a good person, just doing her job."

"I agree. Leave the tabloid alone as long as they agree to never publish a single story about my family. Ever. I just want this to be done and over. If Donnie gets his, I'm happy. Oh, except there's one more thing . . . Francesca. Tell the cops if she is the one who leaked all of this and is willing to testify against Donnie, I won't file a complaint against her. That's how much I want this over."

I look to Elise for approval, and she nods.

"Okay, all clear then," Todd says. "Feel free to go out when you want. But Keith, you'll definitely need to take a driver and guard for a bit until all of this dies down. It won't be instantaneous, but if we're lucky, a Kardashian will get pregnant again and that'll be all the talk and they'll leave you alone." He laughs, and we hang up, looking at each other in shock.

Carsen is the first to break the silence. "Does this mean Elise has to go home now?"

My eyes snap to Elise as I answer Carsen, trying to decipher what she's thinking as I jump in the deep end with no life vest. "No, it means she *can* go home now. But only if she wants. I'd rather she stay here with us. This can be her home now too. If that's okay?"

My words hang in the air, the question a huge turning point in our family. Elise looks at Carsen, the hope obvious in her eyes. Carsen, in all her innocence, seems unaware of the weight of the situation and responds casually. "Cool! I want to finish a few more rows on my coaster tonight before dinner. Pretty sure I'll need your help. And next, I want to try a blanket."

And without a care in the world, she walks back outside and plops down on the lounger, returning to her knitting.

Elise and I let out long-held breaths, and she laughs softly. "Well, I guess that's that. I'd love to stay."

Sarah pats Elise on the shoulder, a twinkle in her eye as she whispers quietly. "Welcome to the family." Sarah heads back into the kitchen to grab a platter of fried chicken and walks outside with it.

As soon as we're alone, I scoop Elise into my arms, holding her tight as I push a strand of hair behind her ear. "I meant what I said. I want you to stay. Tonight, tomorrow, forever," I tell her, looking into those eyes that I know I can't live without. "I love you."

She blushes, the pink lighting up her cheeks and making her look like a sweet angel. "I love you too. And I want to stay. I can't imagine not being here now, with you and Carsen and Sarah. You're . . . home."

Her words hit my heart like sweet arrows, and I take her mouth in a soft kiss as I grab a handful of her firm ass in my hands. It's just the right thing to do. Soft and hard, gentle and rough, all the things she makes me think and feel . . . each one of them is better than the last. And only Elise can draw them all out of me.

There's a tap on the back door and we break apart to see Sarah smirking as she hooks a thumb behind her. "Dinner's ready, lovebirds."

# CHAPTER 29

## ELISE

Hours later, dinner has been eaten, stories have been told, and laughs have surrounded us for hours. Finally, the tension and dread that have underlined the last couple of weeks has fallen away.

After we clean up, Sarah wipes her hand on the dish towel. "Well, fam, I'm off to soak in my bathtub before sleeping for at least twelve hours in my own bed. Now that we're not on lock-down, I'm going to head home. Call me if you need anything."

We say our goodbyes and Sarah leaves. Soon, Carsen crashes out too, falling asleep almost before her head hit the pillow. It's a little slice of heaven when she asked if Keith and I both could tuck her in.

After closing her door, Keith pulls me close, kissing my fore-head as the gravity of what our family could be sinks in. Detouring through the kitchen to snag two nightcap beers, we snuggle on the back porch, talking and looking at the stars.

"I'm going to grab another," Keith says, sighing happily. "I think I've earned it today. Want one?"

"No, thanks. I think I'm going to change into my jammies. I'll meet you back in five?"

Keith heads to the kitchen and I go to our bedroom. Wait . . . *our* bedroom. God, that feels good, and I'm going to love getting used to saying that. Quickly, I dig through the big drawer where I'd dumped the clothes Sarah had brought over for me, looking for PJs. I guess if this is our bedroom now, maybe I'll have to claim more than one drawer in the dresser.

Shuffling things around, I see a flash of red lace. I fish around a bit, pulling out a lacy teddy I'd bought but never worn. Sarah brought just the thing.

Slipping my clothes off, I change into the teddy and check myself in the full-length mirror. *Looking good, Elise. And now it's time to be a little bad.*

Sticking my head out the window, I see Keith below, his back to me as he watches the moon. "Keith, can you help me with something?"

I wait, standing tall and proud in the middle of the room as I hear him come inside, his bare feet still clumping on the carpet. Thank God he's a country singer. He'd never make it as a ninja.

"What do you ne—" Keith asks as he steps inside, but his voice tapers off into a groan as he sees me. "Holy shit."

I smile and arch my back a bit, knowing the pink of my nipples is visible through the fine lace. "I think this might be a bit too revealing. What do you think?"

"God damn, Elise," Keith says, his eyes wide and his jaw still a little slack. "You look sexy as fuck. Turn around, let me see all of you."

I do as he says, turning a slow circle to let him see all of me, but I look over my shoulder, wanting to see his reaction to the tiny string between my ass cheeks.

I don't have to wait as Keith nearly pounces across the room to grab me forcefully from behind. Excitement sends shivers down my body as I expect him to shred the lace, hurl me across the bed, and ravish my body however the fuck he wants . . . but this is Keith, and as always, he's in control.

"You tease me . . . but it's a good tease," he whispers in my ear, running a gentle finger along the edge at my cleavage, smiling as goosebumps break out along my skin. "But you're not going to make me lose control first."

His hips grind forcefully against my body as he turns me around, his full cock already pressing to my clit, but his touch is reverent as he traces along the slim strap at my shoulder.

"Do you like it?"

"Like?" Keith asks, lifting one strap and easing it off my shoulder but leaving my breast still covered. Tracing his finger down my arm, he shakes his head once. "No. I fucking love it."

He reaches behind me, grabbing the tiny thong and pulling it up, making it rub along my pussy as I gasp at the sensation. I feel the bottom slip between my lips, and the string rubs against my asshole, making me shudder as Keith leans down, whispering in my ear.

"I'm going to fuck you in this, this sexy red lingerie that makes me so fucking hard for you. I'm gonna leave it on you and just slip this little string that's splitting your ass over to the side so I can get my cock in your hot pussy. Do you want that, Elise?"

My head nods like a bobblehead, desperate for what he's saying to happen right now. "Fuck yes, Keith. Do it now. Fuck me."

But he steps back, his hand rubbing along the bulge in his jeans, and my pussy gets even wetter, knowing he's gonna fill me with his thick cock. "Oh, Elise. You know better than that. Who's in charge here?"

I bite my lip, knowing this is part of the tease, although it doesn't always feel like a tease . . . it just feels natural. For a second, I'm reminded of him telling me in our first interview that foreplay can be the best part if it's done right, and fuck, does he do it right. "You are."

"That's right, good girl. Get on the bed, on your knees and face down."

I hurry to do as he says, grabbing a pillow to lay my face on as I lift my ass in the air. I can feel Keith move behind me, his presence filling the room and my senses. He pauses behind me, running a gentle, intimate hand over my right cheek so softly that it almost feels like a whisper of wind. "That's a damn pretty sight, your fine ass turned up for me."

He grabs a handful of each of my cheeks with his large hands, kneading and massaging, spreading me open wide to his gaze. "Look how wet your pussy is. I've barely touched you and your cream is soaking down your thighs. Time to taste."

Without letting go of his powerful hold on my cheeks, he bends down to bury his face between my legs, tracing his tongue in a long line up my inner thigh to my center before repeating it on the other side. I shiver at the sensation, so good but not nearly enough. I lift my ass more, tempting him, taunting him, hoping he'll give me what I desperately need.

I should've known better. *Smack*! His hand pops down on my cheek, fire exploding from my ass through my body before re-centering on my desperate pussy. "Bad girl. I know what you want, and I'll give it to you. But only when I'm ready. Until then, let me take my time."

I whine, the heat from the spanking warming my body and leaving me wanting more. *Smack*! He spanks my other cheek and I glare back at him. "You . . . you fucker. You know *exactly* what you're doing."

"Damn right," he says, his eyes never leaving my ass. Keith

gently rubs to soothe the sting, his smile showing how pleased with himself he is for spanking me. "Needed your pretty cheeks to match this lace."

The flash of pain gone, his touch gets rougher again, and he spreads me wide, the thong string pulled off to one side to let him have full access to anything he wants. Holding my breath as he leans forward, ready for his tongue on my pussy, I clench the blanket underneath me to prepare for the expected bliss. But that's not what he does. Instead, he starts on the outside, at the base of my ass before his hot, wet tongue moves toward my higher center, and I feel him flick against my asshole, making me squirm in delight.

He holds me tighter, locking me in place where he wants me. "You're mine, Elise. Every part of you . . . mine."

I nod, overwhelmed by the wonderful sensations of his tongue on my ass, but it's not enough. "Tell me."

"Yours," I moan, my hips bucking uncontrollably even though he has a tight hold on me. "Everything. It's all yours."

"Mmm, good girl," he murmurs, licking me again, his tongue slipping over my ass before moving down to tease at my lips. I spread my knees wider, letting him in deeper, and he takes the invitation, fucking my pussy with his tongue before circling my clit.

"Ohh, fuck . . . Keith . . . feels so good."

He's teasing me, tracing patterns with no sense so I can't expect his touch, making me feel so good without letting it build too high, driving me crazy as he feasts on my body.

He moves a finger to my ass, letting the thick digit press inside slowly and deliciously, never pausing his torture of my clit. Deeper inside he goes, and I feel a sense of being so full, so wonderfully impaled, and this is just the beginning. I push back, wild for more as I moan and cry out, begging him.

He slips his free thumb into my pussy, filling me as he finger-fucks me faster and faster, filling my ass and pussy simultaneously.

Suddenly, he sucks my whole pussy into his mouth, thrashing his tongue across my clit. I explode, my orgasm pounding through me, tremors wracking my body as I bury my cries in the pillow.

I'm still coming when I feel him pull back, his jeans dropping and his hard cock thrusting deep inside me in one long stroke. It sets me off again, and I keep spasming, my walls fluttering around his thickness as he pounds my body relentlessly.

"Fuck, fuck, fuck," I squeal nearly incoherently as my spine fills with fire. I arch and reach back for him, trying to get all of him that I can. Keith is tugging the string of my thong tight over my left cheek, and he grabs my hands behind my back, locking them in place and forcing me to be still for him. "That's it," he says as he roughly, wonderfully hammers my pussy. "Keep squeezing me like that. Let me feel you milking my cock, your pussy sucking the cum out of me."

I squeeze my pussy as hard as I can, wanting to drive him as crazy as he's driving me, wanting him to reach that tipping point where he loses control.

"Harder," I growl as I regain my voice. "Fuck me . . . I want it, Keith. Come in me and fill me up."

He grunts, his hand twisting around the thong, and I feel the lace loosen around my lower half, falling to the bed beneath me as he tears it from my body. Now that his hand is free, he buries it into my hair as he leans over me, still pinning my hands behind me as he covers me with his body to rumble in my ear. "You think you can take me harder, Elise? Be careful what you wish for."

I nod, and he takes my breath away, slamming into me harder than ever before. Holy fuck . . . this man is more than I ever could have imagined, even after all the fucking we've done before. This is right on the line, the undercurrent of pain making the pleasure even better.

I know I'm going to be sore after, and I like the thought that he'll be imprinted on my body inside and out, heart and soul. I'm his forever, and he knows it as he makes me totally his.

"Yes . . ." I choke out in a strangled cry as my body tightens and explodes in another orgasm, his name a prayer locked behind lips frozen in exhilaration, caught in the waves of pleasure spreading from my pussy out to my fingers and curled toes.

Somewhere in the haze, I hear him behind me, his voice trembling as he's on the edge too. "Just like that, Elise. Fucking milk me like a good girl."

I have just enough energy left to squeeze him in a vise grip, giving him all I have.

"Shit, so tight . . . it's so good," Keith grunts. His cock swells, and I feel him slap into me a final time, his cock exploding deep inside me, the warmth of his seed coating my insides and making me softly weep in satisfaction.

As we pant, trying to catch our breath, I collapse to the bed, Keith still on top of me and inside me. Gathering me in his arms, he kisses my cheek, tasting my tears. "You okay?" he whispers, concerned. "I didn't hurt you, did I?"

I smile, moaning happily. "So much better than okay. So much better."

I feel the rumble of his laughter at my back, and he kisses my shoulder before slowly pulling out. I feel the loss instantly and wish he were inside me still. I'm too exhausted to look up, but I hear Keith pad to the bathroom and walk back to the edge of the bed.

"This might sting for a second."

I hiss as he presses a wet washcloth to my sore pussy, but almost as soon as the shock of discomfort starts, it passes and a soothing warmth takes its place.

"Mmm, that feels good. But you might have to kiss it all better."

"Normally, I'd give you a smack for that sass, but maybe I'll take mercy on you for now."

I chuckle, looking at him from half-hooded eyes. "Maybe just save it for later?"

"I can definitely do that."

After a minute or two, the washcloth loses its warmth and Keith sets it aside, gathering me to curl up to him as he wraps his arm around my shoulders.

He covers us over with the blankets, tracing his thumb along my shoulder. "I love you."

I look up at him, seeing the honesty, the depth, the truth in his eyes and knowing it's all we ever need to say.

"I love you too, Keith."

# EPILOGUE

## ELISE

I can't believe how nervous I am, sitting in the dressing room backstage. It's the first night of Keith's new summer concert tour, and it wasn't until I looked back that I realized he's always started his summer tours in his home state, Idaho.

Some investigative reporter I am. Luckily, since I quit my job with *The Daily Spot*, I've been doing freelance reporting so I was able to come along. Freelancing has been better than I could've ever hoped, letting me work on whatever stories interest me. With Keith and Carson's permission, I even did a whole new in-depth profile on our new family, and *Rolling Stone* snatched it up at a good premium. Not quite *The New York Times*, but you really can't get much more respect in the music industry media.

Ironically, the tabloids have left too. With no more secrets—well, none that are that big, my wonderfully aching ass tells me—the buzz of intrigue has died off. There's just nothing there for the paparazzi to pick clean.

I'm even doing a weekly blog post for a country music site called *Life on the Road with Keith Perkins*. So even while we're on tour, I get to work and spend time with Keith. It's the best of both worlds. Paparazzi still show up in droves for awards and concerts, but it's settled down enough so that we can live pretty quietly at home.

Carsen is safely back at school, at least for another week until her summer vacation starts, and then she and Sarah will join us on the tour starting in San Diego. Best of all, Keith and I can usually sneak out for coffee without hassle as long as he skips the cowboy hat and wears the Clark Kent getup.

I've come to like the faux nerd version of Keith, and we've definitely put those glasses, along with some of my wigs and disguises, to good use over the last few months. He plays my nerdy computer repair guy in glasses and a polo, or I'll pretend to be his personal lap dance stripper thanks to the moves I saw at Maggie's gig. Keith says it's sexy to have a blonde one minute and a brunette the next, and I'm thinking of ordering a short red wig for some extra spice. I think a red-haired version of myself might be a bit more bossy, and it'll be fun to see if Keith can handle that. Ha!

But today, Keith is in full cowboy mode in his tight jeans, plaid button-down shirt, hat, and boots. He looks hot as hell and I'm reminded again how lucky I am that everything has worked out this way.

It could've been very different. If I hadn't written the initial article. If we hadn't given in to our attraction. If we hadn't gone public with our story. Hell, if Donnie hadn't tried his blackmail schemes.

There are a thousand what-if's, but they've all led to this moment right here. We're happy, in love, with our careers doing well . . . and I've got my very own dominant sexual beast of a country music star to satisfy every desire I could ever imagine.

There's a knock at the door, and from the other side, I hear the head roadie, a balding, leather vest-wearing guy holler in his smoke-lunged voice, "Fifteen minutes to stage time!"

Jim, Shane, and Eric stand, moving toward the door. "All right, man. See you in ten next to the stage for our pre-show cheer to kick off this year's tour," Jim teases.

As they leave, I turn to Keith, who's shaking his head good-naturedly. "Oh, I need to see this cheer! That's definitely going in the first story about the tour."

Keith grins, shrugging. "Of course, but you know, I think I'm going to need to read these posts before you make them live. This isn't all-access, so I might need to make sure you're not telling all of my dirty secrets."

I can hear the teasing heat in his voice, and I come close, whispering breathily in his ear. "Oh? And do you have some dirty secrets, Mr. Perkins? Please tell me . . . I'll do *anything* if you'll tell me."

"I might have one or two secrets left in me," he rumbles, his voice just on the line between teasing and sexy. "Want to hear one?"

I bite my lip, looking at him with faux-innocence as I nod. He spins me, shoving me flush against the door and whispering hotly in my ear. "My secret is that I'm gonna fuck your pussy with my fingers, make you come all over my hand. And then I'm going to play my concert with your taste, your scent marking me. When I wave to the crowd, it'll be you I'm thinking about. Your fucking cream so sweet on my fingers as I blow kisses to all the fans. Take off your panties, Elise."

I rush to do as he says, yanking my maxi skirt up and pulling at my thong. Keith grabs my wrists, stopping me in my tracks. "Wait. I didn't know you had that on. You know how much I like those."

I do know. That's exactly why I've taken to wearing them

more frequently. Keith caresses my bare cheeks, humming happily. "Leave it on."

I nod, and keeping my skirt gathered in my hands, I press my cheek to the cool wood of the door, arching my back and pressing my pussy closer to Keith. He stands behind me, wrapping his arms around me and dropping his hands to my hips, urging me open some more.

I spread my legs a little wider, giving him access, and feel him chuckle behind me. "Oh, no, you're gonna spread those pretty pussy lips for me. Hold your skirt with one hand and then open yourself for me. I need one hand for your sweet little clit and one to fuck your pussy."

I do as he says, and as soon as he touches me, I cry out softly, knowing this room might not be soundproofed. "Oh, fuck, Keith. That feels so good."

He goes fast, his fingers moving across my clit in hard sweeps, and I feel his cock grinding against my ass, turning me on until I'm soaked and I want more. "There's not enough time. I want—"

Keith interrupts me, tugging on my ear with his teeth. "You've got three minutes, Elise. Then I'm walking out that door for the show. I want your cum on my fingers. You need to get there. Squeeze my fingers and imagine it's my cock filling you up and come for me like a good girl."

He shoves his fingers deep inside me, pressing them forward to my front wall, his other hand grinding against my clit. It's so good, and all I need is to fall off the edge, gasping and coating his hand. It's hot, intense, dirty, quick . . . but sometimes, that's just as good as the times we've spent hours slowly teasing each other to multiple orgasms.

Before my vision even clears, I'm spinning and dropping to my knees as I wrench Keith's jeans open. I look up and give him a flirtatious smirk. He's not the only one who can tease his partner. "Two minutes and you're walking out that door, Mr. Perkins. You need to come down my throat before then. Or else."

"Or else what?" he growls, gasping lightly as I lick his shaft from base to tip.

"Like you said, you're walking out that door. So get there, cowboy," I say as I wink at him.

Before Keith can respond, I take his whole cock deep in my mouth and suck with everything I have, immediately bobbing up and down on his cock and loving the intoxicating musk of his natural scent. Keith groans loudly, planting his palms on the door behind me and spreading his legs wide as he tries to fuck my face. But I'm faster, holding his hips, slurping and hollowing my cheeks as I suck, hungry for him.

I squeeze his balls, tugging gently as I hum, gazing up at him with the innocent look that I know he loves. He groans, his orgasm rocketing through him, and he shoots jet after jet of sweet warmth down my throat and I swallow, satisfaction buzzing in my head as I take every drop like the good girl I am.

He pulls back, yanking me up from the floor to kiss me fiercely. "Damn, Elise. Now I'm gonna be thinking about burying my cock in your pussy the whole damn show."

I wink, dabbing at the corners of my mouth like a lady. As if I missed a single drop. "It'll probably be your fastest show ever. Don't forget to blow kisses to the crowd."

Keith lifts his hand to his mouth, inhaling deeply and then licking a taste of my honey from his fingertip. "Mmm, I have a feeling this is gonna be a great show."

He tucks his shirt back in, helping me adjust my skirt so we both look more or less put together. Hopefully, no one will be able to tell we just fucked backstage. Then again, this is music . . . this might not be out of the ordinary.

We speed-walk through the dark curtained hallways and I remember the first concert I went to where Keith fingered me in a jealous fit backstage. It all seems like a dream, so perfectly impossible but somehow true and real.

"Okay, you ready?" Jim asks when Keith joins them. "Pain don't hurt!"

"Glory never dies!" Shane adds.

"And chicks dig scars!" the others yell, making me laugh.

"Kick some ass!" they all finish, heading out on stage to the cheering crowd. I'm just as loud, but this time, though, I'm just off stage. Which in some ways is better. I can see my man more easily.

Keith grabs the microphone, looking out on the crowd. "Hel-loooo, Boise! Are you ready to sing along with an old home-town boy?"

He leans an ear out, listening to them scream wildly. "That's what I thought!"

I watch as he brings his fingers to his mouth, blowing a big kiss to the crowd before looking over at me and winking. I almost melt, and I'm glad nobody can see me swoon.

God, this man is so damn sexy and amazing. And most impor-tantly, he's *mine*.

I watch transfixed as he sings song after song, working the stage like a master. It's a bigger setup than the small shows I've seen at home, and it's exciting to watch him use the space, flirting with the audience as they watch him with rapt atten-tion, singing every word back to him.

Knowing the big closing is coming soon, I'm surprised when I hear the music play on with a soft beat as Keith takes off his guitar, handing it to a stagehand.

He approaches the mic and pulls off his hat, wiping his forehead. "Hey, Boise. You mind I do something a little different tonight?"

Yelling back their agreement, he continues. "You see this yellow scarf tied up on my microphone?"

His fingers run along the length of yellow fluff tied to the top of the stand and hanging down to almost brush the stage. I blush, knowing why it's there but not noticing it before.

"Well, it was made for me by someone really special to me. She joked one night that I could tie it to my mic like Steven Tyler, a little rock star style for this country boy. In fact, she dared me that I wouldn't do it. And you know what I had to do, right?"

I can hear a mutiny of voices yelling back, mostly seeming to agree that Keith had to do it. I laugh, thinking of Keith saying, "hold my beer," but I still get warm and fuzzy inside because Keith did put the scarf I'd knitted for him on his mic and promised he'd do it every show for the whole tour.

"That's right. I put the damn scarf on the mic, because contrary to some folks' opinions, I'm not a stupid man. And when your woman tells you to do something, you'd best do it. When she dares you to, well then, you damn sure better do it!"

There are some hoots and hollers, and I grin. That's right . . . his woman. And he makes it sound like I'm in charge. If they only knew.

"So the woman who made this scarf for me is here tonight. You think I could bring her out and introduce you to her?"

My jaw drops as Keith looks over at me, waving me onstage. I shake my head no, honestly terrified. I'm not shy, but shit, this is on another level. There are thousands of people out there. No fucking way. I'm the one behind the camera and keyboard, writing the stories.

Keith grins, talking to the crowd again. "Oh, looks like she's shy, but I promise she isn't. She just needs a little incentive. Hey, Elise?"

I glare at him, and he smirks, "I *dare* you to get that fine ass out here with me."

Fuck, he knows I'm coming out there after his whole speech about my daring him and his following through. I take a deep breath and step out onstage.

The wall of supportive sound that hits me as I step awkwardly out helps unlock my knees, and as I give a little wave, I even hear a few wolf-whistles, which helps even more. Still, it seems like Keith is miles away as I walk the few yards to him in the center of the stage.

As soon as I'm close enough, he takes my hand, pulling me to his side and kissing me fully . . . in front of everyone. But it settles the swarm of butterflies in my belly a bit, even as it starts another type of fluttering in my body.

There's some noise again, but it seems to be a mix of cheering, more wolf-whistles, and a lot of 'awws.'

Keith releases me, spinning me out to let the whole crowd get another look at me. "So everyone, this is my woman, Elise. Elise, this is . . . everyone."

The crowd goes wild again, and I see lots of people waving, but even more phones being held up, recording this craziness. "So, I've got one more song to play for you, but I thought maybe you could help me with something first."

Keith moves the microphone out of the way and looks at me, our eyes locked as he slowly drops to one knee. The crowd roars again, a physical force that nearly knocks me over as my head spins. From the corner of my vision, I see a two-man crew run onstage with a camera and a boom mic above us and realize they're beaming us to the big jumbotron screens for the audience.

*Oh. My. God. What is happening? Is he doing what I think he's doing? Oh, my God.*

Keith takes my hands in his, looking up at me. "Elise, I wasn't looking for you. I didn't think this was in my cards, at least not for a long time, maybe never. But you came into my life, full of sass and refusing to take no as an answer. And we somehow fit together perfectly. You have given me so much . . . your heart, your trust, your love. And you have mine too . . . all of me. I love you and I want to spend the rest of my life making you as happy as you make me. Elise Warner, will you marry me?"

From somewhere, he's pulled out a ring and is holding it at my fingertip, his eyes shining hopefully. The tears are already rolling down my face as he waits, the shock and beauty of the moment overwhelming me.

I can't get a word out. My head's spinning so much, so I nod. "Yes, Keith. God, yes!" I finally whisper. "I love you."

He slides the ring on my finger, and I can't even see it as he swoops up, hugging and spinning me, and I can finally breathe, joyful laughter filling the air as I cling to him. "I love you so much, Keith."

He sets me down, and I realize the crowd is still going crazy, a deafening roar of celebration coming from every direction.

*Holy shit, I just got engaged on stage at a concert. My fiancé's concert. Whose life is this?*

Keith grabs the microphone again, still holding my hand. "Thanks, everyone. I think that went okay. What do you think?" he teases.

They cheer again, and Keith looks back, giving some sort of signal. The stage lights dim, and I see two stagehands come out, one with Keith's guitar and another with a stool. I think at first that Keith is going to sit down and sing, but he gestures to me instead.

I settle on the hard stool, thankfully remembering to sit up straight as Keith strums a few chords. "All right, Boise. I started this new song when it seemed like everything that could go wrong had gone wrong. It was angry, it was bitter . . . a real country song."

That earns a few laughs, and Keith continues. "But when I looked at the things that really mattered, that was all I needed to realize just how lucky I am. The song changed . . . because Elise changed me."

The first notes are soft, and anyone who doesn't know Keith might think they're plaintive . . . but this is the Keith I've been able to get to know more over the past few months, the one who is controlled, and reflective . . . and who just asked me to marry him.

*In the darkest of nights*
*When I'd near given up hope*
*You held me close*
*And you saved me*

*As the storm raged on*
*I had no fight left*
*You stood, sheltered me*
*And you saved me*

*You showed me love*
*You showed me light*
*You taught me pain was worth it*
*If you were the prize*

*It's a whole new world*
*It's a beautiful day*
*As long as you're by my side*
*It'll be a helluva a ride . . .*

**The End. Thank you for reading. If you enjoyed the book, please leave a review!**

**If you haven't read Dirty Talk, continue on for an excerpt! It is where Elise was first introduced! It is also a complete standalone.**

# EXCERPT: DIRTY TALK

KATRINA

"Checkmate, bitch," I exclaim as I do a victory dance that's comprised of fist pumps and ass wiggles in my chair while my best friend Elise laughs at me. I turn in my seat and start doing a little half-stepping Rockettes dance. "Can-can, I just kicked some can-can, I so am the wo-man, and I rule this place!"

Elise does a little finger dance herself, cheering along with me. "You go, girl. Winner, winner, chicken dinner. Now let's eat!"

I laugh with her, joyful in celebrating my new promotion at work, regardless of the dirty looks the snooty ladies at the next table are shooting our way. I get their looks. I mean, we are in the best restaurant in the city. While East Robinsville isn't New York or Miami, we're more of a Northeastern suburb of . . . well, everything in between. This just isn't the sort of restaurant where five-foot-two-inch women in work clothes go shaking their ass while chanting something akin to a high school cheer.

But right now, I give exactly zero fucks. "Damn right, we can eat! I'm the youngest person in the company to ever be promoted to Senior Developer and the first woman at that level. Glass ceiling? Boom, busting through! Boys' club? Infiltrated." I mime like I'm sneaking in, shoulders hunched and hands pressed tightly in front of me before splaying my arms wide with a huge grin. "Before they know it, I'm gonna have that boys' club watching chick flicks and the whole damn office is going to be painted pink!"

Elise snorts, shaking her head again. "I still don't have a fucking clue what you actually do, but even I understand the words *promotion* and *raise*. So huge congrats, honey."

She's right, no one really understands when I talk about my job. My brain has a tendency to talk in streams of binary zeroes and ones that make perfect sense to me, but not so much to the average person. When I was in high school, I even dreamed in Java.

And even I don't really understand what my promotion means. Senior Developer? Other than the fact that I get updated business cards with my fancy new title next week, I'm not sure what's changed. I'm still doing my own coding and my own work, just with a slightly higher pay grade. And when I say slightly, I mean barely a bump after taxes. Just enough for a bonus cocktail at a swanky club on Friday maybe. *Maybe* more at year end, they'd said. Ah, well, I'm excited anyway. It's a first step and an acknowledgement of my work.

The part people do get is when my company turns my strings of code into apps that go viral. After my last app went number one, they were forced to give me a promotion or risk losing my skills to another development company. They might not understand the zeroes and ones, but everyone can grasp dollars and cents, and that's what my apps bring in.

I might be young at only twenty-six, and female, as evidenced by my long honey-blonde hair and curvy figure, but as much as I don't fit the stereotypical profile of a computer nerd, they had to respect that my brain creates things that no one else does. I think it's my female point of view that really helps. While a chunk of the other people in the programming field fit the stereotype of being slightly repressed geeks who are more comfortable watching animated 'girlfriends' than talking to an actual woman, I'm different. I understand that merely slapping a pink font on things or adding sparkly shit and giving more pre-loaded shopping options doesn't make technology more 'female-friendly.'

It's insulting, honestly. But it gives me an edge in that I know how to actually create apps that women like and want to use. Not just women, either, based on sales. I'm getting a lot of men downloading my apps too, especially men who aren't into tech-geeking out every damn thing they own.

And so I celebrate with Elise, holding up our glasses of wine and clinking them together in a toast. Elise sips her wine and nods in appreciation, making me glad we went with the waiter's recommendation. "So you're killing it on the job front. What else is going on? How are things with you and Kevin?"

Elise has been my best friend since we met at a college recruiting event. She's all knockout looks and sass, and I'm short, nervous, and shy in professional situations, but we clicked. She knows I've been through the wringer with some previous boyfriends, and even though Kevin is fine—well-mannered, ambitious, and treats me right—she just doesn't care for him for some reason. So my joyful buzz is instantly dulled, knowing that she doesn't like Kevin.

"He's fine," I reply, knowing it's not a great answer, but I also know she's going to roast me anyway. "He's been working a lot of hours so I haven't even seen him in a few days, but he texts me every morning and night. We're supposed to go out for dinner this weekend to celebrate."

Elise sighs, giving me that look that makes her normally very cute face look sort of like a sarcastic basset hound. "I'm glad, I guess. Not to beat a dead horse," *—too late—* "but you really can do better. Kevin is just so . . . meh. There's no spark, no fire between you two. It's like you're friends who fuck."

I duck my chin, not wanting her to read on my face the woeful lack of fucking that has been happening, but I'm too transparent.

"Wait . . . you two *do* fuck, right?" Elise asks, flabbergasted. "I figured that was why you were staying with him. I was sure he must be great in the sack or you'd have dumped his boring ass a long time ago."

I bite my lip, not wanting to get into this with her . . . again. But one of Elise's greatest strengths is also one of her most annoying traits as well. She's like a dog with a bone and isn't going to let this go.

"Look, he's fine," I finally reply, trying to figure out how much I need to feed Elise before she gives me a measure of peace. "He's handsome, treats me well, and when we have sex, it's good . . . I guess. I don't believe in some Prince Charming who is going to sweep me off my feet to a castle where we'll have romantic candlelit dinners, brilliant conversation, and bed-breaking sexcapades. I just want someone to share the good and bad times with, some companionship."

Elise holds back as long as she can before she explodes, her snort and guffaw of derision getting even more looks in our direction. "Then get a fucking Golden Retriever and a rabbit. The buzzing kind that uses rechargeable batteries."

One of the ladies at the next table huffs, seemingly aghast at Elise's outburst, and they stand to move toward the bar on the other side of the restaurant, far away from us. "Well, if this is the sort of trash that passes for dinner conversation," the older one says as she sticks her nose far enough into the air I wonder if it's going to be clipped by the ceiling fans, "no wonder the country's going to hell under these Millennials!"

She storms off before Elise or I can respond, but the second lady pauses slightly and talks out of the side of her mouth. "Sweetie, you do deserve more than *fine*."

With a wink, she scurries off after her friend, leaving behind a grinning Elise. "See? Even snooty old biddies know that you deserve more than *meh*."

"I know. We've had this conversation on more than one occasion, so can we drop it?" I plead between clenched teeth before calming slightly. "I want to celebrate and catch up, not argue about my love life."

Always needing the last word, Elise drops her voice, muttering under her breath. "What love life?"

"That's low."

Elise holds her hands up, and I know I've at least gotten a temporary reprieve. "Okay then, if we're sticking to work, I got a new scoop that I'm running with. I'm writing a piece about a certain famous someone who got caught sending dick pics to a social media princess. Don't ask me who because I can't divulge that yet. But it'll be all there in black and white by next week's column."

Elise is an investigative journalist, a rather fantastic one whose talents are largely being wasted on celebrity news gossip for the tabloid paper she writes for. I can't even call it a paper, really. With the downfall of actual print news, most of her stuff ends up in cyberspace, where it's digested, Tweeted, hashtagged, and churned out for the two-minute attention span types to gloat over for a moment before they move on to . . . well, whatever the next sound bite happens to be.

Every once in awhile, she'll get to do something much more newsworthy, but mostly it's fact-checking and ass-covering before the paper publishes stories celebrities would rather see disappear. I know what burns her ass even more is when she has to cover the stories where some downward-trending celebrity manufactures a scandal just to get some social media buzz going before their latest attempt at rejuvenating a career that peaked about five years ago.

This one at least sounds halfway interesting, and frankly, better than my love life, so I laugh. "Why would he send a dick pic to someone on social media? Wouldn't he assume she'd post it? What a dumbass!"

"No, it's usually close-ups and they're posted anonymously," Elise says with a snort. "Of course, she knows because she sees the user name on their direct message, but she cuts it out so that it's posted to her page as an anonymous flash of flesh. Look."

She pulls out her phone, clicking around to open an app, one I didn't design but damn sure wish I had. It's got one hell of a sweet interface, and Elise is using it to organize her web pages better than anything the normal apps have. It takes Elise only a moment to find the page she wants.

"See?" she says, showing me her phone. "People send her messages with dick pics, tit pics, whatever. If she deems them sexy enough, she posts them with little blurbs and people can comment. She also does Q-and-As with followers, shows faceless pics of herself, and gives little shows sometimes. Kinda like porn but more 'real people' instead of silicone-stuffed, pump-sucked, fake moan scenes."

She scrolls through, showing me one image after another of body part close-ups. Some of them . . . well damn, I gotta say that while they might not be professionals or anything, it's a hell of a lot hotter than anything I'm getting right now. "Wow. That's uhh . . . quite something. I don't get it, but I guess lots of folks are into it. Wait."

She stops scrolling at my near-shout, smirking. "What? See something you like?"

My mouth feels dry and my voice papery. "Go back up a couple."

She scrolls back up and I read the blurb above a collage of pics. *Little titty fuck with my new boy toy today. Look at my hungry tits and his thick cock. After this, things got a little deeper, if you know what I mean. Sorry, no pics of that, but I'll just say that he was insatiable and I definitely had a very good morning. ;)*

The pictures show a close-up of her full cleavage, a guy's dick from above, and then a few pictures of him stroking in and out of her pressed-together breasts. I'm not afraid to say the girl's got a nice rack that would probably have most of my co-workers drooling and the blood rushing from their brains to their dicks, but that's not what's causing my stomach to drop through the floor.

I know that dick.

It's the same, thick with a little curve to the right, and I can even see a sort of donut-shaped mole high on the man's thigh, right above the shaved area above the base of his cock.

Yes, that mole seals it.

That's Kevin.

His cock with another woman, fucking her for social media, thinking I'd probably never even know. He has barely touched me lately, but he's willing to do it almost publicly with some social media slut?

I realize Elise is staring at me, her previous good-natured look long gone to be replaced by an expression of concern. "Kat, are you okay? You look pale."

I point at her phone, trying my best to keep my voice level. "That post? The one right there?"

"Oh, Titty Fuck Girl?" Elise asks. "She's on here at least once a month with a new set of pics. Apparently, she loves her rack. I still think they're fake. Why?"

"She's talking about Kevin. That's him."

She gasps, turning the phone to look closer. "Holy shit, honey. Are you sure?"

I nod, tears already pooling in my eyes. "I'm sure."

She puts her phone down on the table and comes around the table to hug me. "Shit. Shit. Shit. I am so sorry. I told you that douchebag doesn't deserve someone like you. You're too fucking good for him."

I sniffle, nodding, but deep inside, I know that this is always how it goes. Every single boyfriend I've ever had ended up cheating on me. I've tried playing hard to get. I've tried being the good little go-along girlfriend. I've even tried being myself, which seems to be somewhere in between, once I figured out who I actually was.

It's even worse in bed, where I've tried being vanilla, being aggressive, and being submissive. And again, being myself, somewhere in the middle, when I figured out what I enjoyed from the experimentation.

But honestly, I've never been satisfied. No matter what, I just can't seem to find that 'sweet spot' that makes me happy and fulfilled in a relationship. And while I've tried everything, depending on the guy, it never works out. The boyfriends I've had, while few in number considering I can count them on one hand, all eventually cheated, saying that they just wanted something different. Something that's *not* me.

Apparently, Kevin's no different. My mood shifts wildly from self-pity to anger to finally, a numb acceptance. "What a fucking jerk. I hope he likes being a boy toy for a social media slut, because he's damn sure not my boyfriend anymore."

"That's the spirit," Elise says, refilling my wine glass. "Now, how about you and I finish off this bottle, get another, and by the time you're done, you'll have forgotten all about that loser while we take a cab back to your place?"

"Maybe I will just get a dog, and I sure as hell already have a buzzing rabbit. Several of them, in fact," I mutter. "You know what? They're better than he ever was by a damn country mile."

"Rabbits . . . they just keep going and going and going," Elise jokes, trying to keep me in good spirits. She twirls her hands in the air like the famous commercial bunny and signals for another bottle of wine.

She's right. Fuck Kevin.

DERRICK

My black leather office chair creaks, an annoying little trend it's developed over the past six months that's the primary reason I don't use it in the studio. Admittedly, that's probably for the better because if I had a chair this comfortable in the studio, I'd be too relaxed to really be on point for my shows. Still, it's helpful to have something nice like this office since it's a hell of a big step up from the days when my office was also the station's break room. "All right, hit me. What's on the agenda for today's show?"

My co-star, Susannah, checks her papers, making little check-marks as she goes through each item. She's an incessant check-marker, and I have no idea how the fuck she can read her sheets by the end of the day. "The overall theme for today is cheaters, and I've got several emails pulled for that so we can stay on track. We'll field calls, of course, and some will be on topic and some off, like always. I'll try and screen them as best I can, and we should be all set."

I nod, trying to mentally prep myself for another three-hour stint behind the mic, offering music, advice, hope, and sometimes a swift kick in the pants to our listeners. Two years ago, I never would've believed that I'd be known as the 'Love Whisperer' on a radio talk segment called the same thing. Part

Howard Stern, part Dr. Phil, part DJ Love Below, I've found a niche that's just . . . unique.

I started out many years ago as a jock, playing football on my high school team with dreams of college ball. A seemingly short derailment after an injury led me to do sports reporting for my high school's news and I fell in love.

After that, my scholarships to play football never came, but it didn't bother me as much as I thought it would. I decided to chase after a sports broadcast degree instead, marrying my passion for football and my love of reporting.

I spent four years after graduation doing daily sports talks from three to six as the afternoon drive-home DJ. It wasn't a big station, just one of the half-dozen stations that existed as an alternative for people who didn't want to listen to corporate pop, hip-hop, or country. It was there I received that fateful call.

Looking back, it's kind of crazy, but a guy had called in bitching and moaning about his wife not understanding his need to follow all these wild superstitions to help his team win.

*"I'm telling you D, I went to church and asked God himself. I said, if you can bless the Bandits with a win, I'll show myself true and wear those ugly ass socks my pastor gave me for Christmas the year before and never wash them again. You know what happened?"*

Of course, everyone could figure out what happened. Still, I respectfully told him that I didn't think his unwashed socks were doing a damn thing for his beloved team on the basketball court, but if he didn't put those fuckers in the washing machine, they were sure going to land him in divorce court.

He sighed and eventually gave in when I told him to wash the socks, thank his wife for putting up with his shit, and full-out romance her to bed and do his damndest to make up for his selfish ways.

And that was that. A new show and a new me were born. After

a few marketing tweaks, I've been the so-called 'Love Whisperer' for almost a year now, helping people who ask for advice to get the happily ever after they want.

Ironically, I'm single. Funny how that works out, but all the good advice I try to give stems from my parents who were happily married for over forty years before my mom passed. I won't settle for less than the real thing, and I try to advise my listeners to do the same.

And then there's the sex aspect of my job.

Talking about relationships obviously involves discussing sex with people, as that's one of the major areas that cause problems for folks. At first, talking about all the crazy shit people want to do even made me blush a little, but eventually, it's just gotten to be second nature.

Want to talk about how to get your wife to massage your prostate? Can do. Want to talk about how your girlfriend wants you to wear Underoos and call her Mommy? Can do. Want to talk about your husband never washing the dishes, and how you can get him to help? I can do that too.

All-in-one, real relationships at your service. Live from six to nine, five days a week, or available for download on various podcast sites and clip shows on the weekends. Hell of a lot for a guy who figured *making it* would involve becoming the voice of some college football team.

So I want to do a good job. And that means working well with Susannah, who is the control-freak yin to my laissez-faire yang. "Thanks. I know this week's topics from our show planning meeting, but I spaced on tonight's focus."

Susannah nods, unflappable. "No problem. Do you want to scan the emails or just do your thing?"

I smile at her. She already knows the answer. "Same as always, spontaneous. You know that even though I was a Boy Scout, being prepared for this doesn't do us any favors. I sound robotic when I read ahead. First read, real reactions work better and give the listeners knee-jerk common sense."

She shrugs, scribbling on her papers. "I know, just checking."

It's probably one of the reasons we work so well together, our totally different approaches to the show. Joining me from day one, she's the one who keeps our show running behind the scenes and keeps me on track on-air, serving as both producer and co-host. Luckily, her almost anal-retentive penchant for prep totally doesn't come across on the air, where she's the playful, comedic counter to my gruff, tell-it-like-it-is style.

"Then let's rock," I tell her. "Got your drinks ready?"

Susannah nods as we head toward the studio. Settling into my broadcast chair, a much less comfortable but totally silent one, I survey my normal spread of one water, one coffee, and one green tea, one for every hour we're gonna be on the air. With the top of the hour news breaks and spaced out music jams, I've gotten used to using the exactly four minute and thirty second breaks to run next door and drain my bladder if I need to.

Everything ready, we smile and settle in for another show. "Gooooood evening! It's your favorite 'Love Whisperer,' Derrick King here with my lovely assistant, Miss Susannah Jameson. We're ready for an evening of love, sex, betrayal, and lust, if you're willing to share. Our focus tonight is on cheaters and cheating. Are you being cheated on? Maybe *you* are the cheater? Call in and we'll talk."

The red glow from the holding calls is instant, but I traditionally go to an email first so that I can roll right in. "While Susannah is grabbing our first caller, I'll start with an email. Here's one from P. 'Dear Love Whisperer,' it says, 'my husband travels extensively for work, leaving me home and so lonely. I don't know if he's cheating while he's gone, but I always wonder. I've started to develop feelings for my personal trainer, and I think I'm falling in love with him. What should I do?' "

I *tsk-tsk* into the microphone, making my displeasure clear. "Well, P, first things first. Your marriage is your priority because you made a vow. For better or worse, remember? It's simple. Talk to your husband. Maybe he's cheating, maybe he isn't. Maybe he's working his ass off so his bored wife can even *have* a trainer and you're looking for excuses to justify your own bad behavior. But talking to him is your first step. You need to explain your feelings and that you need him more than perhaps you need the money. Second, you need to get a life beyond your husband and trainer. I get the sense you need some attention and your trainer is giving it to you, so you think you're in love with him. Newsflash—he's being paid to give you attention. By your husband, it sounds like. That's not a healthy foundation for a relationship even if he is your soulmate, which I doubt."

I sigh and lower my voice a little. I don't want to cut this woman's guts out. I want to help her. "P, let's be honest. A good trainer is going to be personable. They're in a sales profession. They're not going to make it in the industry without either being the best in the world at what they do or having a good personality. And a lot of them have good bodies. Their bodies are their business cards. So it's natural to feel some attraction to your trainer. But that doesn't mean he's going to stick by you. Here's a challenge—tell your trainer you can't pay him for the next three months and see how available he is to just give you his time."

Susannah snickers and hits her mic button. "That's why I do group yoga classes. Only thing that happens there is sweaty tantric orgies. Ohmm . . . my . . ." Her initial yoga-esque ohm dissolves into a pleasure-induced moan that she fakes exceedingly well.

I roll my eyes, knowing that she does nothing of the sort. "To the point, though, fire your trainer because of your weakness and tell him why. He's a pro. He needs to know that his services were not the reason you're leaving. Next, get a hobby that fulfills you beyond a man and talk to your husband."

I click a button and a sound effect of a cheering audience plays through my headset. It goes on like this for a while, call after call, email after email of helping people.

Well, I hope I'm helping them. They seem to think I am, and I'm certainly giving it my best shot. In between, I mix in music and a hodgepodge of stuff that fits the daily themes. Tonight I've got some Taylor Swift, a little Carrie Underwood, some old-school TLC. I even, as a joke, worked in Bobby Brown at Susannah's insistence.

Coming back from that last one, I see Susannah gesture from her mini-booth and give the airspace over to her, letting her introduce the next caller. "Okay, Susannah's giving me the big foam finger, so what've we got?"

"You wish I had a big finger for you," Susannah teases like she always does on air—it's part of our act. "The next caller would like to discuss some rather incriminating photos she's come across. Apparently, Mr. Right was Mr. Everybody?"

I click the button, taking the call live on-air. "This is the 'Love Whisperer', who am I speaking with?"

The caller stutters, obviously nervous, and in my mind I know I have to treat this one gently. Some of the callers just want to laugh, maybe have their fifteen seconds of fame or get their pound of proverbial flesh by exposing their partner's misdeeds. But there are also callers like this, who I suspect really needs help. "This is Katrina . . . Kat."

Whoa, a first name. And from the sound of it, a real one. She's not making a thing up. I need to lighten the mood a little, or else she's gonna clam up and freak out on me. "Hello, Kitty Kat. What seems to be the problem today?"

I hear her sigh, and it touches me for some reason. "Well . . . I can't believe I actually got through, first of all. I worked up the nerve to dial the numbers but didn't expect an answer. I'm just . . . I don't even know what I am. I'm just a little lost and in need of some advice, I guess." She huffs out a humorless laugh.

I can hear the pain in her voice, mixed with nerves. "Advice? That I can do. That's what I'm here for, in fact. What's going on, Kat?"

"It's my boyfriend, or my soon-to-be ex-boyfriend, I guess. I found out today that he slept with someone else." She sounds like she's found a bit of steel as she speaks this time, and it makes her previous vulnerability all the more touching.

"Ouch," I say, truly wincing at the fresh wound. A day of cheat call? I'm sure the advertisers are rubbing their hands in glee, but I'm feeling for this girl. "I'm so sorry. I know that hurts and it's wrong no matter what. I heard something about compromising pics. Please tell me he didn't send you pics of him screwing someone else?"

She laughs but it's not in humor. "No, I guess that would've been worse, but he had sex with someone kind of Internet famous and she posted faceless pics of them together. But I recognized his . . . uhm . . . his . . ."

Let's just get the schlong out in the open, why don't we? "You recognized his penis? Is that the word you're looking for?"

"Yeah, I guess so," Kat says, her voice cutting through the gap created by the phone line. "He has a mole, so I know it's him."

There's something about her voice, all sweet and breathy that stirs me inside like I rarely have happen. It's not just her tone, either. She's in pain, but she's mad as fuck too, and I want to help her, protect her. She seems innocent, and something deep inside me wants to make her a little bit dirty.

"Okay, first, repeat after me. Penis, dick, cock." I wait, unsure if she'll do it but holding my breath in the hopes that she will.

"Uh, what?"

I feel a small smile come to my lips, and it's my turn to be a little playful. "Penis, dick, cock. Trust me, this is important for you. You can do it, Kitty Kat."

I hear her intake of breath, but she does what I demanded, more clearly than the shyness I expected. "Penis, dick, cock."

"Good girl," I growl into the mic, and through the window connecting our booths, I can see Susannah giving me a raised eyebrow. "Now say . . . I recognized his cock fucking her."

I say a silent prayer of thanks that my radio show is on satellite. I can say whatever I want and the FCC doesn't care.

I can tell Kat is with me now, and her voice is stronger, still sexy as fuck but without the lost kitten loneliness to it. "I recognized his cock fucking her tits."

My own cock twitches a little, and I lean in, smirking. "Ah, so the plot thickens. So Kat, how does it feel to say that?"

She sighs, pulling me back a little. "The words don't bother me. I'm just not used to being on the radio. But saying that about my boyfriend pisses me off. I can't believe he'd do that."

"So, what do you think you should do about it?" I ask, leaning back in my chair and pulling my mic toward me. "Is this a 'talk it through and our relationship will be stronger on the other side of this' type situation, or is this a 'hit the road, motherfucker, and take Miss Slippy-Grippy Tits with you?' Do you want my opinion or do you already know?"

"You're right," Kat says, chuckling and sounding stronger again. "I already know I'm done. He's been a wham-bam-doesn't even say thank you, ma'am guy all along, and I've been hanging on because I didn't think I deserved better. But I don't deserve this. I'm better off alone."

Whoa, now, only half right there, Kat with the sexy voice. "You don't deserve this. You should have someone who treats you so well you never question their love, their commitment to you. Everyone deserves that. Hey, Kitty Kat? One more thing. Can you say 'cock' for me one more time? Just for . . . entertainment."

I'm pushing the line here, both for her and for the show, but I ask her to do it anyway because I want, no need, to hear her say it.

She laughs, her voice lighter even as I know the serious conversation had to hurt. "Of course, Love Whisperer. Anything for you. You ready? Cock." She draws the word out, the k a bit harsher, and I can hear the sass, almost an invitation, as she speaks.

"Ooh, thanks so much, Kitty Kat. Hold on the line just a second." My cock is now fully hard in my pants, and I'm not sure if my upcoming bathroom break is going to be to piss or to take care of that.

I click some buttons, sending the show to a song, Shaggy's *It Wasn't Me* coming over the airwaves to keep the cheating theme rolling. "Susannah?"

"Yeah?"

"Handle the next call or so after the commercial break," I tell her. "Pick something . . . funny after that one."

"Gotcha," Susannah says, and I'm glad she's able to handle things like that. It's part of our system too that when I get a call that needs more than on-air can handle, she fills the gap. Usually with less serious questions or listener stories that always make for great laughs.

Checking my board, I click the line back, glad that Susannah can't hear me now. "Kat? You still there?"

"Yes?" she says, and I feel another little thrill go down my cock just at her word. God, this woman's got a sexy voice, soft and sweet with a little undercurrent of sassiness . . . or maybe I really, really need to get laid.

"Hey, it's Derrick. I just wanted to say thanks for being such a good sport with all of that."

"No problem," she says as I make a picture in my head of her. I can't fill in the details, but I definitely want to. "Thanks for helping me realize I need to walk away. I already knew it, but some inspiration never hurts."

"I really would like to hear the rest of the story if you don't mind calling me back. I want to hear how he grovels when he finds out what he's lost. Would you call me?"

I don't know what I'm doing. This is so not like me. I never talk to the callers after they're on air unless I think they're going to hurt themselves or others, and I certainly never invite them to call back. But something about her voice calls to me like a siren. I just hope she's not pulling me into the rocky shore to crash.

"You mean the show?" Kat asks, uncertain and confused. "Like . . . I dunno, like a guest or something?"

"Well, probably not, to be honest," I reply, crossing my fingers even as my cock says I need to take this risk. "We'll be done with the cheating theme tonight and it probably won't come back up for a couple of weeks. I meant . . . call me. I want to make sure you're okay afterward and standing strong."

"Okay."

Before she can take it back, I rattle off my personal cell number to her, half of my brain telling me this is brilliant and the other half saying it's the stupidest thing I've ever done. I might not have the FCC looking over my shoulder, but the satellite network is and my advertisers for damn sure are. Still . . . "Got it?"

"I've got it," Kat says. "I'll get back to you after I break up with Kevin. It's been a weird night and I guess it's going to get even weirder. Guess I gotta go tell Kevin his dick busted him on the internet and he can get fucked elsewhere . . . permanently. I can do this."

"Damn right, you can," I tell her. "You can do this, Kitty Kat. Remember, you deserve better. I'll be waiting for your report."

Kat laughs and we hang up. I don't know what just happened but my body feels light, bubbly inside as I take a big breath to get ready for the next segment of tonight's show.

KAT

I knock on the door to Kevin's apartment, the voice of Derrick the Love Whisperer still running around in my head. I deserve better than to be cheated on.

"Hey, babe," Kevin says when he opens his door. He's still wearing his 'work clothes,' a black tank top with *KH Nutrition* emblazoned on it along with track pants that are just a little tight and normally worn just a little low on his hips when he works out. I've never really understood why he does it, but it's part of his 'thang.' Every Instagram pic and video he does, he whips off the tank, adjusts his track pants in a way that highlights the Adonis belt V-cut of his abs, then flexes and sort of makes a hooting grunt before finishing the show with "KH, Bay-bay!"

I used to think it was sexy, in a musclehead, caveman-ish sort of way. No longer. "Don't 'hey, babe' me," I growl, looking up into his eyes. I'm not in work clothes, so I'm missing the extra inches of height my heels normally give me. But I'm a legit five-two of fury right now, so I don't care if he's nearly a foot taller. "How long have you been fucking her behind my back?"

"Huh?" Kevin asks, but in his eyes I can see he has a damn good idea what I'm talking about.

"Don't act stupid, you son of a bitch!" I hiss, poking him in the chest. "You know exactly what I'm talking about. Titty Fuck Girl. Where'd you meet her, the gym? When you went out shopping for a new smartphone with the money I gave you because you swore you needed the better camera for your Instagram page? How long has it been going on, Kevin?"

Kevin looks up and down the hallway. For a guy whose Internet presence makes him look like a big baller, he's living in a cracker box POS apartment building, and I know he's worried about his neighbors hearing me blab his private business. "Come on inside. We can talk—"

"If you don't tell me how long it's been going on, I'm going to put my knee right in your nuts," I growl. "This isn't a negotiation, Kevin." It really doesn't matter at this point. It's most likely just going to make me angrier, but I can't stop myself.

He looks like he's about to run but sighs. "Fine. I met her a couple of months ago when she came into the gym. I was filming a squat."

"What? So she just walked up behind you to compliment your form and suddenly, you're in bed?" I laugh, realizing just how short I sold myself. He's fake—the tan, the persona, the entire image. Just to get more followers.

Kevin looks sheepish but nods. "She said she'd promote my supps, do some spots on her Instagram feed, and let me shoot some selfies with her wearing a KH tank top."

"So you titty fucked her?" I hiss, shaking my head. Seriously, what the fuck? I can hardly take it as I stare at his chiseled face, wanting so badly to slap him. "Do you realize how ridiculous you sound right now? How stupid do you think I am?"

Kevin looks pouty, the same look he used when he hit me up for four hundred bucks for his new smartphone. "You never believe in me, never think I can be successful even though I work so hard."

It's in this moment that I see it. Though his face is schooled into a puppy dog look, his eyes are alight as he turns the blame back on me, thinking he's pulled one over on me once again. And all the fire leaves me. I'm mad he cheated, but I don't even really like him right now, and honestly, I haven't for a long time but was too afraid to do anything about it.

My voice takes a parental, lecturing tone. "You're not working. You're a lazy ass who spends hours at the gym bullshitting with the bros and thinking some scam is going to magically make you money without your having to actually do anything. But you know what? I looked the other way for too long even though everyone told me you were no good. None of that even matters now. You cheated on me. Done. Game over."

Kevin inhales, trying to stand at his tallest, most imposing. His forearms clench and his biceps start to strain as he puffs up. It strikes me that once upon a time, he'd stand over me like this and I'd find it so damn sexy I'd be instantly wet, but now, his attempt at intimidating me is just ridiculous. "You'll be sorry. You'll never find someone who treats you like I do, who satisfies you like I do."

God, how could I have been so blind? "Like you do? You know, I hope you're right because you treat me like an afterthought, using me as an ATM when you're a little short, screwing around, and blaming me for your lack of success when it's your own fault," I reply, keeping my voice calm but firm, not letting him get an inch on me. I'm not going to raise my voice, to yell or let him think that he's gotten to me, because for some reason, honestly, he hasn't. "And as for satisfied in bed, I have literally never had a single orgasm with you. Ever. I'm not gonna lie, your dick is nice to look at and photographs well, apparently, but you don't even know what to do with it. Sticking it in and out for two minutes before blowing into a condom and then rolling over to gasp while staring at the ceiling doesn't quite cut it, Kev. So yeah, I hope I never find someone who treats me like you do. I thought I could settle for content, just float along and not rock the boat, but I deserve so much more."

Before Kevin can reply, I turn and walk toward the stairs, not wanting to lose my nerve in front of him. It's not until I'm halfway down that the shakes start as the adrenaline leaves me, but I keep it cool until I get to my car.

---

One Week Later

A week since the blow-up with Kevin and I'm surprisingly not upset. Disappointed, sure, but if you end a one-year relationship with someone, shouldn't you feel sad? I've felt a lot of other emotions, anger mostly, but they've faded too. Instead, I'm just left with this . . . I guess more than anything, lack of things to do. I've got more free time on my hands, but I'm not sad or upset.

I guess the lack of depression goes to show how far apart we'd drifted and how unattached I was from him without even realizing it. Really, the most annoying part of this whole thing has been that I've had to change my gym membership because I didn't want drama or to limit myself to when I could or couldn't go based on his haunting the place.

Maybe I never really was in love with him. We'd met at the gym, and he'd been charming and admittedly hot, so when he asked me out, I said yes. Our dating just naturally progressed, and somewhere along the way, we started calling it a relationship, but who knows if he was ever really committed? I was faithful, but that was more out of habit and the fact that I would never cheat than any obvious commitment we had. It's not like he ever put a ring on it.

Even though it had been over a month since we'd been intimate, I'd gone to the doctor for a checkup just to be safe, and luckily, everything was clear. I can't believe he'd put me at risk, but I guess I should've seen it coming considering guys always cheat.

Taking the opportunity to do a purge on everything in my life, I've got the radio turned up and I'm cleaning my apartment like a mad woman when I hear the voice. *His* voice.

It's like velvet-covered gravel, and just a few words make me breathless and hot. "Good evening, listeners. Derrick King here, aka the 'Love Whisperer'. What's happening in your love life? Our focus tonight is on pushing boundaries in the bedroom. What's encouraging and fun? What's demanding and over the line? Call in if you've got something to discuss."

I've gone stock-still, my cleaning completely forgotten as his voice washes over me. I turn it up a little more as I finish sweeping, deciding everything else can wait as I listen.

Over the next few hours, Derrick is surprisingly simple in his answers to callers, who want to try a variety of things sexually but for whatever reason haven't discussed it with their partners. It's almost comical how every call gets into a groove, and it sort of goes like this:

I want to do this crazy thing.

Have you asked your partner?

No.

Talk to them. Maybe they're into it.

But I'm not sure they want to.

How could you know if you don't talk with them? If they are, great. If not, decide if it's a deal breaker and move forward according to your answer. Chances are it's not a deal-breaker if you're not doing it now.

It's funny and spiced up with plenty of little anecdotes and witticisms that leave me grinning, while his voice turns me on even as I'm comforted. I listen to his no-nonsense approach as he advocates conversation and honesty at every turn, and I only wish I had a man like that who'd actually talk and be honest with me.

As the show wraps up, I remember his request for me to call him back and tell him what happened with Kevin. He was probably just being nice and doesn't actually expect me to call, but something about it felt real.

I wait for a bit after the show ends to give him time to get out of the studio and wherever it is he goes after work, and then I call. I'm heading out anyway. I've got a late-night rumbling tummy that can only be satisfied by something cheesy and takeout.

The phone rings several times and I'm about to hang up, mad at myself for being stupidly excited about talking to *The Love Whisperer* again, when he answers.

"Talk to me."

It's the same purring growl. That panty-melting voice of his isn't an act.

"Hey, Love Whisperer. It's your Kitty Kat."

There's a throaty chuckle on the other end, but there's concern in it too, which helps me feel better. "*My* Kitty Kat now?" he asks, and I can hear the smile in his voice. "After a week went by, I wasn't sure if I was going to get that return call. I was starting to doubt whether I had an effect at all."

"You set me straight. Hold on. Let me put you on speaker. I've got this technogeek wonder phone that I love to use speaker on."

"Well, I'm in my office, so this isn't private . . . but tell me, how'd it go?"

I plug my phone into the charging dock in my dash and slip my Bluetooth earpiece in as I fire up my car. "First off, I can't believe I didn't listen to anyone."

Derrick

"I can't believe you're the type to settle for anyone," I reply, relaxing back in my office chair. It's late. Almost nobody is around the studio right now. It's one of the benefits of satellite radio, I guess. You can run a lot more shows pre-recorded. "So he fessed up?"

"He gave me the most ridiculous line of shit ever," Kat says, her breathy voice causing a stir in my pants. What the fuck is wrong with me? "He said that he did it because she was willing to pimp his line of supplements on her Instagram page."

"You're shitting me," I say, rolling my eyes. "What a stupid asshole."

"You're right there. Honestly, I waited a week to call because I wanted to get a clear head."

"I can understand that. So he fed you a line of bullshit, and you chucked his ass out on the street. That's what I wanted to hear."

"Not quite," Kat says. "I went to his apartment to give him the news. No waiting around."

"Good for you," I tell her. "So, that's it? I mean, I like it, but sounds a bit easy, don't you think?"

"Well, he did try to puff his chest out and tell me no man would ever treat me like he did or satisfy me like him. I took a little delight in telling him that I sure as hell hoped not since he's a cheater whom I had to fake it with because he'd never even made me . . ." Kat says with spunkiness before stopping herself short. "Uhm, I mean—"

"Wait, seriously?" I ask in a sputtering laugh. "Is that true? You weren't just busting his balls? Damn, Kat . . . for how long?"

"It's okay," she says, seemingly comfortable talking to me. "My best friend told me to get a dog or a new rabbit. Or both. She's probably right."

"A rabbit?" I ask, my brain half-buzzed from her voice. Fuck me, I need to get laid.

"Well, um, not a bunny rabbit," she replies, her voice becoming even a little breathier. "You know . . . a rabbit."

She makes a buzzing sound, and all of a sudden, it hits me. She's making me seem like an amateur. I talk about sex for a living. I shouldn't be caught off guard like this. Trying to maintain at least a veneer of professionalism, I clear my throat. "Yeah, I can see where that'd come in handy. Take matters into your own hands, so to speak. I've done that myself more than a few times."

What I just said sinks in for both of us, and the tension between us can be felt even over the phone lines. If I could see her right now, I'd swear we'd just crossed a line. And I'd probably see how far I could push to make a move.

Kat can feel it too. "So, uh, yeah, anyway. That was probably an overshare on my part. Sorry about that."

Fuck it. I don't know why I'm doing this, but I'm just gonna go for it. Her sweet voice is doing something magically delicious to me, something about her intriguing me in a way I haven't felt in a long while. Time to jump in the pool and see if she's willing to swim with me. I look around the studio, not seeing Susannah. "Not an overshare at all. I'm just in the middle of picturing you with your new pet bunny, what you would look like spread wide open with your tits pearled up, pussy pulsing around a little toy that can't fill it, and what you'd sound like when you come."

I know my voice has gotten deeper, lust making it even rougher than my usual smooth radio sound, but I can't stop it.

I adjust myself in my jeans, glad she can't see the effect she's having on me right now.

There's a slight hitch in her voice as she adjusts to what I just said. "Derrick, wow. I don't know what to say to that. Fuck."

She's all but whispering by the end of her sentence and I wonder if she's touching herself to let out some tension. I don't even know what she looks like, but I don't care. I want to see her just like I said, maybe in a little skirt that's hiked up so she can show me as I inhale her scent. "You don't have to say anything unless you want me to stop."

I pause, hoping she doesn't say stop because I damn sure don't want to. I barely know this woman, this voice coming through my phone, but she's got me rock hard and on the edge with barely a word. I reach down and undo the button on my jeans, giving myself at least a little room to breathe.

"I think I need to—"

I interrupt, hoping to give her what she wants and needing my own release as well. "What do you need, Kitty Kat? I'll give it to you."

Kat pauses, and I can feel her trembling on the edge before she lets out another deep breath, half moan, half sigh of regret. "I think I need to go. I'm sorry. This is all new to me and I wasn't expecting this tonight. And . . . well, I'm driving. Gotta stay safe. Good night, Derrick."

Before I can say a single thing to stop her, she hangs up. *Damn it, Derrick! You pushed her too far, too fast.* I literally just did a show about listening, not going beyond your partner's limits, and I just blasted past Kat's, lost in my own desire.

My brain is yelling at me, disappointed that she hung up, but my cock is still at full attention, begging for release. I let the image of Kat take over my mind, not even knowing what she actually looks like, but imagining her pink pussy dripping as she rubs a vibrator across her clit.

I reach into my briefs, taking my cock out and grabbing it in one fist, then stroke up and down my shaft, giving me instant relief as I groan. To hell with it. As hot as I am, this will be fast, so the odds of anyone catching me are slim. And if they do, well, they're in for a sight because I can't stop.

I imagine Kat holding the vibe to herself as she slips two fingers into her pussy, thrusting them in and out in time to my own strokes, her eyes hooded with lust and watching my every breath.

In my head, I talk to her, telling her to fuck herself with her fingers. To show me how much she wishes it were my cock filling her tight pussy, how she wants to squeeze and milk me until I fill her up with so much cum that it spills out of her, too much for her little cunt to hold.

The combination of memories of her voice and my own mind filling the gaps and imagining dirty talking to Kat sends me over the edge. I explode, my come coating my hand as I jerk, getting every last shudder from the orgasm as I picture Kat screaming my name as she's lost in her own pleasure.

I glance around my office again, seeing the box of tissues on the corner of my desk. I grab a handful, glad there's something to help clean up this particular spill . . . and damn glad nobody's around to see the mess I've made.

KAT

"Yo, Kat!"

"You already spent that new bonus check?"

I huff, wishing I got a bonus check, but I play along anyway. I give a wave to Harry and Larry, two of my co-workers. "You'll see when the pizzas come in at lunch!" I joke back.

Harry rubs his Monday shirt, a stretched and faded *Pizza The*

*Hut* custom job he got off the Internet. "Just remember, no sausage!"

"That's not what I've heard," I tease, and Harry snorts. He claims to be a ladies-man love machine, but I have more than a sneaking suspicion that's all talk and some serious next-level self-aggrandizing. He's a good guy, though, and he doesn't take anything too seriously.

"Yeah, well, hope you've got another doozy cooked up," Larry says. "My latest game's gonna have me taking your shine soon enough."

I laugh and head to my cubicle. I've finally gotten it exactly the way I want, with triple screens that allow me to code, visualize, and debug all at the same time.

I immediately pull up my next project, an ambitious attempt at totally integrating calendars, social media, and office apps that could turn the whole damn system on its head.

I need to focus because the coding on this is going to be tricky. Integrating all these systems is easy. Doing it without turning someone's smartphone into a brick that works at the speed of a turtle? That's tricky.

As I work, I know I should be focusing on code. Every line has to be correct and every phrase has to be perfect. I can't have any mistakes or any clogs. But instead, my mind keeps wandering back to my phone conversation with Derrick.

The conversation had been nice until it got a little too heated. I mean, he had me half moaning even before he said what he did. I can't believe I just bailed like that.

Sure, I know I was a total coward, but I truly wasn't expecting it and I didn't know what to say. Especially since all of my blood was rushing to my neglected pussy, making me squirm around in my seat and tempting me to pull over right then to take matters into my own hands once again. I was this close to telling him exactly what I needed.

*Face it, Kat, you wanted to,* my mind tells me. *In fact, you wanted him to be there, his silky voice telling you what to do, talking you through every action as his eyes watched you with rapt attention.*

Shaking my head, I try to get back to work, putting in hour after hour of work and making little progress. Coding is a lot like speaking a foreign language. For some people, those folks who get paid big bucks, they can translate on the fly, able to listen in one language and talk in another almost instantaneously.

Others, like me, might be just as fluent in both languages but can't operate in both at the same time. So for me, coding means I have to put my brain in 'code mode' to really get in the groove.

Just as my left-hand monitor flashes me a signal that it's noon and time for lunch, my phone rings. It's my sister Jessie, who's learned to never, ever call me during my work hours unless someone important is dying.

Jessie's always been like a second mom to me. Eight years older, we never really had that period when she was a teen where she thought taking care of her little sister was a pain in the ass. Instead, she looked out for me, making sure I got my schoolwork done and never letting me veer too far off the path into crazy.

She's not some stick in the mud though. Actually, the first time I ever got drunk was with Jessie, and we both have had plenty of good laughs along the way. With hair two shades darker than mine and another three inches on me, she's beautiful and a stellar wife and mom, all the while holding down a full-time job as a risk management specialist for an insurance company.

She's truly Super Woman and everything I want to be when I grow up, whenever that'll be. With my new promotion, I'm at least *halfway* there, the professional success coming more readily than the personal. "What's up in the land of vehicle recall calculations?" I ask her. "Got anything that'll blow up in my face?"

"Very funny," Jess says with a laugh. "Actually, I called to say congrats on work and your promotion. Good job, Sis. I knew you could do it. Acing it at work, and on the home front too? How's Kevin?"

I wonder for a split second if she can read my mind, the professional-personal discrepancy coming out of her mouth just a beat after it crossed my mind. I can tell she doesn't care but feels like she should ask.

"What about Kevin?" I ask, trying to not sound snippy. Hell, maybe I should listen to her more because she was spot-on with him and has been right before about boyfriends too. "There *is* no more Kevin."

"What do you mean?" she asks, and I tell her about our breakup, leaving out the issues with our sex life and focusing on his cheating and my not putting up with it.

When I finish, Jess gives me a little cheer. "Good for you, girl. You're beautiful *and* smart, and there's no reason you should have to put up with any man who can't see that."

"Well, I don't want to be a downer, but not everyone finds a fairytale Prince Charming who loves you like Liam does you. Gonna be honest here. He's the only thing giving me hope that such a man exists in the real world, because all the ones I run into are cheaters, liars, and users looking for a booty call and nothing else."

Jess knows my experience with men so she gives me a pass. "He's out there," she tells me reassuringly. "You'll find him soon. Probably when you least expect it."

Unbidden, my mind jumps to Derrick and how that was so unexpected. But I don't even know him. Not really, just his radio persona, although he did seem genuine and real when he was listening to my drama about breaking up with Kevin.

Of course, he seems to have a bad boy side too. Good guys don't start talking about how they want to watch me toy my pussy on a second conversation unless they've got at least a decent naughty streak running through them.

There's a part of me that wants to get my own bad girl vibe going . . . kind of. I mean, I want to, but my wild child streak is sadly narrow, but maybe I could learn a few things from Derrick.

"Yeah, well," I finally say, not wanting to go down that particular rabbit hole at the moment, pun intended, "either way, I'm single now."

"Sexy and single," Jess replies. "Whatcha gonna do with all that ass inside them jeans?"

"I'm wearing a skirt today, actually," I retort. "But I do need to get some lunch."

"I gotcha," Jess says, letting it drop. "Listen, don't let any of those cretins you work with have a heart attack because your beautiful ass goes walking by, okay? And if anyone tries to grab anything, you break their wrist with one hand and slap a sexual harassment lawsuit on them with the other."

"I will," I promise her, smiling. "See you later, Jess."

"Will do. Call me tonight. We can catch up on Mom," Jess says. "Love ya, Kat."

"Love you too. Bye."

---

Getting home tonight, I can't help it. I find myself listening to Derrick's radio show.

"Good evening, listeners, your Love Whisperer Derrick King here, and tonight, our topic is something that seems mysterious to most men. Some men say it doesn't even exist."

"The stupid bastards," Susannah says with an exaggeratedly venomous tone of disdain, making me chuckle.

"I wouldn't say stupid, just . . . uneducated and in need of some enlightenment," Derrick purrs, making the muscles on the insides of my thighs tremble. Oh, what this man could educate me on.

"So tonight, our topic is The Female Orgasm. We're going to start off with an email. This is from . . . H. H writes that she and her girlfriend have sex often, but she is frustrated that her girlfriend can only climax from a dildo or a strap-on. H feels like that's off limits. What can she do?"

I lift an eyebrow. Derrick's chosen a doozy to start the night. "Sounds like someone needs some dick," I murmur to myself before my body whispers back that yes, it does need some dick.

"H," Derrick says, his voice sure and slightly stern, making my mouth go dry, "first, penetration has nothing to do with sexual orientation. What your girlfriend needs is what she needs. There's nothing wrong with her body saying that's what it likes best. It has nothing to do with how she feels about you as a person or her attraction to you. I'm just going to be straight with you. What your email tells me is that you might need to deal with your own insecurities. Talk to your girlfriend. I'm sure you two will be just fine."

I'm hanging on to his every word, and I idly wonder if perhaps my confession to him last week inspired this topic.

"Susannah's got us another caller, Z. Z, go ahead."

*"Yeah, D, listen . . . I'm trying my best with my lady, but it seems like no matter what I do, she just doesn't get there. Like, we have sex and stuff, and she says she enjoys it, but she rarely has an orgasm. It's messing with my head and I really want to please her."*

In his velvety voice, Derrick tells the caller to take his time and he's gotta build up to the main event with foreplay, not just dive in and pound her and think that'll do it.

"It starts in the mind, talking to her and telling her how sexy she is, what you want to do to her," he purrs. I can't take it anymore. I can feel my nipples tightening in my t-shirt and I cup my left breast, imagining Derrick telling me this face-to-face.

"Cup her face in your hands and kiss her gently at first, then devour her. Move down her neck, maybe tease a little nibble to see if she's into that, and lick along her collarbone. Make it down to her breasts which by now should be full and heavy," he says, and I echo him, massaging both of my breasts. It feels so good I have to sit down on my couch, leaning back and my legs spreading slowly.

"Tease her nipples, palm them and circle your hands, cradle her breasts and lick the nipples until they tighten up, then suck them deeply. If she liked the neck nibbles, maybe light bites or easy pinches here too. Your mileage may vary with that because everyone is different. Make your way down her body, layering kisses with licks and sucks along the way."

"Fuck," I moan, my eyes rolling up as my pussy quivers in anticipation. I let my left hand slide down, cupping myself through my shorts, the heat making me gasp at the first touch. The whole world swims away and all I can hear is Derrick's sexy growling.

"Compliment her pussy and let your hot breath warm her as you let the anticipation build. Then lick her with a flat tongue from slit to clit several times before focusing on her clit for circles. I've heard writing the alphabet with your tongue can be good, and when you find a letter that makes her moan, do that one over and over, but if that's too much, just trace patterns and rhythms. Flat tongue, pointed tongue, fast, slow to see what she responds to best. The answer's easy really, just pay attention to her. Take your time. Take as much time as you need to help her get into it. You'll be able to tell. She's not gonna be shy about it and you'll know. She'll open up like a flower."

I can't take this anymore. I slide a hand inside my panties, rubbing at my lips and wishing it were Derrick. I bet he's got strong fingers that could leave me dripping with desire and a tongue that could write poetry on my clit.

"Eventually," Derrick continues, "slip a finger inside slowly and pull it out, teasing her opening and stretching her. Hell, who knows, maybe two or three fingers or more. Like I said, just pay attention. Curl them toward her front wall to slide across her G-spot if you can find hers."

I follow his words, slipping two fingers inside my soaking pussy and pumping them slowly before finding my G-spot. Derrick's got me so turned on that finding the spot is easy, and each intense stroke leaves my toes curling on the carpet.

"All the while, you finger bang her and you lick and suck her clit like a starving man. It might take a few minutes, it might take a lot longer, but you do what she likes and stick with it until she comes. It'll be the best reward ever, trust me. After that, well, you see what it takes. She'll be open to you. Just listen to her body and be creative. No wham-bam, thank you, ma'am. Most women are more complex than that, all right?"

Susannah interrupts, and I can hear it in her voice that she's turned on too. "Wow, Derrick. That was rather . . . descriptive. Fellas, from a female perspective, let me tell you . . . hell yes to all of that. Hell. Yes."

They laugh, sending the show over to a song, and Mazzy Star's *Fade Into You* comes grooving out of my radio. I keep my fingers going, pumping them in and out and finding all the ways that my body likes it, grinding the heel of my hand against my clit before easing up and brushing it with my thumb.

The whole time, I can only imagine that Derrick's there doing it. I don't even know what he looks like, but holy fuck, I don't know if it matters when a man knows what he knows. My pussy clenches around my two fingers as I strum my clit with my thumb, and I cry out, pushing myself over the edge and coating my hand in my sweet slickness. The orgasm's intense, and I bite my lip hard, moaning his name. "Derrick."

Fuck me. God, I want him to fuck me so badly. When I come back to reality again, I realize the commercial break's over, and I take my hand out of my soaked panties, panting shakily.

Holy Shit, Derrick's cohort is right. Hell yes to all of that. Listening to his voice describe how he gets a woman to come, giving but always in control . . . it's worshipful mastery and I want it.

I want it so badly.

I definitely should not have hung up last night. Kicking myself for my cowardice and the missed opportunity, I click off the radio as Derrick moves on to another caller who apparently wants to know why his girlfriend can't come from anal.

I can't take another answer from Derrick. Not if I want to get any sleep.

**Want to read the rest? Get Dirty Talk HERE!**

# ABOUT THE AUTHOR

Other books by Lauren:

*Get Dirty* Series (Interconnecting standalones):

Dirty Talk

*Irresistible Bachelor* Series (Interconnecting standalones):

Anaconda || Mr. Fiance || Heartstopper

Stud Muffin || Mr. Fixit || Matchmaker

Motorhead || Baby Daddy

*Connect with Lauren Landish*
www.laurenlandish.com
admin@laurenlandish.com

**Join my mailing list (www.laurenlandish.com) and receive 2 FREE ebooks! You'll also be the first to know of new releases, sales, and giveaways. If you're on Facebook, come join my Reader Group!**

Made in United States
North Haven, CT
22 June 2024

53935038R00196